ANDREW TAYLOR

# Death's Own Door

HODDER

First published in Great Britain in 2001 by Hodder & Stoughton
An Hachette UK company

This paperback edition published in 2019

2

A CIP catalogue record for this title is available from the British Library

Paperback ISBN 9780340696026
eBook ISBN 9781444764970

Printed and bound in Great Britain by Clays Ltd, Elcograf S.p.A.

Hodder & Stoughton policy is to use papers that are natural, renewable
and recyclable products and made from wood grown in sustainable
forests. The logging and manufacturing processes are expected to
conform to the environmental regulations of the country of origin.

Hodder & Stoughton Ltd
Carmelite House
50 Victoria Embankment
London EC4Y 0DZ

www.hodder.co.uk

For Tony, with love

# The Principal Characters

DR ANGMER – of Fontenoy Place, Trenalt

BERNIE BROADBENT – County Councillor; cousin of EDITH THORNHILL; 'Uncle Bernie'

THE HONOURABLE CICELY CASWELL – of Fontenoy Place, Trenalt

MR DRAKE – Deputy Chief Constable

JILL FRANCIS – deputy editor of the *Lydmouth Gazette*

IVOR FUGGLE – chief reporter of the *Evening Post*

MAJOR JACK GRAIG – nephew of Rufus Moorcroft

'DRACULA' GRIMES – Detective Sergeant, Lydmouth Division

AMY GWYN-THOMAS – secretary to the editor of the *Lydmouth Gazette*

RANDOLPH HAUGHTON – of Bruton Street, London W1

BRIAN KIRBY – Detective Sergeant, Lydmouth Division

NURSE LINDOR – of Fontenoy Place, Trenalt

GARETH LOYSEY – an artist; and JUNE (née Hudnall) his wife

MR MORGAN – manager of Barclays Bank, Lydmouth

DR LINDSAY PIRK – of Eastville Clinic, Cardiff

GEORGE SHIPSTON – senior partner of Shipston & Shipston, solicitors of Lydmouth

SUSAN SOLLY – housekeeper at Highnam Cottage, Trenalt

RICHARD THORNHILL – Detective Inspector,
  Lydmouth Division; and EDITH his wife
RAYMOND WILLIAMSON – ex-Detective
  Superintendent; and BUNTY his wife

# Chapter One

———◦◦◦◦———

The little train rumbled out of the tunnel. Sunlight broke through the smoke and swept into the compartment. Edith Thornhill glanced out of the left-hand window and saw Fontenoy Place glowing on the hillside farther down the valley.

Nearly there. But she wished she hadn't come.

She turned her head to the other window and there was Trenalt, smudges of grey on the other slope of the valley. The train would be at the station within a couple of minutes. She scrambled to her feet – fortunately she had the compartment to herself – and peered into the mirror beneath the luggage rack. No train smuts, thank God, and her make-up was still as good as it needed to be. She removed the hatpin and rapidly adjusted her hat on her thick fair hair. When the hat was secure again, she straightened her jacket and smoothed her skirt.

What did it matter? No one would know who she was.

The little train slowed. It rattled over a level-crossing and passed a signal box. The platforms slid along the windows. The station seemed smaller and dingier than it had in 1938. There was no longer a tub of flowers beneath the window of the station-master's office. Squealing and hissing, the engine came to a halt.

Panic rose in her throat. There was still time to turn back. Why make herself even more unhappy that she already was?

Edith picked up her handbag, opened the compartment's door and stumbled on to the platform. She would sit in the waiting room until the next train back to Lydmouth. The station-master threw a mailbag into the guard's van. Edith glanced up and down the platform. Doors slammed. A dozen other passengers had alighted but she recognised none of them. Black ties and dark suits told their own story. She hung back, pretending she needed to tie up her shoelace, waiting until they had filed out of the station.

But she couldn't stay here where Hugh had—

Something else had changed. She forced her mind away from Hugh to work out what it was. No one was waiting to meet her: that was it. In the old days, Granny had always walked down to the station. Later, when the arthritis had taken hold, there had always been someone here. Bernie, perhaps, or Jack. Sometimes, best of all, even Hugh.

*Oh God, not Hugh again. Don't think about Hugh. Not now. Not here of all places.*

The other passengers had gone. The train pulled away. The level-crossing gates creaked and swung open. The stationmaster returned to his sanctum. Edith was alone. She hurried away from the edge of the platform. She glanced up, facing away from the village, and saw on the other side of the valley the slate roofs and harsh red bricks of Highnam Cottage. The minutes passed.

Rufus, she thought, Rufus: why *you?*

The door of the office opened. The stationmaster stood on the threshold, turning his gold-braided cap round in his hand. 'Something wrong, ma'am?'

'No – nothing at all, thank you. I was just tying my shoelace.'

His eyes had taken in her clothes. 'You're here for Mr Moorcroft's funeral, I dare say. Through the station yard and up the hill. You can't miss the church.' His mouth moved as if he were about to spit. 'I'd be there myself if I could have got the time off.'

Edith thanked him and hurried out of the station, fleeing from the curiosity in the man's face. She trudged through the sunshine up the hill. The air was hot and still. After a few minutes, Edith felt the prickle of sweat. She knew from experience that soon her face would be pink and shiny. The knowledge that she would not look her best made everything worse. Why was it so hot?

Granny had once said, with a bronchial chuckle, that hot weather killed off old people like flies, much more than cold. Then the following winter she died. But Rufus hadn't been old. According to the notice in the *Gazette*, he had been sixty-eight. She had glimpsed him twice since she had moved to Lydmouth, and the first time she'd hardly recognised him. In 1938 he had looked ten years younger than his real age. When she had last seen him, he had looked ten years older. He hadn't recognised her.

'Excuse me!'

Edith was already turning. At the back of her mind she had been aware of the sound of a car behind her, coming up from the level-crossing beside the station, and known from the change in the engine note that it was slowing. She turned and saw a sleek blue coupé. Sitting at the wheel was a man of about forty with close-cropped dark hair rippling with suppressed curls and glistening with hair oil. He had heavily marked eyebrows and large brown eyes. She thought she might have seen him some-where before but she could not put a name to him. He leaned out of the window, revealing the black tie round his neck.

'Are you going to the funeral?'

Edith admitted that she was.

'Thought so. Like a lift? Time's getting on.'

Edith hesitated only for a second. She did not want to walk up to the village by herself, past Fiddler's Cottage where the road forked and where she had waited in the rain all those years ago, past the village hall where she had had her moment of triumph, past the Hudnalls' house whose windows she had watched surreptitiously for hours from her bedroom in her grandmother's cottage at the corner of the churchyard. She knew she must see all these places. But she would rather have someone else there at the time, someone to distract her.

'Thank you. That's very kind.'

The man got out of the car and opened the passenger door for her. His manners, Edith thought, were a little too good to be true, the gestures a little too exaggerated, but she wasn't complaining. Now she was closer to him she noticed the bags under his eyes and the vertical lines between the eyebrows. She didn't know much about men's suits or about cars, but she thought that in his case both were expensive, like his voice. And the car was a very pretty blue.

'I thought I'd take the short cut up from the river.' The man smiled down at her. 'That was about three-quarters of an hour ago. Don't they have signposts around here? I'm Randolph Haughton, by the way.'

'Edith Thornhill.' His name nudged her memory.

He climbed back into the car. 'You knew Rufus well?'

'Not really,' Edith said. 'But I knew him better when I was a girl. My grandmother used to live in the village.' She shot a glance at him, but he appeared to be concentrating on his steering. 'That was before the war.'

He nodded and to her relief did not ask further questions. 'I've known old Rufus for years,' he volunteered. 'Didn't see him as often as I should have done. You know how it is. Saw quite a lot of him during the war when he was in London for a couple of years. Not so much since then.' His shoulders twitched. 'Too late now.'

Edith realised that they must have passed Fiddler's Cottage already. The village hall flashed by on the right, looking smaller and shabbier than in memory, like the station. Haughton parked at the end of the line of cars along the churchyard wall. The church clock began to toll the half-hour: the service was due to start at eleven-thirty, so everyone else must already be inside.

They hurried along the path to the church door. Edith glimpsed her grandmother's cottage, the stone tiles now replaced with slate, and a garage standing where the pigsty and the outdoor privy had been. In that instant it became a strange place, nothing to do with her or Granny. Time had moved on, Edith thought, and herself with it. She felt unexpectedly relieved.

Haughton took his hat off in the porch, and the way he automatically smoothed back his hair was faintly familiar, like his name. He held the church door open for her. In the nave, the temperature dropped sharply. The organ was playing and the congregation was standing. Faces turned to look at them. Edith was glad she was not alone but part of an apparent couple. She and Haughton slipped into a pew near the back. And at that moment the organ swelled in volume and the congregation burst into 'Onward Christian Soldiers'. She picked up a hymnal and fumbled through the pages.

'Typical,' Haughton whispered. 'Ghastly hymn. Rufus loathed it.'

The coffin was up in the choir, resting on trestles and smothered with flowers. Edith sang mechanically, her eyes scanning the backs of the congregation. People changed so much in fifteen years. She wondered if anyone here would recognise her, and wasn't sure if she wanted them to or not. There was only one person whom she was afraid to meet, but unless he had changed greatly he wasn't here. She began to relax. The church itself was certainly familiar, almost unchanged as far as she could see.

The hymn stopped and a clergyman she did not know said words she didn't listen to. Her mind drifted away. She had told no one she was coming, not even Richard. Perhaps especially Richard. She could not live her life entirely in reference to him, after all. Besides, when she had last seen him, leaving the house after breakfast, she had not known she would go to Rufus's funeral. What would have been the point of telling him? He had other things on his mind these days.

She found herself sitting down, following the herd instinct which afflicts people in churches. A man slipped out of one of the front pews and made his way towards the lectern with its great brass eagle. He was a heavy, broad man, slightly balding, not tall but with a physique which gave an impression of strength. When he reached the lectern, and turned to look at the congregation, she sucked in a sudden breath of air. Haughton glanced at her. Edith stared down at her gloved hands, and felt the blood rising to her cheeks.

So he was here, after all. Jack Graig. As large as life, and several stone heavier than when she'd last seen him. But still Jack Graig.

Edith did not listen to the words he was saying. For all she knew or cared he might have been reading the weather forecast. She heard his voice, though – deeper and firmer than it had been. The rest of the service flowed around her as if it were a stream and she were a rock in the middle of it: and in time the softest water wore down the hardest stone.

*Jack Graig can't be here.*

His uncle had died only a week ago. He couldn't have come back to England in that time, surely? And Rufus Moorcroft had only been an uncle, not a father. They wouldn't have sent him home on compassionate leave for an *uncle*. She felt angry – while she stood, knelt, sat, sang and prayed – angry with herself for giving way to a sentimental impulse, angry with fate, and most of all angry with Jack Graig for having the gall to turn up after all these years.

The mourners followed the coffin and the priest into the sun-filled churchyard. Edith had wondered whether they would allow Rufus Moorcroft to lie here. She and Randolph Haughton fell in at the end of the procession which wound between the gravestones to a part of the churchyard near the northern boundary. There were few headstones here, and a pair of trees, a whitebeam and a yew, created a partial screen. Perhaps this was where they put people like Rufus Moorcroft.

She kept on the fringe of the crowd around the open grave, making sure that she was behind Jack Graig. Probably he wouldn't know her from Adam or, rather, from Eve, but she did not want to put it to the test. She recognised the perpetually frowning features of old George Shipston, the senior partner of the solicitors' firm in Castle Street. Another familiar face belonged to a middle-aged woman in a squashed felt hat.

'Morning, Mrs Thornhill,' said a man's voice at her shoulder.

Startled, she turned her head. 'Brian.'

Detective Sergeant Kirby smiled at her and raised his hat, a new bowler which had left a welt across his forehead. He wore a dark suit with padded shoulders which made him look broader than he was, almost like a spiv. The gay green pattern of his tie clashed with the green silk handkerchief peeping from the breast pocket of his jacket. He was bursting with colour and energy, like an exploding firework.

'Just keeping a watching brief,' he said. 'Not the only one, either.' He had a Londoner's voice, perhaps a generation removed from pure cockney. His eyes flicked away from her, and she followed his gaze to a plump, elderly man trying half-heartedly to suppress a phlegmy cough on the other side of the grave. 'Know who that is? Ivor Fuggle, works for the *Post*.'

Kirby murmured the words in such a low voice that only she could hear him. He smiled and nodded, as though they were casual acquaintances, and moved a yard or two away. Edith had been a policeman's wife for long enough to know exactly what he had been saying, both with and without words.

The coffin was out of sight in the grave. Jack Graig stared down at it. The rector was speaking. Suddenly there was a stir on the edge of the crowd. A tall, thin woman pushed her way into the mourners, taking no more notice of them than if they had been a field full of long grass, and strode through them to stand by Jack Graig. She had straggling grey hair and a long brown raincoat which trailed down to her ankles. Edith saw her face and immediately recognised the high arched brows, the prominent cheekbones and the curving nose.

Poor Miss Caswell. Edith had thought she would be dead.

Another woman followed in her wake. She was shorter, broader and perhaps twenty years younger, her square brown face fretted with worry lines. She took Miss Caswell's arm. Miss Caswell snatched it back. The movement pulled her coat apart, revealing the grey pinafore beneath. She stared into the grave, her face absolutely still except for the tears crawling down her cheeks.

Edith looked away. She wanted to cry too, but she did not know whether it was for Rufus or Miss Caswell or herself – or something sadder and less personal than any of them. Earth pattered on the coffin and Jack Graig blew his nose. The crowd dissolved, following a logic of its own, breaking into knots of people moving slowly through the churchyard, chatting, patting pockets in search of matches. Jack stayed with the rector.

Edith moved quickly away. The sooner she left, the less chance of meeting Jack. To her horror, her eye caught a familiar name incised in stone, and her stomach lurched as though the path beneath her feet had suddenly dropped her into a hole. This was where the Hudnalls lay, father and son, Vernon and Hugh.

The son's grave was enclosed by a marble rectangle like a pair of fire fenders placed back to back. Weeds and grubby chips of marble filled the space between the fenders. At one end was a book-shaped marble tablet with a vase set in it. The vase was empty.

*I bet his blasted sister chose it.*

Edith forced herself to walk on. She did not want to read the inscriptions. She knew what she would see: that Hugh and his father had died on the same day nearly fifteen years ago.

George Shipston was sitting on a bench near the lychgate, a cigar in his mouth. Ivor Fuggle bent over him, talking earnestly. Edith hurried past. Then Brian Kirby was beside her again, the sun glinting on his thick yellow hair, as shiny as fresh thatch.

He smiled at her. 'I didn't realise you knew Rufus Moorcroft.'

'I knew him slightly when I was a girl.'

'So did a lot of people.' Kirby waved in the direction of the grave. 'Not a bad turnout.'

'My grandmother used to live in Trenalt,' Edith said, answering the question which he hadn't asked. 'Sometimes I'd come and stay with her. Mr Moorcroft was very well liked. He did a lot for the village, one way and another.'

'Who's the old woman? The one who turned up at the grave.'

'Her name's Cicely Caswell,' she said. 'She . . . she was a friend of Mr Moorcroft's.'

'Not quite right in the head?'

'She used to be a patient at Fontenoy Place.'

'Sort of nursing home, isn't it?'

Edith nodded. She was glad to see Brian because she liked him, and she was almost certain that he liked her – and not in the way he should like the wife of a superior officer. It was an open secret that he and Joan Ailsmore, a WPC at Lydmouth, were courting. Sometimes that gave her a tiny twinge of jealousy. But her usual pleasure in seeing him was diluted by the fact that she wished they hadn't met here. He would tell Richard that he had seen her. She had nothing to hide, of course, absolutely nothing. But sometimes it would be nice to do things without having to explain why.

'Who's the chap you're with?' Kirby asked in a carefully neutral voice.

'Someone who used to know Mr Moorcroft. We didn't come together, actually. He offered me a lift up from the station.'

Kirby nodded. 'So you don't know how he knew Moorcroft?'

'No, I don't.' Edith's irritation showed in her voice, and she took a step towards the gate.

'Oh – there's old Shipston,' Kirby said. 'Excuse me.'

He walked away, head back, bouncing on the balls of his feet as though they were made of rubber. Edith's eyes travelled in front of him, to George Shipston, who was looking at Miss Caswell. There was something in the solicitor's face that made her shiver. He looked as though he were starving and wanted to devour the old woman to satisfy his hunger.

Haughton came up on her other side, and she turned to him almost with relief. 'I gather they've laid on tea and sandwiches in the village hall. Are you coming?'

'No, I'd better not.' She couldn't avoid bumping into Jack in the village hall. 'I must get back to Lydmouth.'

He took out a cigarette and tapped it on his case. 'Look – I know this must seem strange but haven't we met somewhere before? Here, even?'

'No – I don't—' Edith broke off and stared at him. It was the eyes which gave him away. Middle-aged Randolph Haughton with his ravaged face still had the eyes of someone younger: a slim, dark young man with eyes like a spaniel's. She frowned and plucked the name hesitantly from the past. 'Randolph?'

He froze, the cigarette halfway between the case and his lips. 'By God,' he said softly. 'Edith. Edith Broadbent. The leading lady.'

'It's Thornhill now,' she said automatically. Her heart was racing. Randolph had been a friend of Hugh's. He had come down to Trenalt to stay with the Hudnalls at least twice during that last summer. She hadn't had much to do with him because he had seemed much older and terrifyingly sophisticated. How much had he known about what was really going on?

Randolph lit the cigarette with a gold lighter, his hand trembling slightly. He blew out smoke and licked a shred of tobacco from his lips. Just as he was opening his mouth to speak, his eyes widened and his gaze moved from Edith's face to someone approaching behind her.

'Edith!' The voice was unmistakable – it hadn't changed since Edith was six years old, when she had heard Miss Caswell lecturing a tramp about the virtues of a nice cup of tea while giving him a shilling. The lecture had continued even after the tramp vanished into the public bar of the Bear. 'Did you say Thornhill? But it's Edith *Broadbent*, isn't it? I saw you over there and I thought, I know that face. I never forget a face.'

Edith held out a hand and Miss Caswell shook it briefly, smiling benevolently at Edith.

'You probably won't remember me.'

'Of course I do, Miss Caswell.' She saw the old woman's eyes running over her. 'I was so sorry to hear about Mr Moorcroft.'

Miss Caswell's lips trembled. 'Least said, soonest mended.' Then her face sharpened. 'Though there's a lot I could say.'

Her companion at the graveside walked quickly towards them and took Miss Caswell by the arm. 'Come along, dear, you mustn't go bothering people, especially not strangers.'

'Don't be silly, Lindor,' Miss Caswell said. 'And don't paw me. Besides, this isn't a stranger.'

'Miss Caswell, you—'

'She's Edith Broadbent. I've known her since she was a little girl. She used to come and stay with her grandmother in the cottage over there.' She flapped the skirts of her long brown coat like a bird ruffling its feathers. 'Before your time, Lindor.'

The brown-faced woman glanced at Edith, who nodded and smiled, confirming Miss Caswell's story.

'Have you come back to live in Trenalt?' Miss Caswell enquired.

'No, I live in Lydmouth.'

'Lydmouth! I haven't been there for years. Far too much traffic these days. One hardly sees a horse.'

Lindor touched Miss Caswell's sleeve. 'Dr Angmer won't like it if you overexcite yourself.'

'Dr Angmer is a silly billy. I'm not overexciting myself. I'm meeting an old friend.' The mouth began to tremble again and suddenly the eyes were huge with unshed tears. 'And saying goodbye to an old one. To my *best* friend.'

'That's enough, dear. Really, I think it's time we were getting back. We don't want to be late for lunch.'

'Whyever not?' said Miss Caswell, recovering her cheerfulness. 'It's Tuesday, so that means dried figs.' She stooped towards Edith and lowered her voice a fraction. 'They give us dried figs to keep us regular.'

'Come along, dear,' Lindor said.

'Hello, Miss C., Miss Lindor,' said a new voice, belonging to the woman whose face had seemed familiar to Edith by the graveside. 'You are Mrs Broadbent's Edith, aren't you,' she informed Edith. 'Remember me, dear?' She tugged the black felt hat. 'Susan Solly. I used to help out at Oak Tree House but just before the war I went to help Mr Moorcroft instead. Didn't live in, mind. He was a lovely gentleman. If you ask me, he never really recovered after his wife died. You know it was me that found him? I just couldn't help looking. Too curious by half, that's what my mother used to say to me.' She gazed placidly round the churchyard. 'You know, we were all here on Saturday for the wedding of my sister's youngest. Makes you think, doesn't it? That's what I said to my Ernie. Life and death, you can't have one without the other. Just like a—'

'I wanted to ask you something, Mrs Solly,' Miss Caswell broke in, apparently unaware that Mrs Solly was talking. 'You'd probably remember if anyone would.' She wrapped bony fingers around the other woman's plump forearm and lowered her head to the level of her ear. 'What was the name of the woman who married the White Rabbit?'

'The White Rabbit!' Mrs Solly shrieked with laughter and

then, remembering where she was, choked her mirth and turned it into a cough. 'What are you——'

'Was it Constance? Or was she simply *like* Constance? So easy to confuse the two, isn't it? And I suppose if she's married the White Rabbit, she's Mrs Rabbit now. Constance Rabbit. She's come back now – it was in the paper. You know who I mean. But what's her name?'

Talking with increasing urgency, Miss Caswell drew Mrs Solly aside.

'Oh dear,' Lindor murmured to Edith. 'We didn't want her to come to the funeral, but we couldn't keep her away. Then she took such a time getting ready, I hoped she'd be too late.'

'You mustn't worry,' Edith said.

'So you knew her before the war?'

'Slightly, yes.'

'Do you think she's worse now than she was then?'

'She was always . . . she was always a little unusual, but there was never any harm in it.' Edith looked at Lindor's face and saw the anxiety there. 'I'd say she was doing very well for her age. She must be well into her seventies but she looks very fit.'

'Seventy-five last June,' Lindor said with a note of pride in her voice. 'Now, I must get her back to lunch.'

'Why don't I run you both back in the car?' Randolph Haughton said suddenly. He had been standing silently for several minutes, watching and listening. 'I was a friend of Mr Moorcroft's,' he went on, grinding his cigarette out beneath his heel. 'That's my car over there – the blue one. Not much room in the back, I'm afraid, but at least it's not far.'

'Well, if you're sure – it would be very kind. But what about your sandwiches and——'

'I was leaving in any case. I'm having lunch with a friend in Lydmouth, you see.'

'All right, then. Thank you. She may take a bit of persuading, though. She's got a bee in her bonnet about walking. Good for the health, she says.'

While Haughton and Lindor were talking, Edith watched Miss Caswell. The old lady released Mrs Solly and sidled towards the lychgate. George Shipston was now talking to the clergyman. He laid his half-smoked cigar on the wall behind him, took out an envelope and made a note on it with a silver pencil. Miss Caswell picked up the cigar, squeezed the smouldering tip on to the grass and slipped the remains into the pocket of her coat. Then she walked swiftly away.

The sequence of actions had a practised furtiveness. How could Cicely Caswell be reduced to stealing half-smoked cigars to consume on the quiet like a naughty schoolgirl? Edith could stand it no longer. She wanted to go home to the silent house in Victoria Road. She slipped away from Haughton and Lindor without saying goodbye, planning to leave the churchyard by the other gate because there would be less chance of her departure being noticed. But as she rounded the buttress at the south-west corner of the nave she collided with Jack Graig.

They jumped apart as though their magnetic fields would not allow them to be close.

'Edith,' he said. 'Edith, I hoped . . . I thought—'

'Jack — I didn't expect to see you here.'

'No.'

'I was so sorry to hear about your uncle.'

He nodded. 'It's all very strange.' He shook his head as though confused and then gestured towards the dark crowd in the churchyard. 'I hadn't realised he was so well liked. To tell the truth, I hadn't seen as much of him in recent years as I should have done.' He swallowed. 'Have you come far?'

'Only from Lydmouth.'

'You're living in Lydmouth — I didn't know.'

'For the last few years. We were in East Anglia before that. Cambridgeshire.'

'Cambridgeshire? My wife came from there.'

'Your wife? Your *wife*?'

'Yes – well, to be precise my ex-wife. Look here, you haven't got to rush away, have you? There's tea and sandwiches in the village hall. Or sherry if you prefer. Mrs Solly's laid it on. You will come, won't you?'

If she had not been so surprised, Edith would not have agreed. His *wife*? Instead she nodded and fell into step with him.

'Poor Uncle Rufus,' he said. 'What a way to go.'

'What exactly happened?' she said, desperate for something to say.

He stopped and looked down at her. 'You haven't heard?'

'Only what was in the papers.' And, had she been perfectly honest, what she'd heard in the greengrocer's and in the butcher's.

'They were very kind,' Jack said harshly. 'While the balance of the mind was disturbed – all that rot. Everyone liked Uncle Rufus, you see. Respected him, even. So they wanted to make things as easy as possible. But if you ask me, he was as sane as you or me. So he must have known exactly what he was doing.' He hesitated and looked straight into Edith's eyes. 'And why.'

# Chapter Two

'Sit down, Thornhill,' Drake said. The Deputy Chief Constable was sharpening a pencil, the shavings falling into an ash-free ashtray. 'I wanted to catch you now because I'm driving round the divisions this afternoon,' he announced. 'Nothing like being on the spot to find out how things are getting on.'

'Yes, sir,' Thornhill said.

'And there's another thing. What's all this about the Moorcroft case?' Drake pushed the point of his pencil into the fleshy ball of his thumb and, apparently satisfied, laid it carefully on his blotter. 'Why have you sent Kirby to the funeral? Mr Hendry told me this morning that he thought there was no reason why we should leave the file open.'

'With respect, sir, Mr Hendry hasn't seen Sergeant Kirby's last report.'

Drake's eyebrows, each the colour and shape of a miniature fox's brush, arched. 'Nor have I.'

'No, sir. You were with Mr Hendry and I didn't like to disturb you. But in the meantime I thought I'd better send Sergeant Kirby over to Trenalt.'

The DCC grunted. He was a small, sturdy man with thinning ginger hair. He had spent ten years in India, rising to the rank of District Superintendent of Police. After Partition, he had been seconded to advise the police force of the newly independent Pakistan. During his years abroad, his fair skin had turned a dull uniform red. His appointment as DCC and head of the county's CID had followed soon after Superintendent Williamson's retirement. The word in the canteen was that it was a case of appoint in haste, repent at leisure.

'Why haven't I seen this report?'

'It was left in your secretary's in-tray. That was the normal procedure with Superintendent Williamson.'

Drake looked up. 'I may be instituting some of my own procedures, Inspector. You'd better give me the essentials. I'd understood it was an open-and-shut case of suicide.'

'Yes, sir. So did everyone. And it may be no more than that. But there are one or two loose ends.'

Drake leant across the desk, his small blue eyes bright and hard. 'Man's lost his wife. Washes down a few dozen sleeping pills with half a bottle of whisky. Leaves a considerate little note for the housekeeper. Where's the problem?'

Thornhill shrugged. 'Put like that, there isn't one.'

'No sign of anyone else on the premises,' Drake continued. 'The pathologist comes up with nothing suspicious. Friends say he's been depressed. His GP says he's not surprised Moorcroft snapped. One of those strong silent types, he reckoned, where everything bubbles away inside, out of sight.'

'He hadn't been to see his GP for three years, sir. And then there's the point that his wife died years ago, in 1935. So why kill himself now?'

'Not our problem, Thornhill.'

'According to Sergeant Kirby, Moorcroft had quite a bonfire on the night he died.'

'Natural enough. Personal stuff, no doubt. It's all of a piece with the note for the housekeeper.' Drake sipped black tea from a dainty flowered cup, while his eyes studied Thornhill over the brim. 'We're not trick cyclists, thank God. We're only concerned with what people do, and whether they've broken the law. We don't have to worry about why.'

Thornhill hesitated. 'This bonfire, sir. One or two scraps of paper hadn't burned properly. Sergeant Kirby found part of a receipted bill from a clinic in Cardiff. The Eastville Clinic.'

'Well?'

'Moorcroft's GP didn't know that he was receiving treatment elsewhere. Why burn a bill?'

'You don't act rationally on half a bottle of whisky and enough barbiturates to stun an elephant.'

'We looked through his bank statements and returned cheques. There were no payments to the Eastville Clinic.'

'Then he paid in cash – people sometimes do, you know – or he used another account. No – we let sleeping dogs rest in peace.' Drake looked up, meeting Thornhill's eyes. 'There's one more thing. On quite another subject.'

'Sir?'

'Mr Hendry and I intend to set up a central office of senior detectives for serious crimes.'

Thornhill felt his eyes flicker, and hoped Drake hadn't noticed. 'For the whole county?'

'Yes. It's a more efficient way to use resources. The Standing Joint Committee approved the plan this morning. The office will be run by a detective chief inspector with a team of officers seconded from around the divisions to work under him. The DCI's job could be an external or an internal appointment.'

'Do we know when the office will be set up, sir?'

'The sooner the better, in my view. But it depends on whether we advertise outside the force, among other things.' The Deputy Chief Constable glanced at his watch and stood up. 'Time for lunch, I think. Either way, there'll be an official announcement about the reorganisation by the end of the week. But I'd like you to keep it under your hat until then. I wanted to tell the officers in charge of divisional CIDs beforehand.'

A few minutes later, Thornhill walked slowly down the High Street. He was going to buy a birthday present. The pavements were crowded with shoppers and workers hurrying home to lunch. He bumped into a stout gentleman and muttered an apology. His mind was full of what Drake had said.

A central office for the county's CID would have a profound effect on the entire force. Thornhill wanted to be in that central office, if possible running it, which would mean a promotion to boot. The snag was, every other detective would want to join it too. If they advertised the top job outside the county, they would get a flood of applications. Would the central office be effective? If the scheme went ahead, it wouldn't do much for the morale of the detectives who weren't chosen to join it. He wondered what Superintendent Williamson would think of the idea. He was willing to bet that the old man had already received a phone call from one of his former colleagues.

He drifted into McLean's Bookshop, which was in a side road near the Bull Hotel.

'You sent me a card to say a book I ordered has come in,' he said to the assistant. '*The Blue Field* by John Moore. My name's Thornhill.'

The assistant took her time finding the book, wrapping it up and receiving payment. Meanwhile a small queue built up behind Thornhill. He turned and caught the eye of a tall, thin woman in early middle age. She looked away at once, and examined the blue spines of a row of Pelicans with ostentatious interest. She had a narrow face dominated by a long, slightly crooked nose, and wore a little brown hat with what looked like a small antenna sprouting from its crown. Thornhill guessed she had recognised him. One of the drawbacks of his job was the loss of anonymity which went with it, especially in a town the size of Lydmouth. He had seen her before somewhere – perhaps had passed her in the street. He turned back to the counter to receive his change.

He walked back to Police Headquarters. Instead of going up the steps to the front door, he went around to the car park at the rear of the building. He unlocked his Austin and stretched out his hand to the Oxo tin on the back seat. He wondered what Edith had given him today. Cheese and tomato sandwiches, probably. Sometimes he yearned for ham.

'Richard!'

Thornhill straightened up quickly, banged his head on the roof of the car, and swore. Bernie Broadbent was standing in the porch of the back entrance of the police station, his arm raised in greeting. Bernie was one of the county councillors on the Standing Joint Committee and had probably stayed behind after the meeting for a drink with the Chief Constable.

'I was hoping I would bump into you,' Bernie said as he lumbered down the steps. 'How's my little Edith?'

'Fine, thank you.' Thornhill's wife and Bernie Broadbent were cousins, a circumstance which Thornhill found acutely embarrassing.

'And the children?'

'Camping in Pembrokeshire with Sylvia and her family.'

'James was telling me about poor old Rufus Moorcroft,' Bernie said. He was now on Christian name terms with Mr Hendry, the Chief Constable. 'I'd have gone to the funeral if it hadn't been for this meeting.'

'You knew Moorcroft?'

Bernie shrugged heavy shoulders and fumbled in his jacket pockets for pipe and tobacco pouch. 'I used to know him a bit before the war. Not well – but I saw him occasionally when I went over to Trenalt. My auntie lived there. But you'll know all about her, of course – your Edie's gran.'

Thornhill nodded, though he hadn't been aware that Edith's grandmother had lived in Trenalt; it was possible that she had told him and he had forgotten. He wondered what else he didn't know. Perhaps Edith had even met Rufus Moorcroft.

'Nothing odd about the death, was there?' Bernie said. There was an unexpected note in his voice. He sounded almost jaunty.

'Suicide, as far as we know.'

Bernie stuffed the unlit pipe in his mouth. He looked at Thornhill and for a moment seemed on the verge of saying something else. Then he waved his hand in farewell and strolled across the car park to his Riley.

Thornhill stared after him. At that moment a gleaming BSA motorbike turned into the car park. It thundered to a halt a few yards away from Thornhill. The rider removed his goggles.

'Afternoon, sir,' said Brian Kirby.

'How did it go? Good turnout?'

'A lot of people. At least a couple of hundred, I should say. Did you know he was a war hero?'

'Which war?'

'The first. He was in the Royal Flying Corps or something – won a couple of medals. The rector mentioned it in his address. He seems to have been very well liked in the village. Did a lot for local charities and so on.'

They went into the building together and walked up to the first floor. Thornhill led the way into his little office. He laid the book on the desk and waved Kirby to a chair.

'What about family?'

'There was a nephew there – Major Graig. Seemed a decent enough sort of chap. He's staying at the house.' Kirby's voice hardened. 'Fuggle turned up. Odd, don't you think? Country funerals aren't usually his cup of tea. Even when the dear departed is someone like Rufus Moorcroft.'

'Do you think he knows something we don't?'

Kirby fiddled with the knot of his tie, a new one which Thornhill suspected that WPC Joan Ailsmore had given him. 'The man's got a nose for dirt, I'll say that for him. They say the *Post* pays him a fortune. He made a beeline for the Bear afterwards.' He shifted his chair. 'Oh, and I had a word with

Mrs Thornhill, too. I didn't realise she was going.'

'Her grandmother used to live in Trenalt before the war,' Thornhill said smoothly. Under cover of the desk, he squeezed his left hand into a fist. 'Mr Drake thinks there's no reason to keep the investigation open.'

'Fair enough, I suppose. Oh, but there was one other thing. Before I went to the funeral, I talked to the telephone people. Moorcroft made a trunk call on the night of his death, to a Mayfair number – flat in Bruton Street, registered in the name of Haughton.'

'You tried it?'

Kirby nodded. 'Someone who said she was the maid answered. Turned out to be one of a block of service flats. She put me through to the porter. He said that Haughton had gone away for a few days. Wasn't sure where.'

Thornhill tapped the lid of the Oxo tin. 'Go and have some lunch now. But afterwards, there'd be no harm in phoning Highnam Cottage and asking Major Graig if he knows the man.'

When he was alone, Thornhill pushed the sandwich box aside. He felt uneasy. Why hadn't Edith mentioned she was going to Trenalt? He was annoyed with her. She had no right to conceal something from him. Then it occurred to him that if she had no right then nor did he. It was an uncomfortable thought and he tried to distract himself from it.

He unwrapped the book and sniffed the smell of fresh paper. He wondered whether he dared write something on the flyleaf. Something to make it personal. He uncapped his fountain pen and stared at the virgin page.

While he was waiting for inspiration, another unwelcome thought slipped into his mind. He remembered where he had seen the thin-faced woman before. Surely she worked at the *Lydmouth Gazette*? Among her colleagues was Jill Francis. He shivered. Too close for comfort?

# Chapter Three

Jill Francis saw the elegant blue car as soon as she came into the front office of the *Gazette*. Two schoolboys were peering into the driver's window, their faces rapt as though providence had granted them an angelic visitation.

Inside the office, Randolph Haughton was leaning on the counter, chatting to the receptionist. Just as Jill entered the room, the bell above the street door pinged and Amy Gwyn-Thomas came in, wearing her new beige hat. Jill lifted the flap of the counter for her. With the slightest of nods, the smallest possible acknowledgement of the courtesy, the secretary glided past her. Jill felt momentarily chilled as though a draught had touched her.

'Jill, darling!'

Randolph lunged towards her. He took her hands and kissed her ceremoniously on both cheeks. His gesture managed to imply that if only there had been a muddy puddle before her, he would have been delighted to cover it with a velvet cloak or anything else that came to hand. Behind her, Jill heard a sharp intake of air. Miss Gwyn-Thomas was enjoying the spectacle.

Still holding her hands, he stood back. 'Look, I hope you don't mind my dropping in like this.'

'Of course I don't. You said on the phone you're down for a funeral?'

'Ghastly things. And what's worse is what happens after-wards: I left them having tea and Spam sandwiches in the village hall. You're my excuse for avoiding all that, bless you. Where shall we have lunch?'

'It'll have to be the Bull Hotel, I'm afraid. I haven't much time. But we can walk — it's only a few yards.'

He held the door open for her and she passed into the street. Glancing back, she saw the receptionist and Amy Gwyn-Thomas staring after her, the one curious and the other disapproving.

'Where was the funeral?' Jill asked.

'Trenalt. Do you know it?'

'I've never actually been there.'

'Chap called Rufus Moorcroft. All rather sudden.'

'I know. I'm sorry.'

He grimaced. 'In the midst of life, eh? I hadn't seen him for a while, and now I wish I had.' He took her arm and they strolled down the pavement. 'It's a pretty part of the world — good-looking country . . . I think I might stay in Trenalt for a day or two. There's a nice little pub and they do rooms. I want to do some work, you see, and there never seems to be any peace and quiet in London.'

'Work?'

He glanced at her and grimaced. 'One of my little pieces. The poetry of Robert Herrick.'

Jill nodded. Randolph Haughton had no need to work but he created the illusion that he did in a variety of ways. He spent an inordinate amount of time slaving over literary essays which occasionally appeared in magazines with small circulations. They were generally magazines in which he was a shareholder. He thought of himself as a man of letters, and Jill liked him enough to let him get away with it.

'Who's it for?' she asked. 'Do you know?'

'*Berkeley's*.'

'Really?' Jill knew that her surprise had shown in her voice. 'Well done – you must be pleased.'

*Berkeley's* was a 150-year-old fortnightly journal which mixed political comment with a range of cultural reviews and articles. It was traditionally liberal in slant and had a healthy five-figure circulation.

Randolph paused outside the portico of the Bull. 'Actually, it's mine now. Well, not exactly mine but quite a lot of it is, if you know what I mean.'

Jill nodded gravely. 'How nice. Will you take an active interest?'

'Oh yes. I'd like to see more politics. I think it's grown a bit smug in the last few years and they're not getting the younger readers they used to. Which also means the advertising revenue is beginning to slip.'

Jill nodded, knowing he was probably right. Randolph Haughton was a bad writer but a good businessman.

A few minutes later they were sitting in the hotel dining room with Forbin the head waiter fussing over them. Randolph looked first at the menu and then at the wine list, and his dark, lined face grew sadder and sadder.

'The only thing that's really trustworthy is the steak-and-kidney pudding,' Jill murmured to him. 'And Forbin does have wine which isn't on the list – you could ask him about that.'

He glanced around the vast dining room with its peeling wallpaper, frayed tablecloths and stained carpet. 'My dear – how could you bury yourself somewhere like this?'

'Oh, it has its advantages. Don't grumble, Randolph – remember those Spam sandwiches.'

After they had ordered, Randolph sat back, sipping the sherry that Forbin had found him. 'What's your editor like? Bit of a bumpkin?'

'Philip's a dear. I've known him for years. If he and Charlotte weren't away I'd introduce you.'

Randolph offered her a cigarette. She noticed with approval the snowy-white cuffs of his shirt, the slim gold case and the expensive cigarettes. She liked nice things. Who didn't? She listened as he negotiated with Forbin about the wine, bringing to the task a judicious mixture of authority and flattery, together with a hint of future financial recompense. It was a game, she thought, and Randolph and Forbin both knew the rules. Soon there was a bottle of claret dating from the year of the old king's Silver Jubilee on the table.

Randolph could be an engaging companion and the conversation flowed easily. He talked about people they both knew and about his plans for *Berkeley's*. After the steak-and-kidney pudding, he refilled their glasses and offered Jill his cigarette case again.

'Tell me about work.' He wriggled his eyebrows. 'Village shows and funerals and council meetings?'

'It's not all like that. I'm increasingly concerned with running the paper, actually. And when Philip's away I'm acting editor.'

'But you must find it rather dull. And surely some of the people become a bit tiresome?'

'You get tiresome people anywhere.' But as she spoke Jill was aware that part of her was agreeing with him. 'Oh, all right. I know. In London you can get away from them more easily. Did you notice the woman who came into the *Gazette* office just as I came down?'

He shook his head.

'She's Philip's secretary. She's been in love with him for years, and for some reason she's jealous of me. She can really be quite unpleasant. I think she spies on me.' She stopped, then forced a laugh. She wasn't used to so much alcohol at lunchtime, not these days, and she shouldn't let her tongue run away with her. 'I'm exaggerating, of course, but it can get a little tedious.'

Randolph clucked in sympathy. 'It sounds absolutely frightful. Do you ever feel – well, nostalgic for London?'

'Yes — I suppose I do.'

He stared at her for a moment without speaking.

'Still,' Jill went on, her voice sounding artificially cheerful to herself, 'one can always go up for a night or two. It's not as if London is the other side of the solar system.'

At times, she thought, Lydmouth felt as if it were in another galaxy. At that moment Forbin appeared with the menu. After the waiter had gone, Randolph turned the conversation to politics. He had a wide acquaintance and a taste for gossip, and soon Jill was enjoying herself. A resignation from the Cabinet would soon be announced, and she and Randolph speculated happily about the possible reason.

They decided to take their coffee in the cavernous lounge at the front of the hotel. Randolph went on ahead, while Jill visited the lavatory. When she reached the lounge a few minutes later, she found him sprawling in an armchair with the *Lydmouth Gazette* open on his lap and a cigarette drooping from the corner of his mouth.

'I've seen worse, dear,' he said, tapping the paper. 'You do quite a good job.'

'Not just me,' Jill snapped. 'Philip Wemyss-Brown is one of the best journalists I've ever worked with. There are a few pockets of professional competence outside London.'

He grinned at her. 'You've got such a nice way of being cross.'

She felt herself smiling back, knowing that she had risen to the bait he had dangled in front of her and that both his condescension and her irritation were part of another game, like the one he had played with Forbin but with different rules. A waitress arrived with their coffee and, as an afterthought, Randolph ordered brandy.

'I feel I deserve it. I do so hate funerals.' He glanced down at the newspaper. 'I didn't realise Gareth Loysey lived here.'

'He and his wife moved down a few months ago. They're

living a few miles outside Lydmouth. She grew up in this part of the world. In Trenalt, actually.'

Randolph nodded. 'I know. Her brother was a friend of mine at Oxford, and I met her once or twice before the war — before she became Mrs Loysey. I met him, too — Loysey, I mean. They were courting, or rather she was. Have you met him?'

'Not yet. I'm going to do a piece on him in the next few days, though.' The item in the paper mentioned Loysey's giving a talk at Ashbridge School. 'What do *you* think of his work?'

Randolph shrugged. 'So-so. I saw his last show, as a matter of fact — Rosendale's, Cork Street. I went to the opening — God knows what it cost to put on. All rather vulgar — quails' eggs and Roederer.' He sniffed. 'No, I prefer his older work. To my mind, he's got rather tame since the war.'

'Does he sell?'

'I doubt if he makes much money out of it. Never has, as far as I know. He's probably got private means.'

The brandy arrived. Jill had accepted a glass, feeling she deserved the treat but would probably live to regret it. After the first sip, she blurted out: 'I'm glad you came. It's my birthday. So this feels like a celebration.'

'Many happy returns, darling.' He stood up and planted smacking kisses on her cheeks, much to the delight of the other people in the lounge. 'I wish I'd known it was your birthday — I'd have looked for a present.' He sat down heavily in his chair and lit yet another cigarette. 'Actually, I do have something for you.' He smiled, one side of his mouth higher than the other. 'Not a present — more of a proposition. I wondered if you'd like to give me a hand with *Berkeley's*.'

Jill had taken a mouthful of brandy and surprise made her cough. She dabbed her eyes with a handkerchief. 'Doing what? Something freelance?'

'No. Staff — features editor, in fact. I need someone to pull that side of things together. Someone who knows what I'm looking for.'

'It – it would mean moving back to London.'

'Of course. But if you're worried about accommodation there's no need. A cousin of mine has a house in Lancaster Gate with an empty flat at the top of it. You could have that while you found your feet. For as long as you liked.'

'But I'm out of touch.'

'You'd soon pick it all up again. You haven't been forgotten, you know.' He squinted at her through the cigarette smoke. 'No need to make your mind up now. Sleep on it. I'd see that you didn't lose out financially, of course.'

Jill drained her brandy and smiled at him. 'I must say it's nice to be asked.'

'Say yes and make it even nicer.' He grinned and added in a louder voice for the benefit of any eavesdroppers: 'I could go down on one knee if you like.'

Jill giggled in a way ill befitting a professional woman with a reputation to maintain.

'Another brandy?' Randolph suggested. 'More of that frightful coffee?'

'I really must get back to the office. Some of us have a living to earn.'

Randolph came out with her to the hall of the hotel to say goodbye. He asked for her phone number, and as he was jotting it down the door to the street opened and Bernie Broadbent came in. His heavy face brightened when he saw Jill. She introduced him to Randolph. Bernie's massive hand swallowed the younger man's.

'Pleased to meet you,' Bernie said. 'Can't stop, I'm afraid. Council meeting this afternoon.'

'You're a councillor?' Randolph murmured. 'How awfully public-spirited.'

As far as Jill knew, the two men had never met before. But it seemed to her that a spark of recognition passed between them. She pushed the thought out of her mind, said goodbye to them, and hurried along the High Street. The afternoon air was warm against her face and her head swam.

Too much brandy and too much imagination, she thought — a recipe for disaster.

# Chapter Four

Edith Thornhill stood just inside the door. Screwed to the wall near by was a brass plate commemorating the generosity of Vernon Hudnall and Rufus Moorcroft, which had made it possible to build the village hall in 1938. Most of the mourners had already left. A team of ladies from the Women's Institute were clearing the trestle tables.

The curtains had been drawn across the stage at the far end. Edith remembered the curtains when they were new – a deep and luxuriously soft purple velvet, which had seemed the height of luxury. Now the material was frayed and faded.

She heard footsteps and turned.

'Sorry to keep you,' Jack said. 'Mrs Solly wanted a word. Well, rather more than a word, actually.' He winced. 'She wanted to tell me all over again about finding Uncle Rufus.'

Edith led the way into the sunshine. She wished she hadn't accepted Jack's offer of a lift home. But she had just missed one train and would have had to wait nearly an hour for the next. Besides, Jack said he needed to go to Shipston's office in Castle Street after lunch, and he had sounded pathetically incapable of finding Castle Street on his own.

Directly across the road from the village hall was the Bear. Ivor Fuggle was sitting on one of the benches outside with a glass beside him, writing in a notebook balanced on his knee. He looked up and stared at them. When Edith stared back, he did not look away.

Jack had not noticed. He gestured at a dusty Ford parked in the lee of the churchyard wall. 'Uncle Rufus's old banger. Do you remember it?'

Edith shook her head.

'Nearly twenty years old and it still goes like a bomb.' His voice shook slightly.

He opened the car door for her. He was nervous, she thought, just as he used to be. Neither of them spoke until they were out of the village and on the road to Lydmouth.

'Why don't I drop you off at your house and then go on to Shipston's afterwards?' Jack suggested.

'There's no need,' Edith said quickly. 'I want to do some shopping on the way home.'

They drove on in silence for half a mile. Jack cleared his throat.

'How old are your children?'

Then it was easier. She told him about David and Elizabeth, about where they went to school, and what they were like. And in return, he told her about his son, who was seven and a half years old and lived with his mother, Jack's ex-wife, near Aldershot. 'Of course, I see him as often as I can,' Jack said. 'It's not easy, with the army. I was in Germany before Aden. Though I should be in England for a while now. He'll be going away to school next month. For the first time. Poor little blighter.'

The atmosphere between them eased while they talked of their children. Children were a safe subject, a source of endless contrasts and comparisons, symbols that each of them had other lives, now, and other commitments. She wondered about the ex-wife: what her name was; what she was like; above all, why she was an ex-wife and not a current one.

'It'll be Henry's birthday soon,' Jack said. 'He keeps badgering me for a puppy. He mentions it in every letter he writes. His mother is not keen, though. He's got a rabbit, and she says that's quite enough livestock to be going on with.'

'That reminds me. The White Rabbit.'

'What?' Jack changed gear, causing a screech of protesting metal from the gearbox. 'Sorry.'

'Miss Caswell was talking about someone called the White Rabbit. She couldn't remember his surname. He married someone. Miss Caswell said something about her coming back — the wife, I mean — but I don't know where.'

Jack was silent. She looked at him, wondering if he hadn't heard. Then, with his eyes firmly on the road, he said: 'You remember Hugh? Hugh Hudnall.'

Edith swallowed. 'Of course I do.' She looked down at her hands, watched her fingers turning her wedding ring and her engagement ring round and round. She hoped she wasn't blushing.

'Do you remember he had a sister? June — a bit older than he was. I think she was a half-sister, as a matter of fact.'

'Yes.'

'June had a boyfriend that Hugh used to call the White Rabbit. Floppy hair and bright bow ties. Some sort of artist, I think. I've a feeling they got married in the end. Can't remember the surname but someone must know. Hugh didn't like him.'

'But why did Miss Caswell want to talk to her?' Edith wished she hadn't brought up the subject. How could Jack be so insensitive as to mention Hugh?

'No idea. But the poor old dear's cracked, isn't she?'

'She was very fond of your uncle.'

'He was kind to her. Poor old chap.'

'What do you mean?'

Jack glanced at her for a moment. 'I don't know. I suppose I feel guilty about him — that I didn't make more of an effort to see him or even to keep in touch. The police showed me the note he left. All it said was: "Sorry – just can't go on. I miss Mary and there's nothing left to live for. Sorry to be such a bother." '

'Mary?'

'His wife. She died in the thirties. I hardly remember her.'

Edith looked away. She wound down the window a few inches, suddenly desperate for fresh air. The sadder she felt about Rufus, the warmer she felt about Jack. It was confusing, and she could do without that. She had enough confusion already.

They drove into Lydmouth. Jack had forgotten the layout of the town. Edith directed him along the High Street and from there to Castle Street. Shipston & Shipston occupied what had once been a Georgian town house at the upper end of the street. Jack pulled up outside.

'Are you sure I can't run you home first?' he said. 'I know the way now.'

'No thanks, really – I must do some shopping.' She put her hand on the door handle.

'Edith?'

'What?'

'Why did you never write? I wrote to you, care of your grandmother. Why did you – just leave?'

She looked at him. 'Can't you guess?'

'No – I know it was a shock about Hugh and so on, but—'

'The summerhouse,' she said harshly. 'That summerhouse in the garden at Highnam Cottage.'

He looked at her, his broad forehead as furrowed as a ploughed field. Then his face cleared. 'You thought it was me in there? The day after the play? Is *that* it? Edith – surely you—?'

He stopped abruptly. The pleading expression left his face as though sponged away by an invisible hand. He stared past Edith through the window of the car's passenger door.

Edith turned her head. George Shipston was standing on the pavement, bent down so his face was framed by the window, his head and neck suspended miraculously between heaven and earth. Had he been eavesdropping? How much had he heard? How much had he understood?

'Good afternoon, Major Graig,' the old man said in a voice like a hacksaw cutting metal. Frowning slightly, he looked at Edith. 'I hope I'm not interrupting anything.'

# Chapter Five

It was very hot. A bluebottle cruised through the open sash window and drifted towards the cornice of the big room on the first floor. Despite the open window the room smelled of stale old cigars, like a smoking compartment in an elderly railway carriage.

George Shipston scrabbled in one of the lower drawers of his desk. Jack took advantage of this instant of privacy, loosened the knot of his tie and eased his hard collar away from his neck.

Sounds rose from the ground floor, muffled and remote as though in a dream: the clacking of typewriter keys, like a platoon at a distant rifle range; the hooting of a car horn; Shipston's nephew, Mr Wilfred, talking about tennis in a slow, sleepy voice. There was information to be gathered, Jack knew, there were decisions to be made. But all he could think of was Edith Broadbent.

*Mrs Thornhill.*

For years, she had stayed in his mind, for years she had been eighteen. Now she was different but somehow still the same. She had filled out, and he liked that. It was odd to think of their lives progressing in parallel for so long. Now, suddenly and unexpectedly, the lines had intersected again.

'Yes – here we are,' Shipston said, leaning back in the

wooden armchair behind the desk and fanning his face with a long white envelope. 'I knew I had it somewhere.'

'I'm glad there is a will. When I heard about that bonfire, I was afraid Uncle Rufus might have burnt it.'

Shipston grunted. 'I always advise our clients to deposit their wills with us or in the bank.'

'When did he make it?'

Shipston searched for his reading glasses, which he found eventually on the desk in front of him. He settled them on his nose, picked up the cigar which had been smouldering in the ashtray and stared suspiciously at the envelope. 'We drew it up for him in September 1939. Did a lot of that sort of work in the first year of the war. Concentrated people's minds. He added one or two codicils after the war. Would you like me to outline the terms?'

'Please.'

Shipston prised open the flap of the envelope and slid out the will. His wrinkled hands were shaking as he unfolded it. 'When did you last see Mr Moorcroft, Major?'

'I've been abroad a good deal.' Jack knew he could have made time to come down to Trenalt. 'I think the last time I saw him was at my mother's funeral. That was in '49.'

Shipston nodded his head gravely, as though approving and in some way confirming the inscrutable timing of the Almighty. He sucked on the cigar as if it were a dummy, removed it from his mouth and said: 'First the bequests: there's two hundred pounds to the housekeeper, Mrs Solly – I believe she was at the funeral. The parish church gets the same amount, with the particular request that it should be used to keep the graveyard tidy.'

'My uncle used to mow the grass there when he was younger.'

'Just so. Five hundred pounds to the Royal Air Force Benevolent Fund. A similar sum to the Star and Garter Home in Richmond. And a walnut bureau, believed to be Queen Anne, to a gentleman in London, a Mr Haughton. But the rest of the estate goes to you.' Shipston looked up. His eyes gleamed brightly beneath a tangle of overgrown eyebrows. 'You'll be wanting to know how much, I imagine, Major Graig. Hard to be sure before we get it valued for probate. He had a house in London, of course, which is rented out. All in all, I would expect the gross value to be somewhere in the region of sixty to sixty-five thousand pounds.'

'Good God. I had no idea he was that well off.'

'Indeed.' Shipston sniffed. 'As residuary legatee, I'm afraid you will be responsible for the estate duty.' He pawed at a pile of papers at one side of the desk and extracted a sheet. 'It's a sliding scale, of course. You pay nothing on the first two thousand, then one per cent on the next thousand, and so on. Yes, it becomes quite punitive. Mr Attlee has much to answer for. By the time one reaches the range between sixty and seventy thousand, the Chancellor takes forty per cent.' His cheeks shook, reminding Jack of a gobbling turkey. 'Iniquitous, in my opinion.'

'Yes.' Jack thought in a dazed, circular fashion: *I'm rich. I'm going to be rich.*

'Do you know Mr Haughton?'

Jack blinked. 'Yes – he was a friend of my uncle's. He was at the funeral.'

'I wonder if he's one of the Shropshire Haughtons.'

'What?'

'Middleham Park, near Ludlow,' Shipston said proudly, as though it were his. 'They used to own half the county at one time, I believe.' His cheeks began to tremble again. 'Estate duties have had a ruinous effect on our old families.'

'I've no idea if he's—'

'A most distinguished family too. In fact, I believe they're related to Miss Caswell. Her great-grandmother was a Haughton, if my memory serves me well.'

'That's most interesting,' Jack said, edging forward on his chair. 'Now, what happens next about this will?'

Shipston waved a slightly grubby hand. 'Oh, we apply for probate. You saw Miss Caswell at the funeral?'

Jack nodded. 'Unfortunately I didn't get a chance to talk to her properly. She—'

'Such a tragedy. They were a Wiltshire family. Lived near Rode. Of course the title's died out now. Lord Vauden must be her nearest relation. But I was truly shocked to see her at the funeral.'

'Why? Uncle Rufus had quite a soft spot for her.'

'It was hardly an appropriate occasion for someone with her delicate nerves. No, it was wholly inappropriate. I'm surprised that Dr Angmer allowed it. He's a sound man, in many ways, but in my opinion he's far too easy-going. And one has to think of the look of the thing. Miss Caswell isn't just anybody, after all. And the press were there, too. There was a man called Fuggle, you know, a most unsavoury character.'

'Well, I suppose they report funerals in the local rag, don't they?'

Shipston ignored what Jack had said. His jaws worked up and down as though chewing up a thought so he could spit it out as an articulated sentence.

'The thing is, Major Graig,' he said at last, 'the man's a scandalmonger. One has to think of Miss Caswell. We don't want bad publicity, do we?'

# Chapter Six

On that same afternoon, Tuesday, 19 August, June Loysey was sitting at her desk in the dining room of Grebe House with the *Gazette* spread open before her. She stared at the announcement of Rufus Moorcroft's funeral. She could have recited the words with her eyes closed. She told herself for the tenth time in the last half-hour that it had been wise for her not to go.

Yet there was just the possibility it might have been useful. She might have been a little farther forward if she had gone, and if fate had been on her side. On the other hand, judging by the events of the last few years, fate was anywhere but on her side. It was all so terribly unfair.

Bloody Rufus. Why had he been so stupid?

With a sigh, June pushed the paper aside and drew the pile of bills towards her. She opened the middle drawer of the desk and took out her cheque book. The effort seemed to exhaust her. She stared out of the window. From here you could see the gable wall of the former stable they had converted at great expense into Gareth's studio. If he was going to do any work, any real work, he needed to have things just right. He *deserved* to have them just right. She had always understood that. But getting things just right always cost a lot of money.

She began to leaf through the bills, trying to decide which

should be paid immediately and which could be safely left until another month. There was one from the wine merchant, their old one in Bloomsbury, which made her raise her eyebrows every time she looked at the figure at the bottom of the bill. *Payment at your earliest convenience.* Still, once they settled down, once they'd got over the expense of the move, they would be able to live more cheaply. This was the country, after all, and everything was cheaper in the country. Besides, there were fewer temptations.

She heard the click of the studio door. Four o'clock already. She swept the bills into the drawer, stood up and stretched. Gareth did not like to find her fussing about with the accounts, as he called it. The sprung floor of the dining room creaked beneath her weight as she strode to the door and down the hallway to the kitchen. By the time Gareth appeared, she already had the kettle on and was slicing bread at the table.

'I'm late,' he said. 'I was going through some old sketch-books, and I lost track of the time. It's made me feel quite faint.'

She was by his side in an instant. 'Come and sit down.' She settled him at the table in the window seat, which they used for breakfast and tea. He watched her for a moment.

'June – do you think we could have anchovy toast? I feel I need something a little more substantial than usual.'

She concealed her dismay. 'I always think of that as a sort of winter snack.'

'It gets quite cold in the studio. Do you know, I think my circulation's getting worse. It's a very damp climate down here, isn't it? I'm sure that's not helping. I got so cold I was going to put a hat on. They say one loses most heat through one's head. But I couldn't find the wretched thing.'

'Which hat, dear?'

'The green one – you know, the pork-pie hat with the feather.' He stuck out his lower lip. 'I could have sworn I'd left it in the car. Have you moved it?'

'No,' she said, and turned away so he could not see her face. 'But I'm sure we can find lots of other hats. What about the—?'

'But of course a hat wouldn't solve the real problem,' he broke in. 'This country's damned climate. You never know what it's going to do to you. Why don't we run down to Italy this autumn? I'm sure a little bit of sunshine would do us both the world of good.'

June thought of the bills in the drawer and the latest bank statement with its debits in red ink. 'Perhaps in the spring, dear. We've hardly had time to settle in since the move.'

Gareth had brought his current sketchbook with him and while she prepared the anchovy toast and made the tea his pencil scratched and scraped. The sound gave her pleasure. She was worried about his health, though. The change of scene would do him good. The annoying thing was, she had come so close to solving their little difficulty.

She poured the tea and carried his cup over to him.

He glanced up at her. 'You haven't forgotten about tomorrow?'

'Tomorrow?' She felt a familiar sense of panic rising within her.

'Cardiff.' He snatched a slice of toast and crammed it into his mouth. He added with his mouth full: 'Surely you remember?'

'Oh – of course. When does it start?'

'The private view begins at six. Frankly, I think it's a waste of time – Maitland's work is very overrated. I don't know what Herbert sees in it. Still, ours is not to reason why, I suppose. I'd like to get down there a couple of hours earlier, though. I want to discuss the retrospective with Herbert. I had an idea about how to hang it while I was going to sleep last night.' He tore off another mouthful of toast and stared at her with bright eyes. 'I think we should do it by theme, not chronologically. It would give the critics a peg – something to write about. That's half the battle.'

He was flushing now, June noticed, as he often did when he was excited. Gareth, with his pink skin and his very fair hair, had always reminded her of a little boy. The older he became, the more she noticed the resemblance.

'If you could run me down to Lydmouth after lunch tomorrow,' Gareth went on, 'I'll take the train from there.'

She sat down heavily facing him. The toast smelt wonderful, despite the heat, but she was trying to lose weight so she resisted the temptation. If Gareth went to Cardiff by himself, he would be gone for four or five hours. It gave her an unexpected opportunity. She had assumed he would want her to drive him down there and stay with him the whole time.

'But I'd like you to come and fetch me, if that's all right,' he said. 'Herbert's having a couple of my canvases framed, and it would be tiresome to have to lug them back on the train. Besides, they might get damaged.'

'When would you like me to collect you, dear?'

'Not before ten. It may even be later. We're going out for a bite of supper afterwards. You could just wait outside the gallery.'

'Yes. Would you like some more tea?'

He pushed his cup across the table to her. He lit a cigarette and watched her fetching the kettle from the Aga, topping up the teapot and refilling the cups.

'Herbert mentioned *Lady with Fan* again.'

June's hand went to her throat. 'What did he say?'

'Even though it's so small, he thought it would look particularly well on the half-landing – as long as it was properly lit. So it was the first thing you saw when you went into the exhibition.'

'I'm surprised he's seen it.'

'I showed it to him before the war. He knew Moorcroft slightly, too – he saw it at Highnam Cottage a year or two ago.' Gareth rubbed the tip of his little nose. 'As a matter of fact he suggested we reproduce it for the front of the catalogue. Ironic, isn't it?' He ground out the half-smoked cigarette. 'That's the worst thing about this job. The bloody philistines. And when they own your work, it makes it even worse.'

She touched the sleeve of his jacket. 'You mustn't worry, darling.'

'Of course I worry. I wonder what will happen.'

'To *Lady with Fan?*'

'Do you think you could find out who Moorcroft's heir is? Maybe they'd sell it to us – or at least lend it for the retrospective.'

June patted her husband's arm and withdrew her hand. 'Don't worry, dear.' She wished he would let her pull his head down on her bosom. There were some sorts of comfort he would not let her give him. 'I'll see what I can find out. Where there's a will there's a way.'

He looked up sharply. 'A will – that's a point. I wonder if Moorcroft left one. Had he any family?'

'There was a sister, but I think she died. Her son used to come and stay at Highnam Cottage sometimes. You probably remember him – Jack somebody. He was madly in love with that girl who played the lead in Hugh's play. You remember, the one you said looked like a milkmaid. She wasn't local, but her grandmother lived in the village.'

Gareth Loysey looked up and smiled slowly. 'I remember,' he said with a speed and certainty that made her instantly suspicious, instantly jealous. 'Edith Broadbent.'

# Chapter Seven

The little train pulled out of Trenalt station and groaned and snorted down the single-track line towards the mouth of the tunnel. Councillor Bernie Broadbent waited for the level-crossing gates to open, his hand tapping the steering wheel. Then the train vanished into the side of the hill, and all that was left of it was a wisp of smoke rising into the blue sky.

A swift swooped and zigzagged to the side of the hill. Someone was walking on the path that led over the hill to the old quarry which lay concealed on the other side of it. At this distance the figure was little more than a silhouette, a stick figure. But Bernie knew who it was: Cicely Caswell. He could make out the shape of the long flowing coat. He thought she was hunched over, perhaps with her hands to her face. Maybe she was crying for Rufus. He hooted his horn in a fit of irritation, and at last the gates began to open.

The Riley bumped over the tracks and followed the road south along the valley, gradually climbing. A few minutes later, Bernie passed the entrance to Highnam Cottage. The road was running along the top of the ridge now. Suddenly Fontenoy Place came into sight, serene and golden in its parkland, a couple of hundred yards away on his left.

He had little time for old buildings, which in general he

thought were expensive to maintain and inconvenient to live in. But he liked the plainness and the symmetry of Fontenoy Place for all that. The main house was a rectangular block with short symmetrical wings connecting it to smaller pavilions at either side.

He turned in at the open gates by the lodge. He wondered if there were any truth in the rumour that Dr Angmer was too slack. A notice by the side of the drive requested him to keep his speed below 10 mph. He passed a uniformed nurse pushing a man in a wheelchair. They did not look at him.

The drive led up to a broad, gravelled terrace in front of the house. Two old women watched him incuriously from a stone seat set in the balustrade that bordered the terrace. On the lawn below, a young man in a boater paced up and down, five steps forward, five steps back, talking earnestly to himself.

Bernie parked the car and went up the steps to the front door, which was standing open, revealing a cool dark hall beyond. He rang the bell and waited. As his eyes grew accustomed to the gloom, he saw that institutional debris was scattered across the marble chequerboard of the hall – raincoats, wellingtons, umbrellas, hatstands, and a flock of untenanted wheelchairs. He heard the swish of a door and then footsteps. A woman in nurse's uniform appeared, obviously on her way elsewhere. Stout and middle-aged, she had a face whose texture reminded him of a walnut shell.

Bernie removed his hat. 'Evening. My name's Broadbent. I've come to see Dr Angmer by appointment.'

She sighed. 'All right. You'd better wait here.'

She went through a pair of tall double doors on the right, closing them behind her. Broadbent took her words as an invitation to step into the hall. There was a set of columns on the left, beyond which a staircase rose into the heights of the house. He thought the smell was like a cross between a school's and a prison's. The elegance and the brightness of the sunlit exterior was a sham: the reality was this – a sad, dark place. He heard pots clattering and somebody calling for a nurse in a high, cracked voice.

Then the woman returned. 'You can see him now.' She rushed away, her feet slapping on the stone treads of the stairs.

He went through the doorway. He was in a long tall room, full of light – the sort of room the exterior of the house had promised. At the far end were French windows looking out over a paved terrace and more parkland. There were bookshelves on the other three walls, stretching up to the ceiling. A small man in a dark suit put down a book and rose up from an armchair. He came towards Bernie, his hand outstretched. His body was pear-shaped, with narrow shoulders, short legs and heavy thighs. He had grey hair receding from the temples.

'Councillor Broadbent, this is a pleasure.' Angmer's voice had a clipped quality, as though English were not its first language. 'Do sit down. May I get you a drink?'

Bernie accepted a whisky. Angmer fussed over a tray on a table near the windows. While he poured the drinks, he talked about the weather in obsessive detail. Once they were both settled in chairs, facing each other across the high marble chimney piece, his approach abruptly changed.

'It was kind of you to come at such short notice, Mr Broadbent. I know it must seem a little callous, perhaps, on the very day of poor Mr Moorcroft's funeral. But Sir Anthony and I felt that he would have been the first to get the question of his successor settled as early as possible. And no one, I'm sure, would be more suitable than yourself.'

'I see,' Bernie said warily. 'But perhaps you'd better tell me a little bit more about it before we go any farther.'

'Of course, of course.'

'Who was that woman who let me in, by the way?'

'What? Oh, yes. That is Nurse Lindor.' Angmer gave a little smile and stared down at his whisky glass. 'Rather a rough diamond, perhaps, but her bark is worse than her bite. She is invaluable with many of our more difficult guests.'

'Guests?'

'Oh, yes. That is one of our guiding principles, one of the changes I insisted on when I took over from my predecessor. We don't have residents or patients here – we have *guests*.'

'How long's the place been going? Must be at least forty years.'

'Oh, longer than that. Well over fifty. Longer still, if you go back to the foundation of the Trust itself. We were founded in 1887. The trustees leased a house in Wiltshire. But we outgrew it. When Lord Vauden's father inherited the estate here at the turn of the century, he decided he didn't want to live at Fontenoy Place and he leased it to the Trust. He sold it outright to us in 1919, together with about thirty acres of the park. Death duties, you know. It gives me great pleasure that the present Lord Vauden is one of our trustees. Many of our guests find that element of – of continuity particularly reassuring.'

'A charitable trust?' Bernie said.

'Of course.'

'What exactly is its purpose?'

'We look after those unfortunates who for a variety of reasons are unable to live what one might call a normal life in the world.'

'They pay to live here?'

'Oh yes, indeed. Or rather, in many cases, their families do. One could not run an establishment of this nature without substantial revenues coming in. I should make it clear that our guests have a very varied range of problems.' Angmer rolled his glass between his hands and stared past Bernie to the French windows at the end of the room. 'Some of the older ones are what my predecessors would have labelled moral defectives as opposed to mental defectives. Nowadays, of course, the—'

'Folks like Miss Caswell, eh?'

Dr Angmer's eyes snapped back to Bernie. 'Oh – I hadn't realised you knew her.'

'I had an auntie who lived in Trenalt before the war. Everyone knew her.'

'We've always allowed guests of that type a good deal of freedom. Within limits, naturally.' He waved large, limp hands like flippers as though defining the bounds of their liberty. 'Not that there are many of them left. Nowadays, most of our guests are either mentally unstable for one reason or another or simply very old. So old they can no longer cope by themselves. Some of their problems stem from nervous breakdowns. For example, we still have former officers from the Great War. Some of those have physical problems rather than, or as well as, mental problems. So, you see, we cater for a wide range of guests. I'm responsible to the trustees for the overall direction of the place, both medical and administrative.'

'And who are the other trustees?'

'Besides Lord Vauden and Sir Anthony Ruispidge, we have the bishop and George Shipston, who also handles our legal work. I know Sir Anthony feels that someone with – ah – your business acumen would be very valuable to us. And of course your local connections are another advantage from our point of view. The duties aren't onerous, either. The trustees meet every quarter, usually here. We often combine the meeting with lunch or dinner.'

Bernie nodded and, setting down his glass, levered himself out of the chair. 'Well, I'm glad to have met you, Doctor, and thanks for the drink. I'm flattered to be asked, too. If you don't mind I'll have a think about it and I'll be in touch.'

Dr Angmer conducted him out to his car, talking in fits and starts about a variety of subjects. He was sweating, but perhaps that was from the heat. As they were crossing the hall, Nurse Lindor clattered down the stairs.

'You haven't seen Miss Caswell, have you, Doctor?' she said.

Dr Angmer glared at her. 'She's probably taking a turn in the park. No need to worry.' Once he and Bernie were outside, he added in a low voice, 'That's the trouble with these ill-educated women. They're inclined to panic at the slightest little deviation from routine.'

They shook hands. Bernie drove slowly away. He glanced in his rear-view mirror. Angmer was still standing by the front door, a large pink hand raised in farewell.

He went back the way he had come, past Highnam Cottage, down to the station and then up to Trenalt itself. Instead of taking the road to Lydmouth, however, he pulled over and parked by the churchyard wall. He walked up the steps and threaded his way between the stones until he came to his aunt's grave, a stone's throw from the cottage where she had once lived. The last time he had been here, near the end of the war, there had been fresh flowers around the stone and the earth above her was still gently humped like an eiderdown covering a sleeping person. Now the earth was flattened, and grass grew thickly where once there had been flowers. He touched the top of the headstone for an instant and walked on.

He found Rufus's grave tucked away near the churchyard wall. No headstone here, of course – just a temporary wooden cross from the undertaker and a great, gaudy mass of wreaths and flowers. One of the wreaths had come from him. He had used the meeting of the Standing Joint Committee at Police Headquarters this morning as an excuse to himself not to come to the funeral.

'Who are you?' said a woman's voice behind him. 'What are you doing here?'

He turned round. Cicely Caswell, her face a mixture of haughtiness and fear, stared at him over the top of a large table tomb surrounded by rusty railings. For him not to have seen her before, she must have been crouching behind it.

'Miss Caswell,' he said. 'Do you remember me? Bernie Broadbent.'

She looked puzzled. Then her brow cleared and she waved excitedly towards the row of cottages beyond the churchyard wall. 'You lived over there.'

'Not exactly. My auntie did.'

'Mrs Broadbent. She liked peppermints.' Miss Caswell gradually emerged from her place of concealment, a step or two at a time, glancing from left to right, like a cat on strange territory. A long brown raincoat without a belt trailed from her narrow shoulders almost to her ankles. The coat was unbuttoned, revealing a grey pinafore beneath. She wore a straw hat with a frayed brim but neither gloves nor stockings.

'You've come to see Rufus,' she said. 'Did you know him?'

'Yes. Not very well.'

'He was my best friend.' She looked up at Bernie, studying his face. 'You won't tell anyone, will you?'

'That he was your best friend?'

She shook her head vigorously. 'That you've seen me. I'm not meant to be out. I should be in bed soon.'

Bernie glanced up at the church clock. 'Isn't it rather early for bed?'

'We have to go to bed early. Lindor would be very cross. You won't tell her?'

'No, I won't.' He thought she had aged a great deal since he had last seen her close up. Not her figure, but her face. It was clear that her standards were slipping. Her hands were dirty and wisps of grey hair were escaping from under the brim of the hat. But the voice was the same as he remembered from that summer before the war.

'I must go back, I must go back.'

He wondered whether he should offer to run her back to Fontenoy Place but he was too embarrassed to ask. He wasn't sure he wanted a madwoman in the car. Besides, she wouldn't want a lift. It would make her return too obvious.

'Gentlemen still smoke after dinner, don't they?' she said suddenly.

'Yes — I suppose they do.'

'They smoke cigars after dinner,' she informed him, her tone gathering certainty. 'Mama never allowed them to smoke in the house, though, except in the billiard room. And in the summer, on fine evenings, they smoked on the terrace.' Her lips moved but for a few seconds no sound came out.

'Sorry?' Bernie said. 'Were you saying something?'

'Once I heard them talking about Constance, you know,' she said in a voice that had dropped almost to a whisper. 'And that reminds me: I must make a telephone call. One puts pennies in the slot, you know, and presses buttons. I watched Lindor when she phoned her sister. It's quite straightforward. Would you be so kind as to lend me tuppence? I don't appear to have my purse.'

He took out his purse and shook a handful of change into the palm of his hand.

'A business matter,' she went on. 'Most important. But you mustn't tell anyone that you've seen me. You give me your word?'

He dropped two coppers into the grubby palm of her outstretched hand. 'Of course I won't. Not if you don't want me to.'

She muttered something, staring down at the coins. He thought he caught the word 'Kent'. For an instant, he toyed with the idea of trying to explain to Miss Caswell that tuppence would not buy a very long trunk call to Kent. But before he could say anything, there was a distraction. A large blue car pulled up outside the Bear. It was a beautiful thing. He didn't recognise the make. A slim middle-aged man emerged from behind the wheel.

Miss Caswell scuttled back to the shelter of her grave. 'Who's that?' she hissed. 'He was here before. I had a ride in his car.'

Bernie eyed the sleek lines of the bonnet with a sensation that was somewhere between lust and religious exaltation. 'Why don't I go and find out? I'll keep him occupied, and then you can leave.'

'Yes. That would be kind.' She spoke as if she were the one conferring a favour. 'Well, I mustn't keep you, Mr Broadbent. It's been so nice meeting you again. Give my regards to your aunt.'

She waved at him and then ducked down behind the grave. Only the top of her hat remained in view, bobbing above the top of the monument.

Poor old cow, Bernie thought.

He strolled out of the churchyard and crossed the road to the pub. The car was a Bristol, he saw as he drew closer to it, a streamlined vehicle which made his own Riley seem old-fashioned and mass-produced. He went into the lounge bar. The man was leaning on the counter, waiting for the barmaid to finish with the crowd in the public bar. He turned as Bernie came in and his eyes lit up with recognition.

'It's Mr Haughton, isn't it?' Bernie said. 'We met at the Bull at lunchtime.'

'Of course.' Haughton held out a soft, very clean hand. 'Miss Francis introduced us. Can I get you a drink?' He glanced over the bar. 'When they condescend to serve us.'

'Thanks. That's a lovely car out there.'

The glories of the Bristol, compared and contrasted with those of other cars they had driven, carried them safely through the first five minutes of their conversation. They settled at the table in the bow window, each with a large whisky. Bernie was amused to see Miss Caswell tiptoeing across the road from the churchyard to the public telephone box on the corner.

Haughton saw him smile. 'That's Rufus's friend, isn't it? Rufus Moorcroft, I mean.'

'Yes – I didn't realise you knew Rufus. Is that why you're down here?'

'Yes, the funeral. The old lady was there and I gave her and her – her keeper? – a lift afterwards. I met her once or twice before the war. Talking to her is rather like having an audience with a dowager duchess, eh?'

Bernie nodded. They sipped their drinks and watched Miss Caswell struggling with the heavy door of the telephone box and then wrestling with the telephone directories.

'So – you knew Rufus too?' Haughton said, dabbing his lips with a silk handkerchief. 'Did you know him well?'

'Not that well,' Bernie said. 'But he'll be badly missed around here.'

Haughton produced a gold cigarette case. 'Yes,' he said slowly. 'Funny thing, when people die. It's as if someone's chucked a stone in a pond. The ripples just keep on coming. And sometimes you don't quite know where they'll end up.'

He held out the open cigarette case to Bernie. Their eyes met. Haughton had brown eyes, which reminded Bernie of a pair of velvet curtains his mother used to have. When he was a child, he would rub his cheek against them, marvelling at their softness.

'You know,' Haughton said quietly, 'I've a feeling we've met before. I'm not sure we were introduced, but I remember your face. Were you in Trenalt in the summer of '38, by any chance?'

# Chapter Eight

Jill Francis watched and waited.

Only one of the upstairs windows looked out over the garden at the back of Church Cottage. It was near the head of the stairs. Jill stood beside it, her elbows propped on the sill and a cigarette in her mouth, staring over the wall at the end of her garden at the walled enclosure beyond. Once this had been the kitchen garden of the vicarage next door. Now it contained a mass of sun-dried mud and weeds. Stacked along one wall, where once there had been a row of greenhouses, were bricks, gravel, scaffolding and a large pile of sand which Alice, Jill's cat, found an agreeable amenity.

Waiting like this made her feel like a schoolgirl. She would feel embarrassed if anyone discovered her in this position.

A local builder was in the process of turning the old kitchen garden into a select development of bungalows and small houses. The council's planning department had waved its wand and transformed it into a desirable place to live. Several of the plots had already been sold, including one of the two bungalows whose minute gardens would back against the wall of Jill's own. Set in that wall of crumbling stone topped with old brick was a gate, rotting at the bottom, the wood bleached in the sun, sagging on its hinges.

Jill stubbed out her cigarette. *Come on.* One spent far too much time waiting in this world.

At last she saw movement at the far end of the kitchen garden, where there was another gate leading to Bull Lane and the High Street. It was Richard. He closed the farther gate behind him and walked swiftly towards the nearer gate to Jill's garden. Automatically she patted her hair. He was walking fast and purposefully, not furtively. He kept his head down, and in any case the brim of his hat sheltered his face.

She would have liked to have checked her appearance in the bedroom mirror, but she could not stop watching him. There was a fascination in seeing him when he thought he was alone and unobserved, as if solitude might somehow make him more himself. She waited at the window until she heard the click of the latch on her own gate. She was moving away when she caught another movement at the far end of the garden.

The gate to Bull Lane was opening. Just as Detective Inspector Richard Thornhill left the kitchen garden by one entrance, Miss Amy Gwyn-Thomas came in by the other. At this distance her brimless hat looked like an inverted acorn cup.

Coincidence? Had the Gwyn-Thomas woman seen him?

As she reached the foot of the stairs, she heard Richard closing the back door. Excitement gripped her, taking her as always by surprise. It was as though control of her emotions had passed, unexpectedly and unobtrusively, to someone other than herself. She almost ran into the kitchen. They hugged each other.

'Happy birthday, darling,' he murmured into her hair.

She was relieved because she had feared he had forgotten, and guilty that she had even imagined that he might not have remembered.

Still holding her by the shoulders, he moved a little away from her. 'I've got something for you. Nothing much, I'm afraid.'

She saw the brown paper bag on the table and knew from its shape that it was a book. He picked it up and handed it to her.

There was a watercolour reproduced on the cover: a winding road leading through a patchwork of fields to a village in the middle ground; the village had a church whose spire was almost identical to the one at Eastbury; in the foreground were a few sheep and a signpost; behind the village was a hill with a tower on its summit and, nestling close to the village, a blue field. That was the name of the book – *The Blue Field*, by John Moore.

'I remembered your saying you loved the other two books, and you hadn't got the third one yet,' Richard said. He hesitated, looking into her face. 'You do like it, don't you?'

She opened the book. On the flyleaf, he had written, 'To J. from R., with best love on your birthday'. It was the first message he had ever written for her. She had no letters from him, not even a postcard. Richard was a careful man, even when he took risks.

'Darling, it's wonderful.'

She put her arms around his neck and kissed him hard on the lips. She had in fact bought a copy of *The Blue Field* from Hatchards when she was last in London a few weeks ago. It was under a pile of magazines in the sitting room. His arms locked behind her back. As they were kissing, the arms slipped lower and lower. Then his hands cupped her bottom. He pulled her against him.

Jill turned her head away, disrupting the kiss. 'Richard – not now. We need to talk.'

'It can wait.'

She wriggled out of his arms. 'No, it can't. Come into the sitting room.'

She took his hand and drew him into the hall. He made a half-hearted attempt to encourage her upstairs. She tugged him into the sitting room instead. She pushed Alice off the sofa and they sat down. He took both her hands in his.

'What is it?' he said. 'Something's worrying you, isn't it?'

'It's that Gwyn-Thomas woman at the *Gazette*.'

'Tall, thin woman with a long nose?'

'That's her. She came into the kitchen garden just as you were coming through the gate into my garden. I think she could have been following you.'

His eyebrows ran together. 'Do you think she saw me come in here?'

'I don't know. She might have done. Even if she didn't, she might have seen you go into the kitchen garden from Bull Lane. So when she came through the gate and couldn't see you, she must have worked out there's only one place you could be.'

'I could have gone through the third gate – the one to the vicarage garden.'

'No you couldn't. Some spivs came in and stole one or two tools from the outbuildings the other week, and since then they've kept that gate locked and bolted.'

'She was in the bookshop at lunchtime,' Richard said. 'But that must have been a coincidence. She was already there when I went in.'

'I wouldn't put anything past her.'

He drew away from her. 'Do you think she knows? Or is she just haunting you on the off-chance? Or just to make a nuisance of herself?'

'I don't know,' Jill said. 'But I do know we can't carry on meeting here. It's too dangerous.'

'So that leaves the other place?'

She nodded.

'But it's not particularly safe there, either. And we'll have to find somewhere else when the weather gets colder.'

*Will we?*

Jill looked at the pile of magazines serendipitously concealing her own copy of *The Blue Field*. The magazines were back issues of *Berkeley's*. Randolph Haughton had dropped them at the *Gazette* during the afternoon. Propped on the mantelpiece was his card, with the number of the Bear scribbled on the back and the words: *You'll want to do your research before you make up your mind.*

She stared up at the white rectangle of pasteboard. So was this the choice: going back to London, to a job which was equally likely to lead to either professional triumph or professional failure, but which certainly wouldn't be dull; or staying here, in a town that was gradually smothering her, but with the chance of spending a few snatched hours with Richard Thornhill?

He took her right hand with his left, holding it loosely so she could release it at any time. Richard was good like that, she thought, unusually sensitive for a man to changes of mood and atmosphere. Perhaps the snatched hours were worth any amount of tedium, even worth the attentions of Amy Gwyn-Thomas.

'Jill,' he was saying, 'will you listen to me?'

She dragged her attention back to him. 'What is it?'

'This can't go on. I can't bear seeing you like this.'

A harsh laugh escaped her. 'I'm not sure there's a better alternative.'

'Leave Lydmouth,' he said. 'Let's leave together, I mean.'

She thought of the job Randolph had dangled so enticingly before her. 'That's easy enough for me, Richard. But *you* can't. You can't leave Edith and the children. And it would be the end of your job, too.'

'But not the end of the world.' His face had become very pale, throwing into relief the blue-black of his stubble. 'I could find another job, I could do something else. That's not important. I'd explain the situation to Edith – and of course I'd make sure she and the children wouldn't suffer financially. These days, lots of people are divorced. It's no longer the problem it used to be. And once the divorce came through, then we could marry. We don't even have to stay in England if you don't want to. We could emigrate. Canada, perhaps, or Australia. Make an entirely fresh start.'

Her fingers tightened on his. She knew she would remember this, perhaps always. This was her real birthday present. He had given her something that she had not believed he would be able to give. She knew he meant it, too – Richard was not the sort of man who would make a proposal he did not intend to fulfil. She lifted his hand to her lips and kissed it gently.

'Well?' he said. 'Will you marry me?'

'I don't know, darling,' she said. 'I just don't know.'

# Chapter Nine

The phone was picked up after the second ring. Edith Thornhill's heart lifted with the receiver.

But Brian's voice came down the wires, the telephone making him sound more of a Londoner than ever: 'CID. Sergeant Kirby speaking.'

'Oh, Brian. It's Edith Thornhill.' Her voice sounded as flustered as she felt. She forced herself to speak more slowly: 'I wanted a word with my husband. Has he left?'

'I think he has. He might still be somewhere in the building. I could find out, if you want.'

'No – no, there's no need.' Automatically she covered up for him, for her. 'He said he had one or two things to do on the way home. And it was nothing urgent.'

She said goodbye and rang off. In the kitchen, she sat down with her knitting. Supper was in the oven. The table was laid. She wasn't used to having time on her hands, and she wasn't sure she liked it. Usually the children were there. Even if they were asleep upstairs, they and their needs somehow impinged on her. But at present David and Elizabeth were camping on a farm in St Brides Bay. She worried, naturally, that they might drown, or fall off a cliff, or blow themselves up with a Primus stove or suffer a fatal accident because of her brother-in-law's appalling driving.

That said, the fact they were not here left a hole in her life that no amount of housework or gardening had yet succeeded in filling.

She knitted more quickly – a red-and-white hot-water bottle cover – as though the more stitches per minute she produced, the greater her chance of filling the hole. The children's kittens, Max and Tom, stirred in their basket, alerted by the clacking of the needles.

'Damn,' Edith said aloud to them. 'Damn, damn, damn.'

The cats tumbled out of the basket and stretched. Tom staggered over to her chair and pounced on the ball of wool, which had fallen to the floor. Parted from it, he mewed piteously and wandered towards the scullery, where the food bowls were, with his brother trailing after him. She followed them with her eyes, feeling diminished by their departure. They weren't a substitute for the children but they were better than nothing.

*Funny to think they came from Jill Francis. That woman.*

Edith shook her head vigorously to clear it. She was imagining things. That was the trouble with spending too much time by yourself: too much time to think. And, of course, today had been upsetting. She had only herself to blame for that. Going back to Trenalt had not been a good idea. She had decided to go to Rufus Moorcroft's funeral on impulse, while she was washing up the breakfast things. Perhaps, she had thought, the distraction would do her good. And she had liked Rufus Moorcroft. It had even occurred to her that from Trenalt, which belonged to a past which had nothing to do with Richard or Jill Francis or even the children, she might see things more clearly.

Not things – people. Her husband, for example, and Jill Francis.

Trenalt. She dragged her mind back to the village. As a child, she had thought that the Trenalt valley was a place complete in itself, that unlike other places it didn't need a world around it. In memory, it had always been summer, for the simple reason that she had usually visited it in July or August during the long school holidays. In the early years she came with the rest of the family, later with her sister Sylvia, and finally by herself because at the age of fifteen Sylvia had decided that she did not care for the country.

Several of the shops had closed down since then. She remembered especially the baker's which had occupied what was now a private house beside the Bear. Sometimes Miss Caswell used to buy Lydmouth buns there. She had seemed almost as old then as she did now. She would break them into pieces and walk back to Fontenoy Place, offering sultanas, currants, dried cherries and cinnamon-flavoured fragments of bun to everyone she met. Humans were not the only recipients of Miss Caswell's generosity. Dogs, cats and birds were offered her largesse as well.

'She's touched, that one,' Granny said. 'But she's harmless, poor woman. And she's got a nice heart. So mind you're nice to her. And put your heart into it, my girl. If a job's worth doing, it's worth doing well.'

*If a job's worth doing, it's worth doing well.* That had been Granny's motto. She threw herself into her duties and expected her granddaughters to do the same.

But the last time Edith had stayed in Trenalt, the summer of 1938, everything had been different. Granny had not been well, and spent much of Edith's visit sitting by the kitchen fire and complaining about the cold. Edith had found her grandmother's behaviour inconvenient rather than worrying, and had begrudged the fact that the balance of their relationship had shifted. Granny was there to look after her, not the other way round.

Anyway, Granny's illness had not seemed important. That summer, what mattered was the play. And the new people at Trenalt – Jack Graig, yes, but most of all Hugh Hudnall.

The Hudnalls had moved to the village from Lydmouth the previous spring, so Edith had not met them before. Vernon Hudnall, recently widowed and himself in poor health, had wanted a change, and his doctor had thought that living in a high, airy location might help his bronchitis. Hudnall bought Oak Tree House from the widow of Dr Egward. He knew Trenalt, and Trenalt knew him, because he owned a nearby quarry. But Edith had never met his children.

So nothing had prepared her for Hugh. On the second day of her visit, she went to the baker's to buy buns for tea. On her way back, two men emerged from the darkened interior of the Bear, glasses in their hands. She glanced at them, and then had to tear her eyes away.

They were both young. In the summer of 1938, Jack had only just left school. He was shorter than Hugh but broader. Edith registered his presence but would have found it hard to say what he looked like in half an hour's time. Later she had discovered that Hugh often had that effect on people: he drew their eyes towards him. Saying what he was like did not begin to explain why it was so hard to look away from him: he was slim and tall, with fair hair, very blue eyes and regular features. So were thousands of other young men. On that occasion he was wearing an old blazer with green and brown stripes, a faded shirt with a frayed collar open at the neck, and grey flannel trousers.

He stared at Edith, making no attempt to conceal his interest. 'Georgina,' he said to her.

'Who?' she replied, confused.

He smiled. 'The perfect Georgina.'

'But I'm not. I'm—'

'Come and have a drink, and we'll tell you all about her.'

'I can't. I have to get back.'

Hugh had looked at her for a moment. She had felt as if she were a famous painting that he had travelled miles to see. Then he said, 'You could spare five minutes, surely? You see, I can't let you go now I've found you. I feel I've been looking for you all my life.'

\*　　\*　　\*

The doorbell rang.

Edith's body jerked in the Windsor chair as if an electric current had run through it. The past vanished, leaving her staring at the idle needles on her lap and feeling faintly queasy. She put the knitting on the table and stood up. It was as if she'd been caught out in an indulgence of a mildly shameful nature, like a lonely glass of sherry.

Richard, she thought with both relief and anger. Perhaps he'd forgotten his key again.

But on the doorstep she found Uncle Bernie. As he kissed her cheek, which he did not usually do when they met, she smelled the whisky.

'I happened to be passing,' he said. 'Not a bad time to call, is it?'

'Of course not. Come and have some tea. Unless you'd like something stronger?'

In recent months, Bernie had taken to dropping in with increasing frequency. Edith thought he might be lonely in that big house of his on Narth Road, though the notion of Bernie being lonely, or indeed having any weaknesses whatsoever, seemed faintly absurd. Richard sometimes found his visits tiresome, but she always made him welcome. This was not just because she liked him. It was also because he was in the process of buying this house for the Thornhills. Fairy godfathers needed cherishing.

He went into the kitchen, as he always did, and sat in the Windsor chair by the open window. He asked for beer, so she brought him a bottle from the pantry.

'Richard not back yet?' he said, stuffing tobacco into his pipe with thick fingers.

'He's had to work late quite often recently,' Edith said. 'There's been a lot to do, especially with Mr Williamson retiring and Mr Drake being appointed.' She smiled at him. 'But you know all about that.'

Bernie nodded. He stared out of the window. It was almost as if he had not heard what she had said. She wondered whether he had had more to drink than she supposed, or even if he were ill. Perhaps when Richard returned, she should ask him to drive Bernie home.

'I was talking to someone who knew you,' he said abruptly. 'Man called Haughton.'

She turned her head away from him, and picked up her knitting from the table. 'Mr Haughton? Yes – I went to a funeral today, and I met him there.' She waited for Bernie to say something, but he was silent. She hurried on: 'It turned out that we'd met before the war but I didn't know him well.'

'Rufus Moorcroft's funeral.'

'Yes.'

'I was thinking of going myself, as a matter of fact. But I had a meeting.'

'Miss Caswell was there. Do you remember her? The patient at Fontenoy Place who liked feeding people?'

'Yes. I saw her this evening, too. Poor old duck. She looked like a tramp. No gloves, and her hands were filthy. On the downward slope, I'm afraid. Of course, Moorcroft's death must have hit her hard. She was mooning over his grave. She was always sweet on him, wasn't she?' He sipped his beer, and glanced at her over the brim. 'I suppose you must've got to know Moorcroft quite well before the war. Especially that last summer before your nan died, when you were in the play.'

There was a rising inflection in Bernie's voice, and she knew the remark was not a statement but some sort of question, perhaps an invitation. At that moment, to her huge relief, the telephone began to ring in the next room. She excused herself and went to answer it.

She knew before she got there that it would be Richard, probably phoning to say that he would be a little later than planned. She picked up the phone and recited their number.

'Edith – it's Jack. Jack Graig.'

'Oh.' She stared fixedly at a small plaster bust of Beethoven on the sideboard. The curve of his right nostril had a small chip.

'You were the only Thornhill listed in Lydmouth in the phone book, so I thought it would be you. It was nice to see you again and have a chat. I wonder – would you be free for lunch tomorrow, by any chance?'

Edith thought: *One day, we must buy a piano to go with Beethoven. I'm sure the children are musical.* Tomorrow, between breakfast and supper, was a desert. There was nothing there but an empty space. 'Yes,' she heard herself saying. 'I've got nothing on.'

Now she had agreed, the hesitancy in Jack's voice vanished. He arranged a time to pick her up in the morning and rang off. She said goodbye and went back to the kitchen. Bernie was where she had left him. His glass was nearly empty and the air above his head was blue with pipe smoke.

'Who was it?' he said without looking up. 'Richard?'

He spoke as though he had a right to ask. She didn't like that.

'No,' she said. 'No one important.'

# Chapter Ten

Richard Thornhill spent most of Wednesday morning in Cardiff. He was representing his own force in a meeting designed to facilitate co-operation between five neighbouring CIDs. Co-operation was necessary but this meeting wasn't. Thornhill said little and thought a good deal.

He had woken this morning with the feeling that he'd said goodbye to his old self. He had the exhilarating and terrifying sense that a new person was now inhabiting the shell of the old one. Yesterday, he had asked Jill Francis to marry him.

The consequences of that choice affected everything. At last, he told himself again and again, as the voices droned on and the committee room filled with layer after layer of smoke, he had the chance to make a new start. He and Jill would be together all the time. No more snatched hours. No more lies.

In the meantime, though, there was still his old life with its responsibilities and worries. Above all, he wondered how Edith would take the news. He wasn't sure, but he thought she'd been acting strangely lately. Perhaps it was the absence of the children.

The chairman brought the meeting to an end in just over an hour. Following precedent, the committee members were due to move to a pub with an understanding landlord and continue their deliberations for another three or four hours. The practice was justified on the grounds that you could co-operate much more seriously with a pint in front of you and several pints inside you. Usually Thornhill went along, though he was not a serious drinker, but today he murmured something about work to catch up on, giving the impression that Drake was proving a demanding taskmaster, and slipped away early.

He found the Eastville Clinic in a side street off the Newport Road. He had telephoned ahead so they were expecting him. He would have to play it carefully. Drake had more or less told him to close the investigation into Rufus Moorcroft's death. He did not want to risk news of his visit getting back to Lydmouth.

The clinic was a large, plain Victorian villa standing in a sea of tarmac covering what had once been its garden. It was plastered with stucco painted a pale green, now much weather-stained. The big sash windows were obscured by acres of net curtains. Among the cars parked near the front door were two Jaguars and a Rolls-Royce.

Inside, the building was smarter than its exterior had led Thornhill to expect. It was in the modern style, with thick carpets, bright colours and spindly, angular furniture. What struck him most was the height of the ceilings and the silence.

He asked for Dr Pirk. The receptionist made sure he had an appointment and then showed him to a waiting room, where he sat in solitary state on a long yellow sofa. In front of him was a glass-topped table on which were arranged the current issues of magazines in immaculate columns, a vase of fresh flowers and an empty cut-glass ashtray. One thing was for certain: this place had nothing to do with the National Health Service.

Ten minutes later, a nurse came to fetch him. She gave him a professionally reassuring smile and took him up a broad staircase to a sun-filled landing. They met no one. She tapped on a door at the end of the corridor, opened it without waiting for an answer and stood aside to let him go in. As soon as he was inside the room beyond, the door closed behind him. On one level he would not have been surprised to hear the sound of a key turning in the lock.

'Inspector Thornhill.' A man behind the desk rose and held out his hand. 'I'm Lindsay Pirk.'

They shook hands and Lindsay Pirk waved Thornhill to a group of armchairs which were arranged round the empty fireplace. He was a tall, burly man of about Thornhill's age, with dark hair, fine features and a cultivated voice. He wore a black jacket with striped trousers beneath. There was a red rosebud in his buttonhole, and Thornhill found himself wondering irrelevantly if his wife had picked it for him that morning. Lindsay Pirk offered him a drink, which Thornhill declined.

'Since the patient is dead, the normal rules of confidentiality do not apply,' Pirk said, lowering himself into a chair and tugging at the creases of his trousers to avoid bagging the knees. 'And of course we are always happy to help the police when there's no conflict with our medical duty. However, Inspector, there are delicate features about a matter such as this. One has to bear in mind the feelings of families and friends.' He looked enquiringly at Thornhill, as though waiting for reassurance.

'I'm not sure I understand you, Doctor.'

'In view of Mr Moorcroft's condition.'

'But that's the point. Before Mr Moorcroft committed suicide, he destroyed many of his personal papers. As I explained to your secretary yesterday, we found a receipted bill from this clinic. But we would like to establish why you were treating him in case it has any bearing on his death.'

'His suicide. Yes, indeed, it may well have a bearing.'

He pursed his lips and stared at his white hands with their manicured nails. 'Mr Moorcroft suffered from a personality deficiency. The kindest way to look at it was that he was severely mentally ill. He was homosexual.'

'I see. But he had been married, and—'

'Many of these people are, I'm afraid. To give him his due,

Mr Moorcroft seemed to recognise how repugnant his condition was. I understood from him that he'd fought against it all his life. He told me that he had something of a position in the community, which was why he didn't want to discuss it with his GP.'

'So he came to you for help?'

'That is correct, Inspector. I must have seen him seven or eight times over the last two years. My secretary will give you the precise dates, if you wish.'

'We went through his bank statements and returned cheques. We found no trace of his visits there.'

'He probably paid in cash. That type of patient often does. They want to avoid unnecessary questions at home, you see. You'd hardly want to explain why you needed aversion therapy, for example, over the breakfast table.'

'Aversion therapy?' Thornhill frowned. 'But surely—?'

Lindsay Pirk smiled and shook his head. 'No – I don't mean we paraded naked men in front of him, let alone encouraged him to undertake illegal acts with them. We are a little more sophisticated than that. We show patients like Mr Moorcroft photographs of male nudes and then we give them apomorphine, either by tablet or injection. Like so many treatments, it's essentially very straightforward – we're simply putting into effect the Pavlovian principle.'

'And you find it works?'

'We have a reasonable success rate. If all goes well, as the patient becomes repulsed by his own sex, he becomes increasingly attracted to the opposite one.' Lindsay Pirk leant forward, elbows on knees, nodding as though hammering home his points with his forehead. 'Mr Moorcroft was not an easy subject, I have to admit. We have an apparatus for recording sound on magnetic tape. I used it to make a recording which emphasised the vileness of what he wanted to do. The vileness of what he had *done*. Then we put him in a room with a male nurse, no windows and a stack

of pornographic books. Oh, and I would have encouraged him to
have a few whiskies as well – in general, we find, a little alcohol
increases suggestibility. Then the nurse played back the tape and
we gave him the injection.'

'Morphine? Doesn't that just make them sleepy?'

'No, no. *Apo*morphine. It's a nausea-inducing drug. Very
soon a patient comes to associate the sight of naked men with
feeling violently ill. It's important to make the patient associate
his condition with degradation.'

'I'm not sure I follow.'

'You see, along with the sexual stimulus supplied by the
photographs, we provide the most disgusting physical circumstances we can contrive. The patient starts to be violently ill, but
we don't let him get out of bed, of course, or even give him a
basin. Which means he vomits all over himself, on the sheets, on
the pillows. We don't allow him to clear it up. And then in later
sessions we repeat the treatment as often as necessary.'

Thornhill thought of sad men he had occasionally arrested in
public lavatories. No wonder they were sad, if this was the
treatment doctors provided for them. 'And this . . . this
treatment was effective for Mr Moorcroft?'

'Ah – well, in his case, we made some progress, but it was
clear from what he told us that it was not a complete cure, or
anywhere near it. We had to try the electric treatment – with his
permission, of course. This involves attaching electrodes to the
arms and legs of patients and showing them slides of men and
women. But I'm sure you understand the principle. I don't want
to bore you with the technical details.'

Thornhill nodded. 'Was Mr Moorcroft . . . to your knowledge, was he engaged in any homosexual activity?'

'No. I understood from him that he'd not succumbed often
to these urges, and the instances when he had were many years
ago. It is possible that he was lying. The trouble with inverts is
that their condition has a pernicious moral effect, quite apart

from anything else. You wouldn't believe some of the things I've had to listen to.'

'Would you say that his suicide took you by surprise?'

Lindsay Pirk shook his head. 'It's a heavy burden for someone to bear. And I know Mr Moorcroft was depressed about the length of time the treatment was taking. Science can work wonders, Inspector, but it's no use pretending the treatment is a pleasant one. It's an unpleasant cure for an unpleasant disease.'

'But not in his case a cure.'

Lindsay Pirk smiled, his face serene. 'We must put our trust in science. I have every hope, Inspector, that within a couple of generations the condition will be nothing more than a footnote to medical history.'

# Chapter Eleven

'That painting,' Mrs Solly shrieked over the roar of the Hoover. 'That little one in the funny green frame.'

'What was that?' Major Graig shouted. 'Can't you turn that thing off?'

Mrs Solly raised her voice. 'The one from the study! You know.'

'Turn that damned thing off!' bellowed Jack Graig, and at last there was silence.

The Hoover had masked the approach of the CID's Hillman on the drive. Brian Kirby was standing on the doorstep of Highnam Cottage, part of his mind wrestling with the difficult problem of persuading WPC Joan Ailsmore to let him go all the way. She had allowed him a fair distance down the most delectable road in the world, but he was still a long way from his destination.

Unfortunately there was work to do. Kirby raised his hand to the knocker and then stopped as the meaning of what he had heard sank in. When in doubt, his old boss used to say, eavesdrop.

'The picture was funny too,' Mrs Solly said in her natural speaking voice, which was on the louder side of natural and clearly audible through the open window beside the door. 'Funny peculiar, that is. I always thought it looked like someone having a bilious attack, sort of seen from the inside. But Mr Moorcroft said it was a picture of a lady.'

'I expect my uncle put it somewhere. It'll turn up. We'll talk about it later, if you don't mind, Mrs Solly. I'm late for an appointment.'

Kirby heard footsteps approaching on the other side of the door. He raised the knocker and let it fall with a clatter. Almost immediately the door opened and Graig stared at him. He looked hot and flustered, perhaps because he was too warmly dressed for the weather. He wore a double-breasted tweed sports jacket with a red-and-white spotted cravat round his neck and beige cavalry twill trousers.

'Hello. What can I do for you?' he barked.

'My name's Kirby, sir. Detective Sergeant Kirby, Lydmouth CID.'

He began to produce identification, but Graig waved it aside. 'You were at the funeral, weren't you?'

'Yes, sir.'

There was a roar in the house. Kirby glimpsed Mrs Solly edging towards them, artfully giving the impression that the Hoover was towing her and she had no more control over it than she would have had over a bucking bronco.

'Come outside,' Graig said. 'It's quieter.'

He led the way across the drive, through a little shrubbery and on to the lawn beyond. At the far end of the lawn, Kirby knew, where the ground began to drop, was the summerhouse, with the site of the bonfire a little below it. He had brought Joan here last week, in the line of duty, of course, and she had loved the view.

Graig stopped on the lawn. 'I thought you chaps had finished.'

'Just tying up one or two loose ends, sir. I happened to be passing through Trenalt, and I hoped you wouldn't mind if I dropped in.'

'I can only spare you a moment. I've got to go out.'

'One small question. I tried to phone you yesterday afternoon, in fact, but you weren't in. And the question's about a phone call, too. It seems that on the evening before your uncle died, he tried to phone a Mr Randolph Haughton. Flat in Bruton Street, in London. I wondered if you knew Mr Haughton, and why your uncle might have wanted to talk to him.'

Graig looked away, in the direction of the summerhouse. 'Haughton?' he said, scratching his head behind his left ear. 'Yes – he was an old friend of my uncle's. He was at the funeral yesterday.'

'And where is he now, sir? Gone back to London?'

'No, he was going to stay at the Bear for a night or two. I offered him a bed here, actually, but he didn't want to impose. And he said he had some work to do.'

Kirby had taken out his notebook and was jotting down this information, as much to impress on Major Graig the official nature of these proceedings as for any other purpose. 'And what sort of work might that be?'

'I believe he writes articles of some sort. I've no idea why my uncle wanted to phone him.'

Kirby's pencil snapped. 'Mr Moorcroft was probably feeling low, sir. Natural enough to want to phone a friend.'

'Would you like to sharpen that pencil, Sergeant? I've got a knife on me.'

Graig fumbled in his jacket and produced a slim penknife with a flat stainless-steel handle. He opened it and passed it to Kirby, handle first. It was a fussy gesture, Kirby thought as he sharpened the pencil, noticing as he did so how sharp the blade was. It was almost as if Graig were trying to distract him.

He closed the penknife and returned it to Graig. They walked back to the house and said goodbye on the drive. Kirby drove slowly down to the station and up the other side of the valley to the village. The blue Bristol was parked outside the Bear. Kirby asked the woman who answered the door for Mr Haughton. She showed him into a parlour overlooking a little garden at the back of the building.

At a rickety writing desk in front of the window sat the slim, dark-haired man with whom Edith Thornhill had spent so much time at the funeral. He glanced up, smiled at Kirby and waved at a chair. He was writing on a sheet of lined paper with a gold pen. He wrote a few more words, carefully blotted what he'd written and capped the fountain pen. Then he turned back to Kirby.

'Sorry to keep you waiting. I knew if I didn't get it down, I'd lose it. The person from Porlock problem. Heaven knows how much literature we've lost because of that.' He smiled. 'Not that I call what I'm doing literature, of course.'

Kirby nodded, wondering what Porlock had to do with it. In Somerset, wasn't it, and that was miles away. 'I just wanted a quick word about Mr Moorcroft, sir,' he said. 'I'm Detective Sergeant Kirby, Lydmouth CID.'

He was puzzled, and gratified, to see confusion flash like lightning across Haughton's face. Then the older man picked up a gold cigarette case and held it out to Kirby.

'Thanks,' Kirby said, taking a cigarette.

'And how can I help you?' Haughton said smoothly.

'Were you aware that Mr Moorcroft tried to phone you on the evening before he died, sir?'

Haughton showed no sign of surprise. 'Yes. The porter left a message. I was dining with friends that evening, and it was rather late when I got back to the flat, so I didn't phone him. Not then.' He leant forward to light Kirby's cigarette. 'I wish to God I had, of course.'

Kirby accepted the light. 'You didn't think it worth coming forward and telling us this?'

Haughton blew out smoke. 'There seemed very little point. It wasn't as if we'd actually talked.'

'Would you say you were close friends?'

The other man paused, the cigarette a few inches from his lips, smoke spiralling up to the low ceiling. 'We were good friends, but perhaps not close ones.'

'He must have been older than you, sir. Had you known him long?'

'We met before the war. We had a friend in common. I saw him occasionally during the war, when he was up in London. You know he worked at the Air Ministry? But I haven't seen so much of him since then. We kept in touch, though.'

'You wrote to one another?'

'Oh yes.' Haughton examined the end of his cigarette, and added casually, 'Perhaps you found some of the letters?' He laughed. 'I never keep letters myself, but some people do.'

Kirby said nothing for a moment, sensing that he had an advantage, but uncertain why. Then: 'How did you hear that he had died? Who told you?'

'It was in *The Times*, Sergeant. As was the date of the funeral.'

'And you decided to stay for a while?'

'I was planning to spend a week out of town in any case.' Haughton gestured towards the paper and the open books on the desk. 'There's some writing I have to do, and I wanted peace and quiet.' There was a hint of reproach in the voice, which had the Olympian certainty of a BBC announcer's. 'So I thought I'd combine that with coming to the funeral.'

Kirby asked a few more questions but got nowhere. Underneath the appearance of calm, Haughton was rattled. Ten to one the reason was completely insignificant. The trouble with posh people like Haughton was that their upbringing had left them with a shell of self-confidence which could be hard to penetrate unless you knew where the cracks were and where to apply leverage.

As Kirby was leaving, he tried one last question. 'Were you surprised at the news, sir?'

Haughton spread out his hands. 'Of course I was. You don't

expect a man you've known for years to kill himself. I suppose he was lonely. One thing puzzled me, though.'

Kirby waited. With some people, silence was the best goad.

'Why now?' Haughton's voice was quiet, as though he were talking to himself. He looked up. 'If Rufus was going to kill himself, I'd have expected him to do it earlier. When . . . when something tragic had happened – for example, when his wife died. But why kill himself *now*?'

# Chapter Twelve

Before she left the office on Wednesday morning, Jill Francis succumbed to temptation, opened her handbag and took out *The Blue Field*. She reread the inscription on the flyleaf. 'To J. from R., with best love on your birthday.' The sentimentalist in her hoped he had used a permanent ink. She snapped the bag shut and went to powder her nose before leaving. When she returned for her hat and gloves, Miss Gwyn-Thomas looked up from her type-writer.

'Oh, Miss Francis, there was a phone call for you. Councillor Broadbent wondered if he could have a word.'

'Now? Was it urgent?'

Miss Gwyn-Thomas studied the blank sheet of paper in her typewriter. 'I'm afraid I couldn't say.'

Because you didn't take the trouble to find out, Jill thought, knowing that Miss Gwyn-Thomas had a genius for finding ways of being quietly obstructive. She said, 'Do you know if he's at Netherfield or at his office this morning?'

'I don't know, Miss Francis.' Miss Gwyn-Thomas moved swiftly to protect herself from a possible accusation of incompetence. 'He rang off before I could ask.'

Jill thanked her and went into the editor's room, closing the door behind her. No one answered when she phoned Netherfield, so she tried the works. Bernie's secretary put her through straight away.

'Jill – good of you to phone back so soon. I wondered if I could have a word.'

'What about?'

'Not something I want to talk about over the phone. I could come and see you.'

'Unfortunately I'm just about to go out. What about lunchtime? We could meet at the Bull.'

'Not exactly private.' He sounded edgy. 'Would you have time to drop in at the office at some point today?'

Jill glanced at her watch and made some swift calculations. 'Would about half-past twelve suit you? It may be a little earlier or later – I can't be exact.'

'Perfect, Jill. I appreciate it.'

Bernie probably had a council-linked story for her. When it suited him, he had a talent for quietly liaising with the press.

A few minutes later, she was driving out of town. She followed the road north until she reached Drybury, a small village nearly halfway between Lydmouth and Ross. She asked at the post office and was directed to Grebe House, which stood in a couple of acres of its own grounds about half a mile to the west of the main road. It was a small Regency house, freshly painted and standing in trim gardens. If Randolph Haughton was right, and Gareth Loysey wasn't making much money by his painting, then he must have private means.

Jill rang the bell. The door was answered by a large, clumsy woman in her late forties, who was wearing a cotton sundress with a bright floral pattern. There were patches of sweat under the armpits and her swollen eyes suggested she had been crying. But there was no mistaking her enthusiasm for the press.

'Miss Francis from the *Gazette*?' the woman asked, beaming. 'My husband is expecting you, of course.' She smiled, exposing a rather grubby set of dentures. 'He doesn't often give interviews, you know.'

Jill smiled and allowed herself to be ushered into a sun-filled drawing room.

'Do sit down. I'll tell my husband you're here, and make some coffee.'

With her head lowered, Mrs Loysey bustled out of the room, jarring her thigh against the arm of the sofa. Jill looked at the pictures, a mixture of oils and watercolours. A minute passed. Then another. Jill began to grow impatient. At last she heard shuffling in the hall. A man in a corduroy suit came into the room, wiping his forehead with a red silk handkerchief. He was small and had once been fair. He had a balding head, shaped like an egg, a pink complexion, small grey eyes, and prominent ears with very large lobes. His ears and his teeth looked as though they had been designed for a much larger head. Jill had never seen him before yet something about his appearance nudged her memory.

'Miss Francis.' He seized her hand and shook it vigorously. 'I'm so sorry to have kept you waiting. I had a sketch I had to get done. You must've thought me so rude.'

'Not at all,' Jill murmured, which was untrue.

'June will be bringing us some coffee in a moment, so let's get comfortable. Would you like to sit near the window? The light's better and I think you'll find that chair quite comfortable.'

He asked her anxiously about her journey with a concern that would have been appropriate if she'd come from the other end of the country. Once she was settled in a chair, he perched on the window seat, placed his hands together in the attitude of prayer and said, 'And now, Miss Francis, I'm all yours.'

Despite herself she giggled. At that moment they heard the rattle of crockery in the hall. June appeared with the coffee. Jill noticed there were three cups on the tray.

'June, my love, might I ask you a favour?' Loysey said in his high, musical voice. 'We're rather short of petrol. Do you think you could pop down to the village now and top her up?'

'Oh, we could do that this afternoon.'

'Yes, we could – but you know how I worry when I've got an appointment.' He turned to Jill. 'I have to go to Cardiff this afternoon,' he went on. 'That's why we couldn't manage this afternoon for the interview. Someone's private view. One of those things one cannot get out of.'

'And Gareth is also going to discuss his retrospective,' June said in the bright determined manner of a mother thrusting a reluctant infant into the limelight. 'The gallery's being so insistent. They just wouldn't take no for an answer, would they?'

He smiled at her. 'And that's why the petrol's so important, darling. You know they sometimes shut the garage after lunch. By the way, has my hat turned up? The green one? I think I left it in the car. I wore it when we went to the Pickerings, the Sunday before last.'

'I'll have another look in the car. But are you sure you didn't leave it at the gallery?'

'Quite sure, dear.'

He smiled at her again as she left the room, and Jill saw her blushing.

Once his wife was out of the way, Gareth poured coffee and passed Jill a cup. 'Sorry to bore you with these domestic details. Have a biscuit? No? Do smoke, by the way. Now, fire away.'

'The *Gazette*, of course, is a local paper,' Jill began.

'So you would like to have a local twist to your story, Miss Francis. I do understand. We lived in London for many years but my wife was born and bred in Lydmouth. I'm sure plenty of people still remember the Hudnalls. Her father – Vernon Hudnall – was a man of some substance. By the time I knew them, of course, they'd moved away from Lydmouth itself to Trenalt.'

Jill nodded, and wondered whether Loysey had heard about the suicide.

'So, in a very real sense,' Gareth continued smoothly, 'this is a return home for us. I asked June to marry me in Trenalt, you know. We did most of our courting there and in Lydmouth. So the area has always held a special place in our affections. And after a while, you know, one tires of the bustle of the city. Hence our decision to return.'

Loysey talked very fluently, needing few prompts. Jill took it down in shorthand. He had done this before, she thought, given journalists what they required with the minimum of fuss. The material was all here. All she would need to do when she got back was edit her notes and type them up. She quite liked the little man, she decided, despite his egotism. He had charm, intelligence and a sense of humour. You could forgive a great deal of selfishness for the sake of those qualities.

'Yes,' he was saying, 'I've been under pressure for some time to have a retrospective, so when Herbert Reece-Williams suggested it again, I was ready to listen. It seemed particularly appropriate, too, to mark our return to this part of the world. We've even had one or two approaches about setting up a permanent exhibition locally. Of course, at this stage, I'd better not mention the institutions. That wouldn't be fair.'

'Do you have the material for an exhibition? In your own possession, I mean.'

'That's most perceptive of you, my dear. That's the great problem with a retrospective or any other major exhibition, when one has achieved — how can I put it? — a reasonable degree of popularity. So much of one's work is in private collections. And, not unnaturally, it can be difficult to arrange the loans. One of my portraits from just before the war is a case in point. *Lady with Fan* — it marked quite a turning point for me. But whether the — ah — current owner will permit us to borrow it for the exhibition is another matter.'

As the interview was winding down, June Loysey returned, glancing at her watch when she came into the room and again when she asked whether anyone wanted more coffee. She had lunch to serve, Jill guessed, and then she needed to drive her husband down to Lydmouth in time for his train. She was a woman who lived under the tyranny of time, as well as that of Gareth Loysey.

Both the Loyseys came out to say goodbye when Jill left. A muscle was jumping in June Loysey's cheek. Gareth opened the door of Jill's car with a bow. The gesture should have seemed ridiculous, but it had an element of self-parody which made it amusing instead. His sharp little eyes darted into the car.

'Oh – I see you read *Berkeley's*, Miss Francis.'

'Yes.' Jill had put several copies on the back seat of the car, meaning to flick through them while she ate her lunch.

'There cannot be many of us in Lydmouth who do.'

'Perhaps not,' Jill said. 'Thank you for the coffee, Mrs Loysey.'

She started the engine and let out the clutch. As she drew away, she glanced at her hosts and waved at them. Gareth and June Loysey were standing arm in arm. Gareth had raised a hand in farewell and was smiling. June was looking down at him – she was slightly taller – her face flushed and grim. Jill suddenly realised why Gareth Loysey's face looked familiar.

It was not because she'd seen a photograph of him, let alone met him. It was simply a generic resemblance. Gareth Loysey looked like a rabbit.

# Chapter Thirteen

By eleven o'clock, Edith had finished the jobs she needed to do and decided that everything else could wait. She wandered into the garden and sat on a bench near the roses. It was clear that Wednesday was going to be another warm day. She felt nervous about what lay ahead, but also fatalistic. At least it would give her something else to think about. Something other than Richard and the possibility that he was more friendly than he should be with Jill Francis.

Heavy and empty, the morning surrounded her like a rising tide. Edith watched a bee moving with clumsy efficiency from flower to flower. It was as if the present were conspiring with the past. There had been a bee in the play. Not a real bee, of course, but a fictional one which flew in and out of the script.

'Think of it as a sort of Cupid,' Hugh had said. 'Cupid in a striped waistcoat.'

Edith blinked. Since Rufus's funeral, since she had talked to Jack and seen Hugh's grave, the memories had flooded back. Hugh had made his joke about the bee during one of the rehearsals in the village hall. Everyone had laughed, because it was Hugh's play and everyone liked Hugh.

The village hall was so new that it still smelled of paint. Passers-by put their heads inside to marvel at it. A fund for building the hall had been in existence for as long as Edith could remember. People had waited for it so long that its reality was taking a while to sink in.

What had brought it about, according to Granny, was that Hugh's father, Vernon Hudnall, had made a large contribution to the fund to coincide with his move to Trenalt. Mr Moorcroft had promptly matched the sum. Suddenly the building committee found that they had more than enough money at their disposal.

'We could do with a few more like Mr Hudnall and Mr Moorcroft,' Granny had said. 'They say the hall cost nearly six hundred pounds, and most of it came from them. They haven't scrimped, either, I'm glad to say. If a job's worth doing, it's worth doing well.'

The hall went up on a piece of land beyond the church, near the entrance to the village's playing field. During that first summer it was in regular use for cricket team teas, social events, as a branch of the county library, and to house the Scouts' bazaar when it was threatened by torrential rains at the end of July. It was also – and most importantly as far as Edith was concerned – the home of TADS, the Trenalt Amateur Dramatic Society.

This was a new organisation, founded by Hugh Hudnall, fresh from dramatic triumphs at university. Their first performance was to be a play entitled *The Forest Rebel*. Hugh Hudnall had written it, and he was also the director and was playing the title role. Mr Moorcroft was the stage manager, which in practice meant he did most of the organisation.

Granny approved of all this, rather to Edith's surprise, even the fact that Edith was joining TADS and was going to be embraced in public by a young man. Hugh and Jack Graig came round to see her about it. Hugh treated Granny as if she were seventeen rather than seventy-three, and Granny liked it. Despite her ill health, she became quite lively while they were there, almost flirtatious. She liked a nice play as well as anyone, she told

Edith after they had left, and she knew it must all be above board because Mr Moorcroft was involved.

So, to her mingled delight and consternation, Edith found she had no choice: she was going to play Georgina Marfell, the daughter of a local farmer. The plot, Hugh explained to her, was based on a historical episode. It was a love story, too, with touches of humour. And, Hugh went on, it was even more than that. It was about the age-old struggle between capital and labour. One had only to look at what had happened so recently in Spain to see how frightfully relevant it all was.

In 1831, riots had broken out in the Forest protesting against the enclosure movement and the consequent loss of commoners' rights. For four days, the rioters tore down fences and jeered at attempts by local magistrates to stop them. Then a squadron of the Third Dragoons arrived. The ringleaders were arrested. They were held temporarily at the Bear in Trenalt on their way to stand trial in Lydmouth. Lord Vauden of Fontenoy Place had been one of the magistrates who had summoned the dragoons to deal with the rioters.

One of the ringleaders was a young man named Warner Jackson, who – unknown to the magistrates – had been courting the daughter of a farmer living within the parish of Trenalt. The ringleaders escaped from the outhouse in which they were kept. Local legend had it that Georgina Marfell, the farmer's daughter, had smuggled in the key to them. One of the soldiers was killed in the escape, and it was said that Warner Jackson struck the fatal blow.

All the ringleaders except Jackson were caught and hanged. According to Hugh's play, Jackson had concealed himself in the Forest where, with the help of Georgina, he pursued a Robin Hood existence helping the poor and weak until Georgina had raised enough money to smuggle him out of the country. She had planned to accompany him, but in Hugh's version of the play, she died of brain fever on the eve of his departure.

Hugh said that the bee was a symbol of the working man, and it appeared in various scenes. One of these — Edith's favourite — took place during the play's Robin Hood phase. Georgina was afraid of being stung and Jackson hid her under his coat, which led to a particularly exciting embrace.

According to Rufus Moorcroft, Jackson had been a well-known local troublemaker. Georgina Marfell may have had a hand in his escape but she had nothing to do with him afterwards. He was arrested two days after he murdered the dragoon. The authorities tracked him down to a house of ill repute near Bristol docks.

'Nonsense,' Hugh said when Rufus told them this. 'History got it wrong. It so often does. My play isn't about what happened. It's about what ought to have happened.'

Edith had liked Rufus, who treated her with grave courtesy, as he treated all women. She described him to her sister in a letter as being like Sir Galahad in middle age, but with a proper haircut and the DSO rather than a sword and a shield. (She had been rather proud of that turn of phrase.) She particularly approved of the way he was kind to poor Miss Caswell, who had a habit of dropping into the village hall during rehearsals and trying to feed him Lydmouth buns.

'Rather quaint, isn't it?' Hugh had murmured to Edith and Jack Graig on one of these occasions. 'The poor old duck's in love with him.'

Jack's face had turned almost as red as the dragoon's tunic he wore. The notion of love, Edith had noticed, seemed to embarrass him.

'Don't be unkind,' said June Hudnall, Hugh's half-sister. 'Of course she's not in love with him.'

Hugh grinned at her. 'Whoops. I'd forgotten you were our resident expert on love these days.'

Then it had been June's turn to blush. 'I can't stand here chatting. Someone's got to fill the tea urn.'

She hastily turned away. She was a big, heavy woman, several years older than Hugh. It was an open secret that she worshipped a small, fat artist named Gareth Loysey, who sometimes came down to stay with the Hudnalls.

One afternoon, after the rehearsal, Hugh proposed a picnic tea. He had the knack of coming up with an idea and making it sound like the most desirable thing in the world. He decided they should go up to the field at the top of the quarry. 'It's like the top of the world up there,' he said. 'We shall be as gods.' Only Hugh could make a remark like that and not sound stupid and pretentious, partly because you could see from his face that he was teasing everyone, including himself.

He and Jack raided the baker's while Rufus drove back to Highnam Cottage and fetched a Primus stove, a kettle and a picnic basket. They met at the picnic site. Most of the party had walked from the village. There was a field path which led round the head of the valley, crossing behind the imposing stone parapet of the railway tunnel and then up to the top of the hill. Vernon Hudnall still owned the land on which the quarry stood, though it was no longer used, and the small meadow beside it at the brow of the hill.

During the walk Edith had been consumed with jealousy. The emotion was physical in its intensity: pain ebbed and flowed in her belly as though a savage parasite were devouring her from within. The reason for this was that Hugh walked ahead, taking no notice of her, talking intently to a friend who had come down for a few days. Randolph was dark and good-looking. According to June Hudnall, he was very rich. Like Hugh, he had just finished his final year at Oxford.

Edith had spent a lot of that summer feeling jealous. So many people – Randolph, Rufus, Jack, even old Mr Hudnall – seemed to have a prior claim on Hugh. It was so unfair. She knew that, if she only had the chance, she could soon show Hugh that he needed no one else but her.

Gareth Loysey had been in the procession too, towed along like a captured prize by June Hudnall. Edith wasn't sure what to make of him. He seemed nice enough, though not particularly eccentric considering he was an artist. But she never really got to know him because whenever Gareth started talking to her, June always turned up and somehow the conversation never took place.

It was only now, Edith thought, as she remembered across a fifteen-year gap, that she began to see what had been going on. She had not been the only one to feel jealous that summer.

They had been in the middle of a spell of fine weather. She knew the meadow beside the quarry from childhood walks. Rufus was already there. He had found an accidental windbreak in the form of a crescent-shaped pile of stones, earth and rusting iron objects whose original purpose was impossible to guess. Here he was setting up the Primus stove.

While they waited for the water to come to the boil, they sat and lay around on the grass, chatting and in some cases smoking. It was then that Cicely Caswell appeared. She came from the direction of Highnam Cottage and Fontenoy Place, following a footpath that went round the other side of the valley from the village.

'Here comes trouble,' Hugh murmured to Randolph. 'But she's a sweetie, really.'

Rufus stood up and chatted with her. He excused himself when steam began emerging from the kettle's spout. He crouched down to make the tea, offering Miss Caswell a cup.

She accepted. For a moment she stared at the view. Then she drifted back to the group of picnickers, smiling vaguely. Edith thought she might be coming to talk to her. To her surprise — and everyone else's — she went up to Gareth Loysey.

'Mr Loysey,' she said. 'I'm not sure we've been introduced. I'm Miss Caswell of Fontenoy Place.'

He stood up at once and shook hands with her. June made a

noise, perfectly audible to the whole party, which sounded like *pah!* and reminded Edith of steam spurting from the safety valve of an engine.

'They tell me you're an artist, Mr Loysey,' Miss Caswell went on.

'Then they tell you correctly,' he said.

'I wonder – do you accept commissions?'

Gareth had glanced round, perhaps looking for help. 'Well . . . yes, I do. Sometimes.'

'Can you do portraits?'

'I can do anything you like.'

'Good, good. In that case, I should like to commission you to paint a portrait.'

He raised his eyebrows. 'Of whom?'

'Of myself.'

So there it was: one more ingredient to the recipe that had poisoned the summer. More than a single summer, Edith thought, as she sat on the bench in her garden. She wondered what had happened to the portrait. Perhaps Jack would know. She looked at her watch and realised with a start that she had been sitting outside for far too long. Panic poured over her. She rushed into the house to get ready.

The trouble was, she thought as she frowned at her face in the mirror on her dressing table, Jack had changed. He wasn't a boy any more. He was a rather nice-looking man, and an army officer. So one wanted to look one's best when one saw him. One owed it to oneself. Of course, she could never forget what had happened, or forgive him for it. But that was another matter.

In the event, she was ready long before Jack arrived. When at last she opened the door to him, he spread out his hands in apology.

'So sorry I'm late.'

'It really doesn't matter.'

'Oh, but it does. Punctuality is the politeness of princes, as

Rufus used to say. I was on the verge of leaving when one of your husband's colleagues came to call. That's what delayed me.'

'Oh? Who?'

He stood in the doorway while she put on her hat. 'Plainclothes man called Kirby,' he said. 'Wearing an extraordinary tie. I think I saw his face at the funeral.'

'Yes, he was certainly there.' Edith felt annoyance on Brian's behalf because of the remark about the tie. 'What did he want?'

'He was asking about your friend Randolph Haughton.'

'I wouldn't say he was my friend, exactly.'

'Sorry – I seem to be putting my foot in it, rather.' He wrinkled his forehead – rather attractively, Edith thought – and smiled at her. 'May I start again?'

She smiled back at him. 'I dare say it's my fault. For some reason I'm feeling a bit on edge today.'

'I don't know about you, but funerals often have that effect on me.' The smile left his face. 'Do you know what the sergeant told me? Rufus tried to phone Haughton on the night he died. Couldn't get through.'

'It seems perfectly natural he should want to talk to a friend.'

'Yes. But it shook me a bit. Makes one wonder, doesn't it? If Haughton had been there, maybe Rufus wouldn't have killed himself. Or if *someone* had been there he could talk to. Perhaps he was simply lonely. If – if I'd seen more of him in the last few years, perhaps he wouldn't have killed himself.'

Edith saw the unhappiness in his face and liked him for it. For an instant she rested her gloved hand on his arm. 'You mustn't think like that, Jack – promise me you won't. It wasn't your fault.'

He stared at his arm, at the place she had touched. He said in a gruff voice, 'Where would you like to have lunch?'

'I know,' Edith said. 'Let's have a picnic.'

# Chapter Fourteen

Broadbent and Jones occupied a sprawling site off the main road between the centre of Lydmouth and the satellite hamlet of Edge Hill to the north of the town. At the southern end of the site was a modern block of offices, with its own entrance. Jill parked the *Gazette*'s Ford Anglia between Bernie's Riley and an old navy blue Austin saloon.

A receptionist showed her upstairs to the anteroom of Bernie's office. His confidential secretary was tapping away at a typewriter. Bernie was there, too, and so was old George Shipston.

'Jill, come in.' Bernie smiled. 'George is just leaving.'

Shipston looked grimly at her.

'Have you two met? This is George Shipston, Jill. George, this is Miss Francis, who edits the *Gazette* when Philip Wemyss-Brown has got his mind on golf, which seems to be most of the time these days.'

They shook hands. She had seen him in court occasionally, and, more often, at the sort of civic and social functions that she had been obliged to attend as a reporter.

'Francis?' Shipston mumbled, glowering at Jill. 'We used to act for a family of that name who had a house near Abergavenny. Are you related to them, by any chance?'

'I believe my father had some cousins in that part of the world. But I've never met them.'

'Very nice people. Do send them my good wishes when you're in touch.'

Jill said she would, though as far as she knew her father had not heard from them since she was a girl. But it seemed a shame to disappoint the old man. He shuffled downstairs, with an unlit cigar in one hand and his briefcase dangling from the other.

'No calls, Freda,' Bernie said to his secretary. He held open the door leading to his own private office and waited for Jill to pass through.

It was a large room with plate-glass windows overlooking the works itself. She stared down at a dozen buildings of varying sizes. Scattered among them were piles of materials — anything from neatly stacked pipes to what looked like a small mountain of scrap metal. Men scurried to and fro across the yard. The windows were double-glazed but sounds filtered through — clangs, shouts, the roar of engines, the penetrating pulse of a telephone.

'It's like an ant-hill.' She glanced up at him. 'Sorry — I don't mean to sound rude.'

'Don't be sorry.' Bernie struck a match and relit his pipe. 'It's exactly like an ant-hill. Looks a complete muddle but in fact they all know what they're doing.'

'And so do you.'

He laughed. 'They work better for knowing I'm up here looking down on them. And if I'm not up here, I'm down there. It's the only way to do it. You can't manage a crowd like this by remote control. Won't you sit down? Can I get you a drink?'

She declined the drink — yesterday's indulgent lunch with Randolph was still fresh in her mind. She sat down in an easy chair beside a coffee table at one end of the office. While Bernie poured himself a small whisky, she looked around. The room was neat and impersonal, like Bernie's house, Netherfield.

'Saw that obituary of Rufus Moorcroft in the *Gazette* the other day.' Bernie sat down beside her. 'Was that you?'

'No – we had it on file. Philip wrote it.'

Bernie raised his glass to her. 'Chin-chin. I suppose you've got an obituary for me somewhere on file.'

Jill smiled and said nothing.

'I knew Moorcroft a bit,' Bernie went on. 'Before the war, it was. My auntie lived in Trenalt and I bumped into him sometimes when I went to see her. He helped organise a play Edith was in – you know Edith, of course.'

Jill looked sharply at him but Bernie's face was half obscured by smoke.

'Funny play – meant to be historical, but it was really left-wing claptrap dressed up in funny clothes.'

'That doesn't sound like Mr Moorcroft.' She wondered when Bernie was going to get to the point – or whether this saunter down memory lane was in fact the point.

'Oh, it wasn't his play. Chap called Hugh Hudnall wrote it. And acted in it. Summer of '38, it was, a few months before Auntie died. Edith was in the play too – she supplied the love interest.'

Jill didn't want to talk about Edith Thornhill. 'Hudnall? That rings a bell.'

'Not surprising. Before the war old Vernon Hudnall had his finger in a lot of pies around Lydmouth. He was Hugh's dad. They used to have a house up near the park before they moved to Trenalt. None of them left now. Except the daughter.'

Something in Bernie's voice alerted her, rather than the words. 'What happened to Hugh?'

'He died too.'

'The war?'

Bernie shook his head. 'Before that. An accident.' He lifted his glass and swallowed half the whisky as if it were medicine to cure sadness. 'But that's all water under the bridge.'

Jill looked at him. 'Why did you want to see me, Bernie? Has it got something to do with Rufus Moorcroft?'

'In a way. Or with Hugh Hudnall, in a sense, though nothing ever happened. All part of the background — you see, my background.'

'I wish you'd come to the point.'

He grinned at her, revealing strong, yellow, crooked teeth. 'I've never done this before, see? I'm nervous.'

She smiled back. 'You? Nervous?'

'Promise you'll hear me out?'

'Of course I will. But I wish you'd stop being so mysterious.'

'All right.' Bernie swallowed the rest of his whisky. 'Will you marry me?'

# Chapter Fifteen

'Sir? May I have a word?'

Drake had his hat and stick in his hand. 'Will it take long? My wife has guests for lunch and they're expecting me.'

'No, sir,' Thornhill said. 'At least, I hope not.'

Drake opened the door to his office again and led the way inside. He didn't sit down and he didn't offer Thornhill a chair either.

'I thought you were meant to be in Cardiff.'

'I was, sir. The meeting ended early.'

Drake said nothing. The little blue eyes glinted below the fox-brush brows.

Thornhill wondered if the DCC knew that these meetings usually continued in the pub until well into the afternoon. He said, 'When we were talking about Rufus Moorcroft's suicide yesterday, I mentioned we'd found part of a receipted invoice from a clinic in Cardiff among the ashes of his bonfire. I – ah – dropped in at the place on my way home.'

'I thought we'd drawn a line under the Moorcroft business.'

'Yes, sir. But I happened to be passing. So I thought I might as well have a word with them.'

There was another silence. Drake used silence as Superintendent Williamson had used a raised voice. He hadn't actually ordered Thornhill not to visit the clinic. On the other hand, he had made it quite clear that he saw no reason to continue the investigation.

'Well?' Drake snapped. 'I don't want to be later for lunch than I have to be.'

'Moorcroft was receiving treatment for homosexuality.'

Drake's lips tightened.

'The doctor I talked to told me that Moorcroft usually managed to repress his urges. But there had been a period of – of activity some time ago.'

'Moorcroft would hardly admit he was spending three nights a week cottaging in Cardiff, would he? Quite apart from anything else, he would have known there would be legal implications.' Drake threw his hat and cane down on the desk. 'You'd better sit down.'

'I wonder if that explains why Ivor Fuggle was at the funeral.'

'Who?'

'He's a journalist on the *Post*, sir.'

Drake had copies of the local papers on the side table near the fireplace. He picked up the *Post*. There was a signed article by Fuggle on the front page.

'F-U-G-G-L-E and he pronounces it *Fewgle*?'

'Yes, sir.'

Drake snorted at human vanity. 'So what's the significance of his being at the funeral?'

'He's got a nose for scandal. He's unscrupulous, too.' Thornhill looked at the carpet. 'We have a good relationship with the *Gazette*, which on the whole is responsibly run. The *Post* is another matter – largely because of Fuggle.'

'Damned perverts,' Drake said. 'Nothing but trouble.'

'I beg your pardon?'

'Queers,' Drake said harshly. 'It's not just what they do to each other, though that's bad enough, God knows. No, there's the extra problem that they attract crime like blood in the water attracts sharks. It doesn't help that most of them are of low moral fibre to begin with. And they're easy prey for blackmailers, too. I had a case in my district during the war. Nasty business. Some of the victims were British. There were even a couple of officers.'

'There's nothing to show that there's anything more than one man here, sir.'

'I wouldn't be so sure, Thornhill. Queers tend to cling together in my experience. People think this sort of thing's reserved for the big cities, but it goes on everywhere, believe me. Perhaps it's as well you sent Kirby to the funeral. Were there other homosexuals there?'

Thornhill wondered how one recognised them unless they wore the clothes of the opposite sex or dyed their hair orange. 'Hard to know. Mainly local people, I gather, including my wife – her family used to live in Trenalt.'

'Better have a word with her. On the QT.'

'Yes, sir. There was Moorcroft's nephew, of course, Major Graig. And Sergeant Kirby tells me that there was a man from London, too – Randolph Haughton.' For an instant he hesitated. 'Sergeant Kirby says that Moorcroft tried to phone Haughton on the night before he killed himself.'

'There you are, then,' Drake said. 'You'd better check with the Yard. Pound to a penny this chap Haughton is another of these perverts. If we're going to have them on my patch, I want to know all about them. And then I want to persuade them to go somewhere else.'

# Chapter Sixteen

'Lydmouth buns,' Jack Graig said. 'Yes, they were one of the things I used to dream about during the war. I was in a POW camp for the last eighteen months, you see, and I had the strangest dreams in that time, mainly about food. I've had nothing like them before or since. The dreams, that is, not the buns.'

'You were a prisoner?' Edith said. 'It must have been terrible.'

'It's over now. I dreamed about food because we were always hungry. Those buns had so much dried fruit in them they'd probably qualify as iron rations. I remember Uncle Rufus saying that they ought to be standard issue for polar explorers.'

Edith laughed. They walked on, side by side, the silence between them as comfortable as an old coat. They had left the Ford parked just off the road on the outskirts of Trenalt and cut across a field to the footpath which led from the village up to the quarry. When Jack had asked where they should go for their picnic, she had said 'Why not the quarry?' without thinking about it beforehand, simply because it had been there in her mind. And he had said, 'What a good idea. I saw a peregrine falcon up there when I was a kid.'

Edith found it strange not to have to put someone else first — Richard or the children. She had not been back to Trenalt quarry since that picnic in the summer of 1938. It occurred to her with the force of a revelation that sometimes you had to go back if you wanted to lay ghosts.

She liked the way Jack had fallen in with the idea as if it were the most natural thing in the world. He had sat in the kitchen of Victoria Road, chatting to her and smoking, while she made sandwiches and a flask of tea. On the way, he had stopped the car and bought beer, fruit and biscuits.

The footpath was climbing now. Jack had the basket over one arm but once or twice he held out his other arm to help Edith over an obstacle. The ground beneath their feet began to tremble very faintly.

'It's a train,' Edith said. 'Hurry.'

'What?'

'It's what we used to do when we were children. It was a sort of game. There's a train coming through the tunnel. If we hurry, we'll get to the parapet over the opening just before it comes out.'

He grinned at her and they began to stumble up the path. At one point she slipped and almost fell but he seized her arm. 'Steady the Buffs,' he said, and it seemed such an exquisitely amusing thing to say that she laughed aloud. They reached the mouth of the tunnel and leaned, panting for air, against the sun-warmed stone of the parapet.

The rumbling became thunderous. Suddenly a great gout of steam and smoke bellied out from the mouth of the tunnel. The little engine rattled and snorted into the sunshine, towing two carriages behind it. They watched it clattering down the single track, slowing and hissing as it approached the station.

'You've got a smut on your cheek,' Edith said.

Jack put his hand up to his right cheek.

'Not that one – the other.' Edith stretched out a hand and then, realising what she was doing, dropped it. 'I suppose we should carry on,' she said quickly. 'You must be starving.'

They walked on, more slowly now because of the heat.

Gradually Edith relaxed. She had always had a soft spot for Jack, despite the fact he'd been so gauche. It is hard to dislike someone who so obviously likes you. She liked him even better now he was older. It had been considerate of him to park the car outside the village, too. Trenalt itself would have been too public, and he must have guessed she would not want to go with him to Highnam Cottage. Or with anyone else for that matter.

The effort of the climb had made beads of sweat stand out on his arms and neck. He was very muscular, she noticed, certainly in the bits she could see. She found herself wondering what his body was like under his shirt. But as soon as she caught her mind wandering on to that subject, she directed it to something safer.

The ground levelled out. They reached the little meadow at the edge of the quarry. The footpath continued along the ridge towards Highnam Cottage and Fontenoy Place. The meadow was not only smaller than Edith remembered but a different layout as well. If memory could doctor the appearance of a field, for no obvious reason, what else could it do?

'The same place?' Jack said, pointing at the crescent-shaped heap of spoil. It was more overgrown than it had been and now looked natural, not man-made. They waded towards it through knee-high grass which rustled like water.

'Going to rack and ruin,' Jack said cheerfully. 'Look at the state of that fence over there.'

'Someone comes here, though,' Edith said. 'There are tracks through the grass.'

At least half a dozen trails zigzagged across the meadow, some more deeply marked than others.

'Too big for fox. Probably ramblers, unless sheep get up here.'

They reached the heap in the middle of the field. Grass and weeds sprouted among the stones. An elder tree had grown up at one end and Edith unpacked the picnic in the partial shade afforded by its branches. The pink fronds of rosebay willowherb swung slowly to and fro in the breeze like submarine plants swaying to the rhythm of the ocean. There were dusty nettles and briar roses. In its own way the place was beautiful, and a world away from the carefully ordered garden of 68 Victoria Road.

'Do you know,' she said, 'I was surprised to see you yesterday. I thought you'd be in Aden.'

He looked up from the beer he was opening. 'How on earth did you know I'd been posted there?'

'The wife of our vicar. She told me a few weeks ago that her brother had been in Aden and met a man whose uncle lived near Lydmouth. He'd asked her when he wrote if she knew someone called Rufus Moorcroft. She didn't, but she thought I might. So then I knew it must be you.'

'They're sending me to Germany now,' he said. 'I was due some leave, too. So as it happened I was in London when Rufus died.'

'What a pity.'

'Yes.' He jerked the cap from the bottle and looked at her. 'I was going to ring him in a day or two. I wish to God I'd—'

'Don't,' Edith said. 'Please don't. You couldn't have known.'

'Any more than you could have known I'd be at the funeral?'

They didn't talk much as they ate and drank. There was more than food to digest. Afterwards, Edith felt drowsy and comfortable. She leaned back against the trunk of the elder and watched Jack, sprawling on his side in the grass a few yards away from her, lighting a pipe.

A pipe gave a man a rugged, dependable air. She wished Richard smoked a pipe. But Richard didn't like smoking. Or did he? She no longer felt she really knew him. And, once you started feeling that about the person you thought you knew best in the world, you started thinking it about yourself, too.

For example, Edith thought, what on earth was she doing, a married woman and a mother, sharing a picnic with a divorced man in a field? She stared up at the huge, blue dome of the sky.

All she could see was the sky and the long grass. It was as if she and Jack were alone on a green-and-blue planet. Hugh had said the field was at the top of the world. And then he had added, 'We shall be as gods.'

'Penny for them,' Jack said.

She started. 'My thoughts aren't worth a penny.'

They listened to another train coming out of the tunnel, the sound so faint it might have been miles away.

'Oh, damn,' Jack said in a quiet, hard voice. 'Someone's coming.'

Edith looked up, panic rising. Then she saw who it was. 'It's only Miss Caswell.'

'Even so,' Jack said, getting to his feet. 'I wouldn't like there to be any — well, gossip.'

Edith flicked a strand of hair from her forehead. 'She's not the type to gossip. Or she used not to be, anyway.'

Miss Caswell had seen them and was heading directly for the place where they sat, the skirts of her raincoat swishing against the grass. The coat was open, revealing the same grey pinafore underneath. She had worn a grey pinafore when Edith was a child, too — perhaps the same one. In those days, all the patients at Fontenoy Place had worn uniforms, like convicts.

'Edith,' Miss Caswell said. 'How nice — and with Jack, too. Poor dear Rufus was very fond of you both.' She beamed at them, which brought a brief radiance to her long, plain face. 'I know he would have been so glad to see the pair of you together.'

Jack and Edith exchanged glances. Miss Caswell was distracted by the sight of the picnic. Jack offered her a biscuit and a drink. She accepted with indecent alacrity. Soon she was sitting with slovenly elegance on the grass. She peeled off much-mended black gloves, revealing pale, long-fingered hands, and began to munch her way through the remains of the food. She talked in fits and starts, though never while she was eating.

'I was walking over from Fontenoy Place — I could see you

coming up the path, though of course I couldn't recognise you from that distance . . . Rufus and I used to come here, you know. It was quite our favourite spot. And I keep my trousseau here as well.'

'I'm sorry,' Edith said, thinking she had misheard. 'Your what?'

'My trousseau, dear. But I shan't need it now, I'm afraid.' Her lips tightened for an instant. 'Constance didn't need her trousseau either, in the end. The other one, I mean. Did you know she became a nun? One doesn't have to have clothes and bed-linen for Jesus, does one? – let alone embroidered napkins as an aunt of mine did, so perhaps one of the sisters had the trousseau. Were there sisters? We didn't know them, you see – one wouldn't, he inspected something, I believe – not police, factories. There was a story to the effect that his father was the Duke of Kent, which would have made her the Queen's niece, in a manner of speaking.'

'Miss Caswell,' Edith said gently, 'I'm not sure what we're talking about.'

'My trousseau, dear. Which reminds me, you must know Mr Broadbent.'

'Bernie? Yes – he's a sort of cousin.'

'Your grandmother's nephew by marriage,' Miss Caswell said, suddenly lucid. 'He used to visit her quite often before the war. He's done rather well for himself, they say. He was kind enough to lend me tuppence the other evening.' She put down a half-eaten sandwich and extracted a purse from the pocket of her raincoat. 'Would you repay him for me, dear? Let me give you the money while I remember.'

The purse was made of fine chain mail with a silver clasp. She opened it and found two pennies which she passed one by one to Edith.

'I'm sure there's no need,' Edith said.

'One should always pay one's debts. All sorts of debts. I remember my mother telling me that when I was quite a little girl.' Sandwich in hand, she looked benevolently from Edith to Jack. 'I hope you won't consider I'm being rude, but I think you make a lovely couple.' And she smiled at Edith. 'I know! You must have my trousseau. There's no point in my keeping it, is there? Not now.'

The offer should have been awkward and embarrassing, Edith thought, as well as mystifying. But instead it was sad and gracious. 'Actually,' she said, beginning the long haul of an explanation, 'I'm already—'

'It's just over there,' Miss Caswell said, waving her left arm as though hailing a taxi. 'At the back. I'll show you where in a day or two, dear. If you don't mind I'd like to tidy things up first. I want to pass it on to you in tip-top condition.'

'It's very kind, but—'

Miss Caswell was consulting her wristwatch. 'Now, I must rush. I have an *assignation*. Not with a nun, though. But please don't tell Lindor. And please don't tell her about the money, either. She doesn't like it when I borrow money, unless it's from her. But unfortunately she's not always there. No, Jack dear, no need to get up.'

She climbed to her feet with surprising agility and waved farewell to both of them. They watched her walking rapidly through the grass. It was hard to tell where she was going. She looked like a scarecrow in motion.

'Do you think I should go after her?' Jack said quietly. 'Take her back to Fontenoy Place?'

Edith shook her head. 'They seem to let her wander about more or less at will. And everyone knows her around here. She's not going to come to any harm.'

'I suppose not. I hope . . . I hope you didn't mind what she was saying.'

'About the trousseau and so on? No, of course not. She meant well – but she got hold of the wrong end of the stick. No one's fault.'

'Yes, you're right.' He hurried on, perhaps anxious to move the conversation to a safer subject: 'What was all that about Constance?'

'I haven't the slightest idea. She always was strange, and I suppose as she gets older she gets stranger. I hadn't realised that . . . that she was so fond of your uncle.'

'That's been going on for a long time.'

'Yes, but we used to laugh about it. It was hard to take it seriously.'

'She did. Do you remember that painting she got that artist of June Hudnall's to do? And Rufus had to pretend to like it?'

Neither of them spoke for a moment. Jack picked up an apple, a Beauty of Bath which had just come into season, and turned it over and over in his hand. Suddenly and almost furtively, he glanced at her.

'Would you like to share this?'

'All right.'

What did another little intimacy matter? Why did it feel like a form of intimacy to agree to share an apple with Jack? She watched him unfolding a little stainless-steel penknife. He removed the peel in one spiralling continuous movement.

'She loved him so much,' Edith said, feeling tears coming from nowhere and filling her eyes. 'Miss Caswell and Rufus. Why? What was the point of it?'

The blade stopped. Metal sparkled against the pale green of the apple's flesh. Jack looked at her.

'Look,' he said. 'Leaving Miss Caswell aside for a moment. There's something you should know, and there's no reason why I shouldn't tell you now. That last afternoon, the day after the play. Do you remember? In the summerhouse. When—'

'Jack,' Edith interrupted. 'Someone else is coming.'

He broke off and twisted his head to look behind him. A man was walking across the meadow, following the line of the footpath to Highnam Cottage and Fontenoy Place. Even at a distance they could see he was making heavy weather of the walk. He was a plump, elderly man, fanning his face with his hat and looking towards them. Edith recognised him.

'Oh no,' she whispered. 'I think he's seen us.'

'Who? Who is he?'

'He was at the funeral. Brian Kirby pointed him out to me. His name's Ivor Fuggle, and he's a journalist.'

# Chapter Seventeen

The manager's sanctum was on the left of the banking hall, separated from the public part of the building by a secretary's office. An etiolated clerk with a sluglike, almost translucent complexion showed Richard Thornhill into a little waiting room immediately outside the manager's door.

'So sorry, Inspector. Mr Morgan is running late. I'm sure he won't be more than a moment – can I get you a cup of tea while you wait?'

Thornhill told the man not to bother. He was left alone with a pile of magazines. A couple of minutes later, the door opened, and a large woman came out, stumbling on the edge of the waiting-room carpet and then regaining her balance. She wore a perky little hat with a half-veil, whose daintiness had the effect of accentuating her awkward movements. Her lips trembled when the manager said goodbye to her. She appeared not to notice Thornhill.

'Sorry to keep you waiting, Inspector.' Morgan held out a soft, white hand. 'Do come in.'

The office was warm and quiet. The visitor's chair still had heat from the woman's body. The room smelt strongly of her perfume, with a hint of perspiration underlying the scent.

Mr Morgan sat down behind his high mahogany desk and pushed a box of cigarettes towards Thornhill. 'Smoke?'

'No, thank you.'

Morgan took a cigarette and lit it with a silver lighter. 'Now – what exactly can we do for you?'

'As I said on the phone, I wondered if I might have a word about the late Mr Rufus Moorcroft. I believe he had an account here.'

'It's rather irregular,' Mr Morgan said. 'Normally, in cases like this, I would have to refer an application of this nature. The executors might feel—'

'I'm sure they might, sir. And very right and proper too.' Thornhill had learnt, painfully and slowly, how this game was played in Lydmouth. He had learnt, too, that there was no point in trying to hurry it. 'The thing is, following the standard procedure would take time – perhaps several weeks. If what we find needs to be used in evidence, obviously we would have to make a formal approach to both the bank and the executors. But, for now, all we need to do is to discover whether a possibility is worth exploring further.'

'Quite so. And, I suppose, if there were any way quietly to expedite the affair, that would save time and effort for all concerned – the police and the bank, not to mention Mr Moorcroft's excutors themselves?'

'Exactly, sir.'

Thornhill watched Morgan pretending to consider. He remembered his former boss, Superintendent Williamson, saying, 'You'll never have a problem with old Morgan, not if you go about it the right way. He's a great man for back-scratching, and he likes it when Mr Hendry gets his wife to send him and his missus a personal Christmas card.' At the time, Thornhill had rather despised Williamson's methods. Now he was beginning to wonder whether they might not have a purpose.

'I can't see the harm in it if you were to ask me one or two questions – just to indicate the areas the police are interested in –

and if I were then to answer – in general terms and off the record, of course,' Mr Morgan was saying. 'After all, it would be in everyone's best interests.'

'Yes, sir.'

'The spirit of the law, rather than its letter,' Morgan mused. 'A private conversation is not the same thing, after all, as revealing confidential records.'

'No, indeed. For example, would it possible to say whether Mr Moorcroft had more than one account with you?'

Morgan's voice became brisk and for the first time acquired a Welsh intonation. 'A current account and a deposit account. He had an arrangement by which a certain amount from the current account was paid into the deposit account every month. He'd made no withdrawals from the deposit account for about five years. The current balance is very healthy – a little over six and a half thousand pounds.'

Thornhill's lips pursed in a silent whistle. 'And the current account, sir?'

'Always in credit, usually by about fifty to a hundred pounds. A model customer, in many respects. He had a regular income paid into it from several sources – his pension, one or two investments, that sort of thing.'

'What about the outgoings from the current account?'

'You want to know if there were unexpectedly large withdrawals? Irregular payments?'

'That sort of thing, sir. Anything that struck you as unusual. Over the last two or three years, say.'

Morgan opened a drawer and took out a folder. He had prepared for this, and their conversation before he agreed to help had been nothing more than a ritual to preserve the outward decencies. Holding the file ostentatiously at an angle so there was no opportunity for Thornhill to glimpse its contents, he skimmed through sheet after sheet of paper. Thornhill waited, saying nothing. He wondered how often Morgan had done this for Williamson or other police officers. It was like watching an actor in a play near the end of a long run.

'There's nothing that stands out. He came in once a week to draw cash, or occasionally sent in his housekeeper with a cheque instead. There were the normal bills, usually paid monthly. He was a man of habit, Mr Moorcroft. I wish all our customers were as good at managing their money.'

'Did you keep a strongbox for him?'

'No. It might be worth your asking his solicitors about that if you haven't already done so. Shipston & Shipston, I believe.'

Morgan had nothing useful to add. Thornhill stood up to leave. Morgan shook his hand again with quiet enthusiasm.

'I understand Mrs Thornhill is related to Councillor Broad-bent,' he said as he showed his visitor out. 'I hadn't realised. Small world, eh?'

And getting smaller every day, Thornhill thought, at least in Lydmouth. He walked through the hot afternoon from the High Street up to Castle Street, where Shipston & Shipston had their office. Though he had not mentioned it to Morgan, he had already made an appointment to see George Shipston.

One of the clerks took him up to the big room on the first floor. The atmosphere was grey with cigar smoke.

'Thornhill?' Shipston said, not bothering to stand up. 'Things are always changing in this town. In my opinion, it's a pity that Ray Williamson has retired. Sound man, Williamson.'

While the old man was talking, Thornhill advanced into the room. The big partners' desk was cluttered with papers, among them a bank statement with several entries in red ink.

'You'd better sit down, I suppose,' Shipston said in a voice like a creaking hinge. 'But I can only spare you a minute.'

The chair was hard and unstable. Thornhill sat well forward on it, with his feet planted on the floor. He was used to a certain type of person trying to bully him. It was a common reaction to a police officer – people were either too aggressive or too submissive.

'I understand the late Mr Rufus Moorcroft was one of your clients.'

'That is correct, Sergeant.'

'Inspector. I understand that he was a wealthy man?'

'I don't think it would be appropriate for me to comment on that.'

'Then perhaps I should discuss the subject with his nephew?'

'By all means.'

Thornhill let a silence lengthen. It was hot and stuffy in the room. He noticed that the old solicitor's hands were trembling slightly. He said, in a gentler voice, 'Had you known Mr Moorcroft long, sir?'

'Over twenty years. Which for a lawyer, of course, is not a particularly long time. He came to us when he and the late Mrs Moorcroft moved down to the area.'

'Do you know why they chose to move to Trenalt?'

'I believe Mrs Moorcroft took a fancy to the place. They had a house in Wiltshire before that – not far from where Miss Caswell's family came from, as a matter of fact.'

'Miss Caswell?'

Watery eyes stared across the desk. 'Miss Cicely Caswell. She lives near Trenalt but she comes from a most distinguished Wiltshire family. She's related to Lord Vauden.'

Thornhill thought it wiser not to ask who Lord Vauden was or had been. 'Did you hold a strongbox or anything of that nature for him?'

'Ask Major Graig.' Shipston ran his fingers through his hair, which was scanty but greasy. His face changed, as though an invisible deity had rearranged the features in a slight but significant manner. 'Poor old Moorcroft,' he said softly, to himself. He picked up a half-smoked cigar from the ashtray and lit it carefully with a match.

'Why poor, sir?'

'Some lives are touched by tragedy.' The old man peered at the glowing tip of his cigar as though the past were written there. 'Mrs Moorcroft died young. Then there was that sad business with Hudnall's boy before the war. Long before your time. And of course poor old Vernon Hudnall himself on the same occasion. He collapsed in Moorcroft's arms, you know. Ray Williamson handled it. Only a sergeant then. Sound fellow, Williamson, bit of a rough diamond, but sound.'

'What business was that exactly?' Thornhill asked.

'Eh? What?' Shipston's head snapped round sharply, as though jerked by a spring, and he stared at Thornhill. The spell was broken.

'You mentioned something to do with the Hudnalls, sir.'

'It's a matter of public record, Inspector. I don't see why you should expect me to enlighten you. Unless you have something pressing to ask me, I would be grateful if you'd allow me to get on.' He flung out an arm, indicating the desk overflowing with files and papers and books. 'As you see, I have much to do.'

Thornhill walked back to Police Headquarters. The general opinion was that George Shipston was going senile. The trouble was, it was not a steady descent. Like a yo-yo, he kept rising up again, as though gathering energy for the next descent. You never knew whether he was going to be cantankerous or merely irrelevant. He switched unpredictably from one mode to the other.

*Another damned old man.*

One way and another, Lydmouth was a town dominated by old men. In some ways, the whole country was the same. Things would be different, Thornhill thought, if one emigrated to one of the dominions. Out there, in Canada or Australia, New Zealand or South Africa, thousands of miles away from this claustrophobic little country, there would at last be room to breathe. And if Jill were with him, they could do anything.

When he got back to Police Headquarters, he went up to the CID Office. Kirby was at his desk, the phone clamped to his ear. He raised a hand in greeting when he saw Thornhill in the doorway and continued talking. A moment later he tapped on the door to Thornhill's office.

'I've just had a phone call from Major Graig, sir. Moorcroft's nephew. The housekeeper at Highnam Cottage thinks there's a painting missing from the study.'

'Thinks or knows?'

'Mrs Solly – that's the housekeeper – is sure it was there when she was last at the cottage, which was the Friday before Moorcroft killed himself. Major Graig said it wasn't there when he arrived at the cottage, which was a couple of days after the death.'

'Why didn't he report it then?'

'Because he didn't know it was missing. He hadn't been down to stay with his uncle for years. And Mrs Solly thought at first it might have been moved. It was only when she mentioned it to Major Graig this morning that they both realised it must be missing.'

'What sort of painting – is it valuable?'

'A little portrait in oils in a green frame – about nine or ten inches square. By a modern artist who used to visit Trenalt. You wouldn't have thought it could be particularly valuable, would you? We're not talking Rembrandt or something. But according to Mrs Solly, Moorcroft said it was worth a few bob now. The major remembers it quite well. He says it's called *Lady with Fan*.'

# Chapter Eighteen

Sitting in the editor's office at the *Lydmouth Gazette*, Jill Francis stared at a photograph of Philip and Charlotte Wemyss-Brown which stood, framed in silver, upon the desk. The Wemyss-Browns were in the South of France for the summer. She was very fond of them, but sometimes she begrudged the amount of time that Philip now took off. They had recognised in Jill someone who could bear responsibility, so they shovelled it on to her shoulders. The more she thought about it, the less appealing the prospect of becoming increasingly mired in the day-to-day running of a provincial paper became.

She got up to find a cigarette. Once it was lit, she stood at the window, staring down at the High Street. Old George Shipston drove by, erratically but fast, in the large Austin which looked almost as old as he was. They shouldn't let him drive still, Jill thought; one day he was going to have an accident. For an instant, she glimpsed his face through the windscreen. He looked like Mr Punch on the verge of tears.

She stubbed out the cigarette and walked up and down the office, trying to work off her restlessness. There was some excuse for it, at least. One didn't usually have a proposal of marriage to think about, let alone two.

Richard Thornhill was in love with her. Bernie Broadbent,

however, wanted her to marry him purely as a business arrangement. She knew why. He of all men needed a wife. And she
recognised that, in Bernie's eyes, she had a number of advantages.
She thought it probable that he intended to be chairman of the
county council before too long. His political ambitions might
not end there. A wife who could act as a hostess, who knew how
to handle journalists, would be an advantage. No doubt Bernie
wanted a lady, as well. In his way, he was a realist, just as she was,
and she liked that in him.

'We're both grown-up,' he had said. 'There's no reason why
we shouldn't treat this as a simple business arrangement.
Separate rooms, of course. I wouldn't interfere. Not in any
department.'

Interfere with what? Could Bernie have got wind of what was
going on between Richard and herself? She was beginning to
realise that one couldn't keep a secret in Lydmouth, or not for
long. On the whole, she thought it probable that Bernie didn't
yet know. In his own way, he loved Edith Thornhill and her
children as much as he loved anyone. They were the nearest thing
he had to a family, to a posterity.

'I'd make a settlement on you, at marriage. Yours absolutely.'
He had stared at her through his pipe smoke, and she had
wondered how far he saw into her, whether he sensed her
weaknesses, whether he realised how much she hungered for a
decent income and the little comforts that came with it. 'You'd
not find me ungenerous, Jill, in any way.'

So there it was: an arrangement which would allow her to
have her cake and eat it too. On the one hand, she would be
expected to act as Bernie's hostess, to provide social lubrication
to the mechanics of his career, and perhaps to prevent people
murmuring about him being a bachelor. In return, she would be
wealthy, and have far more freedom to do what she wanted than
she had now. She could take a little flat in town, for example, and
there would be no reason why Richard shouldn't come up and

see her there, far from the whispering tongues and watchful eyes of Lydmouth.

*But wouldn't that make me a kept woman? Is that really what I want?*

She was aware that around her the building was emptying. Instinctively she glanced at her watch. No one was leaving early. Between them, she and Philip had the *Gazette* running very smoothly — too smoothly, perhaps; there were no longer any challenges.

Her mind went back to Bernie. There was a challenge there, though: what was all that business about the Hudnalls? Something had started him up, and she wasn't sure what.

There was a tap on the door. Miss Gwyn-Thomas came in with the afternoon's letters for her to sign. Jill sat down and uncapped her fountain pen. Miss Gwyn-Thomas hovered.

'Oh, Miss Francis? Would it be all right if I take an extra hour at lunchtime tomorrow? I thought if I stayed on this evening, I could do the minutes now, and the filing as well.'

'I should think that would be all right.' Jill looked up, forcing herself to make conversation, at least to try to be pleasant. 'Nothing too ghastly is it, like the dentist?'

'No – I've got an appointment with an estate agent. I'm going to put in an offer for one of those new bungalows in Vicarage Gardens.'

'That sounds exciting.' Jill signed the last letter and passed the sheaf back to Miss Gwyn-Thomas. 'You'll be nice and central.'

'Yes, and with all mod cons. They say they're going like hot cakes already. I'll put these in the post, shall I, when I leave?'

The secretary clattered out of the room, wobbling slightly on her high heels. As the door closed behind her, Jill swore under her breath. Amy Gwyn-Thomas as a neighbour? It didn't bear thinking about. Almost certainly she would buy the nearest possible bungalow to Church Cottage.

A few minutes later, Jill left the room. A procession of echoes dogged her footsteps. With only the two of them here, the building revealed another side of itself. A tap dripped in the little kitchen. Shadows were beginning to gather in the corners. The clacking of Miss Gwyn-Thomas's typewriter pursued her down the stairs.

She followed the corridor to the back of the building, where she unlocked a door giving on to a flight of stairs leading to the basement. The smell of old paper and damp rose up to meet her. At this level, the air was cool. The walls of the largest of the cellars were lined with metal shelves on which rested the back files of the *Lydmouth Gazette*, stretching back to 1886. Jill had once heard Miss Gwyn-Thomas telling a cub reporter the room was haunted.

She switched on the light and put on a pair of dusting gloves which she kept in her handbag. She worked her way round the shelves until she came to 1938. The year was still in relatively good shape – many of the piles had suffered from careless searchers or the depredations of mice. Jill pulled out the issues relating to August and spread them on the table in the middle of the room. She skimmed through the brittle pages in the glare of an unshaded light bulb. Almost immediately, she found what she was looking for. It was the lead story on a front page.

## FATALITIES AT TRENALT STATION

### DOUBLE TRAGEDY FOR RESPECTED LOCAL FAMILY

Lydmouth and Trenalt are reeling from the shock of two unexpected deaths last night. Local businessman Mr Vernon Hudnall collapsed at Trenalt station and died on the way to hospital. A few minutes earlier, his son Hugh fell to his death beneath the wheels of a train from Lydmouth. Police are still investigating the full details of the tragedy.

Mr Hudnall, a well-known local businessman, had recently moved from Salisbury Road, Lydmouth, to Oaktree House, Trenalt. His son Hugh, 21, had just completed his studies at

Oxford University. Friends are looking after Miss June
Hudnall, Mr Hudnall's daughter . . .

'Miss Francis?' Miss Gwyn-Thomas called down the stairs.
'There's a telephone call for you. I'll put it through to the
front office, shall I?'

Jill went quickly up the stairs. In the front office, she closed the
door leading to the rest of the building and picked up the phone.

'Hello.'

'Jill – it's me.'

A wave of emotion washed through her at the sound of
Richard's voice. She couldn't have analysed the wave, though it
had elements of pleasure, fear and desire.

'Can you talk?'

'So-so.'

'I just wondered—' He broke off and then went on in a rush,
'Darling, have you had time to think about it? Will you marry
me?'

'I'd have told you if I had.'

'I thought you would.' He made a sound like a strangled
laugh. 'To tell the truth, I just wanted to hear your voice. I'm not
trying to put pressure on you.'

'I know you're not.'

'I wish I could see you as well as hear you. I tried to phone
you at the cottage. Are you working late?'

'Yes. There's a lot to catch up on.' She kept her voice level
but she wanted him so badly that she clenched her hands until
the fingers shrieked with pain. And she was worried about the
danger of an eavesdropper. 'I'd better go.'

'What about this evening?' he said.

'Nine o'clock?'

'All right.'

She put down the phone. Had Miss Gwyn-Thomas recognised Richard's voice?

She went out of the front office. She could not hear the tapping of Miss Gwyn-Thomas's typewriter. Perhaps the secretary had moved on to the filing. Then, to her dismay, Miss Gwyn-Thomas appeared at the head of the stairs to the basement.

'Oh! There you are, Miss Francis. I wasn't sure how long you'd be, so I thought I'd better turn out the light down there. Mr Wemyss-Brown was quite concerned about our last electricity bill.'

'Thank you,' Jill said, her alarm increasing. 'How kind.'

Her gratitude sounded as implausible as Miss Gwyn-Thomas's story. Hoping that she was worrying for no reason, Jill went back to the basement. As far as she could see, nothing had been touched, and anyway there could not have been much time for prying. At the most, Miss Gwyn-Thomas would now know that Jill had been looking up the details of the Hudnalls' deaths in August 1938.

*The handbag?*

It was where she had left it, hanging by its handles from the back of the chair she had been sitting on. She opened it. The thought of Miss Gwyn-Thomas pawing through its contents made her feel physically ill. Not that there was anything particularly private inside. Even *The Blue Field* was only a book.

Except for that inscription: *To J. from R., with best love on your birthday.*

But even if Miss Gwyn-Thomas had seen it, surely she could not have recognised Richard's handwriting? There was nothing to connect R. and the book with Detective Inspector Thornhill.

Jill went back up to the editor's office. The secretary was on her knees in front of the filing cabinet and did not look up as she passed. Jill worked for another hour. Miss Gwyn-Thomas poked her head into the room to say she was going home now if there was nothing else she could do. The quietness of the building settled around Jill like a cloak. Her concentration was beginning to slip away from her. She decided that she, too, had had enough.

She walked home, made herself a pot of tea and tried to settle with *The Blue Field*. She felt too restless to focus on the words on the page, let alone to decode their meaning. For weeks, she had had the sensation that her life was wandering deeper into a cul-de-sac. Suddenly the apparently blind alley had opened out and she found herself staring at four possible futures.

For a start, she could stay at the *Gazette*, stay at Church Cottage, and let her affair with Richard move to whatever resolution fate had in store for it. Or she could move to the flat in Lancaster Gate and, courtesy of Randolph Haughton, try to rebuild her old London life with all its excitements and pitfalls. Or she could marry Bernie Broadbent, become, in the eyes of the world at least, a lady of leisure, and continue to see Richard Thornhill in London, if she were lucky. Or she could throw caution and common sense and perhaps common decency to the winds and go away with Richard to build a new life in a country she had never seen.

She was tempted to have a drink. That would never do. You never found solutions at the bottom of a glass of gin, she informed herself sternly, only more problems; far better to have some healthy exercise. The desire for alcohol diminished as she put on her hat and gloves. She let herself out of the back door, crossed the garden and slipped through the gate in the wall to the building site beyond.

Except it wasn't yet a building site. It still offered glimpses of what it had been, the ruined kitchen garden of the vicarage next door. It was a place in transition. Like her, Jill thought, it had left its past but not quite found its future.

She picked her way towards the second gate at the far end, wondering where Miss Gwyn-Thomas's bungalow would be. A moment later, she slipped into Bull Lane and strolled up to the High Street. She would go down to the river, she decided, and perhaps walk upstream along the towpath. If she tired out her body, perhaps she would tire out her mind as well.

On one corner of the junction of Bull Lane with the High Street was the Bull Hotel itself, and on the other was a block of public lavatories, with a telephone box in front of it. Jill glanced idly at the telephone box as she passed. The brimless hat and the nose were unmistakable. She looked again. Then she hurried on, suddenly uneasy.

Nothing to worry about, she told herself. That was the trouble when one was nervy, one started adding two and two and making five. Or even six or seven.

She crossed the road without looking where she was going, and the horn of a car blared at her. She turned down Lyd Street towards the river.

Even so, surely it was odd. Miss Gwyn-Thomas had been standing in the phone box with the receiver pressed to her ear. That in itself was strange, because Miss Gwyn-Thomas had said she was going home. And, if she needed to make a phone call, she could have phoned from the office, or from her home.

There was also the point that Miss Gwyn-Thomas was known to be careful with money, especially when it was her own, so much so that some of the junior staff at the *Gazette* called her Miss Gwyn-Scrooge behind her back. So why had she been wasting two of her hard-earned pennies in a public telephone box?

Finally – and most disturbingly – there was the newspaper which Jill had glimpsed, pressed under Miss Gwyn-Thomas's arm. Just a glimpse, but that was more than enough. Jill was a journalist and identified without conscious thought the mastheads of newspapers as sailors identified the rigging of ships.

Why had Miss Gwyn-Thomas been carrying a copy of the *Evening Post*?

# Chapter Nineteen

———◦◦◦———

'Another bottle of beer, Richard?' said ex-Detective Superintendent Raymond Williamson. 'Or would you prefer Scotch?'

'Not for me, thanks.' Thornhill's glass was still half full.

'What about some potato crisps?' Without waiting for an answer, Williamson bellowed: 'Bunty!' His voice returned to normal. 'By the way, I think you'd better call me Ray, eh? No need to stand on ceremony, is there? Not now I've retired.'

'Okay – ah – yes.' Thornhill stopped himself from adding 'sir' just in time. 'Now, about the—'

'Crisps,' Williamson said firmly. 'Maybe nuts. Or sausages. Or those little puffy things with prawns. Or those little biscuit things you put lumps of cheese on and so forth. Have we got any of those for Richard?'

'Yes, dear.' Bunty Williamson stood at the open French window, clinging to the back of an armchair and swaying gently as if standing on the deck of a ship riding a slight swell. 'What about some cheese straws?'

'Yes, yes.' Williamson waved her away. 'Whatever you like.' He turned back to Thornhill. 'To be honest, I don't know how I managed to fit in a job all these years. You wouldn't believe the amount of time the bloody garden takes. And I've got one or two other jobs on the go, too. I'm thinking of building a potting shed down there – see? Just to the left of the vegetable patch.'

'As I said on the phone, sir—'

'Ray,' Williamson said.

'Ray – it's the Hudnall business in 1938 I'm interested in.'

'Ah, yes.'

'The file went up in smoke when headquarters had that direct hit from an incendiary near the end of the war. But I understand you were the investigating officer, and I thought—'

'The Hudnall railway accident – I remember it very well.' Williamson seemed to fill out as he spoke. 'You know what it's like – sometimes a case helps to get you noticed. I'd just passed my inspector's exams and when the next vacancy came along, which was in the autumn the war started, they offered it to me. Not that there was anything very complicated about the investigation. No, it was more a matter that the case showed I could use tact if the situation needed it. You know as well as I do, Richard, police work isn't just about stamping around in a big pair of boots.'

'So why was CID involved? That's what puzzled me. It seemed like a straightforward accident on the one hand and a natural death on the other.'

'It wasn't quite as straightforward as it seems.' Williamson leant forward and tapped Thornhill on the knee. 'For one thing, young Hudnall was—'

He broke off as Bunty tottered on to the patio, carrying a tray laden with snacks. She had made up with quantity for any shortcomings in quality or presentation. There were cheese straws, little biscuits, olives and a great many nuts. As she put down the tray, it tilted in her hands and peanuts and almonds pattered on the paving stones. Thornhill caught an olive in midair and then restored order as best he could. Bunty watched him, the fingers of her left hand pleating her skirt against her thigh.

'I think I might go and lie down, dear,' she said to Williamson. 'Would you mind?'

'Of course I wouldn't mind.' He waved her into the house and with the same hand scooped up several of the biscuits and crammed them into his mouth. He washed them down with a mouthful of beer. 'Ah – that's better. Help yourself, Richard. Now, where was I?'

'The Hudnalls. Reasons why CID got involved.'

'Young Hudnall – what was his name?'

'Hugh.'

'That's the one. He was queer. It wasn't well known around here, but I'd heard a whisper. I had a word with a chum at Oxford – young Hugh had been at college there – and they knew all about him. One of the nancy boys. Never been arrested, my chum said, but several of his friends had. So that put a different complexion on it. We had to go carefully – especially because he was old Vernon's son.'

Thornhill frowned. 'I don't follow.'

'Before your time. Your Edith might remember them, though. Vernon Hudnall was quite a big man in Lydmouth at one point. His dad was a builder. Made his pile before the Great War. Vernon kept that going and built up a lot of sidelines as well. He had a quarry over Trenalt way and a share in some brickworks up in the Midlands. He owned a sawmill up in the Forest, too. He sold up most of it in the thirties. Cyril George bought the building firm. Vernon had a house over in Trenalt and they went to live there. He was a widower by then, but a daughter kept house for him. And young Master Hugh was at Oxford. Fat lot of good that did him.'

From the room beyond the French windows came the small, unmistakable explosion of a cork emerging from a bottle.

'Anyway, Vernon had a history of heart problems, and his GP wasn't surprised when he dropped down dead after having a shock. But still. We wanted to make sure there were no other . . . no other factors.'

'And then the boy?'

'Well – to be perfectly honest, I always wondered if it was suicide not accident. Couldn't live with himself any longer. A lot of these queers are very unstable, you know. He'd been in some sort of play the evening before, up at the village hall. He'd been drinking, too. Maybe he thought they didn't clap him enough or something. So he got depressed enough to think he was going to make them sorry even if he killed himself doing it.' Williamson shrugged heavy shoulders. 'Sounds crazy, I know, but the point is, they're not normal, are they? You can't expect them to act sensibly, like you or me. If you ask me, it'd be better to lock them all up. If you leave them on the loose, they're a menace to everyone, themselves included.'

'There was no suggestion he was under any other sort of pressure?'

'Blackmail, you mean?' Williamson groped for his pipe and then remembered that it wasn't there because his doctor had forbidden him to smoke it. 'No sign of it.'

'But you checked,' Thornhill murmured.

Williamson nodded. 'Nothing official, nothing on file. I spun the daughter some tale about needing to see her brother's room – you know the sort of thing, "Routine procedure in these cases, ma'am" – and I had a good poke around. Nothing. No unexplained withdrawals from his bank account. Not even any dirty pictures. In fact, you wouldn't have known he was a bloody pansy.' A frown flitted across Williamson's heavy features. 'Turned out he used to box when he was at Oxford. Had one of those things they give them – what do you call it? – a half-blue? But there's absolutely no doubt he was queer.'

'Can you remember what actually happened on that evening – the sequence of events?'

Williamson screwed up his face. 'It was a foul night, I

remember that. Rain was coming down in buckets. Old Vernon Hudnall went into Lydmouth for a dinner. Big function at the Bull. He travelled up with a friend from the village – that chap who died recently, the one who'd been an ace in the Great War – Moorcroft, that's it.' Williamson hesitated before adding in a lower voice which held what might have been a note of pleading: 'And is that why you're here, Richard? Something about that doesn't smell quite right?'

'I'm not sure. Perhaps.'

Thornhill felt as though he were sinking deeper and deeper into a swamp of unreality: this was not the sort of conversation he was used to having with Ray Williamson; to an eavesdropper, judging their relationship only by this conversation, they might have been friends. From the house behind them came the tinkle of breaking glass. Williamson appeared not to have heard it.

'Bloody awful night. Wind and rain – more like an autumn gale than August. The do at the Bull was for an ex-servicemen's charity. Anyway, the dinner finished and Hudnall and Moorcroft caught the last train back from Lydmouth. Hugh came down to meet them.'

'He drove down to the station?'

'The Hudnalls hadn't got a car. He was well on the way to being roaring drunk by then. We had several witnesses who'd seen him in the Bear. Celebrating that play of his, I suppose, or drowning his sorrows. Anyway, it was a dark night. The station wasn't well lit. It's a tiny place. No one was on duty at that time of night. There was a goods train going down to Cardiff about ten minutes before the passenger train with Hudnall and Moorcroft. Young Hugh fell on the line. The train went over him and carried on.'

'No one noticed?'

'No reason why they should have done. It was a filthy night, remember. If you've ever travelled in the cab of an engine, you'll know how bloody noisy they are. Hugh was probably uncon-scious by the time the train went over him.'

'Surely there would have been a jolt or something?'

Williamson shook his head. 'Think about it. Fifty or sixty tons rolling along at twenty or thirty miles an hour. Fireman's shovelling coal and the driver's peering ahead trying to see the next signal through the rain. I doubt if they felt a thing.'

'No witnesses?' Thornhill asked. 'No one saw him fall or the train coming into the station?'

'No one. Then, a few minutes later, along comes the train from Lydmouth. As luck would have it, it came to a halt just in front of the body. The driver had hysterics. Moorcroft and Hudnall came over to see what the fuss was about. And when Hudnall saw his son – what was left of him; he was in several pieces by then – the old man just keeled over. The boy was wearing his college blazer, one of those stripy affairs – I reckon that's how his dad recognised him. Never recovered consciousness. Lucky Moorcroft was there. He was the only one who kept his head. They got an ambulance for Hudnall but he died before he reached the hospital.' Williamson hesitated. 'Why are you asking all this, Richard? Do you and Drake think it's got something to do with Moorcroft topping himself?'

'I don't know.' He saw the disappointment in Williamson's face and rushed on: 'Really. You know what it's like – when someone dies, you start lifting up stones. And then you have to make sure what you find underneath hasn't any bearing on what's happened.'

Williamson drained his glass. 'Another beer? No?' He picked up one of the bottles beside the deckchair and wrenched off the cap. 'How's he doing, then? Drake, I mean?' The old man's eyes were full of a curiosity like hunger. 'I hear a lot of conflicting stories.'

'Early days, yet.'

'He doesn't know Lydmouth,' Williamson went on. 'Always a drawback. Of course, you were like that when you first came. But you soon learned, Richard – I give you that.'

It was meant as a compliment, but Thornhill didn't want to take it as such.

'Sure you won't have another beer?'

He looked at his watch. 'I'd better not. I should be going.'

'You and Edith must come round for supper one night. Catch up on the gossip, eh?'

'Thanks. I'd like that,' Thornhill lied. 'Don't move, Ray — I can see myself out.'

There was another tinkle of glass from the house.

Williamson levered himself to his feet. 'I'd better go and have a look at Bunty. I'm worried about her, to tell the truth. Not been herself lately.'

'I'm sorry to hear that.'

'Old age, Richard. You think it's never going to happen to you — and then it bloody does. Take my advice — live for today. When tomorrow comes, try not to be there.'

He shuffled in down-at-heel slippers into the house. Thornhill followed. They crossed the sitting room and went into the hall. There was no sign of Bunty. Williamson opened the front door.

'There was one thing, Richard. One thing about Hugh Hudnall which didn't come out at the inquest. Wasn't in the file, either, because my boss reckoned it didn't count as hard evidence. The quack thought he might have found a bite mark.'

'A *what*?'

'A bite mark. But it was hard to be sure. It was on the left wrist, and the cuff of the jacket and the wristwatch strap were confusing things.' He chuckled. 'Talking of which, the watch was still working. About the only thing that was. Swiss-made job, real quality.'

'The bite mark, Ray?'

'Just one indentation really, scraped the skin a bit. But the quack reckoned someone could have bitten him.'

'A dog?'

'No idea. You could only see one tooth mark. An incisor, maybe. But it was recent. And there was another thing that struck me, though no one else seemed to think it very important.'

The old man waited anxiously for Thornhill to ask him what it was. His eyes were pale and watering, fringed with pink folds of slack skin.

'And what was that?'

'No umbrella.'

'Pardon?'

'No umbrella. It was a bloody awful night, Richard, remember? Raining cats and dogs. The idea was, Hugh comes down to the station to meet his old dad and take him safely home. I know he was half cut but surely the young fool would have remembered to bring an umbrella?'

# Chapter Twenty

After dinner on Wednesday evening, Dr Angmer worked in his study at Fontenoy Place. He was expecting a caller, he told his housekeeper, but said she need not wait up. He was a considerate man, he liked to think, and he also liked to think that his staff loved him for it.

Slowly the great house around him quietened. The guests settled for the night, many with the help of chemicals. The mentally unstable slept in the east wing, the others in the west. During the day, they ebbed and flowed through the central block of the house where some of the common rooms were – the guests' drawing room, for example, the main dining room and the former ballroom used for indoor exercise.

His visitor was late. He hummed as he wrote steadily at his desk. He was collating notes he had made about individual patients (in this context they were no longer guests) for an article he hoped would eventually appear in the *Lancet*. His working title was 'Some Effects of Diet on the Psychopathology of Old Age'. He wondered whether there might be room for a supplementary paper on medication in a few months' time.

The clock on the mantelpiece, a present from the grateful daughter of a former guest at Fontenoy Place, chimed nine. Dr Angmer heard the knock on the front door as the sound of the last chime was dying away. The knocking continued as he crossed the hall. He opened one leaf of the great front door.

'I'm late,' George Shipston snarled, breathing heavily, his hand on his chest. 'Damned car ran out of petrol.'

'It doesn't matter at all.' Dr Angmer beamed at his visitor with professional benevolence. 'I've been working, and I'd quite lost track of the time. Come and sit down and get your breath back.'

Shipston staggered as he came into the hall but recovered his balance at once. 'Like a fool, I came on that road from Eastbury. More like a cart track, if you ask me. You should get on to the council about it. I left the car where it was and began walking back to Eastbury because it was nearer than coming on here. I must have gone at least a mile before I remembered that I had a can of petrol in the boot of the damned car.'

'Come and sit down, George. I think I'd prescribe a whisky and soda.'

Shipston grunted and sank into one of the chairs by the fireplace. He watched Angmer mixing the drinks. While he was waiting, he took out his case and pulled out a cigar, which he rolled round and round in his fingers. Angmer gave him his whisky but he did not drink it.

'Fact is,' Shipston said haltingly, 'I suppose I was in a bit of a state.'

Dr Angmer sat opposite his guest and looked at him with calm interest. He had already registered the grubby collar, no longer as stiff as it should be, and the hair that needed a trim. Now he noticed the patch of stubble under the right jaw and the scuffed toes of the black brogues. He had been wondering about George Shipston for some time. He would not have been altogether surprised if one of George's younger relations had begun making discreet enquiries about possible vacancies at Fontenoy Place.

'I wanted to have a word about Miss Caswell's trust fund.'

'With me?' Dr Angmer raised his eyebrows. 'I thought—'

'Yes,' Shipston interrupted. 'I know I shall need to talk to Lord Vauden as well. But I thought I should have a word with you first. As you know, her father set up the fund to pay her fees here, with a little pocket money left over. Fifty years ago, the amount he settled was considered generous. The trouble is, fifty years is a long time. We've had two world wars since then, damn it, and the pound has taken quite a beating.'

'Ah.'

'There is also the point that we may soon be forced to raise the fees for Fontenoy Place. That will make the – ah – the disparity even greater.'

'Perhaps Lord Vauden could approach Miss Caswell's relations.'

'And ask for more money? The trouble is there aren't any near relatives left. Most of her cousins have never heard of her. She's been out of circulation for more than half a century.'

'Perhaps Lord Vauden himself—?'

'I shall have to talk to him, of course. But I doubt if he can help financially. He's not a rich man.'

Dr Angmer sipped his whisky and stared at George Shipston, wondering why his visitor was quite so agitated. 'I'm sure we can come to an arrangement for the short term, if necessary, to give you and Lord Vauden time to put her affairs on a better footing.'

Shipston at last put his cigar in his mouth. He lit it and tossed the match into the empty fireplace. He stared up at the clock.

'Forgive me,' Dr Angmer said, 'but this seems to be worrying you a great deal.'

Shipston sighed. His eyes slid down from the clock to Angmer's face. 'I . . . I feel responsible, I suppose. Together with Lord Vauden, and his father before him, I've looked after Miss Caswell's affairs for the better part of forty years. And I . . . I would not like her to live in straitened circumstances.'

He lifted the whisky glass to his mouth with a hand that trembled. A barn owl screeched in the park.

All in the mind, no doubt, Angmer thought. Perhaps there was another paper for the *Lancet* here. 'Some Observations on the Preoccupations of the Elderly: a Gerontological Approach.' In his mind he roughed out some of the many topics one might cover: the fear of running out of money; the growing importance attached to minutiae; inappropriate sexual behaviour of the senile male; the increased mortality in elderly patients with depression/dementia; the interest in – in some cases, obsession with – the movements of one's bowels.

Dr Angmer smiled at George Shipston and raised his glass in a toast. So the old fool had his uses after all.

# Chapter Twenty-one

———◆◇◆◇◆———

Jill's thoughts were like a crowd of people all shouting at once in different languages. She switched off the engine of the Ford Anglia and for a few precious seconds let the silence pour like mist through the open window.

She glanced at her watch. A quarter past nine. She was late. She locked the car and set off up the track, glancing over her shoulder every now and then to make sure no one was in sight. The air was soft and warm, smelling faintly of the conifer plantation higher up the hill. She quickened her pace. The Forest offered privacy. At this time, there were even fewer people than usual likely to be about. Richard said the poachers tended to come later, after the pubs had shut.

She turned to the left on to a path which zigzagged down through oaks and sweet chestnuts. Her footsteps were silent on the spongy ground. Sixty yards later, she came to the clearing. It formed a shallow depression in the side of the slope. Once they had found a stag standing by itself in the middle. As soon as it saw them, it bounded away.

To Jill's surprise, Richard had not arrived. Normally she was the one who was late. He left his car farther down, tucked out of sight on a piece of waste ground off one of the lanes, and walked up from below. She perched on the trunk of a fallen chestnut tree, uprooted in a gale the previous autumn, and lit a cigarette. A few minutes later, she glimpsed him moving silently through the trees. He came towards her, his face dark and intent, walking so fast he was almost running. She stubbed out the cigarette and stood up. He touched her cheek. For a moment neither of them spoke. Then he put his arms around her and she felt, growing inside her, the familiar sensation of furtive urgency. His hands slid down her back, pulling her towards him.

'I'm sorry I'm late,' he murmured. 'I went to see Williamson, and it was hard to get away. It was extraordinary. He welcomed me like the prodigal son.'

'He's lonely, I expect.' She smelled the sour tang of beer on his breath as they kissed. She tore her lips away from his. 'Why did you go and see him?'

'This Moorcroft business.'

'The suicide in Trenalt?' She knew so little about his life and she was hungry for information. 'I didn't know you were taking an interest in that. How does Williamson come into it?'

'There was a fatal accident in Trenalt before the war, and Moorcroft was slightly involved in that. Just possible there might be a connection, but the file was destroyed during the war, so I had to go and ask Williamson about it.' His hands tightened their grip.

'Hugh Hudnall. Fell under a train in August 1938. His father saw the body lying on the line and died of a heart attack.'

He pulled away from her. 'Good God — where did you get that from?'

'Bernie Broadbent mentioned it this morning, and I looked it up in the back file this afternoon.'

'Well, I bet Bernie didn't know this: Hugh Hudnall was homosexual, and so was Moorcroft.'

'And that somehow has a bearing on Moorcroft's suicide?'

'Perhaps. That's the trouble with queers from our point of view — it's not just their . . . their illness. It's everything that goes with it. The way they live, the other crimes they attract. Everything from blackmail to drugs.'

'But it's hardly their fault. It's only because it's against the law.'

'Of course it's their fault. They've got a choice.'

'People don't *choose* to be homosexual.'

'They choose to commit homosexual acts. To break the law.'

'Personally I can't see why it should be against the law. And what's the law got to do with it in any case? You might as well put people in prison for eating chocolate.'

'Oh, surely, Jill — if you knew anything of these people—'

'But I do.'

'What?'

She pushed herself away from him. 'I know a number of people who are homosexual. Some of them are my friends.'

Richard stared at her, his face bewildered. He looked like a child who has just discovered that Santa Claus does not in fact exist.

'Have you read the obituary we did for Rufus Moorcroft? Seen the letters we've had about him? Have you talked to people who knew him? He won a couple of medals in the First World War. He supported every good cause you can think of. He's probably done more for Trenalt than anyone in recent history. You won't hear a bad word against him. Except, possibly, from you.'

She felt herself crumpling and turned away. She had thought that one of the features that distinguished whatever was between herself and Richard was that they didn't quarrel. It had been a belief depending on hope rather than experience, perhaps, but nonetheless important for that. It was important because it was in a sense part of the justification they both needed.

Anyway, she hated quarrelling. But not as badly as she hated the thought that Richard could talk such evil nonsense. Behind Hugh Hudnall and Rufus Moorcroft were Bernie Broadbent and Randolph Haughton.

*They are people, for God's sake,* she wanted to shout, *people adrift in a world whose laws they never made: just like you, Richard, just like me.*

She felt his hands on her shoulders. She turned towards him and, eyes screwed shut, rested her forehead against his collarbone. She felt him stroking her hair. He wasn't wearing a tie. She lifted her left hand and touched the hollow at the base of his neck.

'I'm sorry,' he said. 'I didn't want to upset you.'

'That's not the point,' she muttered.

'I know.'

She slipped her arms around his waist and squeezed him against her. It wasn't that their bodies were treacherous – it was merely that they had their own truths.

'You're turning people into criminals,' she said, angry with herself now. 'They don't choose to prefer people of their own sex. And even if they did, what would it matter? It's so bloody whimsical. It's like putting people in jail because their skin's a different colour or they go to a different church from yours.'

'The police don't make the laws, darling. It's part of my job to uphold them.'

'It's no part of anyone's job to uphold unjust laws, is it?'

He said nothing for a moment, but he did not move away. Then, 'Let's sit down.'

They perched on the fallen tree, still clinging together. She no longer wanted to make love with him, not now, she was sure of that. But she had no idea what she did want. There was even a part of her which would have liked to prolong this moment for ever – this time before the decisions were made, this time when they were sitting together, their arms around each other, not speaking.

'I – I shouldn't stay long,' she said. 'I'm expecting a phone call.'

She sensed the tension in him and knew he wanted to ask from whom.

Instead he said: 'I was hoping you might have had time to think by now.'

'About us going away together.' There was no point in being coy. 'About us marrying.'

'Yes, of course. You know that's what I want.'

She laid a hand on his leg. 'Richard – I'm sorry, but I need more time to think about it. Nothing's straightforward at present.'

'No, I know that.'

She stood up and then swooped and kissed his cheek. 'Miss Gwyn-Thomas is going to buy one of the bungalows behind the cottage. And I think she recognised your voice when you phoned me at the office today. It was unlucky – she happened to be working late, and picked up the phone.'

He looked up at her, his face in shadow.

She bent and kissed him again, this time on the mouth. Then she walked quickly away up the zigzag path which led to the car.

# Chapter Twenty-two

'The whole place seems odd somehow,' Jack Graig said, enunciating his words with care. 'Whole damn caboodle – the cottage, the village, everything. Not unpleasant, but *odd*. Have you ever had the sort of dream when you're in a house you think you know well, and suddenly you find rooms you hadn't noticed before? Or sometimes it's a garden – you find whole areas you never noticed. Yet they're familiar too, as well as being strange, as though you'd known them a long time ago and then forgotten them. Damn it, I'm not explaining this very well.'

'You're doing very well,' Randolph Haughton said. 'Do you want me to run you back in the car?'

They were standing outside the Bear. The bar was closed, and although technically they could have continued drinking as Haughton was a resident, neither of them had wanted to.

'To be perfectly honest,' Jack went on, 'that's why I thought I'd come up to the village. Get a bit of company. You know?'

'I know. What about that lift?'

'I'd better walk. Clear my head.'

'Mind if I come with you part of the way? I'd like to stretch my legs.'

'Sure.' Jack waved his hands expansively. 'Be my guest.'

Both men had swallowed a good deal of alcohol that evening, but Haughton was used to it and Jack was not. The younger man wasn't exactly drunk, though. To Haughton's experienced eye, Jack had reached the stage when to the person concerned everything, including yourself, seems a little larger than life. The outside observer notices instead that while you are still making perfect sense, most of the time, you have to make an effort not to slur your words. While you can still walk in a straight line, if necessary, you have a tendency to bang into tables and prop yourself up against walls. There was a distinct possibility that, if allowed to walk home by himself, Jack would end up in the ditch.

'Yes,' the younger man went on, growing more enthusiastic as the idea seeped farther into his mind. 'Come and have a nightcap, old man.'

Haughton borrowed a torch and a key from the landlord. They walked down the hill to the silent station and up the road on the other side of the valley. There was no traffic. As they crossed the railway line, Jack glanced up at the station.

'Poor bloody Hugh.'

'Sometimes I think it was worse for Rufus.' Haughton turned aside to light a cigarette. 'He felt responsible – God knows why. In a sense I think he never got over it.'

They walked on in silence for another fifty yards. Then Jack cleared his throat and said, 'You knew about, ah–?'

'Yes,' Haughton said.

After another silence, Jack went on: 'I'm going to have to sell Highnam Cottage. Every time I see it, I think of Rufus in the garden. And every time I see the railway station, I think of Hugh.'

'Do you know what else you'll do?'

'Not yet. I could leave the army now, thanks to Rufus. But I don't know if I want to.'

'Early days,' Haughton said. 'No hurry, is there? In some

ways, you know, money doesn't make things easier. It just gives one more choices, and that makes things harder.'

They turned in at the gates of Highnam Cottage and walked up the drive. There was enough of a moon to see where they were going, even without the torch. In silence, they strolled on to the lawn, already slippery with dew, and walked over to the summer-house. Neither of them wanted to go up to the veranda in front, where Rufus had sat as he died. But they stood in front of it and looked out over the view which he had seen before he closed his eyes for the last time. A silver, black and grey world stretched away from them apparently to infinity.

It was a good time to say goodbye to Rufus, Haughton thought. Better than the funeral.

'He wasn't a coward,' Jack said suddenly. 'I didn't know him as well as I should have done, but I do know that.'

'No,' Haughton said. 'That had occurred to me.'

'So he must have had a reason for killing himself, mustn't he?'

'I don't know. People don't always act logically.'

'Can I ask you something?'

'If you want.'

'Were you . . . are you——? Damn it, sorry – none of my business.'

'Am I queer, as the bishop said to the actress?'

'Look, really, I'm——'

'Of course I am. But no, my dear chap, Rufus and I weren't lovers. I had a few passionate moments with Hugh when we were up at Oxford. Didn't last long, but we stayed friends afterwards. One did, somehow, with Hugh. He had a genius for friendship.'

'Yes.' Jack stamped his feet. 'Let's go in, shall we? Time for that nightcap.'

They went into the house by the front door. Jack led Haughton from room to room on the ground floor, turning on lights as they went. In the dining room he opened the sideboard.

'I'm having brandy, I think. What about you?'

'I'll join you,' Haughton said.

Jack picked up the bottle in one hand and a couple of glasses in the other. 'Let's go in the study, shall we? I think it's the room Uncle Rufus used least. It seems — I don't know—'

'More neutral than the others?'

'That's it.'

The study was a small room at the side of the house looking out over the drive. For a while the two men sat drinking in silence.

'How long do you think you'll stay here?' Haughton asked just as the silence was beginning to become oppressive.

'I'm not sure. I'll have to sort out this place at some point. Also, there are one or two friends — What's that?'

There was the sound of a car outside. Jack got up and went to the uncurtained window. He pressed his face against the glass. A pair of headlights were shining straight at him, dazzling him. A horn hooted.

'Who the hell can that be at this time?'

He went into the hall just as the knocker tapped twice on the front door. Standing in the little porch beyond were a large, middle-aged lady and a small man with prominent front teeth. The woman lunged towards Jack, who automatically took a step backwards.

'It's Jack, isn't it?' she informed him. 'You probably don't remember me, but I'm sure Gareth's face will be familiar.' She smiled anxiously at Jack and also at Randolph Haughton, who was standing in the doorway of the study. 'Oh — and I see you have visitors — I do hope this isn't too inconvenient.'

'I'm Gareth Loysey,' the man interrupted. 'This is my wife June.'

'Of course,' Jack said. 'June Hudnall. And you're the artist. We've—'

'We were driving back from a private view in Cardiff,' June

rushed on. 'We saw the lights here. The house looks like an ocean liner from the other side of the valley – all the lights blazing. Anyway, I said to Gareth, I'm sure Major Graig – Jack – wouldn't mind if we dropped by for a moment. He'll know we keep country ways down here.'

While she was talking, June edged gradually deeper and deeper into the hall, towing her husband behind her. Gareth's cheeks were very pink and June kept a firm grip on his arm. He took a spotted handkerchief from his breast pocket and dabbed his forehead.

'The painting,' he said. 'The painting.'

'Yes – that's why we popped in,' June said. 'Or rather, I mean, that was one reason. We really wanted to say how sorry we were about Mr Moorcroft. Such a nice man, and I'm sure he'll be sadly missed. I remember how efficient and courteous he was when we were doing that play – I don't think it would have reached a public performance if it hadn't been for him.'

Jack murmured that it was very kind of them to bother. He introduced Haughton. Loysey appeared not to notice him. He was drunk enough to be oblivious of almost everything except the whereabouts of the painting.

'Yes – the painting,' June said while she was still giving Haughton's hand a brisk shaking. 'Did you know that Mr Moorcroft owned one of Gareth's paintings? *Lady with Fan*. He painted it the summer we did the play, in fact. The thing is, there's going to be a big retrospective exhibition of Gareth's work in Cardiff. And the gallery owner's *frightfully* keen on *Lady with Fan*. You see, it marked a turning point. It was the first of a series of portraits he did, whereas before he concentrated on landscapes and abstracts. I remember Gareth once showed some of the preliminary sketches to—'

'What we were wondering,' Gareth said, glaring impartially around the hall, 'was whether we could borrow it from you, or even buy it.'

'You'd be welcome to it,' Jack said. 'The only problem is, it's gone.'

'What do you mean? Did Moorcroft sell it?'

'We don't know. Apparently it was hanging on the study wall only a few days before he died. But it's not there now.'

'Someone's stolen it,' June burst out. 'When the house was empty, they must have seen their chance and—'

'Have you told the police?' Gareth asked.

'Yes – this morning, in fact. That's when I discovered the painting was missing.'

'Are you sure it's gone? Are you sure it's not somewhere in the house?'

'As sure as I can be, Mr Loysey. You'll appreciate that I haven't had time to go through everything yet, but the painting's certainly nowhere obvious.'

'Damn.' Gareth tugged at his wife's arm. 'What the hell are we going to do?'

She patted his hand. 'Don't worry, dear. We'll think of something. Perhaps the police will find whoever took it.'

Gareth grunted. 'They'll be a bunch of bumpkins down here.'

'Look,' Jack said, 'I don't want to seem inhospitable, but it's late. Would you like to leave me your telephone number? I'll give you a ring if I find out anything about the painting.'

June swung back to him. 'Oh – would you? That would be awfully kind. And I'm so sorry we've disturbed your evening. It seemed such a golden opportunity, you see, since we were passing, more or less, and we could see you were up.'

'That's all right,' Jack said.

The Loyseys said goodnight and left.

'I suppose I'd better be leaving myself,' Haughton said.

'Let me freshen your glass before you go.'

They went back to the study. The visitors had had some of the effects of a cold shower on Jack: he felt less drunk and more awake. He topped up their glasses.

'I suppose I should have offered them a drink. Dreadful people.'

'He'd had more than enough already. Do you remember them well?'

'Vaguely. She was a big, blundering girl.' He grinned at Haughton. 'Actually, what I remember most about her was that one tried to avoid her. It sounds awful, I know. Loysey was down there once or twice, too, staying with the Hudnalls. She was always mooning after him. Whereas he gave the impression that no one else really existed except for Gareth Loysey. But you must remember her, too – didn't you stay with the Hudnalls once or twice?'

'I never knew her well. I saw her occasionally that summer, but I wasn't staying with the Hudnalls. I was with cousins near Lydmouth, and I just drove over now and then. I remember the painting, though. Rufus used to have it over that bookcase, didn't he?'

Jack nodded. 'You remember Miss Caswell?'

'Oh, yes – she was at the funeral.'

'Yes. Well, you probably remember she had a sort of schoolgirl pash for Uncle Rufus. She commissioned Loysey to do the painting. It was meant to be a portrait of her, which she could give to him. All terribly romantic, in its own way. I don't know how she managed to pay for it. Loysey took the money fast enough – he was really poor in those days – and then he turned around and bit the hand that fed.'

'Actually it was good.' Haughton hesitated. 'Unkind, but good. It was a strange, surreal likeness of her, but somehow he transformed her.'

'Made her look like something in a fairground freak show. I was talking about it with – with a friend, this afternoon as a matter of fact. All very clever, I'm sure, but it wasn't my cup of tea. I wonder what Uncle Rufus did with it.'

'Probably burned it. Perhaps he didn't want it to be sold and

risk people laughing at Miss Caswell for the rest of posterity.'
Haughton swallowed the rest of his brandy and said, in a quieter
voice, 'That would have been typical.'

'Uncle Rufus pretended to like it, you know. I was there
when Miss Caswell gave it to him. When he was looking at it,
she started crying because she thought it made her look ugly. She
thought it meant that she was ugly too and he wouldn't like her
because of it. And Rufus patted her hand and said he would
always have it on his wall so it would remind him of her.' Jack
left his chair and went to stand by the black rectangle of the
window. 'She blushed, you know – like a girl. She went brick-
red. And then she smiled, and it was like the sun coming out. I'll
always remember that. Christ, what rot one talks at this time of
night. Look, I'm sorry, Haughton, I'm going to have to turn in.'

Haughton was already on his feet. 'Rufus was a good man.'
He put his empty glass down on the mantelpiece. 'That's what
people forget so easily. Goodnight – I'll see myself out.'

Jack stayed by the window. He heard the slam of the front
door and the crunch of Haughton's footsteps on the drive. But
he saw nothing in the window except his own reflection and that
of the room behind him. Sometimes light concealed rather than
revealed.

He wandered around the house, turning off the lights. Now
Haughton was gone, he was no longer sleepy. The evening had
shaken him unexpectedly, just as seeing Edith had done. He
wished she were here now. He would have liked to have talked to
her about Rufus, talked to her about anything if the truth be
known. The sadness for what might have been nagged him like
an ache deep in the bone.

He found a torch in one of the hall drawers, lit his pipe and
opened the front door. The moon was gone, masked by a bank of
clouds. The night had the true darkness you see only in the
middle of the country or in the middle of the sea. The air had
cooled considerably.

Draping a coat round his shoulders, he crossed the drive to the lawn and went down to the summerhouse again. You could see lights from here — remote specks of gold from upper windows far in the distance. There were stars too, cold as ice. Had Rufus seen all this as he sat dying? Would Edith like this view at night? The despair built up within him, mounting higher and higher. He knew he had to do something, or else something within him, something vital, would burst.

By now his eyes had grown partly accustomed to the night. Below the summerhouse was a dark mass of bushes. He found his way down to the path, a ribbon of paler darkness which ran through it. A moment later he reached the garden gate. He raised the latch with a click like the cocking of a gun's hammer.

For an instant he paused and listened. Then he stepped on to the footpath beyond.

# Chapter Twenty-three

On the night of Wednesday, 20 August, the Thornhills did not get to bed until almost midnight. This was partly because Richard was late home. In the last few months he had often been late. At first Edith had accepted this without question. Recently, however, it had become another item — and quite a large item — to add to her growing list of misgivings.

At about half-past eleven, she went upstairs, changed into her nightdress and washed. She came back down to make a final pot of tea. She heard Richard in the bathroom above her head. Edith wished the children were back at home. It was as if she were only partly real without them, which was not a comforting thought. It was also true that their routine gave a shape to the day, a shape which sometimes irked you when they were there but which you missed when they weren't.

There was too much unoccupied time. Too much time to think.

A few minutes later, Richard wandered into the kitchen, his unshaven chin, rumpled hair and striped pyjamas making him look like an escaped convict in a cartoon. Tom, who had been playing with a scrap of paper on the floor, ran towards him, mewing as though his tiny heart were breaking. Richard scooped him up in one hand. The kitten dug his claws into the pyjama jacket and began to purr loudly.

'Would you like the tea here or upstairs?' Edith asked.

'I don't mind. Here?' He sat down at the table and Tom climbed up to his shoulder and then hauled his way up on to the top of Richard's head. 'Damn this animal,' he said, lifting the kitten gently down to his lap. 'Oh — by the way.'

Edith put his cup of tea on the table in front of him. 'Yes?'

'That funeral you went to.'

'Rufus Moorcroft's?' What other funeral had there been?

'Yes. I didn't realise you'd known him.'

'I didn't know him well. And I hadn't seen him for years.'

'You didn't mention you were going to the funeral.'

'I didn't know I *was* going,' Edith said, stirring her own tea with unusual thoroughness. 'It was one of those impulses. I saw the notice in the newspaper on Tuesday morning.'

'Had you seen him since we moved down here?'

*What am I? One of your suspects? One of your criminals?*

She straightened the newspaper on the table. 'No. Or rather, I'd seen him once or twice in the street, but I hadn't talked to him. But I knew him before the war, when I used to stay with my grandmother in Trenalt. I saw Brian at the funeral. Are you . . . well, are you taking an interest in how he died? Officially, I mean.'

'Just one or two loose ends. So you knew him quite well before the war, did you?'

'Not that well. He did a lot in the village. He knew everyone and everyone knew him.'

'Like a sort of squire?'

'Not really. There was no them and us about it. He was just — just part of the village. He helped with the play.'

'You were in the play too?'

She smiled, suddenly reliving that moment of proud terror she had experienced when Hugh told her that he wanted her as his Georgina. 'It was called *The Forest Rebel*. A man called Hugh Hudnall wrote it. He lived in the village with his family. Rufus was the stage manager. Why are you asking me all this?'

'I told you — just loose ends.' His face was as blank as a mask. 'Did you know a friend of his called Haughton? Randolph Haughton.'

'Yes — he came to the play. I didn't know him well but I met him again at the funeral. I think he knew Hugh at Oxford.'

The play — she remembered its only public performance as well as she remembered anything. She thought it probable that she had never felt so happy in her entire life. What she had enjoyed the most were the courtship scenes. She had first encountered Hugh, in his guise as the heroic Warner Jackson, while picking blackberries in a glade of the Forest. A bumble-bee had landed on her bare arm, giving Warner the opportunity to apply first-aid with his lips. Later, when she helped him to escape from the soldiers, he had kissed her. More kisses followed when she helped conceal him in the Forest while she raised money to pay for him to flee the country. The final scene, where Edith, as Georgina, lay dying of brain fever, urging her lover to leave the country without her, had been particularly satisfying.

Best of all, after the play Hugh had kissed her. Not as Warner Jackson but as himself.

'Edith, you were marvellous. I couldn't have had a better heroine.'

She had almost fainted with joy. A few minutes later, Randolph Haughton had come up to her and congratulated her on her part in the play. She had been impatient with him, because she wanted to be alone with her memory of what Hugh had said and done.

'Hugh was just like this at Oxford, you know,' Randolph had said. 'Method acting — if he had a part he'd stay with it in real life as well. It could get quite confusing for everyone, including himself sometimes.'

It was only afterwards that Edith had realised that the words were a warning, not small talk. And it was only much later still that she recognised that Randolph Haughton had taken the trouble to warn her out of simple kindness.

'I met someone else who was in the play,' Edith said to Richard. 'Jack Graig — Mr Moorcroft's nephew.' She sat down with her tea in the Windsor chair, lifting Max, who had been sleeping there, on to her lap. 'He's in the army now.'

'Oh yes?' Richard sipped his tea. 'Must be quite strange for you — seeing these people you haven't seen for years.'

'In a way.' She swallowed too much tea and burned her mouth. She felt she ought to be open with Richard. But she didn't know what she wanted to say, nor how to say it. It was as if she and Richard were playing a game while unfamiliar with both the rules and the penalties.

'So you knew Hugh Hudnall? Were you in the village when he died?'

'Yes, I was staying at my grandmother's. It turned out to be my last night there.' She bowed her head over the cup. 'It was terrible. Bernie came and took me away the next morning. I was glad to leave. Everyone was so upset.'

'Understandably.'

She waited for him to continue what she thought of as the interrogation.

Instead he smiled and said, 'Why don't you get up to bed? I'll wash up the tea things for you.'

She thanked him and went upstairs. On the way her anger mounted as she thought about what he had said. Not about Hugh or Rufus or Jack or Randolph Haughton. About washing up.

*I'll wash the tea things for you.*

For *me*?

But wasn't the washing up for him, as well?

# Chapter Twenty-four

'A body on the line?' Jill said into the telephone. 'Where?'

A few hundred yards away, in Police Headquarters, Sergeant Fowles sucked air through his dentures. 'Just outside Trenalt station, miss.'

'Who is it?'

'Can't say. That's all I know so far. And that came by a roundabout route.'

There was an ominous note of injury in the man's voice. Jill thanked him effusively and rang off. Sergeant Fowles was Philip Wemyss-Brown's particular friend at Police Headquarters. It had taken well over a year for him to persuade Fowles that when he rang the *Gazette* with some useful little titbit, he could pass it on to Jill instead if Philip were not there. But Jill felt that, as far as Fowles was concerned, she was still on trial.

She flipped open her address book and found the number for the rectory at Trenalt. The rector's sister, who kept house for her brother, was the local correspondent of the *Gazette*. The phone rang but no one answered. Jill glanced at her watch – it was only a little after nine.

A body on the line at Trenalt might be worth no more than a couple of inches at the bottom of page one. On the other hand the village had been in the news lately and there was the curious coincidence of that other body on the line in 1938. Thanks to Fowles, the *Gazette* might have a start over the competition. It was a fine morning and she did not want to be cooped up in the office. Moreover, the outing would be a semi-legitimate distraction from the background murmur of her worries.

She dropped a shorthand pad in her bag and found her hat, gloves and car keys. Miss Gwyn-Thomas was chatting with the receptionist in the front office.

'Yes, one of those new bungalows behind the vicarage. Not cheap, I don't mind telling you, but very nice.' She saw Jill coming in and added, 'Lovely views, too. Quite unexpected.'

'What views?' Jill asked.

'The hills outside town, Miss Francis.'

'How nice for you. I'm going down to Trenalt for an hour or two. I'll phone if I'm going to be late.'

When she reached the car, she took the Ordnance Survey map from the glove box and checked her route. Trenalt lay on the old road from Lydmouth to South Wales, which followed the high ground. She started the engine and drove down the Chepstow road out of town. A few miles to the south, she turned left off the main road. The car climbed steadily higher. On her right, to the west, was a gradually widening view of Wales, mile after mile of green hills. At last the road levelled out and she saw before her the spire of the parish church.

Jill drove slowly into the village. The streets were deserted. She turned left into a narrow road winding down to the little station in the valley below. Almost at once she saw signs of activity.

There were two police cars and an ambulance parked in the station yard. A footpath ran parallel with the line northwards from the station in the direction of Lydmouth. It was too narrow for cars, but there were a number of people walking along it towards the mouth of a tunnel in the distance.

Jill left the Ford Anglia beside one of the police cars and

walked along the footpath. She heard a car coming down the hill and glanced over her shoulder. To her annoyance, she saw an elderly Humber with a scrape along its side drawing into the yard. Someone had tipped off Ivor Fuggle too.

A small crowd clustered around the mouth of the tunnel. The opening itself was screened off. Brian Kirby was there. For an instant he met her eye, gave the slightest of nods and then turned away.

*Does he know about me and Richard?*

A man in his thirties, broad-shouldered and beginning to lose his hair, was looking down from the parapet above the tunnel entrance, as if half eager and half afraid to discover what all the fuss was about.

Jill heard footsteps behind her and caught a familiar whiff of sweat, hair oil and cigarettes.

'Miss Francis – what a pleasure.'

The fruity voice was unmistakable. Jill turned. Ivor Fuggle beamed at her, revealing a mouthful of false teeth.

'Who is it?' Jill asked.

'What?' Fuggle leant forward, fiddling with his hearing aid. 'Who is it?'

Jill nodded.

'I don't know. But I've just established that the Bear will open its doors to thirsty drinkers like ourselves at eleven o'clock. Come and have a drop of the stuff that cheers and inebriates, Miss Francis. We can compare notes, eh? We ladies and gentlemen of the press must stick together. I have a good deal of local knowledge which you may lack and, of course, you have your – ah – special relationship with the police.'

He smiled at her again and pushed his way unceremoniously into the crowd. Jill stared after him. There went another very good reason why she should consider leaving Lydmouth.

'All right, then,' one of the uniformed policemen at the mouth of the tunnel was saying. 'There's nothing to see at present, and you'd make our job a lot easier if you'd all disperse. If you please.'

Jill noticed Kirby slipping round the screens and into the tunnel.

There were running footsteps on the path. Suddenly a woman thrust herself into the crowd. She was middle-aged, broad rather than fat, with a wrinkled brown face. Her eyes were screwed up into slits, and she wasn't wearing a hat. Jill thought her dress might be some sort of uniform. She put her head down and plunged through the crowd like a rugby player charging through the opposing pack of forwards.

One of the police officers moved towards her, his arms outstretched to form a human barrier.

'Who is it?' she said, her voice somewhere between a gasp and a shout.

'Can't say at present, I'm afraid, Miss Lindor. Now – it'll help us all if everyone stays calm and moves back from the tunnel. Now come—'

Nurse Lindor ducked and plunged under his arm. She cannoned into another officer, knocking him out of her way, and ran round the edge of the nearest screen.

For an instant there was silence – the sort of silence, Jill thought, you get when a child falls, the silence before the consequences make themselves known.

Then the screams began. It was as though the tunnel had at last found its voice. Out of its mouth came a series of wails, a long ululation rising steadily in pitch and volume.

# Chapter Twenty-five

Bernie Broadbent changed his cars as other men changed their suits. Out on the drive were his latest purchases, a Riley and a Wolseley. Thornhill's little Austin, looking like the poor relation, was parked between them. And there was at least one other car, Thornhill thought, possibly two, out of sight in the double garage.

'I think Edith may have been sweet on him,' Bernie said. 'A lot of the girls were.'

Thornhill turned away from the hall window. The idea of Edith being sweet on someone else gave him a twinge of jealousy. In theory it was completely irrelevant to his current emotional state, just as a twinge from an old sporting injury was irrelevant to a middle-aged man of sedentary habits. It was irrational, too – the man was dead, after all, and Edith had known him long before she met Thornhill. Not for the first time, he wished he had his emotions under better control.

'Hugh Hudnall was very good-looking,' Bernie was saying. 'But it wasn't just that. He was one of nature's charmers. You know?'

Bernie broke off to light his pipe. His voice had thickened as he talked about young Hudnall, and Thornhill wondered if they had been friends. Bernie must have been well over ten years older than Hugh but villages made unexpected friendships.

'Let's go outside,' Bernie said. 'This place makes me feel shut in.'

He opened the front door and they went out into the drive and walked round the side of the house to the garden beyond. Netherfield was a big, airy modern house, white as a wedding cake, and not the sort of place, you would think, that would induce claustrophobia in anyone.

They strolled down the lawn towards the little river at the bottom of the garden.

'What made it worse was that it was me that told her,' Bernie went on. 'We'd arranged that I would collect her from her gran's and take her into Lydmouth for some shopping. First thing I saw when I drove into the village that morning was the local copper – Joseph somebody, I expect he's retired now, or dead. He beckoned me over and asked if I'd heard. Then he told me. So I'd hardly found out myself before I had to tell Edith. God, it was awful. The two of them, father and son in the same night. And we'd seen them both the day before at the play. Heard about that? He was the hero and she was the heroine.'

Bernie puffed vigorously on his pipe. Of course he would have been upset, Thornhill thought – not so much because Hugh Hudnall was dead, probably, but because of the effect it would have on Edith.

'How did she take it?' he asked.

'Went white as a sheet. Except for two spots of colour in her cheeks. Like a clown's make-up. But she said she was all right. Her gran said it was best she went home, back to her mum. So she packed up her stuff and I put her on the train at Lydmouth the same morning. She cried a little in the car, mind, but she didn't say anything about it. I tried to talk to her – better out than in, I thought – but she wouldn't have any of it.' He stopped and swung round to face Thornhill. 'But why are you asking *me* all this? Hasn't Edith told you? And anyway, why is it important now?'

'It's not a subject . . . not a subject she really wants to talk about,' Thornhill said, picking his words as he might a path through a minefield. 'An unhappy memory, and all that. Anyway, I thought you might know more. The thing is, we've just heard that there was another death on that patch of line. Last night some time.'

'Who was it?'

'An old lady called the Honourable Cicely Caswell. Used to be a patient at a lunatic asylum near by.'

'Oh, Christ.' Bernie stared at him. 'I knew her, too. Everyone knew Miss Caswell. She lived up at Fontenoy Place. It's a sort of private nursing home. She'd been there longer than anyone else, I think – staff or guests.'

'Guests?'

'That's what they call the patients. They're very hot on that. They try to run the place like a cross between a private house and a hotel. There's another thing – Miss Caswell wasn't mad.'

'But I thought they all were.'

Bernie shook his grizzled head. 'Some of them, yes. Most of them are just too old to look after themselves. They or their families pay for them to live there.'

'You're very well informed.'

'They've asked me to be one of the trustees. To replace that chap Moorcroft.'

'I see. And how did Miss Caswell fit in?'

'When the place was set up at the turn of the century, they looked after what they called the morally defective as well as the mentally defective. They weren't choosy as long as the families could pay the bills.'

'Morally defective? What do you mean?'

'People who had a drug habit. Or people whose sexual tastes might land them in prison, likely as not. And in the very early days there were some like Miss Caswell. The unmarried mothers.'

'But that's barbaric,' Thornhill said, startled.

'Being barbaric never stopped anyone from doing anything,' Bernie said. 'She belonged to this grand family which was related to the Vaudens. They had a title, too. When she was seventeen or eighteen, she had a baby, and they mismanaged it — the baby died at birth, but everyone knew about it, so in a way she had the worst of both worlds. I think she had some sort of nervous breakdown, too. The family shut her up and threw away the key. And there she's stayed. Until now.'

'But surely when the parents died——?'

'There was nowhere else for her to go. Anyway, she got used to being there. A lot of them did. Fontenoy Place became their home, the staff became their family. They get institutionalised.'

They came to a wrought-iron bench. Bernie sat down heavily. He knocked his pipe against the heel of his shoe. Two ducks cruised towards him with the expectant assurance of those who are regularly fed at a certain place.

After a pause, Thornhill joined him on the bench. 'What did the honourable make her — daughter of a lord?'

Bernie stared out over the water. 'Something like that. George Shipston can give you chapter and verse.'

'Was she under any sort of restraint? I mean, could she come and go more or less as she pleased?'

'Oh yes, I think so. You often saw her up at the village, sometimes by herself. She used to buy buns and things, and try and feed people, I remember. Everyone knew who she was. They liked her, too, no one would harm her. Even the local louts. They knew they'd regret it if they tried.'

'Why was she liked? Someone like that often becomes a sort of scapegoat.'

Bernie shrugged and examined his hands. 'Despite everything, she was a very nice lady. I think everyone knew that.' He turned and looked at Thornhill. 'God knows, Richard. Some people you like, and some people you don't. She was one of the ones you do.

More like a mascot than a scapegoat, maybe? But I didn't know her well. I can tell you who did, though. George Shipston was one of her trustees and he's also on the board at Fontenoy Place. And she was very fond of one of the nurses there, Nurse Lindor, I think.'

Thornhill took out a notebook and jotted down the names.

'I saw her only a couple of days ago,' Bernie said softly, sounding puzzled, as though her absence had become an insoluble riddle. 'She was fine. What exactly happened to her?'

'We haven't established that yet. All we know is apparently she was run down by a train, probably at some point yesterday evening, near Trenalt station. Tell me, when did you see her? At Moorcroft's funeral?'

Bernie shook his head. 'Later than that – in the evening of the same day. She was in the churchyard, mooning over Moorcroft's grave. She wanted to make a phone call. I lent her tuppence.'

'Who was she going to telephone?'

'I don't know.' Bernie frowned. 'Hang on – I think she said something about someone in Kent. We saw her in a phone box a little later.'

'We?'

'I had a drink with a friend of Mr Moorcroft's in the Bear.'

'I see. Look, this has been very helpful. And I'm sorry to have been the bringer of bad news.'

'Someone has to be.'

Thornhill stood up. 'We may have to talk to you again.'

'Talk away, Richard. I'll see you later. My love to Edith.'

Thornhill left Broadbent sitting by the river and walked back to his car at the front of the house. He was surprised that Bernie had taken the news so badly. He also wondered which of Moorcroft's friends he'd been drinking with – not Haughton, surely? It was hard to see what the two men could possibly have in common.

Just below the surface of his conscious mind moved the

uncharted currents of his affair with Jill, and its implications for Edith, for himself, for the children, as invisible and yet as unmistakably present as the ocean on a dark night.

He drove back to Police Headquarters. The CID's Hillman was in the car park, which meant that Kirby had come back from Trenalt. He went upstairs and found Brian making tea in the little kitchen.

'You want some, guv?'

Thornhill nodded. Kirby splashed milk into two cups and lifted the teapot to pour. There was movement in the doorway.

'Excuse me.' It was Drake's secretary, a tall, nervous woman with faded blue eyes. 'Mr Drake wanted a word with you, with both of you, in fact.'

Thornhill gestured at the teapot. 'Can it wait five minutes?'

'He said right away, I'm afraid. He – he's just been seeing Mr Hendry.'

Kirby and Thornhill exchanged glances. They followed the secretary along the corridor to Drake's office. She tapped on the door of the room that had once been Superintendent Williamson's. Drake was at his desk working his way through a pile of files. The top of the desk looked like a geometric exercise in proportion and parallel lines.

'Ah – Thornhill, Kirby. Sit down. I want you to bring me up to date on this Trenalt business.'

'Sergeant Kirby's just back from the village,' Thornhill said.

Brian flipped open his notebook. 'PC Edwards – he's the local man in Trenalt – he had a phone call from the village stationmaster at a quarter past six this morning. The ganger who walks that stretch of the line had come through the tunnel just north of the station and found a body about twenty yards from the entrance on the Trenalt side. He'd already telephoned Lydmouth and Newport to put a stop on the trains.'

'Single track?' Drake said, making a note.

'Yes, sir. Edwards reported it to Divisional HQ and then

went to have a look. He . . . he confirmed the remains were human.' Kirby swallowed. 'And in two parts.'

There was a pause while the three men digested the last words.

'But the parts belong to the same person, I assume?' Drake said, his voice dry. When Kirby nodded, the DCC went on, 'And Edwards made an identification?'

'Yes, sir. Not so much the face but the general appearance, especially the clothes . . . a grey pinafore and a long brown raincoat. He waited for reinforcements and they were in place by seven-thirty, but because of the circumstances they had to take their time. No road access, for example, and – ah – working conditions weren't easy.'

Thornhill could well believe it. As a young constable he had been called to the scene of a suicide at Cambridge railway station. What he had seen that morning – the disjointed limbs, the blood, the look of surprise, the glimpses of bone and tissue, scattered among the rubbish that gathers on a railway line in a busy station – all this had lingered in his memory like the flavour of rotting food on the taste buds. For weeks afterwards, he had looked away when passing a butcher's window.

'Uniformed said they thought we should have a look. Unfortunately word reached the press. People from the *Post* and the *Gazette* turned up while I was there.'

'Does that mean we've got a leak?' Drake said sharply. 'I don't like the sound of that at all.'

'Perhaps,' Thornhill said.

'It could have been someone in Trenalt,' Kirby pointed out. 'Or someone on the railway.'

'In this instance, yes.' Thornhill was still looking at Drake. 'But it's not the first time, sir. News has a habit of reaching the local press a little sooner than it should.'

Drake made another note.

'And there was another complication,' Kirby went on. 'One

of the nurses from Fontenoy Place – a Miss Lindor – forced her way into the tunnel and had a fit of hysterics.'

'We'd better get someone else to do the formal identification,' Thornhill said. 'Dr Angmer, perhaps.'

'She actually tried to lift the – the body. Apparently she was very attached to Miss Caswell.' Kirby's face was harassed. 'The journalists lapped it up.'

'There's something else they're going to like,' Thornhill said. 'Sooner or later, someone's going to tell them that a young man fell under a train at Trenalt station in '38.'

'Coincidence,' Drake said.

'Of course. But they'll soon find someone to say the line is haunted. Cursed.'

The DCC grunted. 'They certainly would in India.'

'There's another thing,' Thornhill went on. 'I don't know if it's relevant but Councillor Broadbent was in Trenalt on Tuesday evening, and he bumped into Miss Caswell. He lent her tuppence for a phone call.'

'Who would she want to phone?'

'I don't know. You wouldn't have thought she'd have much contact with the outside world.'

'Fontenoy Place?' Kirby suggested.

'Check it,' Drake ordered. 'Why hadn't the people at Fontenoy Place reported her missing?'

'They might not have noticed she wasn't there,' Thornhill said. 'She might simply have got up early. According to Councillor Broadbent, she wasn't under restraint. For what it's worth, he also thinks she was well liked in the village.'

'All right.' Drake took a sip from the cup of black tea. 'Now – when did she die?'

'We don't know yet, sir,' Kirby said.

Drake's eyebrows arched. 'I'd have thought that's the one thing you would know. Surely you've got hold of the train times?'

'She was last seen yesterday evening.' Kirby consulted his

notebook. 'At about eight-thirty or a little afterwards. Four trains went through the tunnel in the next hour or so. The eight-forty-three to Lydmouth, the nine-twenty-three to Newport, and the nine-forty-three to Lydmouth. That's the times they left Trenalt station. Plus one goods train going down to Newport, which passed through Trenalt station at nine-fifty-two. Last train of the day. It's possible one of those killed her. But of course we don't yet know if she died last night. It might have been early this morning. In which case it would have been either a goods train going to Newport at one minute past six or the first passenger train of the day to Lydmouth at nine past.'

Thornhill stirred. 'That's assuming she was still alive when the train hit her.'

Drake stood up and went to the window. He peered down at the High Street below as if checking for eavesdroppers. Kirby glanced at Thornhill. The silence lengthened.

'Very well,' Drake said softly. 'Now I'll put another side to this.'

He spoke so quietly that Thornhill had to strain to hear him. The DCC turned slowly and faced the room. His blue eyes glowed in his blank red face. Drake, Thornhill realised with a sudden thrill of recognition, was quietly but unmistakably furious.

# Chapter Twenty-six

Naughty was a nursery word. Edith Thornhill clung to it like a guilty secret. Not that she had done anything that deserved even that description. It was more that, after what seemed like years of tiresome rectitude, there hovered on the edge of a hypothetical future the possibility of something different.

She wouldn't do anything she shouldn't. Of course not. But it was nice to play with the idea in her mind. Wasn't it strange how something that didn't exist could make you feel happy?

The pleasure was a solitary one. For once she was glad when Richard had left the house. She washed up, made the beds, flicked a duster over the more dust-prone surfaces, cut flowers for the sitting room and the kitchen, and tied up a parcel of linen for the laundry. The most mundane domestic tasks had acquired a strange fascination. The morning was warm but not oppressively so — exactly as the British summer was meant to be but rarely was.

She got ready to go out with more care than usual, spending far more time in front of the mirror than she usually allowed herself. There was a bus stop at the end of Victoria Road, but on this occasion she decided she would walk into town. She wanted the exercise. She had to do something with the mysterious energy fizzing through her body.

In the High Street she visited the newsagent's, the butcher's, the greengrocer's, the grocer's and the ironmonger's. She paid bills, placed orders, complained about a late delivery and held three animated conversations about the weather. Gradually the shopping bag on her arm grew heavier.

Last of all, she came to the baker's, where she placed her order for the following week. As she was paying her bill, she caught sight of the Lydmouth buns. There was a tray of them, freshly baked. She bought six. She thought that if naughtiness had a smell, it would be like that of the buns — sweet, spicy and freshly baked.

Shortly after half-past eleven, she went to the Gardenia for her cup of coffee. This was one of the treats that she tried to work into the week's household budget. Her favourite table near the window was free. She ordered a tea cake to go with the coffee and settled down to add what she had spent that morning to the notebook in which she kept her domestic accounts.

Twenty minutes later, she was about to ask for her bill when a thin and painfully genteel voice impinged on her consciousness. The speaker was a woman two or three yards behind her. It was not the voice itself which hooked her attention but one or two of the words it uttered.

'Yes, it'll be very select. I'm going to have one of the bungalows right at the back, so it will be lovely and quiet, right in the middle of town. You'll never guess who my next-door neighbour's going to be. Miss Francis — our lady deputy editor.'

Edith heard the manageress murmuring a question.

'No, she lives over the wall at the back in that funny little house next to the vicarage. She only rents it, of course. Rather old-fashioned inside, I should think. Probably damp, as well.'

There was another murmur.

'Well, Mrs Browning, you know me,' the first woman went on. 'I was never one to gossip.'

The voice dropped to a whisper. Edith realised that she was stirring her cup of coffee, a cup that contained nothing but dregs.

'Still, it's not very nice, is it, not in a town like this.' Outrage had raised the volume to its previous level. 'What people get up to when they're in London is nobody's business. No one can claim I'm not broad-minded. But London's London, I always say, and Lydmouth's Lydmouth. Of course, I could see it coming. When you get a woman taking a job away from a man, and not doing it very well, you often find that standards are slipping in all departments, if you take my meaning.'

This time there was a sharper edge of curiosity to Mrs Browning's reply.

'No, I wouldn't like to say. But there's no denying there's been a lot of tittle-tattle, some of it involving a married man, and I'm afraid there's going to be more before it's over.' The reedy voice dropped to a whisper. The words were no longer distinguishable, only the sound hissing through a pair of lips like water seeping from a leaky tap.

Then came a moment's silence. The silence, Edith thought, that follows a revelation.

'Really?' Mrs Browning said, her voice loud, surprised and clear. 'But—'

Then came another silence.

Mrs Browning knew Edith's name. Mrs Browning knew who her husband was. Mrs Browning might have stopped the conversation in mid-flow because she had suddenly realised Edith was listening. Two facts, Edith thought, and a probability.

Something must have shown in Edith's face because the waitress chose that moment to pause by her table and ask if everything was all right. She said yes, thank you, and asked for the bill. Meanwhile the conversation behind her resumed. This time Mrs Browning and her customer, both perfectly audible, were chatting about the royal family.

Edith paid her bill, leaving a larger tip than she would usually have done so she would not have to wait for the change. In the doorway, however, she forced herself to turn.

'Goodbye,' she said to the manageress. 'Thank you.'

'Goodbye, Mrs Thornhill.' The expression on Mrs Browning's face, a blend of pity and curiosity, confirmed everything. 'See you next week.'

The other woman glanced round. Tall and thin, she had a long, slightly crooked nose which might at some stage in her life have been broken and badly set. Perched on her head was a brimless beige hat with a stalk like an apple's protruding from the top. Edith recognised the face but could not put a name to it.

Despite the heavy bag of shopping on her arm, she walked all the way back to Victoria Road. Taking the bus would expose her to other people. She did not want them to look at her or talk to her. She walked quickly, with her head bowed. Thoughts darted through her mind, mysterious and half glimpsed, like fish moving in the bottom of a pond. The tea cake and coffee lay heavily in her stomach. Perhaps she would be sick. She wondered if there would be enough hot water for her to have a bath.

At the house, she dropped her handbag in the porch when she was trying to find the key. Her hand was shaking so much that it took a small lifetime to push the key into the lock and turn it.

She let herself into the cool, dark hall, slammed the door behind her and leant against it, as though the weight of her body would keep out the crowd of jeering people that were trying to get in. People like the woman in the horrible hat. Her breath was coming in ragged gasps that tore her chest.

By mistake she had left ajar the door between the kitchen and the hall. Max and Tom nosed through the gap and cantered over the dark linoleum towards her. She knew what they would do in a moment — try to climb, as though her legs were a pair of tree trunks, their claws digging for purchase into the material of her stockings and the skin beneath.

The threat of a ruined pair of stockings was one of the few things which at that moment could have penetrated her misery. She bent and in one swift movement scooped both kittens up to her chest. They climbed higher on to the natural shelf of her breasts and began to lick her neck. She carried them into the kitchen and sat down by the window.

Max began to chew her hair, while Tom made the final ascent to the crown of her head, where he stood, claws fully extended, purring. Tears rolled down Edith's cheeks. She could not wipe them away because the bag containing her handkerchief was still in the hall, and in any case she needed both hands to prevent Tom from falling off. She looked out over the garden she had struggled so hard to make. *Why did I bother?*

Then the doorbell rang.

Tom, startled by the sound, fell off Edith's head and landed on her lap on top of Max. Max licked him absent-mindedly. Tom bit his brother's ear.

She was sorely tempted not to answer the door. She might so easily have been out shopping. What would it matter? Who would know?

Nevertheless, she lifted the kittens from her lap and stood up. Life had to go on, somehow. Besides, it might be a neighbour who had seen her coming in or a boy with a telegram announcing dreadful news about the children. A tea towel was airing on the rail by the boiler and she used it to dry her face. She stared dispassionately at herself in the mirror over the mantelpiece. Her make-up would pass muster.

The doorbell rang again, and her courage faltered.

She forced herself into the hall, making sure the kittens were shut in the kitchen. She would have liked to have hidden away for ever in a dark cave where no one could find her and nothing could hurt her. In any case, she knew without consciously thinking about the matter at all, that she had to continue to pretend she was a normal person living in a normal world where people kept the promises they had made and acted in normal, tried-and-tested ways that everyone recognised were for the best in the long run.

As she passed the mirror set in the hatstand, she glanced at her reflection again. She was shocked to see how ordinary she looked. She smoothed her skirt and opened the front door.

Jack Graig was standing in the porch. 'Edith – I hope this isn't inconvenient.'

'No.' She took a step backwards, holding open the door. 'Would you like to come in?'

'Are you sure?'

'Of course.'

She guessed what he was thinking, and liked him for it. There were some people in Lydmouth who did not approve of married ladies letting strange men into their houses when nobody else was there. She led the way into the sitting room at the front. She was conscious of the shabbiness of the sofa, a hand-me-down from Richard's aunt – and the threadbare state of the carpet just inside the door. But at least she had dusted and aired the room after breakfast and the roses in the bowl on the windowsill had been cut that morning.

She sat down in one of the armchairs and Jack sat opposite her. He turned his cap round and round in his hands as if it were a steering wheel. There were patches of pallor on his face. With a lurch into anxiety, she hoped he wasn't ill. In an instant she had given him an incurable tropical disease and buried him in one of the vacant plots near Rufus Moorcroft's grave in Trenalt churchyard.

'Perhaps I should have telephoned,' he was saying, his voice thick and jerky. 'But I thought, in the circumstances . . . I suppose you haven't heard?'

'Heard what?'

'About Miss Caswell.'

Edith shook her head. She noticed that Jack's blazer needed a good brush and that a thread of cotton dangled from the left cuff of his shirt.

'I'm – I'm afraid she's dead.'

Edith stared at him. Her mouth opened but no sound came out.

'I'm sorry,' he went on. 'I know it's a shock, especially with me blurting it out like this. But I – I thought it might be worse if you saw it in the paper or something.'

'Yes, yes – thank you.' Edith tore her eyes away from his face. 'But how did it happen? She seemed perfectly all right when we saw her yesterday. Was it a heart attack or something?'

Jack shook his head. 'An accident.'

There was another silence. She looked up at him and saw the Adam's apple rise and fall in his throat as he swallowed.

'She . . . she seems to have been knocked down by a train.'

For a moment neither of them spoke. It was as if they were both shouting the same two words at the tops of their voices.

*Like Hugh.*

'Was it at the station?' she asked.

'Just inside the tunnel. I suppose she must have wandered in there last night or early this morning and – Edith, it must have been very quick – she can't have known what was happening.'

'She must have heard it, though, felt it coming towards her.'

'Don't think about it.'

'She . . . she . . . she didn't deserve this.'

'No.'

'The trousseau,' Edith said suddenly. 'Do you remember?'

He spread out his hands. 'Yes. Though to be honest I wasn't sure she knew what she was talking about. I certainly didn't.'

'Nor did I. But whatever it is, she gave it to me yesterday. It's almost as if she knew.'

'That can't be true.'

'No, I suppose not. I expect it was simply that she didn't need it any more, wasn't it? Because your uncle had died. It doesn't mean she was intending to do away with herself.' Hungry for reassurance, she looked at him. 'Does it, Jack? Does it?'

'Of course it doesn't. She wasn't the sort to kill herself. That generation was taught to grin and bear it.'

'When – when was she found?'

'Early this morning. Mrs Solly told me when she came up to the cottage. The police are down there now – with an ambulance. The mouth of the tunnel has been sealed off, and Mrs Solly says they're running a bus service while the line's closed.'

Edith sat in silence for a moment. She stared at the roses, their colour a deep red, darker and softer than blood. There would be another funeral. She was aware that Jack was sitting very still: waiting for her. For the first time she allowed herself to say the words in the privacy of her mind. *He still likes me.* The knowledge gave her a sense of power. She turned her head and looked at him. Funny to think that he hadn't changed. But she had.

'Jack – I think we should do something about Miss Caswell's things. The ones she mentioned. Her . . . her trousseau.'

'Do what?'

'We can't just leave it there. It's – it's a sort of loose end that she's left behind. The least we can do is make sure it's tied up neatly.'

'Do you think it actually exists?'

'Something does. Shouldn't we look for it? If it contains nothing but rubbish, we can at least make sure it's disposed of properly. I can't bear to think of people laughing at her. And if there's anything valuable, we can pass it on to her heirs.'

Edith wondered at her own vehemence. A phrase from a Kipling poem slipped into her mind: sisters under the skin. But what did she have in common with the Honourable Cicely

Caswell? A trousseau? Jack probably thought she was being hysterical, but she didn't care.

'All right,' he said. 'I think I understand what you mean.'

He was so down-to-earth about it, so obliging, that she could have kissed him as he sat four-square, hands on knees, in Richard's armchair.

'Anyway,' he went on, 'if that's what we're going to do, when would you like to have a look for it? I could drive you over there now, if you liked.'

'Would you? Would you really?'

'Of course.' He stared back at her, his face so solemn he might have been agreeing to something much more serious. 'The real problem will be where to look when we get there. If we're lucky, she'll have found a hiding place near where we had the picnic. But if we're not so lucky, it could be anywhere. Down in the quarry, even.'

Edith stood up. 'We'd better take something to eat — it will be lunchtime soon. I'll bring some fruit, shall I, and some bread and cheese, and . . . and . . . I happened to buy some Lydmouth buns when I went out this morning.'

A quarter of an hour later, Edith was sitting beside Jack in the Ford. Neither of them spoke much on the drive to Trenalt. She thought briefly about Richard, about those beastly things the woman in the Gardenia had hinted, and about her ghastly brimless hat with its silly little stalk on top. The news of Miss Caswell's death had not made what happened less horrible than it was before. But it had temporarily numbed the memory. Perhaps Jack was helping too, if only by occupying some of her attention.

As they were nearing the village, Jack said, 'We'll leave the car where we did yesterday, shall we? No point in advertising the fact we're up there.'

'Yes,' she said. 'But won't they see us when we walk up to the field by the quarry? The path goes over the parapet of the tunnel.'

'We can get there another way. There's another path, which takes you higher up the hill. It's a bit steeper, but it's not much longer. I hope——' He broke off, concentrating on steering the car off the road.

'Hope what?' Edith said when Jack had turned off the engine.

'Eh? Oh – I hope we don't meet that journalist fellow this time.'

Edith thought he had been going to say something else but she didn't press it. They left the car and walked over stiles, through sunlit fields, up rock-floored paths which the summer had turned into cool green tunnels. When the way was broad enough, they walked side by side. In the direct sun, it was very warm.

The ground levelled out. They were back at the top of the world. They followed the track through the beaten grass to the place where they had had their picnic.

'Search first or have a drink and something to eat?' Jack asked.

'I don't mind,' Edith said. 'It doesn't matter.'

Jack put down the basket with their food in a patch of shade at the foot of the mound of spoil in the middle of the field. The mound was shaped roughly like a segment of orange and, on its outer curve, it was in places over six feet high. He straightened up and caught her looking at him.

'Edith,' he said. 'What's wrong?'

She looked at the grass. 'Nothing.'

'Of course there is.' His voice had suddenly roughened. 'You've been crying, haven't you? You'd been crying before you heard about Miss Caswell.'

'No. Just a touch of hay fever.'

'I don't believe you. Look, I know it's none of my business, but you know if there's anything I can do to help, you simply have to say.'

To her horror, she felt the tears sliding down her cheeks once again.

'Edith,' Jack said. He touched her forearm and then snatched back his hand as if her skin were burning hot.

The sound of his voice and the touch of his hand made her cry harder than ever. She felt his arms circling her shoulders. She lowered her head and rested it against his chest. She kept her own arms folded, pressed against her breasts, a flesh-and-bone barrier between herself and Jack. Her body heaved in time with the sobs. For a few seconds she abandoned herself to the peaks and troughs of grief. There was even a sort of consolation in the knowledge that she had so little control over her actions.

When she stopped, it was not because her grief had come to an end. It was simply that an unwelcome but powerful thought insinuated itself into her mind. *I must look a terrible mess.* Close behind this came another: *Jack's got his arms around me. Jack's hugging me.*

Edith gulped for air like a stranded fish and pulled herself away from him. He smelled of pipe tobacco, she noticed, and – not unpleasantly – of sweat. She looked up at his anxious face and thought how ugly she must seem to him now.

'I'm sorry,' Edith muttered. 'I don't know what – what happened.'

'I think you should tell me what's wrong now,' he said gruffly, staring over her shoulder. 'You know what they say about a trouble shared. We're old friends, so it's perfectly all right.'

She knelt down and started to unpack the basket. 'I . . . I think Richard – my husband – is seeing someone. A woman.'

Jack crouched down beside her. 'You think he may be having an affair?'

She glanced at him but saw nothing in his face except concern. 'Yes – I heard someone gossiping about it in the café this morning. She didn't say so in as many words, but it was obvious what she meant. She may even have known who I was, I don't know.'

'But, Edith, this is only gossip. Was your husband's name actually mentioned?'

'No. But the woman didn't need to. I know who she meant. Anyway, the thing is, she — she wasn't telling me anything I didn't know already.'

'So you already knew?'

'I — I knew Richard had to see quite a lot of her, the woman they were talking about, and I sometimes wondered if he liked her. She's very smart, very attractive, and . . . oh, there've been signs. I've been going around with my eyes closed. That's the trouble. And that horrible woman made me see.'

'You may have misunderstood.'

'No. It's like a jigsaw puzzle. All the pieces have been there but she made me put them together. Which was the one thing I'd been trying not to do.'

'Still, from what you say, you don't actually *know*. Lydmouth's such a small place that tongues are bound to wag. Ten to one it's just hot air.'

She shook her head. 'I wish I could believe you.' She swallowed and then plunged on: 'It's like Hugh all over again. I feel as if everything is always going to go wrong, as if everything I touch is doomed.'

'That's nonsense.'

'Is it? First Hugh — and, in a way, you.' She saw the twist of pain on his face and wondered briefly why his unhappiness made hers worse. 'And now Richard. I'm tired of it. Where does it end?'

Her voice sounded shrill and childish in her ears. She abandoned the basket and stood up. She wasn't thirsty and she wasn't hungry any more, especially not for Lydmouth buns.

Jack said, 'Edith, I think there's a mistake. I—'

'What does it matter?' she interrupted. 'Everything's happened now. You can't go back and change it, can you? Why don't we look for Miss Caswell's things? At least we can do *that* properly.'

She walked away from him, round the end of the artificial hillock, cutting off the conversation. The plumes of rosebay willowherb nodded in the breeze. Nettles sprouted among scrap metal and stone. A weather-bleached cigarette packet lay half buried in a heap of caked ashes partly enclosed between three rocks. Kids must have made a fire, or perhaps a tramp. It was hard to imagine other people here.

Twenty yards away was the fence that guarded the edge of the quarry – a fence in name rather than in fact since it was hard to think of any animal, large or small, which in its present condition the fence could have kept out. Miss Caswell had been an agile and energetic woman for her age, and if she had hidden her trousseau down there they were going to have a difficult job.

Edith heard Jack coming up behind her and set off towards the fence, accelerating rapidly to widen the gap between them. How on earth, she wondered, could she have talked like that to a man who was the next best thing to a total stranger? To a man, moreover, who—

'Edith! Have a look at this.'

Reluctantly she turned. Jack was tugging at a dead branch which poked out from the back of the mound. She walked slowly towards him. With one hand he lifted the branch and with the other he pulled out a rusting cylinder of metal with irregular holes punched in its side. He looked up as she drew near.

'Is this it? I'm not sure it was worth finding.'

'What is it?'

'Half an oil drum,' Jack said. 'Looks like it was used as a brazier at some point.' He dug into it and pulled out a brown hessian sack. He glanced at Edith and risked a joke: 'Bit like Father Christmas, eh?'

She smiled automatically, as one did when a child made a

joke because not to show amusement would be discourteous. 'What's in it?'

He held the sack open and she peered inside. The smell of stale tobacco rose to meet her. She saw what might be a trowel, tiny flecks of coloured paper, a large brown envelope, a green hat and a bundle of grey wool; and beneath these were other things, a jumble of objects gathered with magpie logic for a purpose that no longer existed.

'Edith, what you were saying earlier . . .' Jack's voice sounded strained, as though forced out of a tight, hard place deep inside him. 'About everything going wrong, and – and mentioning me. I think you must have made a mistake.'

'When?' She did not look at him but continued to stare into the sack.

'The day after the play. That last afternoon – that's what you meant, just then, wasn't it?'

She backed away from both him and the sack. 'I don't know what you're talking about.'

'I think you do. The summerhouse.'

*How dare you?*

She stared down at the long grass. Memories welled like spring water from the tangle of green beneath her feet. By an effort of will she had spent the better part of fifteen years ignoring them. Was that why they were now so unbearably vivid?

The last afternoon in Trenalt – that was when she had learned once and for all that loving was dangerous for the simple reason that men were not to be trusted.

The lesson had been all the more painful because at the time Edith had been riding on a swell of triumph after the play and Hugh's kiss. Two other performances were scheduled. Anything had seemed possible. She had even got as far as choosing her bridesmaids and devoting serious consideration to the matter of children's names. So when she saw the rector's wife delivering the parish magazines after lunch, she had naturally volunteered to deliver the ones to the houses on the hill to the station and to Highnam Cottage on the other side of the line. Edith liked the rector's wife and wanted to use up some of her energy. Also, she had seen Hugh walking up the hill beyond the level-crossing, which meant there was a respectable chance that she would meet him at the cottage. More than anything in the world she wanted to be with Hugh.

'Edith,' Jack said, almost shouting, obstinately in the here and now, his voice penetrating the dark enchantment of memory. 'Won't you listen to me? Please.'

*Listen?* That was the trouble, she had listened. If she hadn't listened on that summer afternoon, the day after the first and as it happened the only performance of *The Forest Rebel*, her life would have been very different, and perhaps other people's lives as well.

The weather had turned at last. The air had been heavy with the approaching rain. She had reached Highnam Cottage but no one answered when she rang the bell and she guessed that anyone who was there would be down at the summerhouse, probably having tea. She rang the bell again, and when there was still no answer, she left the parish magazine on the shelf in the porch and walked across the lawn.

The veranda faced away from her. She did not call out. She wanted to surprise them. In a moment, she was so close she could have touched the back of the summerhouse if she had stretched out her hand.

She heard Hugh laugh.

Something in the sound made her stop. She knew how Hugh laughed, but this was different.

'Darling,' she heard him say. 'Just stop talking and kiss me.' Hugh's voice had been like a caress made sound. 'And then we're going to have to do something about your little badge of manhood. It's going to burst if we leave it standing there much longer. Not so little, either. Now Jack—'

Edith had fled. She had run soundlessly across the lawn, down the grass verge beside the drive and into the lane.

As she ran, she wept.

'Edith,' Jack said in a hoarse voice, moving towards her, his hands outstretched. 'We need to settle this, once and for all.'

So now she ran and wept. What else was there to do when people betrayed you? Time telescoped. Then and now slid together like overlapping tubes. Once again she was running from Jack and Hugh. What did it matter that Hugh was now a ghost?

'Stop. Just for a moment. *Please.*'

Jack's footsteps thudded behind her, and the long grass rustled in his wake. Edith heard herself whimper. She stumbled round the end of the mound and stopped as though she had run into an invisible wall.

Five yards away from her was the squat figure of Nurse Lindor, shoulders hunched forward, striding towards them. Edith made a wordless noise in the back of her throat.

*Where does grief end and anger begin?*

'And what do you think you're doing here?' Miss Lindor saw Jack beyond Edith, and the oil drum and the sack beyond him. 'Prying into what doesn't concern you?'

# Chapter Twenty-seven

Flecks of rain beaded the windscreen of the Austin as Richard Thornhill drove through Edge Hill. It was late on Thursday morning and he was in a foul temper. This was not only because of his inconclusive meeting with Jill the previous evening, which had left him feeling frustrated in more ways than one. He was almost equally annoyed to be wasting his time on a job that could have been entrusted to the rawest detective constable.

He hated a case like this, where outside influences warped the conduct of the investigation. During her life, Miss Cicely Caswell had been insignificant – at most an embarrassment to those who knew her. In death, however, she had become a damned nuisance.

Drake, talking in a clipped, coldly furious voice, had told Thornhill and Kirby that the Chief Constable was taking a personal interest in this matter. Both the leader of the county council and the chairman of the Standing Joint Committee had been on the telephone to Mr Hendry. Miss Caswell's cousin, Lord Vauden, was so concerned that he planned to drive down to Lydmouth at the weekend, where he would stay with Sir Anthony Ruispidge, another member of the Standing Joint Committee – and, like Lord Vauden, a trustee of Fontenoy Place.

The Lord Lieutenant of the county, who had been in the army with Lord Vauden, had sent a telegram requesting to be kept informed of developments. The pathologist was coming up from Cardiff later today to do an urgent autopsy at the RAF Hospital.

Thornhill's life had been further complicated by another phone call to Mr Hendry, this time from a minister of state at the Home Office. The minister's brother-in-law was Herbert Reece-Williams, owner of the Cardiff gallery which was mounting the retrospective of Gareth Loysey's work.

'I gather the minister feels that if this painting vanished – what's it called? *Lady with Fan?* – it would be a tragedy for British art. Or his brother-in-law thinks so, which in this case comes to the same thing. And Mr Hendry thinks we can't rule out the possibility that the disappearance of the painting is connected in some way with Moorcroft's suicide and the death of Miss Caswell. So you'd better go and see this artist fellow, Loysey. Yes, you personally, Thornhill. Show him we mean business.'

Drake had been too loyal, or perhaps too canny, to voice his dislike of all this. He didn't have to. The chilly undercurrents in his voice made it clear how he felt.

'In other words,' he had said quietly at the end of his meeting with Thornhill and Kirby, 'this isn't simply one of those cases where justice has to be seen to be done. What we really have to ensure is that no one can subsequently criticise this police force on any grounds whatsoever. Is that understood?'

Thornhill reached the village of Drybury and asked directions to Grebe House. The sight of it, standing freshly painted, surrounded by trim lawns, increased his irritation. People like the Loyseys, living comfortable lives in comfortable houses, should not be allowed to tweak a police investigation to their advantage. Perhaps it would not be such a wrench to leave the force after all.

The first surprise of the interview was that he recognised the woman who opened the door.

'Mrs Loysey?'

She nodded.

He showed her his warrant card. 'Detective Inspector Thorn-hill, Lydmouth CID. We're looking into the possible theft of a work of art, madam. One of your husband's paintings.'

She nodded. '*Lady with Fan.*'

Thornhill was sure it was the woman he had seen in the bank – the one who had come out of Mr Morgan's office with her lips trembling. She showed no sign of having recognised him, but that did not surprise him.

'I wonder if I could have a word with Mr Loysey?'

'He's very busy.'

'And I understand he's also very keen to get this picture back.'

'Yes – yes, of course. It's just that he doesn't like to be disturbed when he's working. But come in. I'll let him know you're here.'

As they were crossing the large, airy hall, a door at the far end opened and a chubby little man came out with a cup of coffee in one hand and a cigarette in the other. 'Who is it, June?'

'It's a policeman, dear. I wasn't sure if you had time—'

'Of course I've got time to talk to a police officer.' Loysey grinned at Thornhill. 'Hello. I'm Gareth Loysey.'

Thornhill introduced himself again.

'That's splendid,' Loysey said. 'You certainly haven't wasted any time, Inspector. I suppose there's always a chance that Moorcroft burned the painting before he died. I understand he had a bonfire. But I can't believe he'd be such a philistine. Personally I think it was stolen.'

'Do you have a photograph of it, sir? Something to give us an idea of what we're looking for?'

'I can do even better than that. I've got my preliminary sketches. There's a photograph too. Come and have a look – they're down in my studio. June, dear, could you bring the inspector some coffee?'

He led Thornhill out of a half-glazed side door and along a gravel path to a small stable yard. The loose boxes and coach house were now used partly for storage and partly as a sitting room. Inside, an open staircase of polished wood led to what had once been a series of lofts. The Loyseys had raised the ceiling and put in tall north-facing windows.

'Take a pew, Inspector.'

There was a large black-and-white photograph of Loysey on the coffee table. It was a head-and-shoulders shot. Thornhill picked it up and looked at it while the artist rummaged in a large maroon folder.

'I don't usually leave photographs of myself lying around.' Loysey chuckled. 'Much as I'd like to. The *Gazette* are doing a piece about me, and I got the photograph out for them. Ah — here we are.'

He extracted three drawings and a photograph from the folder. He laid them on the coffee table and stood back, his head on one side.

'Though I say so myself, I've done worse.'

Thornhill stared at the sketches. The subject was certainly recognisable as a face, though it was strangely warped as though it lay in a puddle of water. On one of the sketches, swirls of watercolour lay in streaks across the skin. The mouth of the sitter was open in a near-perfect oval. Lipstick circled the lips but did not cover them, creating the impression that the face had a second mouth. She rested a fan coyly against her cheek. Perched on top of the head was a small hat with a pink ribbon trailing from the brim. The woman reminded Thornhill, incongruously, of his daughter Elizabeth pretending to be grown up with one of her mother's hats.

'I understand this is a portrait, sir. Who was the sitter?'

'An old lady who lives in a sort of nursing home near Trenalt.'

'Fontenoy Place?'

'That's it. My wife's family used to live in the village before the war. The lady commissioned me to do a painting of herself for Mr Moorcroft. Strange woman – definitely something missing from the upper storey. Her name's Miss Caswell. There was a rumour in the village that when she was a girl she had an affair with Lord Salisbury. Frankly, when I knew her, it was hard to imagine her having an affair with anyone, let alone a highly respectable Victorian prime minister.'

'Have you any idea who might have wanted to steal the painting?'

'It's worth a few bob, so it might have been stolen by someone who knew what they were doing. But it did occur to me – I hardly like to say this, Inspector – that Miss Caswell might actually have pinched it herself. When I knew her, she worshipped the ground Mr Moorcroft trod on. She's not exactly mentally stable, after all, and possibly when she heard he had died, she decided to take back the painting. Just a thought – I don't mean to tell you how to do your job – but it might be worth asking her.'

June Loysey came in with the coffee. Her husband picked up the drawing so she could lay the tray on the table.

'I'm afraid we can't ask Miss Caswell anything,' Thornhill said. 'She's dead.'

Mrs Loysey sat down heavily on the sofa. 'But . . . but what happened?'

'She seems to have been knocked down by a train. It probably happened last night or early this morning.'

'I can't believe it.'

'Good God,' Loysey murmured. 'The poor woman. That's frightful, isn't it, June?'

His wife dabbed her eyes with her apron. 'I'm sorry – it's quite a shock, really. We used to know her quite well before the war. Everyone in the village did. How . . . how did it happen?'

'We don't know yet.'

Mrs Loysey stood up. 'I . . . I'd better leave you to it. Let me know if you'd like some more coffee.'

She left the studio, slamming the door behind her, and they heard her footsteps walking rapidly down the path towards the house.

'I wish I'd had time to prepare her for that,' Loysey said. 'There's no way you could know, Inspector, but her brother was killed on that stretch of line back in '38.'

'What exactly happened to him?'

'It's a sad story. His father indulged him. There'd been quite a lot of trouble of one sort or another while he was up at Oxford. Anyway, he came down to the station to meet his father one night. He'd drunk far too much, yet again, and he seems to have fallen under the train. But that wasn't the end of it. His father actually saw the body. Poor old chap. He had a heart condition. Just keeled over. So for poor June, it was a double loss.'

'I'm sorry.'

'All water under the bridge now. But try not to worry my wife about it unless you really have to. She finds it very distressing.'

Once again they heard footsteps through the open window. Mrs Loysey tapped on the door and opened it.

'There's a telephone call for you, Inspector.'

He followed her into the house. The telephone was on a table in the hall. He picked up the receiver.

'Thornhill.'

'There's been a development, sir,' Kirby said. 'The SOCOs have found traces of blood on the rails at the entrance of the tunnel. Several yards away from where the body was found.'

Thornhill glanced around him. Mrs Loysey had gone into the kitchen and closed the door behind her. He murmured into the telephone, 'If the train was travelling in the Lydmouth direction—'

'Yes, sir – the collision could have happened at the mouth of the tunnel, and the body might have been pushed up along the line. But there's a problem with that. The SOCOs found some more blood. It was on top of the parapet above the start of the tunnel.'

# Chapter Twenty-eight

Late on Thursday morning, Bernie Broadbent paid a call to Police Headquarters. A detective constable took down the details of his meeting with Miss Caswell in Trenalt churchyard. A WPC brought him a cup of coffee. Afterwards, the Chief Constable gave him a glass of sherry in his private sitting room.

He left the building by the back door into the car park. Thirty yards in front of him, a slim, dark-haired man was threading his way through the parked vehicles. Then Bernie saw the rakish blue car.

'Mr Haughton,' he called. 'Lovely day.'

Randolph Haughton turned, smiling. 'Mr Broadbent – have they been grilling you too?'

'More like a light toasting.' Bernie wished his tailor could produce a sports jacket like Haughton's. On the other hand, in order to set it off you needed a figure to match. 'Are you in a hurry? I owe you a drink.'

Haughton glanced at his watch. 'What a good idea. Let me fetch some cigarettes from the car.'

The two men walked over to the Bristol. Bernie ran his finger along the gleaming paintwork.

Haughton stretched his arm through the open window,

opened the glove compartment and took out a cigarette packet. As he straightened up, he caught Bernie's eye.

'Lovely car,' Bernie said, and cleared his throat.

'Fancy a spin? We could always have that drink in a nice little country pub.'

'Why not?'

They climbed into the car. There was a pile of *Berkeley's* on the back seat. When they had had a drink at the Bear on Tuesday evening, Haughton had mentioned his magazine. Bernie had bought a copy the next morning. Too wordy for his taste, he had thought, but no doubt very clever.

'Have you done lots of writing in Trenalt?' he asked.

'A little. Not as much as I hoped. Too many distractions.'

Bernie directed them out of town by the Eastbury road. As the houses dropped away behind them, Haughton glanced at him.

'I imagine the police were talking to us about the same thing?'

'Miss Caswell?'

'Yes – don't you think it's rather odd they're investigating what happened to her so thoroughly? I mean, I'm no expert on police procedure, but surely it's a straightforward case of accident?'

'I suppose they have to be sure,' Bernie said. 'As it happens I saw the Chief Constable this morning. Between ourselves, I gather Miss Caswell's family have been breathing down their necks.'

Haughton nodded. For a while they drove in silence. Bernie glanced at the hands on the wheel – long-fingered and well manicured, very different from his own. Haughton's head turned towards him and Bernie rapidly looked away.

Haughton said, 'I, ah, I've had her up to a hundred on the straight, you know. Solid as a rock, even at that speed.'

'What's the engine?'

'It's a six-cylinder job – based on the BMW two-litre. Why

don't you take the wheel in a moment? See how she handles for yourself.'

'All right.'

'She was an extraordinary woman,' Haughton said, reverting abruptly to Miss Caswell. 'You wonder what she would have turned into if she hadn't—'

'If her family hadn't locked her away for fifty years,' Bernie said.

'Just so. Frightening, isn't it, what people will do in the name of respectability.'

'She was very friendly with Rufus Moorcroft, wasn't she?'

'I asked Rufus about that once,' Haughton said. 'He made a joke of it. Said they had something in common, like a pair of castaways on a desert island.'

'What?'

'Like a pair of castaways on a desert island: those were his exact words.'

'Sort of square pegs in round holes?'

Haughton looked at him and this time Bernie did not look away. 'That's what brings a lot of people together,' he said. 'Don't you find?' He went on without a change of voice or expression: 'I wonder who she was telephoning when we saw her. The police asked me about that.'

'Me too. I thought she said something about ringing someone in Kent.'

'That's odd.' Haughton took his foot off the accelerator and the car began to slow down. 'From where I was sitting, I could see her in the phone box. She was looking up a number in the directory.'

'But that would make it a local number.'

'Precisely. But I suppose she might have made two calls. Or I might have been mistaken.' He braked gently, and the car glided into the mouth of a farm track. Haughton felt for the door handle. He looked at Bernie, raising one eyebrow. 'Your turn?'

Leaving the engine running, he got out of the car. Bernie followed suit. Haughton smiled at Bernie as they passed, walking round the back of the car. Bernie climbed into the driving seat and ran his hands round the steering wheel.

'By the way, do call me Randolph,' Haughton said. 'All my friends do.'

'I'm Bernie.'

'The controls are all pretty obvious,' Haughton went on. 'You might want to work the gear-stick through the gate before you set off, though. They always have their own feel, don't they?'

Automatically, Bernie pushed down the clutch and dropped his left hand on to the gear lever. Haughton's hand was resting on it. Their fingers touched.

'Sorry,' they said simultaneously.

'I'll show you, shall I?' Haughton said.

Their eyes met. Neither man smiled.

'Yes,' Bernie said. 'You do that.'

# Chapter Twenty-nine

By the time Jill left Trenalt, it was nearly lunchtime. She had interviewed several villagers, including the rector. She had had a long and fruitful conversation with the stationmaster, who was keen to talk to her mainly because she worked for the *Gazette* rather than the *Post*. The man hated the *Post* and all who worked for it because, when they had printed the report of his mother's funeral, they had misspelt her surname, muddled up three couples among the mourners, and left out nearly a third of the people who had attended.

All in all, she was feeling mildly pleased with herself as she walked down the rectory drive towards her car, which was parked by the churchyard wall. She had more than enough material here. According to the rector, Miss Caswell had been the daughter of a peer and had a number of well-known, though remote, relations, including Lord Vauden. Editors and readers liked titles, so Miss Caswell's family connections increased Jill's chance of supplementing her always inadequate income by selling the story elsewhere.

'Miss Francis?'

Jill paused, her hand on the door of her car. She had seen Fuggle sitting outside the Bear, glass in hand, but had hoped he hadn't noticed her.

'Miss Francis,' Fuggle repeated, lingering over the name as he rose unsteadily to his feet. 'Let me buy you a drink. The press should stick together, eh? What shall it be?'

'No, thank you, Mr Fuggle. I really should get back.'

'One moment, my dear. I'd like to drop a word in that shell-like ear.'

Still with his drink in his hand, he crossed the road. He was a big, plump man, and he loomed over her, standing so close that she took a step away from him. There were food stains on his jacket and his trousers had not been pressed for a very long time. The beer in his glass swayed near the brim as he leant towards her. His mouth widened into an approximation of a smile, revealing false teeth and sending a waft of foul air towards her nostrils.

'Share and share alike, my old mother used to say,' he intoned. 'I noticed you had quite a chat with that old fool of a stationmaster.'

Jill nodded. 'Excuse me, Mr Fuggle, but I really must be—'

'Co-operation. That's the name of the game these days, Miss Francis. What did he have to say for himself, then?'

'Would you please get out of my way, Mr Fuggle? I want to get into my car.'

He placed his free hand on the roof of the car and leant proprietorially against the door. 'Listen, Miss Francis. There's no point in you burying your head in the sand. You know and I know you're in a very vulnerable position. Nothing to worry about, of course, as long as it's all among friends.' He paused and gave her another smile. 'I wonder what the police are thinking about this one? Perhaps you could help me, eh? I know you've got your constabulary sources.'

'If you don't get away from my car, Mr Fuggle, I'm going to call a constable and then you can find out exactly what the police are thinking.'

He made a sound almost like a growl, deep in his throat. For an instant, Jill thought he was going to spit at her feet. Instead he shrugged.

'Have it your own way, Miss Francis.' He shambled away from the car. As he was crossing the road he looked back at her for a moment. 'But don't say I didn't warn you.'

Jill was trembling so much that the car stalled at her first attempt to drive away. She knew Fuggle was watching. She drove slowly through the village. Instead of taking the road to Lydmouth, she turned down to the station again. The gates at the level-crossing stood open. The station itself was deserted. A small crowd milled around the mouth of the tunnel. The ambulance was still there, which must mean that they had not been able to move the body yet.

She drove slowly onwards. The sun had slipped behind clouds. Rain was forecast. The road climbed up the other side of the valley. She passed the end of the drive leading to Highnam Cottage – a plain, rather ugly red-brick house rather than a cottage, incongruous in its rural isolation, as utilitarian as a sewage plant or an engine shed.

Why did Fuggle hate her so? Professional rivalry was understandable, but his attitude to her went a long way beyond that. She was used to having to deal with men who had a generic hostility towards women working in journalism. But Fuggle's malice belonged in another category. No doubt he was trying to exorcise his own demons, but that was little comfort to Jill. Somehow he knew about her and Richard. She thought of Miss Gwyn-Thomas. But surely the woman's loyalty to the *Gazette* and to Philip Wemyss-Brown would have been stronger than her desire to hurt Jill?

In any case, the source of Fuggle's knowledge was of secondary importance. The real question was what he was going to do with it.

The road had straightened out, and was now running along the line of the ridge in a broadly southerly direction. She saw the lodge gates of Fontenoy Place fifty yards ahead on the left-hand side and began to slow. When she came closer, however, she noticed that the gates were closed. She pulled over on to the tarmac apron in front of them. A curtain twitched in one of the lodge cottages.

Jill got out of the car. A large middle-aged man wearing an open-necked shirt and corduroy trousers came out of the cottage.

'Yes?'

Jill smiled at him. 'I'd like to see Dr Angmer, please.'

'No visitors at present except by appointment.'

'My name's Miss Francis. I work for the *Gazette*.'

'He said no one who worked for the papers. If you want to see him, miss, you'll have to phone up first.'

The man nodded to her and went back into the lodge. Dr Angmer had reacted quickly, Jill thought, wondering if Fuggle had got here before the gates were shut. She was not surprised by Dr Angmer's decision. Discretion would not be itemised on the bills, but it was part of what you would pay for if you sent your unwanted nearest and dearest to Fontenoy Place.

She drove on, following the lane which wound over the hills and down into Eastbury. From there, the main road ran parallel to the river up to Lydmouth. As she was accelerating out of Eastbury, she saw a familiar blue car approaching from the opposite direction. She wondered what Randolph Haughton was doing down here. She raised her hand and waved as the car passed. But the occupants of the Bristol did not notice her. As the car flashed past, Jill saw that Randolph was in the passenger seat. Bernie Broadbent was driving.

*Well, well. Stranger things have happened.*

By the time Jill got back to the *Gazette*, it was lunchtime. She wasn't hungry – Fuggle had killed her appetite. She went up to the editor's room to work up her notes into a piece on Miss Caswell's death. To her relief, Miss Gwyn-Thomas was out.

She worked solidly for three-quarters of an hour. At the end of that time, she went down to the front office to talk to the receptionist who handled the advertising coming off the streets. On her way down the stairs, she passed Miss Gwyn-Thomas returning from lunch. Neither of them spoke.

She was talking to the receptionist when the door to the street opened.

'Miss Francis! This is serendipity indeed.'

She looked up. 'Mr Loysey. Good afternoon.'

He bustled into the front office. He was wearing a broad-brimmed straw hat, a floppy bow tie and a loose jacket. Dressing the part, Jill thought. He swept off the hat, placed it on the counter and sketched a bow.

'I've brought you that photograph, dear lady.' He opened the envelope he was carrying and laid the photograph on the counter, angling it so the two women could see it. It must have been at least ten years old. 'Cecil Beaton took it for me a couple of years ago. Not a bad likeness, people tell me.'

'It's wonderful,' Jill said, knowing he was angling for praise. 'It'll do perfectly.'

Loysey smiled, almost simpered, pushing his front teeth even farther forward than nature had designed them to be. 'June says it makes me look as if I have a high philosophic brow.'

'Crammed with all sorts of interesting metaphysical speculations, no doubt,' Jill said, tiring abruptly of soothing the little man's conceit. 'Well, thank you for bringing it in, Mr Loysey.'

He leant on the counter, his face as bland as a perfect servant's. 'Tell me, is there any more news about poor Miss Caswell?'

'Not really,' Jill said, automatically stonewalling.

'The poor dear lady,' Loysey said. 'Her death has quite upset June. Did I mention she was the original model for *Lady with Fan*? I do wish we could find that painting.'

The door behind Jill opened and Amy Gwyn-Thomas came into the front office to fetch some figures from the receptionist. The two women murmured like cooing doves at the far end of the counter.

'Yes,' Loysey went on, his bright, intelligent eyes fixed on Jill's face. 'You might even be able to work that in when you write about Miss Caswell, perhaps? One of those elements which could give a touch of colour to what must have been rather a boring life. Poor lady,' he added, perfunctorily. 'Not that it was always boring, by all accounts. You've heard the story about her child?'

'Yes,' Jill said, turning away from him. 'But I doubt if we shall mention that. Not really relevant, is it?'

'Few journalists have the decorum that distinguishes those who work for the *Gazette*, Miss Francis.' He smiled at her and picked up his hat. 'Do you know who they say the father was?'

'Miss Caswell's?' Jill said, wilfully misunderstanding.

'No – the father of Miss Caswell's child. A child who, fortunately perhaps, died at birth.'

The telephone was ringing. The receptionist broke away from Miss Gwyn-Thomas and answered it. Jill hoped it was for her.

'They say the father was the Prime Minister, Lord Salisbury. Seems most implausible to me, but you never know, do you? These Victorians got up to far more than we generally realise.' He laughed, a high, nervous sound which was almost a titter. 'Just like us, one might say, eh?'

'It's for you, Miss Francis,' said the receptionist.

Jill murmured goodbye to Gareth Loysey and picked up the telephone receiver.

'Miss Francis.' The wires worked a mechanical magic that turned Ivor Fuggle's voice into a parody of itself; he sounded like a ham actor trying to convey menace and, unfortunately, succeeding. 'I wondered if you'd reconsidered. Time's running out, you see. For you, that is.'

Jill broke the connection. The doorbell pinged as Loysey left the front office. Jill glanced over her shoulder and discovered that Amy Gwyn-Thomas was watching her.

# Chapter Thirty

Clouds had gathered over the hills to the south-west and were advancing steadily over the sky. The three of them walked swiftly along the footpath in single file like a Red Indian patrol. They did not glance behind them. Lower down the hill, a small grey car came over the level-crossing by the station and began to drive up the lane towards Highnam Cottage and Fontenoy Place.

Nurse Lindor was first, then Edith Thornhill, with Jack Graig following behind. Edith felt ridiculous — as though her behaviour were more appropriate for a trespassing child running away from an angry farmer.

The three of them had been standing in the field by the quarry, near the oil can containing Miss Caswell's trousseau, when Jack had pointed out the two blue shapes walking slowly up the footpath that led up from the parapet of the tunnel to the quarry. The policemen had their heads down, searching the path. Without a word, Jack had pushed the oil can back into its hiding place and pulled a fallen branch over it. He knew, Edith thought, that its pathetic contents were private, and that they — or rather Miss Caswell — should not be exposed to people who would laugh at them.

Suddenly Nurse Lindor stopped. She sniffed. 'Them coppers,' she muttered. 'Interfering so-and-so's. My poor Miss Caswell.'

Edith took her arm. The older woman had a complexion like the skin of a withered apple stored too long in the loft. Nurse Lindor screwed up her eyes. The creases deepened and moisture gleamed on the lashes.

Jack cleared his throat. 'I don't want to hurry you, but it's going to pour in a moment.'

'The police are only doing their job, I suppose,' Edith said.

'Their job? Taking her away from them that cared for her? That's no job for a Christian to do.' Her voice rose to a wail. 'Why wouldn't they let me stay?'

She began to sob. Edith drew her to the side of the path and took a folded handkerchief from her handbag. Nurse Lindor snatched the square of linen and scrubbed her eyes as though trying to rub them out. Edith glanced behind her. Jack had stopped too, and he was looking sheepish, as men so often did when women wept. They were out of sight of the policemen now.

'There, there,' Edith said automatically, as one would to a child with a grazed knee. 'It's all right.'

'I should have stayed with her.' Nurse Lindor gulped. 'I shouldn't have left her.'

'Left her where?' Edith asked.

'In her room last night. Sometimes I stayed and talked to her, helped her undress and wash. It could take ages because she always liked to be clean. Unlike some of them. But she told me to go and I did because Mrs Warsnip was playing up again and I knew we'd have to change the bedding. And to tell the truth, I was tired enough as it was. The poor dear would keep going on about things.'

'Going on? What about?'

'Some sort of nonsense about Constance.'

'Who's she?'

'I don't know. Maybe her sister or something. But she said it was like Constance. It was like Constance all over again.'

Edith said, 'Constance married the White Rabbit.'

'You what? Are you trying to make a fool of me?'

'No – that's what Miss Caswell said. I've just remembered. It was at Mr Moorcroft's funeral. You were there.'

'She was always saying things like that.' Nurse Lindor frowned, but her anger had left as suddenly as it had come. 'She said Constance killed him but she didn't mean to. Not really.'

'Killed who? The White Rabbit? Mr Moorcroft?'

'How should I know? She was always going on about things. Lived in the past, half the time, either there or in the pages of some novel she was reading. But there was no harm in her, truly.' She swallowed noisily. 'She said that they would have been the Duke's grandchildren, if the story was true. But she didn't think it was. And that Constance became a nun.'

'Listen,' Edith said. 'She was an old lady. I expect she was a bit confused sometimes. You've had a terrible shock. Why don't we take you back to Fontenoy Place?'

'And what are you doing with Major Graig?' Nurse Lindor's tears had vanished and her face was hard and suspicious again. 'Poking around in Miss Caswell's things. I know she used to hide stuff up there. She thought I didn't, but I did. There was no harm in it, mind – she just liked collecting odds and ends, like a kiddie, really. I won't have you poking around.'

'It's all right.'

'No, it's not.'

'Major Graig and I were friends a long time ago. Before the war. I used to stay with my granny in Trenalt, and he stayed with Mr Moorcroft. We met Miss Caswell yesterday, and – and she said she wanted us to have her things. That's how we knew where they were.'

'Why?'

Edith swallowed. 'She called them her trousseau. I—'

'Her trousseau?' Nurse Lindor's lips trembled. 'Oh, bugger it.' She looked astonished, as if at the sound of herself swearing. 'She was saving it for her and Mr Moorcroft.' She turned aside and blew hard into the handkerchief. Then she turned back to Edith. 'So why did she give it to you and the major? You're not courting. You can't be – you're married.'

Edith knew her colour was rising. 'I think she misunderstood.' She felt the first drops of rain on her arm. 'Look – it's starting to rain. We'd better get you home.'

'I can find my own way, thank you.' Nurse Lindor looked from Edith to Jack. 'Not courting, eh? Miss Caswell may have been a bit strange at times, but she saw farther than most people do.'

She stormed off along the path. The rain was coming down fast, the drops of water heavy and warm. Within seconds, Edith felt it soaking through her blouse.

'We can't go back to the car,' Jack said. 'The police are still up there. We'd better go to the cottage. Anyway, it's nearer.'

Edith felt a twinge of revulsion. Highnam Cottage was the last place she wanted to go. But if they stayed here they would be soaked. The prospect of going back and meeting some of Richard's colleagues was even less appealing.

'She was upset,' Jack went on. 'Nurse Lindor, I mean. Didn't know what she was saying.' Despite the rain, he stared westwards at a misty, grey horizon and made no attempt to move. 'Nothing to worry about, in my opinion.'

'We're going to get soaked if we hang around here much longer,' Edith said. 'We'd better run.'

They splashed through the swiftly forming puddles. Jack went first and Edith, staring at his square back and his stiff legs, thought how ungracefully adults ran and was glad she was behind him. They came to the gate leading into the garden of Highnam Cottage, and Edith glimpsed the roof of the summer-house beyond the trees. Jack held open the gate for her.

Now she was in front. Panting, she ran past the summer-house, across the lawn and on to the drive. To her horror, just as she reached the shelter of the porch, the front door opened.

Mrs Solly backed out of the house, key in one hand and basket in the other. She jerked round and saw Edith. She shrieked.

'Hello. I'm afraid—' Edith began.

'Oh – you gave me quite a turn. Oh, Lord, you have got caught in the rain. Lucky I brought my brolly. Hello, Major.'

The three of them squeezed into the little porch.

Mrs Solly looked them up and down with interest. 'Clean towels in the airing cupboard. Oh, good – the rain's slackening.'

Jack cleared his throat. 'I'd offer to run you back, Mrs Solly, but the car's on the other side of the hill. We were having a walk—'

'Don't you worry. A little bit of rain won't do me no harm. Are the police still there with poor Miss Caswell?'

Jack nodded.

'The poor dear. I could hardly believe it. There's a curse on that line, if you ask me. That's what they're saying down at the station. First Mr Hugh, and now her. When I saw her on Tuesday at Mr Moorcroft's funeral, she looked as though she'd live to be a hundred. Mind you, she was rambling a bit. She wanted to get on the blower to someone. So I said, where does she live, dear, and she said, Constance lives near the road. Funny old duck. I suppose all the folk she used to know had driveways. Anyway, I mustn't stand here chatting. Gordon's waiting for his dinner.'

Mrs Solly stepped out of the porch, raised the umbrella and set off down the drive. The rain had slackened to a fine drizzle.

Nurse Lindor knows, Edith thought, now Mrs Solly does too. In an hour or two, the news that she was here alone with Jack would be around the whole village.

'Come in.' He cleared his throat. 'I'll get you a towel and show you where the bathroom is.'

He was brisk to the point of rudeness, which made it easier. Edith followed him upstairs. Jack gave her a large pink towel, opened the bathroom door for her, offered to find her a jersey if she wanted one, and clattered downstairs.

Edith dried herself the best she could. She was not as wet as she feared and a little dampness wouldn't harm her. She combed her hair and powdered her nose, literally and figuratively. The bathroom was like a sanctuary. No one could reach her here – not Jack, Mrs Solly, Nurse Lindor or even Richard.

The lower half of the sash window contained stained glass, but the upper half was clear. She stood on tiptoe and looked out. Below her was the lawn, with the summerhouse and its surrounding shrubbery beyond. Her eyes grew hot, and she knew that she wasn't far away from tears, absurd though this was.

All those years ago, she had run across that lawn feeling doubly betrayed. At the time, she had thought that Hugh Hudnall had merely pretended to like her, pretended to be a little in love with her, to divert attention from the revolting things he was doing with Jack. Now she thought it might not have been as calculated as that, though perhaps Hugh had been one of those people who habitually make their friends feel more important to them than they really are. That did not make the double betrayal any less hurtful: not just Hugh, because Jack had pretended to like her as well.

But now the confusion had become intolerable because Jack still seemed to like her, and that made no sense. Hugh was dead. She was a married woman. Perhaps he felt guilty for what he and Hugh had done.

She shut her eyes to hold back the tears. Instead of comforting darkness, she saw her youthful self running across that lawn, running away from the summerhouse and what was happening there. Somehow she had reached Granny's cottage, somehow she had managed to pretend nothing had happened. If Granny had not been ill, she would have noticed, but illness had made her self-absorbed. After supper, Edith had pleaded a headache and had gone out again.

She shook her head, not wanting to remember what had happened next. Carefully she dabbed her eyes with the towel and examined her face in the mirror. After applying a little more powder, she braced herself, unlocked the door and went downstairs. She found Jack in the kitchen making coffee. He had changed into dry flannels and an open-necked shirt.

'Are you all right?' he said. 'Not too damp?'

'Fine,' she replied automatically. Then, to her horror, she heard herself saying: 'I couldn't stop thinking about the evening Hugh died.'

He put the jug of coffee very carefully on the table. 'I saw you.'

'You saw me?' She stared at him. 'When?'

'When you came here. When you went up to the summer-house, and then you ran away as though——'

'You can't have seen me.' She sat down. Her legs were trembling.

'Why not?'

'Because you – you——'

He sat down opposite her and she saw his face changing as the realisation hit him. 'You thought I was in the summerhouse,' he said slowly. 'Of course – that explains it.'

'Then where were you?'

'Here.' Jack jabbed the stem of his pipe at the ceiling. 'In the bathroom. Thinking about you if you really want to know.'

'But I rang the bell. You didn't answer.'

'I was busy.' He looked down at his hands and cleared his throat. 'You know.'

A bubble of laughter, the next best thing to hysteria, burst out of her. 'Powdering your nose?'

He grinned. 'As they say. But afterwards, I was washing my hands and looking out of the window, and there you were like an answer to a prayer. You were walking across the lawn, smiling.' He hesitated. 'Then you stopped by the summerhouse. And a moment later you ran back across the lawn and down the drive. I — I saw your face.'

Edith looked down at the deal table and traced a knot in the wood with her forefinger.

'What happened?' he said. 'You must have heard something.'

'I — I heard Hugh. And — and I thought he was with you. But he *must* have been with you. He said your name.'

'He was with Rufus. What exactly did he say?'

'He wanted a — a kiss. And he said, *Now Jack.* I'm absolutely sure. Then I bolted.'

'It can't have been me with him,' Jack pointed out. 'Because I couldn't have seen you if I was in the summerhouse, or even heard the doorbell. You rang the bell twice, didn't you?'

'Yes, but—'

'If Hugh said my name, it doesn't mean I was there. Perhaps if you'd heard the whole thing, it would have been something like *Now Jack is out of the way, we might as well make the most of it.* I'd told them I was going to read in the house. Actually, I felt I was in their way.' He picked up the jug, poured a cup of coffee and pushed it across the table to her. 'Hugh and Rufus were having an affair that summer. They were homosexuals. Does that shock you?'

'Yes, of course. Well . . . I suppose so.' She frowned. 'I don't know. Rufus was—'

'Rufus was a good man.' He ran his fingers through thinning hair. 'I'd been at boarding school, and I suppose that sort of thing wasn't so strange to me as it would have been for you. I knew what was happening. There were signs . . . But I don't think they *knew* that I knew. I was terrified that everyone else would find out. Especially you.'

She bowed her head again. Jack poured his own coffee and lit his pipe. For a while neither of them said anything.

Edith murmured, 'I was such a fool – you see, I . . . I thought I was in love with Hugh.' She moistened her lips. 'I don't think I ever cried as much as I did that evening. Funny how everything matters so much when you're young.'

Jack's hand twitched, as though he wanted to touch her. 'I wasn't very happy myself.'

She looked at him.

'That was the last time I saw you,' he said in a voice without emotion. 'Anyway, what did you do?'

'I went back to Granny's. Later that night – do you remember how it rained? – I went outside. I seemed to spend hours crying. Just couldn't stop.' Her eyes were heavy with tears. 'I think I must have heard Hugh. Just before he died.'

'Heard him? What do you mean?'

'Do you remember Fiddler's Cottage? That house between the village and the station – where the road forks? It's been repaired now, but no one was living there before the war, not for years. I went there, you see, when I was crying. I stood in the porch for shelter. I heard people running down the hill to the station. One of them must have been Hugh. Then the next morning, my Uncle Bernie came and told me he was dead. That made it worse, don't you see? If I'd been there, out in the road, rather than hiding in the cottage, I could have stopped him. I could have held his arm and stopped him falling off the platform, I could have——'

'That's nonsense,' Jack said. 'You didn't even know who was running. You didn't know what was going to happen. Anyway, why didn't the other people do something?'

'Person. They ran past a moment or so later. Or it could have been Hugh who ran down second, I've no idea. All I know is that it feels my fault.'

'It's not,' Jack said flatly. He screwed up his face. 'Have you mentioned this to your husband? As a police officer, I mean.'

She shook her head. 'Why should I?'

'I don't know. Just in case.' His pipe had gone out, and he struck a match. 'It's just that I went to the inquest on Hugh. And I'm sure that one of the points they made was that no one else was on the station.'

'The second person may háve been going to Highnam Cottage or Fontenoy Place.'

Jack shrugged. 'You haven't touched your coffee.'

Edith added sugar and sipped the lukewarm liquid. Jack smoked. She looked out of the window and to her surprise saw sunshine.

'It's stopped raining,' she said. It seemed like a miracle.

'Come and look at the view,' Jack said, dropping the pipe in the ashtray. 'It's always nice when you have sunshine after rain. The dust settles and everything gleams.'

They went out of the back door, through the little yard and round the side of the house. Side by side, they strolled into the garden and, because the grass was wet, followed the stone-flagged path that ran round the edge of the lawn. Jack glanced at Edith as they approached the summerhouse. She nodded slightly.

Here was the veranda, where the view stretched round for more than two hundred degrees, where Rufus had been with Hugh, where Rufus had died. The weather-stained wooden platform, the railings, the wicker chairs – everything looked so small and shabby, she thought, and entirely – *unbelievably* – untouched by what had happened here. They stopped at the foot of the steps.

'I must go back and sort out Miss Caswell's things,' Edith said in a voice that wobbled slightly.

'There's no hurry. The police have already searched the field by the quarry, and no one else is likely to go up there. Besides, everything will be wet. Better let it dry off.'

'I suppose so.' She looked at the view to avoid looking at him.

'Lovely, isn't it?' Jack said, and she realised he was standing very close to her. 'It's like the world's beginning again. Washed clean.'

For another moment, Edith stared at the folds of land that rippled away to the horizon. Then, at last, she looked up at Jack. It seemed entirely natural that he should bend his head and kiss her on the lips.

# Chapter Thirty-one

The weather could hardly have chosen a less convenient time for a heavy summer shower. Reports filtered back to the CID Office in Lydmouth. The tunnel itself was not the problem. But the rain had come too swiftly for the SOCOs to build an effective shelter over the area immediately in front of the opening. The parapet above the arch and the footpath behind it had been drenched in ten minutes.

It was all of a piece, Richard Thornhill thought: few investigations in his experience had been as unsatisfactory as this. You didn't know where one case ended and another began, or even whether some of them were worth investigating. There was the complication of people with more influence than sense pulling strings. He also had the feeling, not uncommon since his move to Lydmouth, that most of the community knew more about everything than he did and had every intention that things should remain that way. And now the weather was trying its hardest to hamper their search for evidence.

Unable to face the police canteen, Thornhill went out to the Gardenia for lunch. At Hendry's insistence, Drake had arranged a press conference for two o'clock. It would be a waste of time probably, but Hendry was not going to leave himself open to criticism on any front.

On his way back from the café, the Welsh rarebit he had eaten lay heavily on his stomach. He had eaten too fast, and in any case he was so tense it seemed to be affecting his ability to digest his food. A large black car, a pre-war Austin whose design seemed better suited to horses than the internal combustion engine, pulled up outside the Bull. George Shipston, cigar clamped between his teeth, climbed painfully and slowly out of the driver's seat. On impulse, Thornhill put on a burst of speed. He drew level with the car as the solicitor was closing the door.

'Mr Shipston. May I have a word?'

The old man appeared not to have heard. His shoulders were hunched and he was staring at the pavement. His face was puffy.

Thornhill raised his voice. 'Mr Shipston?'

He raised his head and glowered at Thornhill. 'What do you want?' He gave no sign of recognition.

'I'm Inspector Thornhill, sir. I came to see you yesterday.'

'Oh, yes.' Shipston's cheeks were flushed but he was white around the lips. He edged away, as though from the threat of violence. 'I'm in a hurry. I can't talk to you now.'

'You've heard the sad news, sir?'

Shipston paused. He opened his mouth but no words came.

'About Miss Caswell.'

'Tragic,' he mumbled. The cheeks trembled. 'Last of her generation. Lord Vauden's most distressed.'

'You knew her very well, sir, I understand. I wondered if you had any idea what she might have been doing down by the tunnel.'

His face filled with panic. 'What? How should I know?' His voice was high and cracked. 'I . . . I really must go.'

Shipston put his head down, clutched his cigar and stumbled into the Bull Hotel. Thornhill watched him go, feeling an unwelcome pity. What was wrong with the man? Grief for a valued client, an old friend? Senility? Or something else?

He walked on. It was almost two when he reached Police Headquarters. Despite himself, he felt excitement rising – a sensation which had something of the anxious urgency of panic. He pushed open the door of the conference room on the ground floor. It was not crowded. There were in fact more police officers than journalists. Jill was not among them. He wasn't sure whether to feel relieved or saddened. At least he wouldn't have to worry about showing his feelings in public, or about wanting to touch her.

Drake and Kirby were there, together with two other CID officers, three from the uniformed branch and a woman clerk who perched on a chair in the corner with a shorthand pad on her knee. There were only four journalists – a junior from the *Gazette*, Ivor Fuggle from the *Post*, the man from the Gloucester *Citizen* and an old man who acted as a stringer for several newspapers in South Wales. The Chief Constable had accorded this case more importance than the press were willing to do.

'I'll introduce you,' Drake murmured to Thornhill. 'Then it's over to you. Keep it brief.'

At the stroke of two, Drake stood up, thanked everyone for coming with patent insincerity, and handed over to Thornhill. It was hard to imagine Superintendent Williamson ever relinquishing the limelight voluntarily. Thornhill wasn't sure whether Drake was less greedy for glory than his predecessor, or whether he was allowing Thornhill to take a leading role in case the investigation ended in disaster and CID needed a scapegoat. He was about to begin when the door opened and Jill Francis slipped into the room.

Stumbling over his first words, Thornhill described the circumstances, as far as they knew them, surrounding Miss Caswell's death. He emphasised that the police were keen to talk to anyone who had seen her in the twenty-four hours before her demise. When he had finished, he asked for questions. He was not surprised to see Ivor Fuggle lifting a hand.

'We had a suicide in Trenalt last week, Inspector. Do you think there's a connection?'

'We have no evidence to suggest there is,' Thornhill said.

'But I understand Miss Caswell knew Mr Moorcroft.'

'It would be surprising if she hadn't done. It's a small village.'

'Is there any truth in the story that she was in love with him?'

'I'm not in a position to comment on that, Mr Fuggle.'

The stringer from South Wales came in with a question about railway safety. The man from the *Citizen* wanted to know which train had killed Miss Caswell. All the time, Thornhill was on edge, waiting for Jill to ask him something.

Fuggle raised his hand again. 'Slight change of tack here – we've been hearing rumours that the CID is going to set up a special office for serious crimes. Can you confirm that? Or rather, can Mr Drake?'

'We're not in a position to discuss this at present,' the Deputy Chief Constable said primly. 'But there will be an announcement on the subject soon.'

'And will the announcement reveal who's going to run it?'

'We shall all have to wait and see.' Drake glanced around the room. 'Next?'

There were no further questions and Drake swiftly brought the conference to a close. Thornhill suspected that the DCC thought it as much of a waste of time as he did. Jill was the first to leave the room. Not once had she met Thornhill's eyes. He felt cheated.

'Miss Francis was very quiet today, wasn't she?' Fuggle said to Thornhill as they met by the door. 'I wonder why that was.'

Thornhill shrugged. 'You'd better ask her.'

Fuggle gave a chuckle that sounded like bubbling oil. 'I might just do that. Seen anything of Moorcroft's nephew, by the way – Major Graig?'

Thornhill hid his surprise. 'No. Why?'

Fuggle smiled. 'Just thought you might have done, that's all. In view of Miss Caswell and Mr Moorcroft. One thing's for sure, though – it's all happening in Trenalt these days, isn't it? Must be something in the air. Or the water.'

The old journalist lit a cigarette and ambled off. Thornhill followed him out of the room. Jill was standing in front of a notice-board, apparently studying the latest information on swine fever or the dates of the quarter sessions or possibly both. She looked up.

'Inspector?'

'Yes, Miss Francis?'

'Will you be applying for the new position Mr Drake mentioned?'

'I can't comment on that either, I'm afraid.' His mouth dry, he drew nearer to her. No one was in earshot. Fuggle had left. 'This evening?' he murmured. 'Seven-fifteen?'

'Possibly, Inspector.'

'I think Fuggle knows something.' In a louder voice he added, 'If there are any developments, we'll let you know.'

She smiled at him. 'Thank you, Inspector. Good afternoon.'

Thornhill smelled her perfume. He forced himself not to watch her leaving. Instead, he went upstairs, breathing heavily as though he had just run for a bus. Kirby was waiting for him in the CID Office.

'Mr Drake's compliments, sir, and he'd like a word with us. Have you heard the news? It came in while we were downstairs. The SOCOs have got a generator and a decent set of lights down in the tunnel now and they've been having a look at the floor. They say there's no doubt about it: the old woman was dragged inside before she was run down.'

'Are they sure?'

'Yes, sir. Someone else must have been involved.'

'Would that stand up in court, if necessary?'

'They think so.' Kirby's features twisted as if he had glimpsed something he didn't want to see. 'But it's not just that she was pulled into the tunnel. It looks like she tried to crawl out afterwards. But the train got her first.'

# Chapter Thirty-two

On their way to Trenalt in a police car, they passed an ambulance and a police motorcyclist travelling in the opposite direction. Neither Thornhill nor Kirby commented on them but they both knew what they meant. What was left of Miss Caswell would soon be at the mortuary in the grounds of the RAF Hospital in Lydmouth.

When they reached Trenalt, they drove straight down to the station and parked in the yard.

'Dracula's still there even if the lady isn't,' Thornhill said, glancing through the window at the other vehicles.

'I'm not complaining,' Kirby said. 'Not in this case.'

Leaving the driver with the car, they walked along the footpath to the mouth of the tunnel. Most of the crowd had dispersed – and those who were left were mainly children from the village, keeping an eye on proceedings from a safe distance while a uniformed constable kept an eye on them.

The entrance, Thornhill thought, was unexpectedly grand: it sliced into the side of the hill, the sides faced with blocks of red sandstone. The tunnel itself was almost cylindrical, the curving walls lined with four courses of brick. He glanced up at the parapet, a good twenty-five feet above the permanent way.

The constable saluted. 'Sergeant Grimes is in there, sir.'

Thornhill nodded. An area just beneath the parapet was covered with a small tarpaulin. Part of the parapet was covered with another one.

He followed Kirby through the screens into the glare of the lights beyond. It was cool after the warmth outside. The walls, glistening with moisture and pockmarked with shadow, curved inwards into the ground at their base, like the battering at the foot of the ruined gatehouse of Lydmouth Castle. The rails on their wooden sleepers drew Thornhill's eyes through the light and into the darkness beyond. The SOCOs in their overalls were standing in a cluster about twenty yards away. The rails and the left-hand side of the tunnel had been taped off.

'Afternoon, sir,' Grimes called down the tunnel. He detached himself from the others. 'That's it, keep to the right, please. All the marks are on the other side of the tracks.'

A second after each word, its echoes bounced from side to side of the tunnel. Farther in, two of the other SOCOs were talking quietly, and the sound of their voices was like waves breaking on a distant rock. Thanks to the light behind him, Grimes appeared even taller and thinner and darker than nature had already made him. He was popularly known as Dracula because of his appearance. He was a sweet-tempered teetotaller who spent much of his leisure time constructing model aeroplanes from balsa wood, in theory on behalf of his two sons.

'What have you got for us?' Thornhill asked.

'More than enough, I'm afraid. I'll show you. You saw the tarps outside?'

'Yes. Where you found traces of blood?'

'That's it. Do you want to see under them?'

'Not now.'

Grimes led them up the tunnel. They passed another, larger tarpaulin covering a section of line and the area between the rails and the far wall of the tunnel.

'That was where we found her, sir. Nothing to see now.'

'But I'd like to have a look under this one,' Thornhill said, although it was not entirely true.

Grimes lifted a corner of the tarpaulin and pulled it back, angling it so the light farther up the tunnel fell on the ground it had covered. There was nothing to see besides a pair of rails and a patch of muddy stone chippings, gleaming blackly with oil and damp.

'Where's it gone, Drac?' Kirby said, his voice strained, on the edge of shock. 'Where's the blood?'

'Drains away, Brian, drains away. That's what tunnel floors are designed to do, eh? Oh, there's some still there, I'm sure, but you can't see it properly, not in this light.'

Thornhill felt reprieved, and also guilty; he had expected something worse than this. Grimes lowered the tarpaulin and they walked a few paces deeper into the tunnel. They passed an arched alcove set into the brick, a recess perhaps two feet deep and four feet wide, enough for two men.

'The refuges are about ten yards apart,' Grimes said. 'We're pretty sure she was in the next one, which was on the other side. Looked like more traces of blood on the floor of the recess.'

'So she had some sort of wound either in the refuge or before she got there?' Kirby asked.

'Probably. But it's just possible that the blood came from whoever was with her. Trouble is, Brian, the body's in such a mess that it's hard to tell exactly what happened when. I don't envy the pathologist.' Grimes stopped and pointed a gloved finger at the other side of the rails. 'See that? The marks are clearer there because the surface is a bit looser. Right against the wall of the tunnel there's a sort of shallow continuous hollow. See? If you ask me, someone dragged something along there. Maybe the old woman.' His finger dropped a fraction. 'Now look nearer the rails. There are more marks there, but much more ragged. Some deeper, too.'

'Is that where she crawled?' Thornhill asked.

'That's my bet, sir. Quite mucky down there in places, so she moved nearer the rail because the going was firmer and easier.'

For a moment all three men were silent. Probabilities danced like phantoms in Thornhill's mind. 'Surely the driver would have seen something? Or felt something?' he demanded, his voice harsh and loud in the confined space.

'It's most unlikely – not unless she was actually silhouetted against the light.' Grimes stared at him, thin lips pursed between sunken cheeks, as though assessing Thornhill's probable blood content. 'Tunnels are hostile places for trains, sir. If it was coming from Lydmouth, it was coming round a bend and climbing a slight gradient. Wheels probably slipping a bit because it's always damp down here. My old dad was on the railways, and I've been down a tunnel when a train goes through. The smoke and the noise don't leave room for anything else. And engines don't have headlights – not in this country. The most the driver and fireman would have felt was a tiny jolt. But I'd be surprised if they felt anything at all.'

'What sort of weight are we talking about?'

Grimes scratched his cheek with a long finger. 'They use six-wheel pannier tank engines on this line, usually. One of those would weigh maybe fifty or sixty tons when loaded with coal and water. Then you've got whatever it's pulling. If it was a passenger train, you'd have two or three carriages. It would be old rolling stock – maybe thirty or thirty-five tons each.'

'Christ,' Kirby murmured. 'Bloody hell, Drac, it's like cracking a nut with a bleeding sledgehammer.'

There was another silence. Thornhill thought Brian had changed since he and Joan Ailsmore had started courting. It was as if love had made him suddenly aware of how vulnerable human beings were in their fragile envelopes of flesh and bone.

They walked on until they were opposite the refuge on the other side of the rails. Thornhill stared at it, knowing there was nothing he would be able to find that others had not already found, but knowing nevertheless it was important to be here, to see for himself what this place was like.

At present the circumstances of Miss Caswell's death failed to make sense. They were like a number of fractions which should have added up to a whole but for some reason wouldn't. Suppose someone had killed her. Suppose they had wanted to make it look like an accident. Then why not drag the body a little way into the tunnel and lay it across the line? Instead, all the evidence suggested that Miss Caswell, presumably unconscious or at least restrained in some way, had been dragged into the tunnel and concealed in the refuge like a parcel deposited to be collected later on.

'Which train went over her?' he said to Grimes. 'I know the pathologist will have his own ideas about that, but what's your guess?'

'I reckon she died this morning, sir. I saw her about nine o'clock and she was still pretty floppy. If she'd died eleven hours earlier, when the last train of the evening went through, you'd expect her to have started stiffening up at least.'

Thornhill nodded. Rigor mortis was a notoriously unreliable indicator of the time of death, but its absence in this case made Grimes's assumption reasonable enough. The three men went back to the mouth of the tunnel, passing the tarpaulin. Impelled by God alone knew what instinct for survival, Miss Caswell had managed to crawl a good distance from the second refuge. Her powers of endurance deserved a better reward.

'By the way, sir,' Grimes said. 'I had a word with the stationmaster. Man called Rees. He said there'd been another death on the line about fifteen years ago. Up at the station.'

'Oh yes?' Thornhill glanced at Grimes, keeping his face blank. 'And what's the connection?'

'Miss Caswell, maybe. One rainy night, this young chap who lived in the village had too much to drink and fell off the platform in front of a train. Rees said it always seemed a bit odd to him, because the bloke wasn't the sort who got staggering drunk. The other thing was, he said he'd heard Miss Caswell having a bit of an argy-bargy with him a day or two before he died. They were standing at the level-crossing, waiting for the gates to open, and Rees was near by to the side of the signal box.' Grimes glanced from Thornhill to Kirby. His voice trailed away. 'Just an old story, I expect.'

'They were quarrelling?' Thornhill said. 'Had Rees any idea what it was about?'

'All he could remember was one thing she kept on saying. "Leave him alone, leave him alone," over and over again.'

'So why didn't what's his name — Rees — come forward at the time?' Kirby asked. 'Or did he?'

They had reached the screens at the mouth of the tunnel and their faces were pale in the combination of artificial and natural light.

'No, he didn't. Mainly because he didn't know about the accident when it happened. He'd gone to Margate for his summer holidays, and he met a girl there — the future Mrs Rees, as it happens. He had so much on his mind he didn't bother to get in touch with the folks at home. By the time he'd got back it was all over. Anyway, what was there to say? Until now.' He looked from Thornhill to Kirby. 'The way he told me about it, it was like some sort of ghost story. One of them films that gives you the horrors. You know — the murdered man seeks vengeance so he can rest in peace. But . . . but do you think it could have a bearing on what happened here?'

'Sarge?' a man's voice called from the other side of the screens. 'You there?'

Two uniformed officers were waiting outside. They were among the team making a broad sweep over the hillside above the tunnel. When they saw Thornhill their faces became shuttered and wary. Thornhill nodded to them and jerked his head at Grimes.

'Any luck?' the sergeant asked.

'Nothing out of the way,' the elder of the constables said. 'Someone's had a fire in the field by the quarry. Not recently, though someone's been up there. You can see tracks in the grass. But the only thing worth looking at was this.'

Slowly, with a sense of occasion, he took an envelope from the pocket of his tunic and handed it to Grimes.

'What is it, man?' Thornhill said, impatient at the unnecessary suspense.

The constable coloured. 'A – a penknife, sir. Can't have been there long, because there's no rust on it. There were a few bits of apple, too, but nothing worth saving. The birds had got it.'

Grimes held out the envelope so Thornhill could see inside. The knife was about three inches long. It had a flat stainless-steel handle and two blades.

'Is there something engraved on the side?' Thornhill asked.

The constable cleared his throat. 'Couple of initials, sir. Could be JC or JG.'

'JG,' said Kirby, who was peering into the envelope as well.

'How can you be sure?' Thornhill said.

'It's Jack Graig's. Almost certainly. I sharpened a pencil with it when I talked to him yesterday.'

'Where was it?' Thornhill said to the constable.

'That field by the quarry, sir. Near where the fire was. In the grass.'

'Good work.' Thornhill watched the man blush again. He turned back to Grimes. 'The DCC wants the paperwork on this as soon as possible. Come and see me when you get back to Lydmouth. How long will you be?'

'Another hour, maybe.'

Kirby and Thornhill walked back towards the car.

'According to Mr Williamson, the pathologist found a possible bite mark on young Hudnall's arm,' Thornhill said. 'For what it's worth.'

'A bite mark?' Kirby fiddled with the knot of his tie. 'Sounds right up Drac's street, eh? A film with ghosts *and* vampires. But it makes you wonder. Was Hudnall's death no accident? I mean, queers are like that, aren't they? They're always going in for crimes of passion.'

'Are they? Are they more likely to kill than anyone else? I don't think there's any evidence of that.'

'All right, guv. How about this: he had an argy-bargy with Miss Caswell, and she pushed him off the platform.'

'What are you saying, Brian? And then someone waited fifteen years to have revenge on her? No, it could all be much simpler. It's far more likely that the SOCOs are wrong about the marks on the tunnel floor.' Thornhill hoped for all their sakes that they were.

'Suicide?' Kirby said with an unmistakable note of hope in his voice. 'Could be, eh? She jumped off the parapet. But she only managed to damage herself, so she crawled into the tunnel – and later—'

'How did the blood on the parapet get there, then?'

'Nosebleed.' Kirby beamed suddenly. 'Joan sometimes gets a nosebleed. You just wouldn't believe the amount that comes out. She says that—' He glanced at Thornhill's face and hurriedly changed the subject. 'Anyway, perhaps it wasn't Miss Caswell's blood.'

'So whose was it? WPC Ailsmore's? Maybe she had a stroll up there. The plain fact is, we haven't enough to go on at present. Perhaps the autopsy will help. But in the meantime, the less theorising we do the better.'

That sounded very sensible, and if this had been a normal case, Thornhill knew, there would have been no need for theories ahead of the evidence. But Drake and Hendry were breathing down his neck. Assorted VIPs were breathing down theirs. The only thing they knew for certain about this case was that it wasn't normal.

Their driver started the car engine as they approached. Thornhill and Kirby climbed into the back seat.

'Fontenoy Place, Porter,' Thornhill said. 'You know where it is?'

'Yes, sir.'

'You can drop me there, and then take Sergeant Kirby to Highnam Cottage. And when he's finished, bring him back to Fontenoy Place.'

The car glided out of the station yard.

'You don't think Graig's involved, do you?' Kirby asked.

'I'm trying not to think anything. But we'll have to see him some time, and there's no point in making more of a meal of this than we have to.'

For a moment they sat in silence, watching the valley unfolding as the car climbed away from the station. Kirby fumbled for his cigarettes. He was smiling slightly, probably rapt in contemplation of the lovely Joan. Kirby was rarely short of a girl or two, but Thornhill had never seen him behaving quite like this.

'There's another question,' Thornhill said, thinking aloud partly to avoid dwelling on Kirby and WPC Ailsmore bathed in love's young dream. 'Whether there's a link between Miss Caswell in that tunnel and her friend Moorcroft killing himself. And a further link to the boy falling under a train before the war.'

Kirby's smile vanished. 'I wish it *was* one of them horror films,' he muttered, striking a match so viciously that the head snapped from the stick. 'At least we'd know the whole ruddy business would all be over in ninety minutes.'

# Chapter Thirty-three

Every life has its moments of heart-stopping panic. But Edith remembered nothing as bad as this, even in the last year of the war.

Here she was, awash with a torrent of mainly pleasurable emotions, sitting on the drawing-room window seat at Highnam Cottage with Jack Graig: and there was a police car rolling up the drive towards them. To make matters worse, she even recognised the pink, heavy-jowled face of the driver, Peter Porter, who often drove her husband. Richard had taken an unaccountable fancy to the man.

She gasped, pulled her hand from Jack's and lurched away from the window. She stumbled into the arm of a chair and almost fell. Jack swore and dived after her. She felt his hand on her arm, steadying her.

'Edie . . . dearest—'

'He mustn't see me,' she gabbled. 'He mustn't see me. It's Richard, I know it is.'

Through the open window she heard a door slam and the crunch of feet on the gravel. Almost immediately there was a knock. The front door, she remembered with another sickening spasm of panic, was standing open. Anyone in the porch could see right into the hall.

'I can't go out there.'

'Then you'll have to stay here,' he said. 'I'll take them somewhere else.'

'But what if——?'

There was a second knock on the door. Edith ducked behind a high-backed sofa. Jack patted her arm and slipped out of the room. He pulled the door after him, but the latch failed to engage, leaving the door a few inches ajar. Edith's heart was drumming like a mad thing inside her and she found it hard to draw enough air into her lungs. And suppose she sneezed?

She heard Jack's footsteps crossing the hall.

'Good afternoon,' he said. 'What can I do for you?'

'Just a query, sir. May I come in?'

Brian Kirby's voice, Edith thought. The worst possible person to find her here, apart from Richard himself. But at least not Richard.

'Well, in fact, I was about to go out——'

'I hope this won't take long. I wondered if you could identify this.'

Edith, pressed against the wall, heard the rustle of paper. Then came Jack's voice, sounding surprisingly normal.

'Yes, of course I can. That's my penknife. See? There are my initials.'

'Yes, I thought it was.'

'What? Oh yes, of course – you used it yesterday morning when you were asking me about Mr Haughton. Where did you find it?'

'When did you last see it, sir?'

There was a moment's silence. Yesterday lunchtime, Edith thought – the picnic. She remembered the shine of the stainless steel glinting in the sunlight as Jack had peeled the Beauty of Bath in one continuous movement – the apple they had never eaten because they had seen Ivor Fuggle. It had come from a tree in the Thornhills' garden, their first fruit of the year. What had happened to it?

'I'm not sure when I did last see it,' Jack said. 'But I'm jolly glad it's turned up. My uncle gave it to me when I was a boy.'

'Really?'

'Come to think of it, Sergeant, I do remember looking for it this morning. So I suppose it must have slipped out of my pocket yesterday at some point.'

Jack was a bad liar, Edith thought, and she waited, dry-mouthed, for Brian Kirby to pounce on him.

'Were you up on the path that goes over the railway line? The one that goes from here up to the quarry and then down past the mouth of the tunnel and up to the outskirts of the village?'

'No,' Jack said with the patently false certainty of the bad liar. 'I wasn't.'

*You dear fool.* Edith knew why he had denied it. Because he had been there with her, and he didn't want to implicate her in this. They had fled along the path which ran over the railway line because Ivor Fuggle was coming towards them from the direction of Fontenoy Place.

'By the way, sir — what were you doing yesterday evening?'

'Why?'

There was a short silence. Then Kirby said, 'We're trying to build up a general picture of what was happening in the area during the evening. It may help us work out Miss Caswell's movements.'

'Oh. I see. Well, I was here by myself during the early part of the evening. Had a bite of supper. Then I thought I'd have a drink, and I strolled up to the Bear. Must have been at about seven-thirty. Randolph Haughton and I walked back here at closing time and had a nightcap. And while we were having one, that artist chappy, Loysey, turned up out of the blue. The man who did the painting that's missing — you know, *Lady with Fan*. He was with his wife, June Hudnall that was.'

'They drove over here out of the blue?'

'They were on their way back from somewhere – Cardiff, I think. Loysey was awfully keen to have the painting because of some exhibition. And I told him we couldn't find it, and that I'd been in touch with you people about it. So he and his wife left. And Haughton went a few minutes later.'

'Can you remember when this was?'

'No idea, Sergeant.' Jack sounded irritable now. 'At a guess, I'd say between half eleven and midnight. Whenever it was, it was very dark. I took a turn – a turn about the garden – and noticed the cloud cover.'

Edith realised that she was twisting her watch round and round her wrist and the buckle was digging into her skin. She glanced at the window, suddenly terrified that the pink slab of PC Porter's face might be pressed against the glass.

'Thank you for your help, sir.'

'Not at all.' Jack's relief was obvious, at least to Edith. 'Just let me know if there's anything I can do.'

A moment later, Kirby said in a voice that was harder to hear, perhaps because he was now standing in the porch, 'That penknife of yours, sir – so you've no idea what might have happened to it?'

'No,' Jack said. 'I've told you. May I have it back, by the way?'

'Yes, sir. Sooner or later. But if you don't mind, we'll hang on to it for the moment.'

Edith heard the front door closing and Jack's footsteps crossing the hall. He came into the drawing room and looked down at her crouching behind the sofa, his finger to his lips. For a moment they were rigidly still, as though the slightest movement might betray them. They listened to the slam of a door and the whine of a starter motor. The car drove off down the drive. Edith let out her breath in a long shuddering sigh and stood up, holding on to the back of the sofa. Jack put his arm round her shoulders and for a moment she leant against him. Then she pulled away and went and sat down in one of the armchairs.

Jack picked up his pipe from the ashtray on the mantelpiece, peered into it and then put it in his mouth. 'That was damned awkward.' He struck a match and sucked in the smoke. 'I had to be very careful what I said about the penknife.'

'I know.' She picked at the chintz on the arm of the chair. 'You were protecting me, weren't you?'

He coughed. 'Can't be too careful.'

'Something must have happened to Miss Caswell.'

He tossed the match into the empty fireplace. 'What do you mean?'

'I think if this had been a straightforward accidental death, people like Brian Kirby wouldn't be going round asking questions. He's CID.' She looked away from him. 'Richard's his boss.'

'Do you think the police have found . . . well, something suspicious?'

'I don't know.' She felt her eyes filling with tears. She wished with sudden desperation that she had not gone to Rufus Moorcroft's funeral. Life had been so simple before then. There was much to be said for being straightforwardly miserable. At least you knew where it began and ended.

Jack sat down. 'We – we can't go on like this.'

'No,' she said, wondering what he meant and also wondering what she wanted him to mean.

'I should tell you about my wife. My ex-wife.'

He paused to relight his pipe, and Edith would have liked to have snatched the wretched thing from him and thrown it in the fireplace. 'Mae and I met in the war. I was stationed in North Wales for a time, and she was in the ATS. She was my driver, actually. One thing led to another.' He stared at the smoke.

Edith said carefully, 'You don't have to tell me this. Perhaps you shouldn't.'

'But I want to. We had one of those whirlwind romances. Then they sent me off to North Africa. Simon was born while I was away. I didn't see him until he was nearly two years old. By that time, she'd found someone else.'

'I am sorry.'

'Don't be. Luckily he's a nice chap.' He lit another match and stared at it while it burned down almost to his fingertips. 'I never really felt married, to be honest. So agreeing to a divorce wasn't too hard. Seemed the best thing for Simon, as well. He lives with them, of course. Child's better off with his mother, don't you think? But there it is.'

What he wasn't saying, Edith thought, merely implying, was that to all intents and purposes he was a single man and, also, that he had no objection to children being with their mother.

Jack applied another match to the pipe, which again failed to light. He gave up and dropped the pipe in the ashtray. 'You know I saw old Shipston the other day?'

'Yes.' She remembered that grim face like a bird of ill omen staring down at her and Jack in the car.

'He wanted to talk about the will – Rufus's, I mean. The thing is, most of it comes to me. And there's rather more than I thought there would be. No need to stay in the army if I don't want to. I could resign my commission tomorrow.'

'Yes, Jack,' Edith said. 'But do you want to?'

He looked at her, and his eyes were full of pleading. 'I'm not sure. I – I was hoping you'd help me decide.'

Edith glanced at him and wondered how he would look in twenty years' time. He would be plump and pink and comfortable, she thought: the sort of man who would like his routines and who wouldn't snap at the children. How wonderful it would be not to have money problems. She had worried about not having enough money for as long as she could remember. She thought perhaps that Uncle Bernie might remember her in his will, but that would be a long time hence.

'You see, if you're right, about what you told me – that your husband has . . . well, found someone else, there would be no reason why you shouldn't . . .'

Jack's voice died away. Suddenly Edith felt almost drunk with power. A word or two from her could cause enormous and permanent changes to the lives of so many people.

'I need time,' she murmured.

'Of course you do,' Jack said. 'I—'

'And quite apart from anything else,' she went on, 'there's this business about Miss Caswell.' Edith didn't want to think at present about something that might have been a proposal of marriage. Safer to think about Miss Caswell.

'Terrible,' he said absently.

'Do you remember what Mrs Solly was saying when we met her this morning?'

'I wasn't paying too much attention. Something about Miss Caswell wanting to make a phone call? About her rambling away and not making sense?'

'But there might have been some sense in it. Jack, I think the police should know about that. Just in case. Why don't you have a word with Mrs Solly?'

'Surely there's a danger she would mention—?'

'Seeing us together?'

He flushed, hearing her refer so openly to the fact of their friendship, or whatever the word was which described what lay between them.

'We'll have to take a chance on that,' Edith said. 'And, in any case, I suppose I'd better tell him about the trousseau. Them, I mean – the police.' Now she too was flushing. It was all so hideously embarrassing. Even that wretched word *trousseau*. 'But I'd like to have a look at it myself first. Somehow it hardly seems fair to Miss Caswell to let the police pry into her things. Not without knowing what she had.'

'Do you want to go now?'

Edith looked at her wristwatch. 'There's no time. I need to get back and do something for the evening meal. And I haven't done any housework for days. Besides, your car is still parked on the other side of the village.'

'You can stay here while I fetch it.' Jack looked at her and nibbled his lower lip. 'This is crazy, Edith, isn't it?'

'What is?' she said brightly. 'The idea that someone might have wanted to harm Miss Caswell?'

'No, dearest,' he said, stretching out his hand to her. 'Us.'

# Chapter Thirty-four

A very old man was dozing in a wheelchair parked in the sun-filled angle between the wall of Fontenoy Place and the flight of steps running down from the front door. His eyes opened as Thornhill climbed out of the police car. He watched Thornhill approaching, footsteps crunching on the gravel.

'You a police officer?' the old man said in a voice that sounded like very expensive tissue paper.

'Yes, sir.'

'No uniform – does that mean you're one of these detective johnnies?'

'Yes.'

'Good. And about time too.'

Thornhill stopped beside the wheelchair. 'Why's that, sir?'

'I want you to look very carefully at that fellow Angmer's medical qualifications. I've had my suspicions for some time.'

'I see.'

'And while you're at it, Officer, find out why they haven't taken me for my walk. And why was luncheon sixteen minutes late? It's not good enough.'

Thornhill touched his hat in a gesture that might have been taken as assent, partly out of courtesy and partly as an automatic response to the note of command that the old man's voice still retained, a useless leftover from an earlier stage of his evolution, like the stump of the tail at the base of the human spine.

'Did you know Miss Caswell, sir?' he asked.

'Of course I know her. Everyone knows her.'

'Did you see her last night, sir?'

'Must have done.'

'Why?'

'Well, because I always do. I always see everyone at supper.'

'And what time is that?'

'It's meant to be at six o'clock. Yesterday they rang the bell at three minutes past. It's a disgrace.'

Thornhill caught movement in the corner of his eye. A small, balding man stared down at him. His dark suit was too tight, emphasising the plumpness of his thighs, his narrow sloping shoulders and his tall, thin neck.

'Visitors only by appointment, I'm afraid,' he said in a dry, precise voice.

'I'm Detective Inspector Thornhill, sir. Lydmouth CID. I believe you're expecting me.' He felt in his pocket for his warrant card and held it out. 'And you are?'

'Dr Angmer. I am the Director of Fontenoy Place.'

'You couldn't direct traffic on a rainy Sunday,' said the little man from the wheelchair in a weary voice, as if stating the obvious.

'Ha ha, General.' Angmer smiled at the old man and murmured to Thornhill, 'Wonderful sense of humour for his age but it can get a little trying. You'd better come inside.'

Thornhill followed him into a lofty hall. Pillars stretched up in the gloom. Black and white slabs marched across the floor. He stumbled over a discarded wellington boot.

'Nurse!' Angmer called to someone out of sight. 'Please have this mess tidied up.'

Thornhill realised with a slight shock that they were not alone. Sitting on the bottom treads of the stairs were two elderly women in grey pinafores. They stared at Thornhill and he stared back.

'Go to the activity room,' Angmer cried, flapping his arms at them. 'It's Thursday afternoon, so it's pottery, remember? Never too late to learn a new skill, is it?'

The two women made half-hearted efforts to stand up. Angmer lost interest in them and led Thornhill through double doors into a long room overlooking parkland.

'Do sit down. And I apologise for some of our guests. They can be very trying, I'm afraid. Usually we can cope with that – that's what we're here for. But poor Miss Caswell's death has come as quite a shock to us all.'

Thornhill sat down in a leather armchair. He thought the room looked like the library of a gentlemen's club, not that he'd had any experience of gentlemen's clubs. Angmer seemed to grow in authority here, as though this room – not the rest of the house – were his proper sphere of influence. He sat down opposite Thornhill and smoothed back his scanty hair.

'A tragic accident,' he murmured. 'But what exactly can I do for you, Inspector? I understand, of course, that in a case like this there will have to be an inquest. But I would have thought that everything was quite straightforward.'

'I'm not sure I follow, sir.'

'Miss Caswell was an old, confused lady. She was also physically remarkably robust for her age and liked her own company. It's not been easy to keep an eye on her all the time. This is not a prison. Even so, she must have exercised a good deal of – ah – low cunning to slip out of the house undetected last night – '

Thornhill cut in: 'And when did she slip out of the house, sir?'

Dr Angmer blinked. 'I . . . we have not yet been able to establish that, exactly. She came to supper, the last meal of our day here, which was at six o'clock, as usual.'

'The old man outside told me it started three minutes late.'

'One should not take everything the general says at face value, Inspector. As I was saying, Miss Caswell went up to her room—'

'Is that what she would usually do?'

'Yes. We encourage our guests to use the drawing room after supper. Social intercourse is most important, especially for the elderly. At that age, and with the infirmities that some of our guests have, it can be very easy to slide into isolation. We try—'

'But from what you say, Miss Caswell preferred isolation.'

Two spots of colour had appeared in Dr Angmer's cheeks. 'Miss Caswell had been here a very long time, Inspector. She had her own routines. Naturally we made an effort to keep an eye on her. She was certainly in her room at eight-thirty or thereabouts. We give our guests a cup of cocoa then, just as they are getting ready for bed.'

'So they have their drinks in their rooms?'

'That is correct.'

'I would like to talk to whoever took the cocoa to Miss Caswell.'

'That would be Nurse Lindor. She made quite a pet of Miss Caswell. And, I may say, is very upset by her death.'

'And I would like to see her room, as well, sir.'

'Very well, Inspector. But – I hope you won't mind my asking you this – surely this is rather unusual?' He eased his collar and gave a little laugh. 'I can't believe that the accidental death of an old lady would usually attract the attention of a detective inspector.'

Thornhill stared at Angmer as if he were a laboratory specimen. There was a suspicion of perspiration at the man's temples where the bare skin ran into the hairline. An accidental death at a place like this could be bad for business. Angmer must be terrified that he would be blamed for it, perhaps publicly censored by the coroner. Maybe that was all it was. Or was there another reason why the little man veered between nervousness and aggression?

'Who was responsible for Miss Caswell?' Thornhill asked. 'Apart from yourself, of course. Who paid the bills?'

'The family set up a fund to deal with that long before my time. It's looked after by two of our own trustees, as a matter of fact – Lord Vauden, who is, I believe, distantly related to Miss Caswell, and the solicitor George Shipston. I think he is responsible for most of the day-to-day running of Miss Caswell's affairs. He's been absolutely devoted to her, I may say.'

'May I see Miss Caswell's room now? And meet the nurse who looked after her?'

Dr Angmer leapt to his feet. 'Of course, Inspector. One moment.'

He rang the bell by the fireplace. He told the maid who answered it to ask Nurse Lindor to meet them in Miss Caswell's room as soon as possible. Then he guided Thornhill into the hall.

'And who are the other trustees of Fontenoy Place, sir?'

'Sir Anthony Ruispidge and the bishop.' He shot a glance at Thornhill. 'And Mr Rufus Moorcroft was one as well. Councillor Broadbent will be taking his place, we hope.'

Thornhill felt a sinking of the heart. Was there any pie within a ten-mile radius of Lydmouth that did not have one of Bernie's fingers in it?

Angmer led the way into the west wing of the house, which extended from the central block in a mirror image of the east wing.

'This is where our more stable guests sleep,' he told Thornhill.

'And Miss Caswell was one of those?'

'Oh yes, Inspector. We have some very sad cases in here indeed, very sad.'

Thornhill followed him up to the second floor. From the windows that lit the staircase, he glimpsed the central block of the house, rising like a cliff. When they reached the top of the stairs, the scale of the building changed. A long, low corridor, floored with brown linoleum, and smelling of polish and old age, ran down to the window at the far end. Two rows of doorways faced each other along its length like dancers waiting for the measure to begin. Most of the doors were open. On each of them was a label in a brass holder with the name of its occupant. Thornhill glanced from side to side as they walked along the corridor, glimpsing rooms which varied from cell-like simplicity to the pink profusion of an Edwardian boudoir.

'In this wing, our guests are encouraged to make their rooms their homes from home.' Dr Angmer's words had a mechanical sound, as though his mind were elsewhere. 'Their little nests, as it were. This landing is reserved for ladies. We generally find they take more advantage of the opportunity than the men do.'

Why was it so silent, Thornhill wondered? Apart from Angmer's voice, as clipped as a talking robot's, and the hammer-like blows of their nailed heels on the linoleum, they were surrounded by a deadened silence. He felt claustrophobia rising inside him. The constraints weren't physical. It was a glimpse of a possible future. How could people live in this place?

'Where is everyone?' he asked, his voice sounding flattened, as though the resonance had been sucked into the dead air that swirled around them.

'At luncheon, Inspector. In any case, we don't encourage our guests to skulk in their rooms during the day, unless of course they are unwell.'

Dr Angmer stopped at a closed door next to the tall window at the end of the corridor. He unlocked it and went in. Thornhill lingered for a moment on the threshold. The label on the door said: *The Hon. Miss C. Caswell*. The room was furnished as a bed-sitting room. Against one wall was a narrow iron bedstead covered with a quilt. Sepia-toned photographs of marble statuary, set in dark funereal frames, faced him on either side of the window. Beneath one photograph was a small armchair with horsehair bursting from its arms, and beneath the other was a card table which served as a desk. A small deal wardrobe and a matching chest of drawers stood close together on the wall opposite the bed, as though drawn up for sale in the yard of a junk-shop. The floor was covered with the linoleum used for the corridor. By the bed was a small rug, dark red and blue round the borders, but the nap worn down to the pale warp and weft in the centre.

Dr Angmer stood by the window, his hand resting lightly on the card table. 'Miss Caswell set little store by material possessions.' He coughed. 'By her own choice she preferred to live very simply.'

The windowpanes sparkled. There was no dust. The furniture had recently been polished. The window was open a crack and the air smelt sweet and fresh. Someone had cared about Miss Caswell's material surroundings.

Thornhill stepped to the window and looked out over the park. The railway and the mouth of the tunnel were not visible from here, but he could see the hill where the quarry was. There were three library books on the table and he glanced idly at their spines. A novel by Angela Thirkell. *Jeremy and Hamlet* by Hugh Walpole. And a plump green volume with the title *My Bygone Times*. For Miss Caswell, he thought, the present must have turned in on itself fifty years earlier. Living in this great barracks must have sustained the illusion that the twentieth century hadn't really happened.

'I'd like to have a look at her belongings,' he said. 'Would you mind?'

Dr Angmer waved expansively round the little room. 'Look wherever you wish, Inspector. We have no secrets here.'

Thornhill worked swiftly and methodically through the contents of the chest of drawers. The underclothes and blouses in the top two drawers were old, neatly folded and scrupulously clean; many of them were darned and patched, their colours faded with much washing. In the bottom drawer were cardigans and jerseys. Underneath them were four leather boxes. He raised them on to the top of the dressing table and tried the catch of the largest, which was about twelve by ten inches. It wasn't locked. He lifted the lid and found himself looking at a diamond-and-sapphire necklace with matching earrings, bedded in purple velvet. He tried the other boxes and found more necklaces, rings, bracelets and brooches.

'Good Lord,' Dr Angmer said.

'You didn't know she had these?'

Angmer shook his head. 'We don't spy on our guests, Inspector. I wonder how long they've been there.'

'Do you have a safe?'

'Yes.'

'If I were you, I'd lock these up.'

'You think they're real?'

'Better safe than sorry.'

Footsteps were approaching briskly down the corridor. Thornhill flipped shut the lids.

'Ah,' Dr Angmer said. 'Nurse Lindor at last.'

She hesitated in the doorway. Thornhill thought she looked unwell. Her eyes were puffy. Her hair was escaping from her cap.

'Nurse, this is Detective Inspector Thornhill.'

She nodded, staring beyond Thornhill to the window.

'When there's a tragic accident like Miss Caswell's, the police have to be involved,' Angmer said. 'You must have known her better than anyone. I'm sure you'll be able to answer any questions he has.'

Nurse Lindor gave an almost imperceptible shrug.

'So if you'll excuse me, Inspector?'

Thornhill nodded. 'You'd better take those.' He waved towards the jewel boxes.

'Yes, of course.' Dr Angmer picked up the boxes while Nurse

Lindor watched him. 'I'll be in my room. Nurse Lindor will show you the way if you need me.'

They listened to him walking away. It seemed to Thornhill that Dr Angmer was almost running in his anxiety to be gone. He looked at the nurse and said, 'I'm sorry, but I have to look through her belongings. Just a routine part of my job.'

She nodded again, and he guessed that she knew all about routine jobs that other people found less than pleasant.

Within five minutes he had finished the search. There were no more surprises. Not unless you counted the fact that Miss Caswell had owned so little. She seemed to have brought nothing with her of her past life, except perhaps the jewels, and to have acquired nothing while she was living in Fontenoy Place for half a century.

Thornhill straightened up, smoothing the coverlet over the bed. 'You kept everything very neat and tidy.'

'She always liked things spotless, she did.' There was a note of pride in Nurse Lindor's voice. 'Very particular. Not like some of them here. Liked a bath every day, too, and you wouldn't believe the number of times she'd wash her hands.'

'Was this all she had?'

She frowned. 'What do you mean?'

'I wondered if she had anything stored somewhere else. Perhaps in a trunk?'

'She hadn't any need of *things*.'

'Did you know about the boxes Dr Angmer took away?' She nodded.

'And you knew what was in them?'

'Of course I did. I looked after Miss Caswell for years. They belonged to her godmother, she told me, and she'd left them to her.' She snorted. 'I doubt if she'd thought of them for years.'

Thornhill had seen all he wanted. He asked Nurse Lindor to show him back downstairs. She waited while he locked the door.

Before moving off, he glanced at the window at the end of the corridor. It framed a view of unbroken parkland.

'I wouldn't be surprised if that's how she got out last night.' Thornhill swung round. 'What?'

'She liked a stroll in the grounds, Miss Caswell did.' Nurse Lindor's face was flushed and determined. 'Normally she'd go after supper. They have it early here. Generally I go with her. But last night she didn't. She came up here. She was here when I brought her cocoa. So she must have gone out after that.'

While she was talking, Thornhill moved nearer the window. A black cast-iron fire escape ran beneath it. He craned his head and saw the steps descending to the gravelled path below. The window was large and its sill was no more than eighteen inches from the floor. A simple catch locked the two sashes together.

'She could have got out this way?'

'If she'd gone downstairs normally, someone would have seen her.'

'Was the catch opened this morning?'

Nurse Lindor sighed. 'Might have been. The cleaners come up after breakfast, and they usually open the window to air the corridor. They're meant to lock it afterwards, but they don't always remember. I asked the woman who did up here this morning, and she wasn't sure if the catch was shut or not.'

'But the window was closed?'

'Oh yes. People would notice if it was open.'

They walked slowly along the corridor.

Thornhill said softly, 'I understand you went to the tunnel this morning.'

'I was looking for her. Someone had to.'

'I'm sure a lot of people were.'

'Not like I was.'

'Perhaps not.'

'It's not right,' she blurted out. 'No one should go like that.

And what was she doing there? That's what I'd like to know. She wouldn't go in the tunnel because it would make her all messy. And anyway, she didn't like dark places.'

'We'll do our best to find out. I promise.'

She responded to the gentleness in his voice. 'You'll tell me if you do, won't you?'

'If I can.'

She grunted, unhappy with the reservation. 'Thornhill? There was an Edith Thornhill at — at Mr Moorcroft's funeral.'

'My wife.'

Nurse Lindor glanced at him and looked suddenly away. 'The stairs are through there. This house is a real maze.'

He knew she had been on the verge of saying something quite different. He let it go and followed her down the stairs.

They emerged into the gloom of the pillared hall. A maid was talking to someone at the front door. Nurse Lindor stopped suddenly and looked up at Thornhill. Her face was very earnest. For an instant he glimpsed something else: malice, perhaps, or even anger.

'If you want to know what Miss Caswell was like, Mr Thornhill, you should ask your wife.'

*Or jealousy?*

'Inspector!'

Thornhill turned towards the new voice. It was a man's, and familiar. A small, plump silhouette slipped past the maid and came towards him, hand outstretched.

'Mr Loysey. Good afternoon.'

'We meet again.' Loysey pumped his hand up and down in an excess of bonhomie. He grinned. 'You're a man who can take a hint, I'm glad to see.'

'I beg your pardon, sir?'

'When we were talking about my painting this morning, I believe I mentioned the idea that perhaps Miss Caswell might have had something to do with it. I know it's a long shot, but I wondered if it could be in her room. June and I happened to be passing—'

'No, sir. The painting's not there.' Thornhill was aware of Nurse Lindor beside him, as rigid as Lot's wife. 'You can be sure of that.'

'Perhaps not in her room, but it's a big place. I know I'm clutching at straws, but I really am very keen to get this back.'

June had followed her husband into the hall. She tugged at his arm.

'Miss Caswell wasn't a thief,' Nurse Lindor said, suddenly coming to life. 'That's what you're saying, isn't it? Well, you can go and say it somewhere else.'

She moved towards him, unmistakably hostile.

'Nurse!' said Dr Angmer, who had appeared in the doorway of his room. 'I think that's enough. Inspector, your car's arrived.'

She did not take her eyes away from Loysey. 'She was worth ten of you, whoever you are.'

'I'm sure she was, dear lady,' Loysey said.

'Nurse! Nurse Lindor!' Angmer said. 'Come here, please.'

'She'd no more steal your silly little painting or anything else than a newborn baby would.'

June Loysey pushed herself between her husband and Nurse Lindor. 'Stop it,' she said, her face reddening. 'That's enough. Do you hear?'

The two old ladies in grey pinafores, still perching on the bottom step of the main staircase, began to cry. Dr Angmer walked swiftly across the hall and took Nurse Lindor by the arm. Thornhill wondered if he should put a stop to this, but thought it might be more useful to let it run its course. Somewhere outside the house a car door slammed.

'She's dead, you fool,' Nurse Lindor said, speaking at Loysey through his wife as though she were invisible. 'Does that mean nothing to you? All you care about is your bloody silly painting, and she's lying dead in that tunnel. You're mad, do you hear, you're mad.'

'You be quiet,' June Loysey bellowed. 'Can't you do something, Inspector? Can't you arrest her?'

'Hello-ello?' said a voice which sounded like a fruitcake laced with too much sherry. 'Anyone at home?'

Thornhill looked away from June Loysey to the front door, which was still open. Standing on the threshold was the portly figure of Ivor Fuggle.

'Who are you?' Angmer said, his voice rising higher.

'Ivor Fuggle of the *Evening Post*, sir, at your service.'

'I must ask you to leave at once. Otherwise I shall complain to this gentleman here, who is a police officer. You shouldn't be here – the gates are closed.'

'Not the gates of the back drive, my old chum. I just drove right in, following this lady and gentleman here. And even if you'd closed the gates, I could have hoofed it. It's a right of way, according to my map. Now, all I wanted was—'

'Your bloody painting,' shrieked Nurse Lindor, spittle spraying from her mouth. 'That's all you've got on your mind.' Now her anger had reached boiling point, she was oblivious of anyone in the room except Gareth Loysey. 'What does it matter? She's dead, that's the point. For all we know she was murdered.'

From the doorway came an echo in Ivor Fuggle's voice: 'Murdered?'

# Chapter Thirty-five

Everything became easier with practice, Thornhill thought, even lying. He dropped the phone in its cradle and picked up his hat and gloves. He had told Edith that something had come up and he would be an hour or two late. It was almost as if someone other than himself were arranging these deceptions with such smooth efficiency.

In the corridor he met the DCC, swinging his gleaming attaché case, also on his way home.

'You off now?' Drake asked.

'Yes, sir.'

'Any further?'

'Not really. If we could find an explanation for some of the things Miss Caswell said and did in the last day or two of her life—'

Drake cut in: 'Miss Caswell was in her seventies and by common consent she was off her rocker. She was living in cloud-cuckoo-land. So I don't think the answer's there. What we need is something we can get our teeth into. Someone who saw her last night, for example.' He paused, his bright eyes studying Thornhill's face. 'You look fagged out, man. Go home and get a good night's sleep.'

Thornhill, bemused at the idea of a superior officer who was sufficiently observant to notice how the men under his command were looking, walked slowly down to the car park. It was a little before seven o'clock when he left Police Headquarters. He drove down the hill to the station, over New Bridge, and turned left into Farnock Lane.

A few minutes later, he tucked the car fifty yards down a track leading into the Forest and climbed on foot among the trees. The air was still warm and smelled faintly of the conifer plantation a quarter of a mile to the south. The ground underfoot was dry despite the shower earlier in the day. Thornhill wondered what he and Jill would do, where they would go, when the summer was over and the weather changed.

The clearing was empty. Their arrangements were always provisional, and he knew it was possible that she would not be able to come at all. On two occasions he had waited for her and she had not come. He propped himself against the fallen chestnut tree and wondered, not for the first time recently, whether he should buy some cigarettes; smoking would give him something to do with his hands, an occupation, and there was no reason why he shouldn't take it up again now money was a little easier.

He closed his eyes and tried to rest. Instead, pictures from the day flashed through his mind. He couldn't go on like this for long, he thought – the strain would tear him apart. He opened his eyes to escape from the pictures and saw Jill standing in front of him.

'Richard,' she said in a rush, 'I've been offered a job in London.'

He blinked, disconcerted by her sudden appearance as much as by her words. 'What?'

'I've been offered a job in London.'

'Who by?'

'Randolph Haughton. I knew him quite well when I lived in London.' She hesitated, watching his face. 'No, not like that,' she went on. 'He was a friend — we worked together sometimes. He's just bought a magazine called *Berkeley's*. And he's asked me to be features editor.'

'I know what *Berkeley's* is.' Thornhill rubbed his forehead, listening to the bitterness in his own voice. *What about me?* He said, more gently, 'And will you take it?'

'I don't know. It depends what we do, quite apart from anything else.'

'And what are we going to do?'

'I don't know. I still haven't made up my mind. The thing is, I'm getting scared.'

'Why?'

'Because of people like Ivor Fuggle and Amy Gwyn-Thomas. We . . . we are so vulnerable. All of us — Edith, as well as you and me.'

He turned his head away from her. 'When will you decide?'

'Soon, I promise. You look awfully tired, Richard.'

Her sympathy cut him like a razor. She took his shoulders and drew him towards her. For a while they stood without speaking, his head resting on her breast.

'What is it, Richard? I've never seen you like this.'

He lifted his head. 'It's partly this case. No, that's a lie. I feel as if everything's falling apart. You and me. Living in Lydmouth. The job.'

'What about Edith?'

'I don't know about her, either. She's changed.' He rarely talked about Edith with Jill because it seemed an even worse betrayal than those he already committed so frequently and with such enthusiasm.

'What do you want me to do?'

'Say you'll come away with me.' As he spoke, he wondered whether that was entirely accurate. 'No, I'm not trying to hurry you. I'm sorry — I'm not thinking straight. We're under a lot of pressure because of Miss Caswell's death.'

'Why?'

'Some of her friends and relations have a lot of influence.' He knew she liked him to talk about his work, not because she was a journalist – she was scrupulous about not misusing her position – but because it was a sign that he trusted her. In any case, it was easier to talk about the job than about more painful matters. 'We think that someone else was involved. There may have been some sort of struggle at the mouth of the tunnel. It looks like someone dragged her inside, probably when she was unconscious. And the evidence suggests that Miss Caswell came to at some point and tried to crawl out. That's when the train got her.'

Jill winced. 'That's terrible.'

'We should know more tomorrow after the autopsy. The trouble is, there are so many loose ends. No one seems to have seen her since about eight-thirty yesterday evening.' He laughed, sourly. 'I went to see her room this afternoon. Like a monk's cell. She had a small fortune in Victorian jewellery in her bottom drawer.'

'Who was the last person to see her?'

'A nurse called Lindor. She seems to have acted as a cross between Miss Caswell's keeper and her lady's maid.'

'Gareth Loysey dropped by today with a ridiculous story about her,' Jill said. 'About Miss Caswell, I mean.'

'Loysey? Why did he come and see you?'

She touched him gently on the arm. 'Don't worry. We're doing a piece on him and he came to drop in a photograph. He said there used to be a story going around that Miss Caswell's baby was fathered by Lord Salisbury.'

'Was he one of her cousins too?'

'Probably. But the whole thing was clearly absurd. It couldn't have been the Prime Minister because he was an old man and frightfully upright. And the next Lord Salisbury was a model of propriety, too.'

'Miss Caswell tried to make a phone call on Tuesday evening. Bernie Broadbent lent her some money for it.'

'Bernie?'

'Turns out he's known her for years. He knows everyone. Did you know they've asked him to take Moorcroft's place as a trustee at Fontenoy Place?'

'No. But this phone call—'

'—was also witnessed by your friend Haughton. She said something to Bernie about telephoning someone in Kent, but she only borrowed tuppence.'

'Perhaps she didn't know the cost of trunk calls.'

'Haughton said she was looking up a number in the directory in the telephone box. That would make it a local number.'

'Can't you trace the call?'

'The exchange is automatic now. The trouble is, we don't know how much she was living in some world of her own. How far do we take all this seriously? Mrs Solly – she used to be Rufus Moorcroft's housekeeper – she had a word with the village bobby in Trenalt this afternoon. According to her, when she bumped into Miss Caswell at Moorcroft's funeral, the old lady was trying to remember someone's surname. Someone called Constance, she thought, who was a nun and lived near the road.'

'What road?'

'We haven't a clue. Probably Miss Caswell hadn't, either.'

Jill reached up and kissed him. They stood in silence. The Forest, a place of secret activities for so many species, rustled around them. A rabbit darted into the clearing, saw them and scuttled away, its white tail bobbing like a tail-light.

'The White Rabbit,' Thornhill muttered. 'I nearly forgot. Mrs Solly said that Miss Caswell was looking for the White Rabbit at Moorcroft's funeral.'

'She must have been reading *Alice in Wonderland*. Nothing so very strange about that.'

'It wasn't one of the books in her room.'

'She probably knew it by heart.'

The light was beginning to fade. He felt Jill taking his hands and stroking the fingers individually, as though each were a small animal requiring reassurance. She stirred against him.

'And I can't understand what Edith's up to,' Thornhill said in a rush. 'Why didn't she mention this man Moorcroft before? She's not been herself since she went back to Trenalt. Mrs Solly said she – she was with Moorcroft's nephew this morning, that chap Graig. Up at Highnam Cottage. They told Mrs Solly to talk to the police. Jill, I just don't understand it.'

'Do you know what I think?' she said. 'I think you're dog-tired. The best thing you can do is go home and go to bed.'

# Chapter Thirty-six

Nearly an hour after Richard's phone call, Edith rang Police Headquarters and asked to speak to her husband. She was put through to Brian Kirby, who told her that Richard had left the building some time ago.

She wasn't surprised. The worst thing of all, she thought, was the not knowing, the not being absolutely sure. There might be a perfectly innocent reason for his absence.

'Mrs Thornhill?' Brian said, clearing his throat. 'Can I ask your advice?'

'Of course you can. What about?'

'Suppose someone was buying you a ring, and they didn't have all that much money to spend. Would you rather they went for something that looked good, but only had semi-precious stones in it, or would you want the real thing?'

'The real thing,' Edith said.

'Even though it couldn't be very big?'

'Yes. They wouldn't want to give her second best, would they?'

'No. But it wouldn't be very big at all.'

Edith abandoned all pretence of not knowing what this was about. 'Then why don't you sell your motorbike and get her something really nice? She probably hates it in any case. They're such nasty, dangerous things.'

After a moment's silence, Kirby thanked her and rang off. As Edith was walking back to the kitchen, she was surprised to hear the key turning in the lock of the front door. She wasn't even sure whether it was a pleasant surprise or an unpleasant one.

*Maybe they've had a quarrel?*

She wondered what she would do if Jack came through the door instead of Richard. Would it be better or worse? Something inside her had changed in the last few days, and she was no longer sure what she felt about things. Or people.

From then on, the evening followed a pattern which, outwardly at least, was entirely predictable. Richard apologised with polite insincerity for being late. He changed out of his suit and washed while she dished up the liver and onions, which would have tasted nicer if they had been eaten half an hour earlier. While they ate, they listened to the radio, something on the Light Programme which neither of them wanted to hear but which filled what would otherwise have been the awkward silence. Afterwards, Edith cleared away in the scullery while Richard sat at the kitchen table reading the *Gazette*. She made coffee and brought it in to him. It was at this point that the evening diverged from the pattern.

She sat down at the table, spooned sugar into her cup and said, 'Have you been dealing with that accident which happened to Miss Caswell?'

He looked at her with bloodshot eyes. 'Yes. I suppose you must have known her.'

'Oh yes. When I was a girl and I went to stay with Granny. And I met her at Mr Moorcroft's funeral the other day, and once again after that.' She sipped her coffee, noticing that his eyes had drifted back to the newspaper. 'People are saying there's a curse on the railway at Trenalt.'

'That's nonsense,' he said, with a careful smile to show that he wasn't irritated. 'Why bring that sort of thing into it?'

'Because of Hugh Hudnall dying there, too.'

'He died at the station, didn't he?'

'Yes.' She was amazed that she could mention Hugh's name so coolly. 'But you know what people are like.' She grimaced. 'Do you know, I think I must have heard him going down to the station on the night he died.'

The policeman came to the fore, not the husband: 'You heard Hudnall? Was it something you mentioned at the time?'

'No — because Bernie came and took me home in the morning. I told you, remember?'

'Last night.'

She wondered whether there was a reproach there — last night, but not during one of all the other nights before that, all the other nights of their marriage.

'And anyway, I didn't realise it was Hugh I must have heard until much later.'

'So you were outside? I thought it was raining cats and dogs that evening.'

'Yes, it was.' With a twinge of anxiety, she remembered how quickly his mind could work. 'I got caught in the rain and I had to take shelter in that cottage on the hill up from the station. Where the road forks. Fiddler's Cottage — do you know it?'

He nodded.

'And . . . and I heard running footsteps going down the hill to the station.'

'When was this?'

'I can't remember. It was late, though. It couldn't have been long before the last train from Lydmouth was due.' She hesitated. 'There were two sets of footsteps, actually. I'm not sure which were his.'

'Two?' His tiredness had dropped away from him. 'Are you sure? I didn't realise there was someone else on the scene.'

'There wasn't, not necessarily. There was a minute or two between the two people. Hugh could have been the second one. And in any case, the other person may not have been going to the station. They could have been going to Highnam Cottage or Fontenoy Place. Or to one of the farms on that side of the valley.'

The weariness flooded back into his face. 'Yes. Still, it's interesting.'

'You look all in. Why don't you go up now? I'll finish off down here.'

'I think I might.' He forced a smile. 'You wouldn't mind?'

'Of course not. There's not much left to do.'

She listened to his dragging footsteps on the stairs. Max and Tom, who had been asleep in a multicoloured bundle of fur in their cardboard box by the dresser, chose that moment to wake up and demand food. She was glad of the interruption. She lifted the two kittens up and held them against her breasts. They climbed up to her shoulders and licked her face, purring like a pair of well-tuned engines.

Edith thought of the casserole dish and the coffee pot, the cups and plates and cutlery, all waiting to be washed, dried and put away. How she hated the never-ending stream of dirty crockery that poured into the scullery sink. She placed the kittens, one by one, carefully in their box. She put the coffee cups on the tray and carried it into the kitchen. Rich people would have servants to do this sort of thing.

She wondered – and was ashamed that the thought had crossed her mind – whether Mrs Jack Graig would have to do her own washing-up.

# Chapter Thirty-seven

<hr/>

When Jill Francis walked to work on Friday morning, the first person she saw when she turned into the High Street was Bernie Broadbent. He was standing on the forecourt of Gray's Garage, looking as if he owned the place, which in fact he did.

Bernie had a pipe in his mouth and his thumbs in his waistcoat pockets. Behind him was the workshop, its doors open. His Riley was just inside, paintwork gleaming, the bonnet up. Two mechanics were peering respectfully at its engine. Bernie saw Jill, raised his right hand and waved. He strolled across the road to her, acknowledging with another wave the driver of the butcher's van, which had stopped to let him pass.

This was Lydmouth, Jill thought, where everybody wanted to do Bernie Broadbent a favour.

'Jill, my dear. Lovely morning.'

She smiled up at him. He was looking very well. He offered her his arm and asked if he might walk with her a little way.

'I wondered if you'd had time to give my little proposition some thought.'

'Yes,' Jill said. 'And I'm afraid the answer's no.'

She had not known for sure that that was what the answer would be until it came out. But Bernie was nodding as though it were just what he had been expecting.

'Well, I won't say I'm not sorry,' he said cheerfully. 'But I daresay you're right. The trouble with a business arrangement like that, looked at from all points of view, is that perhaps it's one of those ideas that sound better in theory than they are in practice.'

'I'm glad you're taking this so well,' Jill said tartly. 'Used to being turned down, are you?'

He grinned at her. 'You'd have hated it, wouldn't you?' They had reached the door of the *Gazette*. 'Do you think you'll stay in Lydmouth?'

For an instant, she felt as though he'd punched her. Surely he couldn't know about her and Richard? But his face showed kindness and curiosity, nothing else. She was sure there would have been other emotions if he had known what she and Richard were doing to Edith.

'I don't know.'

'It's a very small world for someone like you.' He tapped his pipe out on the sill of the *Gazette*'s window. 'Maybe I'm poking my nose in where it's not wanted, but I always thought you were running away from something when you came down here. No' – he held up a large hand – 'I don't want to know about it. None of my business. But I wouldn't have thought you're the sort of person who runs away from anything for long.'

'Bernie Broadbent,' she said. 'What's this? An attack of second sight? Or just a dose of homespun psychoanalysis?'

They were smiling at one another now. He raised his hat and said, 'I'd better be getting on.'

On impulse, she rested her hand on his shoulder, raised herself on tiptoe and kissed his cheek. To her delight, he blushed.

'You're a wicked woman,' he said. 'They should lock up people like you.'

She watched him walking back down the High Street to Gray's Garage. There was definitely a spring in his step. She wondered what, or who, had put it there.

She let herself into the office and went upstairs. She was earlier than usual. She walked slowly along the landing towards the editor's office at the end, her mind full of her conversation with Bernie. The office was separated from the corridor by the anteroom in which Miss Gwyn-Thomas worked. The door between the anteroom and the corridor was usually kept closed, because Miss Gwyn-Thomas found the noise from the rest of the building disturbed her while she was working. But the catch on the door did not always fully engage, because the wood had warped. As Jill drew nearer, she noticed that the door was ajar. Through the crack fluted the painfully genteel tones of Amy Gwyn-Thomas.

'Yes, Lord Salisbury. The Prime Minister! Quite disgusting . . . No, I don't think we'll be using it. Yes, really they should have locked her up. Then none of this would have happened, would it?'

Jill pushed the door open. Miss Gwyn-Thomas, seated at her desk with the telephone in her hand, looked up. Her mouth was a ragged hole in a twisted face. Jill took two swift paces and snatched the receiver from her. She put it to her ear.

'— and I wonder what happened to the child, Miss Gwyn-Thomas,' she heard Ivor Fuggle saying. 'I don't suppose you've got anything on that?'

Miss Gwyn-Thomas's hand chopped downwards on the telephone's cradle, breaking the connection. Jill slowly placed the receiver on its rest. The two women looked at each other.

'It's not what it seems, Miss Francis,' Miss Gwyn-Thomas said. 'I realise that—'

'And I realise exactly what's going on. How long have you been feeding information to the *Post*?'

Miss Gwyn-Thomas said nothing. The muscles in her face worked as if she were disintegrating beneath the skin.

'I suppose they're paying you? Is this how you're managing to afford your damned bungalow?'

'That's not true, I promise you, I've never had a penny from—'

'Be quiet.'

Miss Gwyn-Thomas's mouth closed itself, opened itself, closed itself again. Then she said, 'You won't tell Mr Wemyss-Brown, will you?'

'What do you think?'

'You – you've got no proof.'

'You're even more of a fool than I thought you were,' Jill said.

Miss Gwyn-Thomas snapped open her handbag and took out a lace-trimmed handkerchief with a pink letter A embroidered on the corner. She raised her glasses and dabbed at her eyes.

'You're on probation, Miss Gwyn-Thomas,' Jill said. 'I'm going to make up my mind later what I'm going to do about you. And if you've got any sense, you'll do your very best to encourage me to feel merciful.'

Jill lingered just long enough to see the expression on Miss Gwyn-Thomas's face. Then she stalked into the editor's room and closed the door behind her. A moment later, she opened the door again. Miss Gwyn-Thomas was sitting where she had left her, still with her handkerchief raised to her eyes.

'I think I'll have coffee at ten-thirty today,' Jill said. 'And I'd like you to buy me some Bourbon biscuits, please.'

She shut the door, sat down at the desk and tried to work. Five minutes later the phone rang. She picked up the receiver.

'Miss Francis.'

'I'm not sure we've got anything to say to each other, Mr Fuggle.'

'I wouldn't be too sure of that. I just wanted to remind you that people who live in glasshouses shouldn't throw stones.'

Jill slammed the receiver down. She was so angry that she stood and began to pace up and down the room. The thing to remember was that Miss Gwyn-Thomas and Ivor Fuggle had no proof of her affair with Richard. As long as she kept her nerve, they were safe. She told herself this several times and tried to believe it was true.

She lit a cigarette and went to stand by the window. She had a job to do, she had choices to make. She looked down at the shoppers flowing to and fro along the pavements. She knew at least half of them by sight, if not by name. She craned her head and looked to the right. Bernie was still standing on the forecourt of Gray's Garage, talking to one of the mechanics. As she watched, a large blue car glided on to the forecourt and drew to a halt beside the two men. Bernie raised a hand in greeting.

A moment later, he got into the passenger seat of Randolph Haughton's Bristol. The coupé nosed its way into the traffic. Jill went back to the desk and began to make notes for her meeting with the advertising manager later that morning. Her anger had evaporated. She was smiling.

# Chapter Thirty-eight

Watching the methodical butchery of a corpse without losing your lunch or changing colour was a proof of virility. It proved to yourself, and to anyone else who might be interested, that witnessing the dissection of human beings was something you could take in your stride.

There was also the point that Brian Kirby was happy to build up his overtime hours because WPC Joan Ailsmore had gone to see her parents in Birmingham. So when Murray reached Lydmouth a little before nine o'clock on Thursday evening, Brian was waiting to greet him. They had driven straight to the RAF Hospital. The mortuary was in the grounds, tucked away behind a screen of rhododendrons and dusty laurels, and here Murray had worked late into the night. Brian stayed with him.

Thornhill arrived at Police Headquarters on Thursday morning to find his sergeant typing up a report in the CID Office.

'How much sleep did you get?' he asked.

'Nearly two and a half hours, sir.' Brian almost glowed with vitality. 'Never felt better.'

Thornhill compared what he saw before him with the memory of his own face in the mirror three-quarters of an hour earlier: a pale skin, with dark smudges beneath the eyes, and two nicks where he had cut himself while shaving.

'Murray's dictated his report.' Brian leant back and shook a cigarette out of his packet. 'The DCC's stenographer came in early, and she's typing it up now.'

'And?'

'She had a number of injuries before death, probably several hours before.' He put the cigarette in the corner of his mouth and glanced down at a sheet of notes on the desk. 'Her right wrist and clavicle were fractured, so was the hip. Four ribs were cracked. Her jaw was broken, and her cheekbone, again both on her right-hand side.'

'Does Murray think that falling from the parapet over the tunnel could do that?'

'Easily. Apparently she was lucky not to be killed outright.'

'If that's the word you want.'

Kirby struck a match. 'Eh?'

'Lucky.'

'All depended on how she fell, you see. Murray thought it could be that she tried to save herself by holding on to the parapet. That might skew the fall. That would explain why most of the injuries were on one side.'

'It would also fit in with the possibility of a struggle.'

Brian lit the cigarette. 'You know Murray. Not a man to speculate.' He blew out smoke and tilted his chair back on two legs. 'But the blood up on the parapet matches Miss Caswell's blood group. Which is O rhesus positive, so it's not necessarily much help. There are some marks, like specks of oil and coal dust, on her coat and in her hair, and the material has a number of small tears in it as well. We've sent samples down to the lab. But, on the face of it, it looks like Drac Grimes was right. The poor old dear was dragged up the tunnel to the refuge, probably on her back. Murray found bruising on the ankles. Someone towed her like a cart.'

'And when did this happen?'

'That's still not clear, guv. Murray says that part of the problem is in establishing the sequence — which injury happened when. It was all very interesting. Quite educational, I found it.'

Without warning, Thornhill felt his temper slipping out of his control. He snapped, 'But what about when she died? Surely he can put a time to that?'

Brian's eyes showed his surprise. He swung forward, settling the chair on four legs, and waved cigarette smoke away as though trying to clear the air. 'Yes, sir. The early morning. Drac had that right, too. Murray says there's no doubt, even allowing for the fact it's cool down there. Her temperature and the lack of rigor point to the same thing. No hypostasis, either.'

Thornhill went to his own room and shuffled files and papers around his desk until it was nine o'clock. His momentary loss of temper worried him. It wasn't poor Brian's fault. The only person he could fairly blame was himself. It was as though he had divided into two people, pursuing parallel and equally unsatisfactory lives. At work, he had the Caswell case and all its ramifications, with the additional uncertainty about the new office for senior detectives. Worse than that, though, were the messy uncertainties of his private life: the guilt, the way Edith had turned into a stranger, his need for Jill and the simple fact that he still did not know how all this would end.

Would Jill come away with him or not? He thought that if only she would agree, then everything else would be simple. Even his bloody headache would go away.

At nine o'clock he telephoned Fontenoy Place and talked to Dr Angmer. The Director was able to confirm that the monthly cheques which Shipston provided on Miss Caswell's behalf were drawn on an account at the Lydmouth branch of Barclays Bank. Thornhill then rang the bank and made an appointment to see Mr Morgan. At twenty past nine, he was ushered into the bank manager's office. He shook the man's soft, white hand and declined a cigarette. For a moment they discussed the state of the weather and enquired solicitously about the health of each other and of Mrs Morgan and Mrs Thornhill.

'I understand from Dr Angmer at Fontenoy Place,' Thornhill said once these pleasantries were completed, 'that Shipston & Shipston have an account here on behalf of Miss Caswell.'

'Yes indeed.' Morgan smiled, as though pleased to be able to confirm this. 'That unfortunate lady. The Honourable Miss Cicely Caswell. My wife and I were discussing her sad demise yesterday evening. Truly a tragic accident. That is, of course, if it was an accident?'

'That's for the coroner to say, sir.'

There was a spark of understanding in Morgan's eyes. 'I understand the inquest has been adjourned.'

'Yes, sir. We have to explore every possibility, and that takes time.'

'There are two signatories on the account,' Mr Morgan said. 'Lord Vauden and Mr George Shipston. I'm sure either of them would be able to give you any necessary information.'

'Yes, sir. I imagine that Mr Shipston would be responsible for most of the day-to-day transactions?'

'That seems a not unreasonable assumption.'

'Mr Shipston is not as young as he was,' Thornhill said.

'Yes, most men have retired by the time they have reached his age. I daresay he will soon consider relinquishing some of his responsibilities. *Time, you old gipsy man*, as the poet says. We often notice that some of our older customers gradually find it harder to keep track of their affairs. There is a tendency to behave erratically.' He gave Thornhill an unexpectedly mischievous smile. 'Still, the customer is always right.'

'What will happen now Miss Caswell is dead?'

'I couldn't say, Inspector. Usually in such cases, the trust would be wound up and the proceeds would be divided among the beneficiaries.'

'So Miss Caswell would only have a life interest?'

'Well, I couldn't comment on her case, naturally, but I believe that is generally so.'

Thornhill stood up. 'You've been most helpful, sir.'

The two men shook hands again. Thornhill was beginning to like Mr Morgan. Talking to him was rather like reading a poem whose meaning was shrouded in symbols: once you understood the code, the meaning was clear.

He turned right out of the bank and made his way up to Castle Street. Shipston's elderly saloon was parked outside his office. The receptionist, who looked nearly as old as Mr Shipston himself, said that Mr George was busy.

'Would you tell him I'm here?' Thornhill said. 'I need to see him about Miss Cicely Caswell.'

For an instant, the woman's expression changed, tightening with alarm. Then she bowed her head. 'If you insist, Inspector.'

Three minutes later, she returned with the news that Mr Shipston would see him now. She detailed one of the clerks to take him upstairs, as though Thornhill were not to be trusted on his own in the building.

Though it was still early in the day, the room was full of pungent, blue-grey fog. Behind the desk sat George Shipston, hunched forward and seeming smaller than usual, with a cigar in one hand and a pen in the other. The clerk retreated, closing the door noiselessly behind him.

Shipston glanced up at Thornhill and then down at the papers spread out on the desk. Thornhill felt his temper sliding away for the second time that morning. He advanced slowly into the room and stopped at the desk. He rested his hands on its scarred mahogany edge and leaned towards the solicitor. Slowly, as though the effort required immense concentration over a period of time, Shipston raised his head once more.

The old man's face was like a desert, Thornhill thought, pale and flaking, pitted with cracks, the only vegetation arid tangles of untrimmed grey hair. Shipston stuffed the cigar in his mouth and sucked hard. The tip glowed and a grey slug of ash fell to the blotter.

Thornhill took a deep breath, coughed and said, 'We shall want to see all financial records relating to Miss Caswell's affairs, as well as any other documents connected with her, such as her will.'

The old man cleared his throat. 'You're being impertinent, sir. Miss Caswell's affairs are none of your business.' The words were hostile but the tone was querulous.

'We have reason to believe that Miss Caswell's death was not accidental. Would you prefer it if we approached Lord Vauden?'

'I . . . I don't have her papers to hand at this moment.'

Thornhill leaned a little closer. 'I don't believe you.' He knew he was towering over the old man, that there was an element of physical menace. 'So what's it to be, Mr Shipston?'

The solicitor sat back in his chair, widening the gap between himself and Thornhill. 'Was she – did she suffer much?'

'She was run over by a train.' Thornhill fought a desire to snatch the cigar and throw it out of the window. 'She also suffered a number of injuries before she died. I'm afraid I can't tell you more than that at present. Is there a will?'

Shipston nodded. He stretched out a shaking arm towards a bookcase behind the desk. There was a deed box on the top shelf. Breathing heavily, he lifted it on to the desk. The name CASWELL was stencilled in faded white paint on one end.

For a moment Thornhill assumed that Shipston must have got the box out of the firm's strongroom when he heard of his client's death. Then he noticed that the top of the bookcase was covered with dust, apart from the spot where the deed box had stood. Why would the old man keep Miss Caswell's deed box in his own office? He remembered Morgan's carefully chosen words.

*There is a tendency to behave erratically.*

Shipston unlocked the box with a key from his waistcoat pocket. He lifted the lid and took out a long envelope, from which he extracted the will. He glanced at Thornhill, still looming over him.

'I drew this up on her instructions in 1949,' Shipston said, his voice gaining in strength as he dealt with familiar things. 'There are two bequests – a ruby brooch to my wife, and the sum of two hundred and fifty pounds to myself.' He looked up at Thornhill. 'She insisted on that, Inspector, because she appreciated what I had done for her. But in point of fact, she did not have that sum of money available.'

'Who is the residuary legatee?'

'Miss Ethel Lindor. She is on the staff at Fontenoy Place, and Miss Caswell had found her most helpful over the years. But I am afraid that it will be a gesture of affection and gratitude, rather than anything more substantial.'

'I'd like to see the financial records. When the trust is wound up, who will receive the proceeds?'

There was no answer. Thornhill stared like an avenging deity at the bowed head of the old man. The grey, greasy hair needed cutting and brushing. The stiff collar was dirty. Flecks of dead skin were scattered like confetti on the shoulders of the black jacket. The cigar smouldered unheeded. Thornhill opened his mouth to point out that he had no time to waste.

A drop of water fell to the scuffed leather top of the desk. Thornhill, fascinated, stared at it in silence. Soon it was joined by another. Then by a third. They gleamed like stones wrenched out of their setting and forced to shine in isolation.

George Shipston was crying.

# Chapter Thirty-nine

Edith took the bus because the railway line was still closed. She knew Jack would have driven her over, but this was something she wanted to do by herself. The bus dropped her at Trenalt station. She was glad that she met no one who recognised her. Most of the other passengers from Lydmouth were going farther down the line. Those who boarded at Trenalt were strangers to her.

Edith glanced towards the mouth of the tunnel as she left the station yard. There were signs of activity – the screens covering the opening itself, a small crowd held at bay by a solitary police officer. She crossed the line and walked away from the village, taking the road to Highnam Cottage and Fontenoy Place.

Long before she reached them, however, she climbed over a stone stile set in the tall hedge running along the left-hand side of the road. At one time she had known these fields as well as she had known her grandmother's garden. Both she and they had changed in the interim, but there was still enough knowledge left for her to cut across to the footpath running from the quarry, the path she had taken less than twenty-four hours earlier with Jack and Miss Lindor.

She made her way up to the meadow by the quarry, moving warily, like a cat on strange territory. She met no one. When she reached the meadow, she circled its perimeter, partly to make sure that no one else was about and partly because she wanted to defer for as long as possible what might happen next. She glanced into the quarry, down at a stomach-lurching vista of scarred rock, scrubby bushes and weeds. It was much larger and deeper than she remembered.

Movement caught her eye. She looked up. A buzzard hovered, waiting to pounce. She wondered if its prey was, on some obscure level, aware of the menace above it. The skin on the back of her neck shivered, as though she herself were possibly at the mercy of a giant beak and a pair of talons. She thought briefly of Richard, who shouldn't have been a stranger but was, and of Jack, who should have been a stranger and wasn't.

She walked swiftly over to the hillock in the middle of the field. The edge of the oil drum was just visible, exactly where Jack had left it. Edith took a pair of gardening gloves from her basket and put them on. She pulled the rusting metal cylinder away from the heap of spoil.

She did not know whether to feel relieved or disappointed that the police had not found Miss Caswell's trousseau. Jack had left it reasonably well concealed and the police could have had no reason to search this area thoroughly. But life had given little of value to Miss Caswell, Edith thought, and the old woman deserved a little decent obscurity in death. That was another reason why she hadn't asked Jack for a lift. Whatever was in this trousseau might not be appropriate for him to see, let alone the police. Worse still, it might have made them laugh. Miss Caswell must have endured too much laughter in her long life.

She took out the drum's contents one by one, and laid them on the grass. Near the top was a muddy trowel with a few flakes of coloured paper sticking to it. A two-year-old copy of *The Times*, folded over to the crossword with one clue completed, had a partly used box of Swan Vesta matches lodged among its pages. There was a man's tie, red and yellow stripes now faded to shades of brown, with frayed ends, cheap and greasy. A brown-paper bag contained a broken pipe and two part-smoked cigars, at least one of which, Edith guessed, had once belonged to George Shipston.

A sense of urgency, first cousin to panic, made her hurry. Without bothering to examine them, she tossed on to the grass a man's shirt, white with blue stripes, without a collar; a green hat, nearly new, with a jaunty little feather in the brim; a large brown envelope; a paint-stained grey jersey inside which was something rectangular and hard; and two novels which apparently belonged to the county library service – both thrillers, one by Sapper and one by Sidney Horler.

Edith sat back on her heels and surveyed Miss Caswell's legacy. Not really a trousseau at all, she thought – more a series of presents for a man. For one man in particular. She picked up the envelope and shook out its contents, a photograph and a thin leather-bound pocketbook, its covers secured with a catch. The photograph was a studio shot of Rufus Moorcroft. He looked as she remembered him before the war. Younger than his years, very good-looking in that well-bred, understated English way.

Had Miss Caswell pored over it for hours? Had she kissed its monochrome perfection? Edith would burn it, she decided, that and the pocketbook. The hat and the trowel would be useful for someone, but everything else could be thrown away. Perhaps, she wondered with a gleam of humour, the hat would fit Jack.

She dropped the photograph back in the envelope and opened the pocketbook. There were several letters inside, and an Oxford bus ticket. The pages were in loose-leaf format, held in place by a ring binder, most of them covered with a small, spiky handwriting, some in ink and some indecipherably in pencil.

The best thing to do would be to make a bonfire when she got home and burn the lot.

As this was going through her mind, her hands laid out the

letters like playing cards on the grass, the address side of the envelopes upwards. There were five of them, all addressed in the same firm, square hand to Hugh Hudnall. Three had been sent to his father's house here at Trenalt, the fourth had gone to an address in Oxford, and the other to London.

Edith felt suddenly breathless, and the skin on her hands was clammy. This was a split second before the realisation was framed in her conscious mind. She recognised the writing in the pocketbook. She recognised the Greek 'd's and 'e's, and the small and misleadingly regular scrawl. She had seen it often enough on the play script. She thought she might even have seen the pocketbook itself. It had belonged to Hugh. Perhaps he had used it as a sort of journal. He might even have mentioned her in it. She wanted very badly to read it: to know what he had really thought about her. She shuffled the letters together and thrust them and the pocketbook back into the envelope. She tossed the envelope on to the striped shirt.

'Oh God,' she murmured, looking at the envelope as if it might at any moment explode in her face. 'Oh God.'

A movement registered at the edge of her field of vision. Shadows flickered on the sunlit grass. A shiver rippled over the back of her neck.

*The buzzard?*

She swung round with a gasp and looked up. The sun almost blinded her. She had been crouching for too long and her knees were aching. She could not make out who was standing there. The sun was a halo of unforgiving light behind the head of the newcomer. And in the same split second she felt both guilty and vulnerable.

Perhaps, she thought, perhaps I deserve to die?

# Chapter Forty

———◦◦◦———

At first Jill Francis thought the old man was drunk. She was tempted to veer on to one of the other paths that criss-crossed the Jubilee Park to avoid passing him. She had not run away from the office halfway through the morning to cope with other people's problems: she had enough of her own.

But there was no sign of a bottle on the bench or on the ground beside him. And he was rocking to and fro, as though in pain. Perhaps he was ill. Jill swore under her breath and walked briskly towards him.

'Are you all right?' she demanded, rather tetchily because she did not want to have to ask in the first place.

The old man raised his head and with a shock she realised she knew him. George Shipston stared mistily up at her, his face contorted in a frown that made him look like a dyspeptic gargoyle.

He failed to recognise her. 'No,' he said. 'There's nothing wrong. Please go away. I don't know who you are.'

'I'm Miss Francis. We met the other day at Mr Broadbent's office.'

He looked at her again. 'Miss Francis. Of course. I remember your cousins very well. That lovely house near Abergavenny . . .' His voice trailed away. He frowned as though puzzled by his own behaviour. 'You must excuse me.' He made a half-hearted attempt to stand up and then slumped back on the bench. 'I . . . I have recently had some bad news.'

'I'm so sorry, Mr Shipston.' Jill allowed intuition to guide her. 'Miss Caswell?'

He raised a grubby handkerchief to his face and wiped his eyes. 'She was too good for this world,' he said, and his sorrow made the cliché new again.

'I'm sure she was.'

'If people only knew what she did.'

'What sort of things?'

He looked up. 'She swore me to secrecy.' The lips quivered. 'No one else knew, not even Nurse Lindor. But there's no need for secrets now, is there?'

'I wouldn't have thought so.'

'Miss Caswell gave very generously to charity.' The old voice rose and fell in a tuneless singsong. 'She didn't want it known. The Church of England Children's Society. Dr Barnardo's. That sort of thing.'

'Children's charities,' Jill said. 'Was that it? Because of her baby?'

'Yes, yes.' Shipston flapped his hand feebly, as though waving away such an obvious question.

'But I thought her baby died.'

'Of course it did.' Shipston in his sorrow retained much of his normal manner. Yet it must have been the sorrow which made him talk like this. 'There was no doubt about it. I corresponded on the subject with the Caswells' family solicitor. Nevertheless, she thought it possible they might have lied to her, you see. She thought it was just possible that they had put the baby into an orphanage.'

Jill nodded gravely.

'The trouble was, there wasn't any money. Not for that sort of thing. Or rather not in the current account. So what could one do? She had the mildest manners of anyone I ever came across — the perfect lady — but she could be very imperious, you know. Blood will tell. Did you know that her maternal great-great-grandfather was the Duke of Kingston?'

'No,' Jill said, because it seemed to be a question that required an answer. 'I don't think I did.'

He was staring at her in a puzzled way. 'But we've met, haven't we? Councillor Broadbent introduced us the other day.'

'Yes. We mentioned it a moment ago.'

'Of course.' He made another half-hearted attempt to rise. 'You're Miss Francis, aren't you? I remember . . . That delightful house near Abergavenny. Delightful . . .'

'Don't get up, please.'

'Then won't you join me?' The old man shuffled a few inches along the bench. While he waited for Jill to sit down, the flame of social vitality subsided. 'But luckily the money *was* there,' Shipston went on. 'In a manner of speaking. The trust fund, you know. Lord Vauden was very understanding, of course, he signed everything I sent him. I'm sure he agreed, it was perfectly all right. Such a gentleman in the old style. One didn't need to spell these things out.'

'So you withdrew money from the capital invested in the trust fund to allow Miss Caswell to make charitable donations?' Jill said brightly. 'How — how splendid for her to know that the money was doing something useful.'

The frowning face turned towards her. 'Precisely, Miss Francis.' His expression softened into something alarmingly like a simper. 'They were all entirely reputable charities, I need hardly say. I made sure of that. There was a pathos about the situation, Miss Francis, which I confess I found very moving. Poor Miss Caswell. They say that Lord Salisbury was the father of her child, which was nonsense, of course. Some salacious journalist got hold of the wrong end of the stick. The man in question was a former groom of her father's, I understand. The blackguard took advantage of her innocence. Practically forced himself upon her, I've no doubt. They used to meet *in* Salisbury, however. So it wasn't the person, it was the place. That was how the mis-understanding arose. Strange how these misconceptions linger.'

Not the person, Jill thought, but the place?

She said, 'The donations – well, I'm sure Lord Vauden will understand.'

'That is where the difficulty lies, Miss Francis. Lord Vauden will of course understand. Indeed, as I say, I suspect a man of his acuity already has. But the police are another matter. They are, I'm afraid, a very vulgar set of men. They take a dark and as it were legalistic view of human nature. They can be trusted to interpret any action in the worst possible light. A detestable plainclothes officer has been dogging me, these last few days. Things have come to a pretty pass in this country.'

Not the place, Jill thought, but the person?

The old man shuffled his bottom to the edge of the bench and stood up with agonising slowness. Jill held her breath, waiting for him to topple backward on to the seat or forward on to the path but knowing that he would not want her to help him.

Swaying slightly, but free-standing, he looked down at Jill. 'Well, Miss Francis, thank you for listening to an old man.'

'What will you do?'

'Let events take their course. When you get to my age, that is not a difficult thing to do.'

'The money was Miss Caswell's. You did what she wanted with it.'

He nodded. 'You know that, Miss Francis, and so do I. So did Miss Caswell, I'm glad to say.' He raised his hat to her. 'I must go and face the music.'

The perpetual frown softened into something which might almost have been a smile. He tottered away down the path, leaning heavily on his stick. Jill watched him. How strange that such rampant snobbery should produce a devotion like Mr

Shipston's for Miss Caswell. Perhaps, too, they had been right: that helping orphans was a better use of Miss Caswell's money than swelling the bank balances of cousins who had had nothing to do with her while she was alive. She doubted whether Richard Thornhill would agree with her. She wondered what had happened to the groom in Salisbury. Who had exploited whom? Perhaps they had simply been in love with each other.

*Not the place, but the person?*

George Shipston was no longer in sight. Jill watched children playing on the swings and the slide fifty yards away. Their shrill cries stirred feelings she did not want to have. In her own kitchen was a Barnardo's collecting box in the shape of a papier-mâché cottage; and it was her private superstition to stuff at least one coin in the slot every day, a votive offering for the Furies.

There and then, she at last made up her mind.

She could not stay in Lydmouth. Now that Ivor Fuggle and Amy Gwyn-Thomas had wind of her friendship with Richard, it would be too dangerous. Not just for her – after all, she could always move away – but for Richard and Edith. She knew herself well enough to understand that she could not stay in Lydmouth and not see Richard, and she thought he would find it equally impossible not to see her.

The alternative, she had thought, was that she and Richard could go away together. But now she realised that it was not really an alternative at all. She would be shackled for ever to guilt, to the knowledge that she had ruined the lives of Edith and the children. She thought that it was possible that she would ruin Richard's life, as well. He was a man too used professionally to being in the right to take kindly to being in the wrong. She could not imagine him without his job.

So she would accept Randolph's offer and go back to London.

Now the decision was made, she knew that it was the right one. Common sense and common decency pointed her in the same direction. Leaving Lydmouth, by herself, would be better for her and for everyone else. Sadness was easier to bear than guilt. Randolph Haughton had made it almost absurdly easy for her – she would be going to a job that she wanted to do, with somewhere to live and an entire social circle waiting for her. No doubt about it, of course it was the right decision.

Then why, she wondered, as she sat in the sunshine looking out at the green hills beyond Lydmouth, did she feel nothing but a terrible desolation?

# Chapter Forty-one

*Not the person, but the place.*

Now that it no longer mattered very much, Jill had the ghost of an idea. No one had taken much notice of what Miss Caswell had said. But sometimes it is not easy to distinguish madness from eccentricity. Suppose that behind her ramblings had lurked a sort of sense, elliptical and allusive, but perfectly rational for all that.

*Not the person, but the place? Or the other way around?*

Jill walked quickly from Jubilee Park down to the High Street. She went to the library and checked a volume in the Famous Trials series. What she found supported what she suspected, but it was still a long way from proof. This was not a crossword puzzle. One needed more than correspondences, more than cryptic hints.

She went back to the office. Miss Gwyn-Thomas was on the phone. When she saw Jill, she started, blushed and slammed down the receiver.

'There was a telephone call from a Mr Haughton, Miss Francis. He wanted you to know that he's taken a room at the Bull.'

'Is he there now?'

'I'm sure I couldn't say.'

Jill went into the editor's room, closing the door behind her. She wasn't surprised that Randolph had had enough of the bucolic charms of Trenalt. Perhaps Lydmouth had become more attractive recently, too. She found the number of Fontenoy Place and rang up. The phone was answered by a man with a precise voice, who sounded as though he made a habit of opening his lips as little as possible when talking. Jill asked if she could talk to Nurse Lindor.

'I'm afraid that won't be possible. Staff are not permitted to receive personal calls except in emergencies.'

'This is important.'

'We have our rules, I'm afraid.'

'May I speak to the Director?'

'I am the Director.'

Dr Angmer grudgingly agreed to pass on Jill's name and telephone number to Nurse Lindor. Jill did not mention where she worked.

She put down the receiver and sat back in her chair. There was another way to approach this. She dialled Bernie Broadbent's office. Freda, his secretary, confirmed what Jill had already suspected, that Bernie had taken the day off. She phoned him at home. The phone rang on and on. She imagined the sound of the bell filling the great white house on Narth Road. Suddenly it occurred to her that if she had said yes rather than no, that house might have been her home. But the thought made her shiver. Just as she was about to give up, the receiver was lifted at the other end.

'Yes,' Bernie said.

'It's me, Jill.'

'Well, it's nice to hear you, as always, but I'm rather tied up at present and—'

'Bernie, would you do me a favour?'

There was a silence at the other end. Bernie was a generous man when he was in the mood, but the granting of favours was something he took very seriously. And, of course, for all she knew he might literally be tied up. Men had such extraordinary tastes.

'What is it? Can it wait?'

'I need to talk to someone called Nurse Lindor at Fontenoy Place. The Director won't put me through to her. So I wondered if you could help. They've asked you to be a trustee, haven't they?'

'Who told you that?'

Jill's stomach lurched as she realised her mistake. Richard had told her when they met last night. She said, 'You know journalists never reveal their sources.'

There was another silence at the end of the line. Then Jill heard something in the background — something which might have been a man laughing.

'Bernie? Are you still there?'

'Of course I am.' He sounded breathless, but to her relief he did not enquire further about the identity of her source. 'Look, Jill, what exactly are you asking me to do? I can't ring Dr Angmer and say would you mind if this friend of mine comes and has a chat with one of your members of staff. He'd want to know why, and I wouldn't blame him.'

'What about if you went there? The place is practically under siege at present, but he'd let you in. And if there was someone else in the car with you, he could hardly turn them away.'

'Why do you want to go?'

She sensed he was weakening, if only because she had aroused his curiosity. 'Something to do with Miss Caswell. I've got an idea and I want to see if it holds water.'

'About how she died?'

'Not really — not yet. It's more that I think I may be able to make sense of something she said.'

'That's more than I can do with you at present.'

'The thing is, Nurse Lindor may know more than she thinks she does.'

Bernie grunted on the other end of the line. 'Let me phone you back in five minutes. Where are you? At the office?'

A moment later, she rang off. She selected a cigarette from her case. Through the door came the industrious tapping of the keys of Miss Gwyn-Thomas's typewriter. There was work piling up but for once it did not seem important. One day soon, she promised herself, she would learn to be sensible. The telephone rang and she snatched the receiver.

'Jill?' Bernie said. 'Yes, I can take you there. But can we do it soon? I – I've got an appointment for lunch which I'd rather not break.'

'The sooner the better.'

'We'll pick you up in ten minutes, then.'

'We?'

'Your friend Randolph Haughton. I've been having a look at his car.'

He rang off. Jill just had time to powder her nose and delegate as many of her responsibilities as possible before the Bristol drew up outside the *Gazette*'s office. Haughton was in the driving seat. Bernie climbed out and was about to squeeze his bulk into the cramped rear seats. Jill laid a hand on his arm.

'Let me go in the back. Then people will think I'm your secretary or something.'

'What's all this about? Catching spies?'

She smiled at him. 'Frightfully hush-hush, Bernie.'

Randolph turned round and stared approvingly at her as she settled in the back of the car. 'You're looking lovely. I do like the hat.'

So did Jill, but it was nice to have her opinion confirmed by someone else. She said, 'Tell me, is that offer still open?'

'The job? Yes, of course.'

'Then I'd like to accept.'

'Splendid. We must celebrate.' Haughton glanced at Bernie and added, 'Later.'

'Shame you're leaving us,' Bernie said. There was no surprise in his voice and Jill guessed that Randolph must have told him. 'When are you going?'

'As soon as possible.' She pushed away the thought of Richard. 'I don't want to leave the Wemyss-Browns in the lurch with the *Gazette*, of course. But anything I can do there, Philip can do twice as well, so it shouldn't be a problem.'

'Good,' Randolph said, letting out the clutch. 'So we're going to Trenalt?'

'Not a bad thing to do in any case,' Bernie said. 'I want to have a word with Angmer.'

'About being a trustee?' Jill asked.

Bernie craned his head round to look at her. 'Someone's got to do it. This business with Miss Caswell isn't going to do them much good. They'll need all the help they can get. I've been asking around. From what I can gather, most of the real work was done by Rufus Moorcroft and George Shipston between them.'

'I'm not sure how much longer Mr Shipston will be doing it.'

'Oh aye?' Bernie's eyes were bright with intelligence. 'Well, we all have to retire some time. No one's indispensable.'

They were out of the town now, and Randolph took the turning up into the hills. They overtook a saloon car just before a bend. Jill noticed Bernie and Randolph exchanging glances and caught the complicity of shared pleasure.

'There's so much power here,' Randolph said. 'One can do almost anything with her. Extraordinarily liberating, eh?'

Bernie nodded.

Jill wondered if they were talking about the car or something else.

They drove through the village and turned down to the station. At the level-crossing, Jill looked up the line. Two uniformed officers were removing the screens from the mouth of the tunnel. The crowd had dispersed. The Bristol climbed effortlessly up the other side of the valley. The early morning sunshine had gone. Cloud cover was creeping in from the south-west.

'I phoned ahead, by the way,' Bernie said. 'Angmer knows I'm coming.'

The car swept past the driveway to Highnam Cottage. There was another part of the jigsaw, Jill thought, though she was not sure where it fitted in. She had a sudden, dizzying vision of people's lives as a huge network of intersecting lines, a multi-dimensional tapestry stretching through time and space. In some places the fabric was tangled, knotted, stained or torn. How could one ever hope to know where one life ended and another began? Or – here in this seemingly gentle valley – where one death was linked with another?

The Bristol drew up in front of the gates of Fontenoy Place. The gatekeeper peered at Bernie, touched his cap and opened the gates for them. The car rolled up the drive.

'Pretty,' Randolph Haughton said approvingly when the house came into sight. 'Rather like my Uncle Claude's place in Leicestershire.'

'Wouldn't like it myself,' Bernie said. 'Not these days. More trouble than they're worth, these old barracks.'

Randolph smiled at him. 'Then you must see my flat. You're bound to like it – everything's frightfully modern and convenient and labour-saving.'

Jill would have liked to have told them to be careful. Surely what was so obvious to her would be obvious to others?

The car glided to a halt on the gravelled area in front of the house. Three old ladies, sitting on a stone bench set in the balustrade, watched them as they left the car. By the steps up to the front door was a very old man in a wheelchair.

'All this coming and going,' he said. 'There's no need for it. Why can't people stop fussing? I shall complain to Dr Angmer.'

Jill smiled at him as she passed and inclined her head,

acknowledging that she had heard what he had said. He ignored her. She followed Bernie and Randolph up the steps.

'But it's smaller than Uncle Claude's,' Randolph was saying. 'About two-thirds of the size, I'd say.'

'My mam used to say it was rude to boast,' Bernie murmured, pulling the knob of the doorbell.

When the maid answered the door, Bernie asked for Dr Angmer.

'If you don't mind,' Randolph said, 'I think I might stretch my legs. Have a look at the park.'

'Much smaller than Uncle Claude's, I'll be bound,' Bernie said. 'Fine – shouldn't be long.' He winked at Jill, which gave her a shock, and added for the benefit of the maid, 'My secretary can go with you if she wants. She needs the exercise.'

The maid led Bernie away. Randolph and Jill strolled outside.

'He's absolutely gorgeous,' Randolph muttered to her.

'You be careful,' Jill said.

'Oh, I will, dear.'

'You're making him positively skittish.'

'I'm glad to hear it. Now, is there anything I can do or would you like me to fade into the scenery?'

'I think I'm better by myself, thanks.'

Randolph smiled at her. He lit a cigarette and sauntered away.

Jill asked the old man in the wheelchair where she could find Nurse Lindor and was rewarded with a glare.

'Nurse who? Never bothered to learn their names. They all look the same to me.'

The three old ladies were more helpful. Nurse Lindor was one of the members of staff supervising Swedish exercises in the ballroom. The youngest of the trio, leaning heavily on Jill's arm, guided her into the house by a pair of French windows and took her down to a cavernous extension where six women and one man were stretching their limbs at the command of a middle-aged woman resembling a regimental sergeant-major. Two nurses sat knitting on a sofa beside the window.

'I used to do Swedish exercises myself,' Jill's guide told her. 'We had two sessions in those days, one for ladies, one for gentlemen. But then Dr Angmer combined them. It's not right, is it? God made us different, and nothing Dr Angmer can do can change that. Several of us walked out in protest. The one on the left is Lindor.'

The nurse looked up from her knitting as Jill approached. Her brown, wrinkled face was like a wooden mask.

'Miss Lindor?' Jill held out her hand. 'My name's Miss Francis.'

The older woman ignored the offered hand. 'Who?'

'I've just come with Councillor Broadbent.' Jill's conscience gave her the smallest of twinges at the way she had avoided answering the question. 'He's with Dr Angmer now. I wondered if we could have a word in private.'

'What about?'

Jill lowered her voice so the other nurse could not hear. 'Miss Caswell.'

There was still no change of expression. With slow, deliberate movements, Nurse Lindor folded up her knitting, placed it carefully in a bag made of chintz material with wooden handles, and rose to her feet.

'And stretch,' said the regimental sergeant-major behind Jill. 'No, to the *right*, Mrs Scowle, not the left.'

Nurse Lindor led the way outside. Without a word to Jill, she went down a flight of steps to a sunken lawn. She sat down on a bench set into the retaining wall. Jill joined her.

'She liked Bernie Broadbent, Miss Caswell did,' Nurse Lindor said in a casual voice, as though resuming a conversation. 'Funny that: she was always very clear about who she liked and who she didn't.'

The walnut-shell face revealed nothing. But something had changed.

Jill said, 'I'm sorry.'

'Why? You didn't know her.'

'But people I know did. Bernie for one.' She groped for names. 'Mr Haughton. Mrs Thornhill.'

Nurse Lindor snorted. 'No better than she should be, that one. I've seen her with—' She broke off and looked sharply at Jill. 'She's a kind woman, though. Miss Caswell was fond of her. She was a good judge of people, in her own way.'

Jill filed away that hesitation for further consideration. She went on: 'I – I've talked to various people, and everyone says that you were the one who knew her best.'

'That's as may be.'

'There are things that she did and said in the last day or two of her life that seem hard to understand. I know people say that's only to be expected, that she was . . . a little eccentric.'

'They say worse things than that, miss. I've heard them. She was a little queer, I grant you, but anyone would be after the life she'd had. No harm in it, though. But I don't see why I should sit here gossiping about her to you.'

'Because you want to know how she died. And why. So do I.'

'What's it to you? Who *are* you?'

'I work for the *Lydmouth Gazette*.'

'One of them reporters? Like that horrible man last night?'

'No,' Jill said very firmly. 'I assume you mean Ivor Fuggle of the *Evening Post*. I'm not in the least like him. I just want people to know the truth about what happened. I don't think Miss Caswell died by accident.'

'That's what I said all along. She'd never go into that tunnel by herself. And now they're saying she fell on the line. Fell! Pushed, more like.'

'Exactly. But can you help me prove it?'

Lindor stared at her for a moment. She sniffed. 'All right. Ask away. But I'm not saying I'll answer, mind.'

'I know the police were trying to find out about a phone call on Tuesday evening. Miss Caswell used the phone box in the village – Mr Broadbent lent her the money. They think she was trying to ring somebody called Constance who lived in Kent.'

'She didn't know anyone called Constance. Nobody in Kent, either. She didn't know *anyone*, I tell you, except the people here. Oh, I know she had all those fancy relations, but they didn't give a thought to her, or her to them, from one year to the next.'

'She came from Wiltshire originally, didn't she?'

Nurse Lindor nodded.

'I wonder if it was somewhere near the village of Rode?'

'I'm sure I couldn't say.'

'It's just that, if she did, that might explain why Mrs Solly thought she said that Constance lived near the road. Not the road. Just Rode, perhaps.'

Nurse Lindor puffed up her cheeks and then let out a breath of air. 'You might be right. The things she said often made sense if you knew how to understand them.'

'I wonder – would it be possible to see her room?'

'Why?'

'Because I'm trying to understand what made her tick, I suppose.'

Nurse Lindor looked down at the paving stones at the base of the bench. Then, to Jill's surprise, she said, 'I can't see any harm in it. But I can't spare long. It'll soon be lunchtime, and some of my old dears will need tidying up beforehand.'

She led Jill back into the house by a side door. They went up a flight of back stairs and Jill soon lost her sense of direction in a labyrinth of landings, further stairs and unexpected vistas. They walked down a corridor where all the doors were ajar, except the one at the end. Nurse Lindor produced a key from her pocket and pushed it into the lock.

'Dr Angmer took away the key,' she said. 'No one's told him that all the keys on this floor fit all the locks. And he hasn't the wit to work it out for himself. He's got all those letters after his name, that man, yet he's as foolish as a newborn babe.'

She twisted the handle and pushed open the door. Jill followed her into the small, sunlit room. She knew what to expect from Richard. Nevertheless it took her by surprise. Small, clean, neat and sweet-smelling, it seemed vividly personal. Miss Caswell might have been here five minutes earlier. Indeed, in one sense, she hadn't really left.

Jill felt her eyes fill with tears for a woman she'd never known. She told herself not to be mawkish and moved round the room, while Nurse Lindor stood like a sentry in the doorway. Jill knew there were limits to the licence which had been afforded her: she did not pull back the coverlet or pry in the drawers. Instead, she looked at the pictures on the wall, admired the view from the window and glanced at the spines of the library books.

*My Bygone Times.* She picked up the fat green book from the table and opened it at random. As she riffled through the pages, names sprang out at her: Swindon, Wootton Bassett, Devizes, Wilton, Salisbury. *Salisbury.* She glanced at the title page. *My Bygone Times: Memories of a Country Childhood,* by G. H. Anstruther-Marsh, JP, MA (Cantab).

Her pulse quickened. Turning to the index, she ran her finger down the 'I's, the 'J's and the 'K's until she came to *Kent, Constance.*

'I need to be downstairs in a moment, miss.'

'I'm so sorry.' Jill turned with a smile. 'I shan't be a tick – I just need to look something up.'

Nurse Lindor nodded, mollified by the manner rather than the words.

Jill turned back to the book, back to *Kent, Constance:* 298. When she reached the page, she was not surprised to find that the corner was turned down. It was almost as if Miss Caswell were prompting her. Her eyes skimmed down the black blocks of text.

*. . . I was much taken up at this time with my plans for a trip up the Nile with my friend the Honourable Alfred Caswell (later the fifth Lord Fullerton after the death of his elder brother the fourth viscount in 1891).*

*That year there was much talk of the Kent case, one of the most celebrated murder trials of the century. I blush to confess that like other young men in our neighbourhood, though naturally deploring the cause, I felt that our brush with notoriety was a mark of distinction on our locality. The murder took place not five miles away from us, at Road (or Rode) near the Somerset border. My parents knew Mr and Mrs Kent by sight. Mr Kent was an Inspector of Factories. Perhaps in an attempt to improve his standing in the county, he encouraged an absurd rumour that he was the illegitimate son of the Duke of Kent, father of our dear Queen.*

*My friend Lord Fullerton (as he later became) assured me that there was no truth in this story about Mr Kent's parentage. He suspected the man had invented it himself to lend a sense of importance to his position. Few people of any standing would visit the Kents, he told me, because of irregularities in Mr Kent's private life.*

*In June 1860, Mr Kent's four-year-old son Francis was found one morning in an outhouse with his throat cut from ear to ear. The boy's half-sister, Constance, was arrested for the crime but subsequently released for lack of evidence. A nursemaid, perhaps the mistress of her employer, was also arrested and then released. The police were unable to bring the case to a successful conclusion. Afterwards, Constance became inclined towards religion. I do not know whether she actually took the veil; but she certainly lived in seclusion among religious people, first in France and later in Brighton.*

*All this changed, however, in April 1865. Of her own accord, and in the company of a curate, Miss Constance Kent went before the Magistrates at Bow Street and confessed that she had indeed murdered her brother. She appears to have been an unbalanced young woman, jealous of the attention afforded to the children of her stepmother. Nonetheless, there seems no doubt that she had repented sincerely of this most heinous crime.*

*The reader will readily imagine that her sudden confession resuscitated interest in the case, locally as well as in the country at large. My friend*

*Caswell and I, however, had other matters on our mind. At last the day of our departure for Egypt dawned. Few of my readers will remember what it was like to . . .*

'Come along, miss,' Nurse Lindor said firmly. 'I can't wait all day.'

Jill returned the book to the little pile on the table and followed Nurse Lindor out of the room.

'Did you find what you were looking for?' Nurse Lindor asked as they were walking along the landing.

'I found something.'

'Whatever it is won't bring her back. But she didn't get in that tunnel by herself, I'll tell you that.' She stopped so abruptly that Jill cannoned into her. 'And I'll help anyone who can find out who it was. And once I know . . .'

'What?' Jill asked.

'Well, if the police won't deal with them, I will. You want to talk to Mrs Thornhill. I reckon she knows more than she's letting on, her and Mr Moorcroft's nephew. She's up there now, you know. I saw her.'

Nurse Lindor set off again with Jill almost running behind her.

'Mrs Thornhill?' Jill said breathlessly. 'She's up where?'

'Up on the hill near the quarry, of course.' Nurse Lindor looked at Jill. The face no longer seemed like a mask: the lines were cracks that revealed the emotions swirling like lava beneath, the pain, the anger, the need to lash out. 'With her fancy man, I've no doubt, poking around in Miss Caswell's things. Nothing I could do about it because Miss Caswell gave them to her. Didn't give me anything, but what does that matter?'

# Chapter Forty-two

'I *knew* there'd be something.' The woman's face was a dark oval against its halo of sunshine. 'She always liked this place.'

Still crouching, her knees protesting at the strain, Edith said, 'Who – who are you?'

'I am right, though, aren't I? This is Miss Caswell's stuff, isn't it?'

'Yes, but—'

'It's funny to see you after all this time. Edith Broadbent.'

At almost the same moment, a cloud slipped across the disc of the sun. Edith's eyes adjusted. Looming over her was a large, heavy-featured woman. Both the face and the voice were faintly familiar.

'Thornhill now,' Edith said automatically, scrambling to her feet. As she did so, she pushed the folds of the blue-striped shirt over the envelope.

'I met your husband yesterday. The policeman.'

The memory slipped into Edith's mind. 'June. How . . . how are you?'

'As well as can be expected, I suppose.' Mrs Loysey gestured at the oil drum, now lying on its side on the grass. 'So is that where she kept it?'

'I'm sorry – kept what?'

'This stuff.'

'Did she tell you about it, then?' Edith felt unexpectedly jealous. 'Her trousseau?'

'Her——? Oh, yes. She mentioned it the other day. And she told me it was up here, in the field by the quarry where we had that awful picnic. Do you remember it?'

'When did she tell you?'

'At Rufus Moorcroft's funeral.'

Edith blurted out, 'But you weren't there.'

'You're mistaken. I was.' June Loysey hunched her shoulders as if to make herself seem smaller than she was. Even so, she was several inches taller than Edith and several stone heavier. 'I'll just have a look through, if you don't mind,' she went on, and the words came out as a threat. 'Actually, I think the old woman may have made off with something that wasn't hers.'

Without looking at Edith, she knelt beside the oil drum and pawed through the contents of Miss Caswell's trousseau. Her hands were large and red, with nails bitten down to the quick. She seized the pork-pie hat.

'That's Gareth's!' For an instant June looked almost happy. 'Why on earth would she want that?'

Next, she found the bundle wrapped in the grey jersey. She pulled apart the knotted sleeves, revealing a battered music case made of cracked leather. There was a monogram in faded gilt letters on the flap: C.P.C. June tore the case open. Edith glimpsed something green inside.

'Ah,' said June, breathing out the sound as her fingers fumbled with the case. Then she sucked in air. 'No,' she whispered, 'no, *please*.'

'What's wrong?' Edith said.

June held up a green wooden rectangle: a small picture frame with a ragged border of canvas running round its inner edge. 'Oh my God,' she said. 'I can't believe it. I simply can't believe it. The silly cow.'

'But what is it?'

'There was a painting by Gareth in that frame. One of his best. The bloody woman's cut it out. She probably burned it.'

'*Lady with Fan?*'

'How do you know?'

'My . . . my husband told me.'

'Was it him?' June stood up slowly, the pork-pie hat in her hand. 'Or was it Jack Graig?'

Edith tried to laugh. 'Whatever gave you that idea, Mrs Loysey?'

'He's in love with you, isn't he, just as he used to be.'

'Oh, nonsense.'

June snarled, 'Don't play the innocent, you little tart.'

'I beg your—'

'That's the difference between then and now. It used to be Hugh you were after. But now it's Jack. He's got Moorcroft's money, I suppose that's the attraction.'

'I know you're upset, Mrs Loysey, but there's no call for—'

'I was at Highnam Cottage.'

'You were *where?*'

'You heard. And I heard you two billing and cooing yesterday. I was looking for the picture, as it happened. So I parked behind Fontenoy Place and came along the footpath. The skies opened, and I nearly bumped into that Lindor woman. I just had time to look in the summerhouse when I heard you two coming over the lawn. So I dived into the shrubbery. What I heard and saw was quite disgusting.'

She paused to linger on the horror of it. In that moment, Edith remembered what she and Jack had talked about when they were standing by the summerhouse. She had mentioned Miss Caswell's things in the field by the quarry: so that was how June had known where to look, that was why she was here.

'Then the pair of you went back to the house,' June went on

with a whinnying snuffle like an excited horse. 'And I can imagine what happened there.'

Edith looked away. Her legs trembled and she would have liked to have sat down.

'That's shaken you,' June observed with obvious satisfaction. 'I came up here, of course, but I couldn't find it, and it was awkward with all those policemen about. So I came back this morning for another look. I wondered if I might find you here as well.'

'I don't understand. What happened to the picture? How did Miss Caswell get it?'

'She commissioned Gareth to do it – you remember? That summer before the war? Then she gave it to Rufus Moorcroft. But after he died, somebody stole it. I guessed it was Miss Caswell. You know what she was like about Rufus. Who else could it have been?'

'Mr Moorcroft might have burned it.'

'In that case what's the frame doing here? Anyway, she admitted as much to me when I saw her.'

June broke off. Between the two women was an unspoken question. *At the funeral?*

But despite what she claimed June Loysey had not been at the funeral, Edith thought, which meant that she must have talked to Miss Caswell at some other time.

June said, in a rush: 'Either Miss Caswell destroyed it or Rufus did – what does it matter? The point is, it's gone for ever.'

A moment later, and much to her embarrassment, Edith realised that June was crying.

'You mustn't mind so much,' she began.

'But Gareth will be furious,' June wailed, clutching the pork-pie hat to her breasts. 'It was so important to get it back – there's a man who needs it for a big exhibition. Gareth'll be so upset. He's like a little boy sometimes. When he wants something badly, nothing else matters.'

The urge to comfort is as powerful as it is irrational. Hand outstretched, Edith took a step towards June. Her foot lodged in an armhole of the striped shirt and pulled it a few inches along the ground.

'So she got that too?' June said in quite a different voice.

Edith glanced down, following the direction of June's eyes. The brown envelope was now in full view.

'She must have taken the hat at the same time,' June went on. 'They were both on the back seat of the car.'

Edith dived down and picked up the envelope. '*When* did she do this? And where?'

'What does it matter? Just give me the envelope, will you? It's mine.'

Edith moved a step away. 'It does matter. Miss Caswell hardly ever left Trenalt. So that almost certainly means that you must have been here.'

'I was. I told you – at the funeral.'

'But I was at the funeral. You weren't.'

There was a silence. June cleared her throat. 'Well, yes – as a matter of fact I did come over a week or so ago. I drove over one evening to see the old place. A sort of sentimental journey.'

'With that envelope,' said Edith slowly.

June ran her tongue along her lips. 'That envelope belongs to me, dear. There are one or two family mementoes in it. Nothing to do with anyone else. When I was in Trenalt, I called to see Mr Moorcroft about the painting. But – unfortunately he wasn't in. While I was knocking on the door, Miss Caswell must have stolen the envelope and the hat from the back of the car. It's as simple as that. You know how she always haunted Highnam Cottage. Now, may I please have my property back?'

'Are you sure you didn't see Miss Caswell?'

'No, of course not. Please, Edith, I'm awfully tired, and I know Gareth will be worried if I don't get home soon. Just give me the envelope and—'

'The White Rabbit,' Edith said.

'What are you talking about?'

Edith frowned, trying to remember what Gareth Loysey looked like. Big teeth, large ears. 'When I met Miss Caswell at Mr Moorcroft's funeral, she was trying to remember the name of the woman who married the White Rabbit. She thought it might be Constance.'

'I don't know anyone called Constance.'

'According to Mr Moorcroft's housekeeper, Miss Caswell wanted to telephone the woman called Constance. The woman who was married to the White Rabbit. And she borrowed some money from my cousin Bernie and used the public phone box. That was on Tuesday evening. Was it you she phoned?'

'Oh, don't be absurd. You're a sensible, married woman these days, not a silly eighteen-year-old mooning after Hugh.'

Edith felt a chill of anger and let it brace her. 'Suppose she saw you in Trenalt the week before, on the Monday evening? When you came over to see Mr Moorcroft, to ask for that painting. On your *sentimental journey*. And a few hours after you saw him, he killed himself. Why would he do that?'

June lowered her head between her shoulders and drew her thick eyebrows together. 'You can't go around making insinuations like that. I . . . I could have you prosecuted. He killed himself because he was old and lonely – there's no mystery there.'

'But why would he kill himself *now*? Unless you'd told him you'd make sure the whole world knew what was in this envelope.'

'That's a lie.' Swaying, June took a step towards Edith, and then jerked herself upwards as though trying to regain her balance. 'I did mention to Mr Moorcroft that I'd found some letters he'd written to my brother. And I wondered if he might like to have them back. I didn't like to take them in and show him, in case – well, you know what men can be like. Impulsive. But anyway, I suggested he might like to lend us the painting for

the exhibition, and perhaps make a small loan to tide us over –
things haven't been easy since we moved down here. Gareth
needs to be comfortable or else he can't work properly. All I was
proposing was a sensible, simple business arrangement between
friends. Only a *loan*. There was never any threat that I'd show
anyone else what was in the letters and the diary––'

'He killed himself,' Edith said. 'He burned all his papers,
took some sleeping pills and some whisky and just waited to die.
Why?'

*Because it's what people do when they don't want to give in to a blackmailer.*

'How should I know? Nothing to do with me.'

Edith clutched the envelope to her. June Loysey had gone to
see Rufus Moorcroft and a few hours later Rufus was dead. Her
thoughts seethed like a panic-stricken crowd. Perhaps Rufus had
not been the only victim of a blackmailer.

There had been two sets of footsteps running down to
Trenalt station on that rainy evening in August 1938. Less than
an hour later Hugh had been dead, his body mangled almost
beyond recognition by the train which had hit him. A possibility
stirred, so monstrous she recoiled from it – only to find there
was another, equally horrible idea in her mind: what about Miss
Caswell? How had she died?

'Listen, Edith, I can explain,' June said gruffly. 'It's all quite
simple. Miss Caswell rang up out of the blue on the evening of
Rufus's funeral. You're right – she'd seen me at Highnam
Cottage and she'd recognised me. There was a photograph of
me with Gareth in the *Gazette* a few months back. She'd seen that
and knew we were living near by.' She squeezed her eyes shut for
a second and rubbed her forehead. 'She wanted to talk to me
because she knew I'd seen Rufus on the night he died. She
wanted me to tell her what had been worrying him. And she said
she had something of mine, or rather not mine – Gareth's.' She
pointed at the hat which was lying on the ground. 'His name's
inside the brim. You can check, if you want.'

'So you met her on Wednesday evening?'

'No! No, I didn't. I couldn't get away. You might as well let me have that envelope now. It's no use to anyone.'

'Then how did Miss Caswell die?'

'How should I know?' June's voice was rising. 'I don't want to have to tell your husband about you and Jack Graig. But if I have to, I will. It won't do his career much good, will it? And have you got kiddies? Think of the effect it would have on them.'

Edith shook her head. She could find no words to say.

'Just give me that envelope, will you?' June screamed. 'It's mine.'

She began to lumber towards Edith, like a bull building up speed. They were alone on the top of the hill, with the sky arching over them. The meadow around them was empty. The grass itself seemed frozen in time. Nothing else moved except the buzzard still wheeling in slow motion above the quarry.

'No,' Edith said, 'no, no, no.' And she said it for Rufus as well as for herself, and for Hugh and Miss Caswell.

June Loysey charged. Still holding her husband's pork-pie hat, she blundered through the long grass towards Edith. Her face was red but calm and serious. In the split second before she started running herself, Edith thought that there must be a mistake, that really June intended to play some childish game with her.

June was almost on top of her now. Edith dodged an outstretched arm and ran. The other woman was between her and most of the field. Edith could run only towards the quarry. But she was younger than June, probably fitter and certainly lighter. She sprinted along the ruined fence separating the meadow from the edge of the quarry. Behind her she heard pounding feet and heavy breathing. She could not spare the energy to look round, but she thought she was increasing the distance between herself and her pursuer.

Until disaster happened.

Her right foot caught in a length of rusting wire, a fragment from the derelict fence. She screamed as she pitched forward, her momentum pushing her down to the ground with a shock that forced the breath from her lungs. As she fell, she flung out her right arm and released the grip of her fingers.

The brown envelope sliced through the air, turning as it went. It landed on the very edge of the quarry. For an instant it seemed to tremble on the brink. June ran past Edith, the ground shaking beneath her tread, her arms groping forwards as though imploring mercy.

The envelope quivered and slid out of sight.

June reached the edge of the quarry. Edith tried to get up but pain shot up her right leg from the ankle.

June looked back. Her face was so red and distorted it was almost unrecognisable. She lay prone on the side of the quarry, swivelled inelegantly and dropped her legs down. She wriggled over the edge. All the time she stared at Edith.

'No,' Edith said. 'No, June, no.'

From the blue distance above them came the sad squealing cry of the buzzard.

# Chapter Forty-three

'Dear God, man,' the Deputy Chief Constable said. 'You look even worse than you did yesterday.'

'Haven't been sleeping that well, sir.'

'Get the quack to give you some pills, then.' Drake shot out his cuffs and admired their pristine whiteness. 'I daresay this Caswell business isn't helping. I'm seeing Mr Hendry just before lunch, so you'd better bring me up to date. And sit down. You look as though you need every bit of rest you can get.'

Thornhill subsided into a chair. He summarised the results of the autopsy and the findings of the scene-of-crime team. 'So we think someone else was involved in her death. It was the train that actually killed her, of course, probably when she was trying to crawl out towards the light. Dr Murray thinks that she probably spent the night drifting in and out of consciousness. She'd only managed to crawl a few yards from the refuge. It's not easy to tell where she was when the train hit her. But she may have collapsed over the rail.'

'I hope to God she was unconscious when it hit her.' Drake stood up and walked over to the window; he was a man who liked to think on his feet. He stared down at the street and then back at Thornhill. 'I don't understand it. What was this other person up to? If they wanted to kill Miss Caswell, why didn't they just go ahead and do it? Alternatively, if it was an accident, why didn't they call for help?'

'Assuming she was pushed from the parapet of the tunnel, it's possible that the person who did it believed she was dead. As it was, she was obviously badly hurt, and almost certainly unconscious. Her attacker might have thought it a good idea to hide the body in the tunnel. To delay its discovery.'

'We are sure that someone else was involved?' Drake pressed.

'Everything points to it, sir. The marks in the tunnel, Miss Caswell being up the tunnel in the refuge, even the angle she fell.'

Drake raised his eyebrows. 'I don't follow.'

'If she jumped from the parapet of her own accord, Murray said he would have expected her to go feet foremost. So she'd break both legs to start with. If she'd been feeling really suicidal, she might have dived. So that would have been head first. But the pattern of the injuries suggests that she went down at an angle. He reckons that makes it more likely she was struggling when she went over.'

'I don't like this,' Drake said, turning back to the window. 'There's nothing to get your teeth into. No shape to it. Too many ifs and buts. What about motive?'

Thornhill shook his head. 'We haven't really got one. The only person who benefits financially is Nurse Lindor at Fontenoy Place. As far as we can see, she stands to inherit Miss Caswell's jewellery. Rather to everyone's surprise, there's quite a lot of it and it may be quite valuable. George Shipston has been embezzling her trust fund for years, it turns out, but not for personal gain: he'd been doing it for her, so she could play Lady Bountiful to various children's charities. That portrait of hers, the one Moorcroft had, still hasn't turned up.'

'Moorcroft.' Drake walked back to his desk and drummed his fingertips on its leather top. 'Everything comes back to him, doesn't it?'

'Including the death of Hugh Hudnall in 1938.'

Drake scowled. 'We've got enough to do without disinterring the past.'

'Mr Williamson reckons there might have been a bite mark on young Hudnall's wrist. He also points out that it was odd that Hudnall went down to meet his father without an umbrella when it was pouring with rain. There's one other thing. My wife was staying in Trenalt on that night.'

Drake's eyebrows shot up. 'Your *wife?*'

'Yes, sir.' Thornhill tried to keep his voice level. 'This was long before we were married, of course. Her grandmother lived in the village, and Edith often stayed with her. She – she happened to be out that night, and she's pretty sure that she heard two sets of footsteps running down to the station. She didn't come forward at the time because she didn't realise it was important. She went back to her parents the next day, so she wasn't involved in the investigation.'

'Let's hope the press don't get hold of that.' Drake's mouth twisted. 'I'd hate to think what that man Fuggle would do with it.'

Thornhill noticed that Drake pronounced it *Fuggle* rather than *Fewgle.*

'Well?' the DCC went on. 'What's your plan of action?'

'I'd like to do a house-to-house, sir. Someone in that valley must have seen something. After all, it was a summer evening, and it wasn't raining. With your permission, I'll take a team up to Trenalt this afternoon and make a start.'

'Try and find out if Miss Caswell's movements make any sort of pattern. When she went out, I mean. Did she take certain walks, for example? It might be worth searching in case she's hidden the portrait near by.'

'You think she took it, sir?'

'It's certainly possible. Loysey wants it, but if he had it, there'd be no reason for him not to let us know. I suppose the most likely thing is that Moorcroft burned it to save Miss

Caswell's feelings.' He looked up at Thornhill and unexpectedly smiled. 'It complicates our life when people start acting altruistically, doesn't it? We're going round in circles now.'

Thornhill smiled back, and his tiredness lifted slightly. 'The other thing is Miss Caswell's phone call on Tuesday evening. We still don't know who she was ringing, or trying to ring. She rambled on about somebody in Kent, who lived near the road. She said other things, too – but we can't make any sense of it. There may not be any sense to find. No one seems to be able to tell us whether she was eccentric or senile or something in between.'

'And to make matters worse, there may not be a single answer.'

Thornhill nodded. Drake picked up his gloves and took his hat and cane from the umbrella stand in the corner. Thornhill stood up and opened the door for him.

'Don't take this too personally, Thornhill,' Drake murmured as he left the room. 'We can only do the best we can with the materials we have. As long as it is the best, of course.'

He nodded goodbye and strode away down the corridor, taking small steps with his short legs, his heels clicking on the linoleum. Thornhill stared at the rigid spine, the swinging cane and the head tilted back. The little man was like a bantam in a lounge suit.

He shook his head to clear it and went into his own room. He wasn't hungry, but he knew he should eat. First, though, he picked up the phone and dialled the number for Church Cottage. He could not concentrate on this case until he knew what Jill had decided. Uncertainty gnawed him like a canker. She often went home for lunch. But the phone rang on and on.

In his anxiety, Thornhill abandoned caution and phoned the *Gazette*. Miss Francis had gone out, the receptionist told him, and they didn't know when she would be back. Thornhill declined to leave a message.

Finally, in a spirit that came very near to desperation, he phoned his own home number. He wasn't sure why he did it: guilt, perhaps; or the need to take Edith over, one more time, what she had heard and seen in Trenalt on that summer night in 1938; or simply the desire to hear a friendly voice.

Whatever his reason, he was out of luck. He listened to the phone ringing in an empty house. Finally he slammed the receiver down in a fit of temper.

*I can't cope.*

The knowledge of his own fragility overwhelmed him. Everything about himself, everything that had seemed so solid and lasting, was fissured with hairline cracks, and the slightest knock would make the entire edifice of his life disintegrate.

He said to himself, 'For God's sake, man.' The words were unnaturally loud because there was no one but himself to hear them. He snatched his hat and went along the corridor to the CID Office. Brian Kirby was examining something on his desk. It looked like a small green box. He jumped when he saw Thornhill and hastily swept whatever it was into his jacket pocket.

'We need to discuss the Caswell case, Brian,' Thornhill said, hoping he had imagined the note of pleading in his own voice. 'Why don't we have some lunch at the Bathurst Arms?'

# Chapter Forty-four

A keening cry broke through the silence and at last made her stir.

Edith Thornhill raised her head. For a moment she thought it must be the buzzard, its cry louder and fiercer because it was drawing nearer. But it was still high in the sky, floating above the quarry, the meadow and its prey. She let her head drop.

*Not the buzzard — a train.*

They must have reopened the Lydmouth to Newport line. From this field she could not see the railway or even the smoke of the engine. Thousands of tons of earth lay between them, more than enough to soak up the vibration of the train rattling through the tunnel. All she had was the shriek of its whistle. Otherwise she was alone with the buzzard.

Edith was lying on her side, her head pillowed on her arm and the rough grass pressing into the skin of her cheek. The damp was seeping through her light summer dress. Bubbles of panic, fear, worry and disbelief burst like fireworks in her mind. She had no control over her thoughts. They controlled her, and were in turn controlled by what had happened.

'A state of shock,' she mumbled. 'That's all it is. It's all right, it's all right.'

She raised her head again and shouted: 'Help! Help!' Then, a few seconds later, 'Mrs Loysey! June!'

Nothing but silence. Though it was a warm afternoon, Edith felt chilly. And, which made no sense, she was sweating, too, and the sweat was cold, as though the pores that had produced it belonged to a dead person.

*I must think. I must think.*

Surely someone would come to look for her? Or someone would come through the meadow? The trouble was, because of the lie of the land, the length of the grass and the hillock, it was unlikely that Edith would see anyone on the path or that they would see her. Perhaps she should try to crawl round the heap of spoil. How far was it? Fifty or a hundred yards? She had never been good at measuring distances. In any case, it would take for ever. She would have to crawl, just like Miss Caswell had crawled in her tunnel. There was no guarantee that anyone would use the path.

And also perhaps it was wiser to stay where she was?

*All things considered?*

Someone must come. Jack might look for her here, or Nurse Lindor. Richard had no idea where she was, though he might guess it was worth looking in Trenalt. But that could take time. She could be stuck up here for twenty-four hours or longer.

'Stuck here for ever?' Her voice emerged as a whimper, and the sound of her weakness was worse than being alone.

Edith told herself not to be silly, that the shock was making her stupid. A sob wrenched its way out of her. She wept quietly for a few minutes, the tears rolling down her cheek and dripping on to the skin of her arm. She sniffed vigorously. Into her mind came the memory of another time when she had wept, when the world seemed to have come to an end. For an instant, she relived that evening in August 1938, the evening when Hugh betrayed her and Hugh died. But the strange thing was that the two times were not separate but part of one another.

Then, just as she thought she could bear it no longer, she heard the ringing of a bicycle bell.

She jerked her head up. There was the sound again: she was sure it was the double ring of a bicycle bell.

'Help! Help! Over here!'

Someone must be on the path. There it was again – the ringing of the bell. Was it slightly nearer?

'Help! Over here!'

The bell continued ringing, drawing nearer and nearer. Edith continued calling. She was adrift in a world where only sounds mattered. The bell on the one hand, her shouts on the other, drawing slowly together.

Through the long grass came a slim, elegant woman wheeling a bicycle, a large, black, sit-up-and-beg bone-shaker with a basket strapped to the handlebars. The woman's dress swayed from side to side, and she looked cool and refreshed, as though enjoying her summer walk. Draped around her hat was a wisp of black lace, a perky little excuse for a veil which added a note of Parisian chic to perfectly ordinary grey felt.

It was so unfair, Edith thought, suddenly depressed. The wisp of black lace, where you put it, how you wore it – all this added up to something you could never hope to buy, however rich your husband was. How could she ever compete with that?

How could she ever compete with Jill Francis?

# Chapter Forty-five

Jill let the bicycle fall into the grass and ran over to Edith. She was lying on the ground, her body twisted into an awkward position with one leg over the other, her right ankle snagged in a length of rusty wire which curled away from the nearest fence post. Edith Thornhill was caught like a rabbit in a snare.

Jill looked for an instant beyond her, beyond the remains of the fence, beyond the point where the field ended, to the quarry. Men and machines had scooped it out of the hill and now all that was left to show where it had been was a great hole, an absence.

She knelt beside Edith and took her hand, which was cool and damp to the touch. It was a shock to see her like this: with smears of damp on her dress, one of her stockings hanging beneath the knee, her hair in a tangle, and what powder that was left on her pale, shiny face scarred with the tracks of tears like the trails of snails. Edith, Jill had always thought, was one of those people who, should they be injured in a traffic accident and taken to hospital, would prove to have clean underwear beneath their clothes and a freshly ironed handkerchief in their handbag.

Edith tried to smile. 'Thank heavens you've come. I was beginning to think that no one ever would.'

'Are you all right? What happened?'

'My ankle.' Edith's face twisted with pain. 'I was running

away and my foot was caught. I can't get it out. It's absolute agony.'

Jill glanced down at Edith's plump but shapely legs. The ankle with the wire round it was swollen.

'You were running away?' Jill said. 'From what?'

'That woman.' Edith's features trembled and her eyes filled with tears. 'June Loysey.'

'What was she doing?'

'She . . . she was trying to get something I had – trying to kill me, perhaps.' Edith wiped her face with the back of her hand.

'Let me get you a handkerchief,' Jill said.

'There's one in my handbag. It's over there. Can you see? Near the old drum.'

Jill fetched the handbag and at the same time picked up her own, which had fallen out of the basket at the front of the bicycle. Edith sat up and opened hers. She took out a neatly ironed handkerchief, which pleased Jill, and wiped her eyes.

'I'm so sorry,' she said. 'I'm not usually as silly as this.' Her lips began to quiver again. 'That woman terrified me.'

'I'm not surprised. But where is she?'

'She went over there.' Edith pointed. 'Into the quarry. She fell, I think, and it was my fault, really.'

'I'm sure it wasn't.'

'Oh gosh, we must see if she's all right. Can you see her?'

Jill moved warily to the edge of the quarry, crouched down and peered into its depths. She saw June Loysey immediately, fifty or sixty feet below. She was lying on her back, staring at the sky, her dress rucked up, her arms outstretched. Her limbs were entangled with a bramble.

'Dear God,' Jill murmured. She glanced back at Edith. 'I'd better get down there. She may still be alive.'

'There's a way down, a sort of ramp in the next field,' Edith said. 'There used to be a road up there in the old days. When – when you're down there, would you get the envelope?'

'What envelope?'

'There's a brown envelope down there. That's what she was trying to get.' Edith stretched out her hand as if in her anxiety she wanted to touch Jill. 'Please. It's important.'

'All right. If I see it.'

Jill knelt and gently worked the wire away from the ankle. She felt Edith wincing and twice heard her gasp. When at last Jill lifted the leg free, Edith cried out.

'Sorry,' they said simultaneously.

Without another word, Jill left her. She followed the line of the fence into the next field, at the far end of which she found the remains of the quarry's access road, cut into the face of the rock. At the top was a huge concrete plinth which at one time must have served as the base for a crane. Discarded fragments of stone were scattered about it as though a passing giant had broken a boulder in a fit of pique.

Jill followed the ramp, making slow progress because of her thin-soled, heeled shoes. There was a possibility that June Loysey might still be alive, might not be beyond the reach of help. Part of her, however, was already shuddering at the prospect of what she would find.

When she reached the foot of the ramp, Jill stopped for an instant to get her breath back. The rocky floor of the quarry was a different world from the field above. Here was a barren, lunar landscape whose nakedness was enhanced rather than concealed by the occasional sapling or weed that had found somewhere to thrust its roots. She glanced up and saw a bird wheeling in the empty sky.

Reluctantly she moved away from the ramp, picking her way among the rubble. The going was much harder than it had been on the field above. Jill followed a course parallel to the face of the quarry. It was difficult to relate her progress below to the lie of the land at the top of the cliff. She passed a pool of murky rainwater. Suddenly she stopped and stared.

Sitting on a raised slab of rock, as though set down for a moment by its owner, was a green pork-pie hat with a blue feather. When Robinson Crusoe saw the footprint in the sand he must have felt as Jill did now: here was something shocking, inexplicable and mysteriously significant. She picked it up and glanced at the name inside.

*Gareth Loysey.*

A memory wriggled in her mind: when she had gone to Grebe House to interview Loysey, he had asked his wife to look for his green hat in the car.

She continued walking. A moment later, she rounded a spur of rock and stopped sharply, gasping like a landed fish. Not two yards away were two thick legs. Jill's knees were shaking. She took two steps forward. June Loysey's eyes were open and she was staring up at the sky, where the bird still hovered. Her dress had ridden up and a long scratch extended from her left knee up her thigh. Her mouth was open and a solitary fly squatted and fed on a bubble of blood-flecked saliva at the corner of the lips.

Jill swallowed. She swallowed again and then again, with increasing urgency. There was no avoiding it. Her stomach heaved as though a giant hand were squeezing it. She staggered a few paces aside and was violently sick. She continued to retch when there was nothing further to bring up.

Shuddering, she went back to June Loysey. She had seen enough dead bodies in the war for the look of them to be familiar – the skin already acquiring a waxen patina, the sense of absence. Nevertheless she knelt down, took June's wrist and felt for a pulse. Life could survive in the most extraordinary conditions, and life was always worth preserving. The fly detached itself from its lunch and flew away.

She made herself crouch there, the cold wrist wrapped in her hand, while she searched for a pulse that wasn't there. All the while she stared at the empty face and counted the passing seconds. After more than a minute, she let go of the wrist. She stood up, stretched and moved round to the head.

June Loysey had not been beautiful in life and she was worse in death. Jill disliked herself for allowing that thought past her mental censor. She bent down and ran the fingers of both hands gently against the back of the head, taking care not to lift it. She felt her way through the wiry permed hair. Her mind translated the information transmitted to it by her fingertips into another, safer language: shards of china and something soft, yielding and amorphous like jelly, enclosed in a fine leather bag.

She straightened up and saw a sturdy but crumpled manila envelope lying four or five yards away. Glad of the excuse, she left the body and picked it up. The end had not been gummed down and Jill glanced inside and saw letters, a pocketbook and a photograph. She upended the envelope so its contents slid partly out. She recognised Rufus Moorcroft's face from the photograph they had used for the obituary. She glanced at the address on the first of the letters and pulled out the sheet of paper inside.

*My dearest Hugh—*

Hugh Hudnall.

No wonder June Loysey had wanted this so badly. She had wanted to protect her brother's name – or more probably her husband's – from scandal.

Jill walked back the way she had come, picking up the pork-pie hat. Once or twice she glanced upwards to the edge of the quarry, wondering if anyone were watching. The bird had gone. The environment was artificial and it made her feel like a laboratory rat. She hurried up the ramp, desperate to reach more familiar terrain.

Her lungs were pumping like bellows by the time she reached the top – too many cigarettes – and she stood there panting for a moment. When her breathing had returned to normal, she checked her appearance as thoroughly as she could. She wished she had a mirror and a comb with her, but they were in her handbag. Vanity was important: she had seen women touching up their make-up in the ladies' lavatory while the air-raid sirens wailed outside, before going down to the shelters. Only the dead lacked vanity.

Jill walked back through the fields. She did not hurry now. The urgency that had possessed her in the quarry had evaporated. Edith was in the same position. She raised a hand in greeting as Jill appeared.

'Is she—?'

Jill dropped the hat on the grass. 'Yes, I'm afraid she's dead.'

'Poor woman.' Edith turned her head away.

'Could you walk if you rested on me?'

'No. The ankle's horribly painful.'

'Then I'd better go and get help. We'll need some men and a stretcher.'

'Please – not yet.' Edith held out her hand. 'May I look at the envelope?'

Jill gave it to her. She watched Edith emptying the contents on to her lap.

'Why did you come here?' Edith asked. 'How did you know?'

'I was at Fontenoy Place. Nurse Lindor said she'd seen you coming up here.' *With her fancy man, I've no doubt, poking around in Miss Caswell's things.* 'She lent me her bicycle and told me where to come. I couldn't find you, so I rang the bell and hoped you'd call out.'

'Miss Caswell was – was in love with Rufus Moorcroft,' Edith said slowly. 'She put presents for him in that oil drum over there. She called it her trousseau. It was hidden in that pile of rocks. I used to know her when I was a girl, and once Rufus had died she didn't want the trousseau any more. So, just before she died, she said I could have it.' Edith was blushing but she hurried on: 'I thought I'd better come up here and see what was in it. Mainly rubbish, I'm afraid. Rags and half-smoked cigars – that sort of thing. You can see for yourself . . . But there was this envelope. I – I'd just found it when Mrs Loysey appeared.'

'She was actually *searching* for the envelope?'

'Yes — at least I think she was. She was also looking for a painting that used to belong to Mr Moorcroft. One that her husband did.'

'*Lady with Fan*?'

'How did you know?' Edith's voice was suddenly hard.

'I think half the world knew the Loyseys were trying to get that painting back. Mr Loysey wants it for an exhibition, I gather. I interviewed him the other day.'

Edith nodded. 'And June would do anything if it made him happy. She seemed like a mother hen with one chick as far as he was concerned. The picture frame was in the oil drum. But not the picture itself. Presumably Miss Caswell must have cut it out. June went crazy.'

'And the hat was there, too?'

'Yes — Miss Caswell must have found it somewhere. June wanted it, so I let her have it. Why not? She said it was Gareth's. Then she wanted the envelope. She — she knew what was in it.'

There was a silence. Jill waited for Edith to continue, and knew that Edith in turn was waiting for her to say whether she had looked inside the envelope.

Edith was the first to lose her nerve. 'I wouldn't let her have it. She was going to take it away from me, so I ran off.' She waved towards the fence, towards the edge of the quarry. 'I tripped. I tried to throw the envelope into the quarry but it sort of balanced on the edge. June made a grab for it. But she missed and it slid over. It must have caught on something because she leant over and tried to get it.' Edith began to pick a blade of grass apart. 'She toppled over, and I tried to reach her, to help, but the wire had caught me, and moving made it worse. And anyway the pain—' She broke off and buried her head in the crook of her elbow. 'I feel so guilty,' she said in a muffled voice. 'If I'd let her have the wretched thing, she would still be alive.'

'Mr Loysey last saw that hat the Sunday before last,' Jill said.

'I went to interview him the other day, and he was asking his wife about it. He said he'd left it in the car.'

'Mr Moorcroft killed himself on Monday evening,' Edith said. 'The very next day. Miss Caswell hardly ever went anywhere except Trenalt. She hadn't even been to Lydmouth for years. So perhaps the Loyseys came over to Trenalt on Monday. One or both of them.'

'If it had been both of them, you'd have thought Mr Loysey would have seen his hat,' Jill said. 'And he can't have driven over by himself, because he doesn't drive.'

'Miss Caswell used to go for walks in the evening. Especially in the summer. When I was a girl, she used to haunt Highnam Cottage, because of Rufus.'

Jill picked up her handbag, took out a cigarette case and offered it to Edith. 'No – I forgot – you don't smoke, do you?'

'Not now.' Edith went back to tearing the blade of grass into even smaller pieces.

Jill took a cigarette and lit it. She dropped the case in the bag. Too late she realised that there was a book in there: *The Blue Field* by John Moore. She could not help glancing from the handbag to Edith. Had she been close enough to reach it while Jill was down in the quarry? Would she have done so? Prying in someone else's bag was not the sort of action you'd expect of someone like Edith. On the other hand, if Edith had her suspicions about Jill and Richard, that would be another matter.

*To J. from R., with best love on your birthday.*

Jill said, 'Do you think Mrs Loysey drove over to see Mr Moorcroft on the Monday? Just before he died?'

Edith raised her head. Her eyes were bright with tears, though it was impossible to tell whether of anger or sorrow. 'I think she came to blackmail him.' She watched Jill's face carefully. 'Do you understand?'

Jill thought this was like playing a game of poker without knowing what cards were in the pack. 'I think I understand.

Before the war, were Mr Moorcroft and Hugh Hudnall having a homosexual affair?'

Once again Edith blushed. She hurried on: 'But why would she blackmail him? Why now? The Loyseys can't need the money. He must sell his paintings, mustn't he, and they've got old Mr Hudnall's money.'

Jill remembered what Richard had told her about seeing Mrs Loysey in the bank. 'I'm not sure if they are well off. Not now. They live very comfortably, but I don't think he sells much of his work at present. And you know how they tax unearned income these days.'

'That might explain it, then – why Rufus killed himself. So if that woman hadn't come along and tried to blackmail him, he'd still be alive today. She—'

Edith broke off and looked sideways through lowered lashes at Jill. She might as well have finished the sentence. *She deserved to die.*

'If Miss Caswell were hanging around Highnam Cottage, she could have seen Mrs Loysey,' Jill said. 'Probably a few hours before Rufus killed himself. She could have stolen the envelope and the hat from the car for her – her trousseau.'

While she spoke, she was adding this new knowledge to what she already knew or suspected. Constance Kent and the White Rabbit. The second pair of feet running down from the station which Edith had heard on the night of Hugh's death, and which Jill could not admit to Edith that she knew about because the information could only have come from Richard.

'When I saw Miss Caswell at the funeral, she was trying to remember the name of the woman who had married the White Rabbit.' Edith plucked another blade of grass and ran a fingernail slowly down its length, splitting it in two. 'Mr Loysey looks like a rabbit with those teeth. But what about Constance? And – and someone said she was trying to ring someone in Kent.'

'Not someone *in* Kent,' Jill said. 'Someone whose name *was* Kent. Constance Kent.'

'Who?'

'She was a Victorian murderess who lived near where Miss Caswell's family came from, in Wiltshire. Constance Kent killed her young brother.'

Edith's mouth trembled. Tears spilled down the cheeks again. She wiped them away impatiently with her handkerchief. 'June killed Hugh,' she said flatly. 'She killed her brother too. He was always his father's favourite, you know. She hated that. And she was so awfully in love with Gareth Loysey. And it was obvious to everyone that he wanted her money. I wonder—' Her voice trailed away.

'What?'

'I wonder if she tried to blackmail Hugh, as well. You see, I was staying in Trenalt with my grandmother on the night he died. I – I heard two people running down to the station, just before the last train from Lydmouth was due. She might have tried to blackmail him, or just had a row with him, and threatened to expose what he was doing to their father. And he ran down to the station to see their father first. And . . . and she followed.'

Jill poked the stub of a cigarette through the matted grass to the earth beneath. She ground it out. 'We can't prove anything.'

'And now she's dead.' Edith shivered. 'It's like a judgment, isn't it?'

'And what about Miss Caswell? Did she telephone June Loysey after Mr Moorcroft's funeral and arrange a meeting? Why would she want to do that?'

'Because Mrs Loysey had been the last person to see Mr Moorcroft. She loved him – Miss Caswell, I mean. She'd have wanted to know what was wrong with him, why he killed himself.' Edith's voice rose. 'When you love someone, you do want to know, even if it's bad news. Especially, perhaps, if it's bad news. Especially if they kill themselves and you don't know why.'

Jill looked away, aware that the conversation might be operating on more than one level and hoping it was not. 'And Mrs Loysey wanted that envelope and the hat, not to mention that wretched portrait.'

'True love.' Edith hiccoughed. 'Everything she did was for her husband. She must have guessed Miss Caswell had taken the picture. Who else would have wanted it?'

Jill thought back to the discovery of Miss Caswell's body, trying to relate what she knew to the events of Wednesday evening. 'They arranged to meet somewhere near the tunnel. That's a quiet enough place on a summer evening, and they both knew the area well.'

'Miss Caswell wouldn't give her what she wanted.'

'And Mrs Loysey lost her temper.' Jill studied Edith's face. 'Judging by what happened to you this afternoon, and if we're right about what happened to Hugh, she had a streak of violence.' She remembered the possible bite mark on Hugh Hudnall's wrist, information that ex-Superintendent Williamson had passed on to Richard, something else that she must not mention to Edith. 'She probably thought Miss Caswell was dead, and she pulled her up the tunnel to give herself more time to get away. I think you were lucky to escape.'

'Jill,' Edith said, and the use of the Christian name was in itself an olive branch, 'what are we going to do with this?'

Jill looked down at the envelope. 'I suppose the police will have to have it.'

'Need they? Does everyone have to know about Hugh and Rufus? What use would it be to anyone?'

'The police aren't anyone.'

Edith made a sound between a groan and a laugh. 'I wouldn't be so sure, not in Lydmouth. It's not an easy place to keep secrets. You must have noticed that by now.'

Once again Jill had the uneasy sense that Edith was saying two things with one set of words.

'It's not as if Rufus and Hugh were hurting anyone,' Edith said in a rush. 'Not really. Not like that woman there. What they were doing was . . . was just between themselves.'

'Yes,' Jill said. 'I agree.' She thought of Bernie Broadbent and Randolph Haughton and the thousands, perhaps millions, like them.

'All we need do is hide that wretched envelope,' Edith said. 'No one would ever know. They'd think that Mrs Loysey had come here looking for that silly painting, which is true anyway, so we wouldn't even be lying.'

It was a pragmatic way to approach an ethical decision, but it had its attractions. Jill said, 'In that case, how did Mrs Loysey come to——?'

'Fall?' Edith said. 'That's easy. She was trying to get the picture frame. People will think she didn't realise the picture had gone.'

'Where is it?' Jill said.

'Over there, near the oil drum.' Edith sat up straight, her face glowing with excitement like a child's, and pointed. 'There should be an old music case near by. It was inside it.'

Jill fetched the case and the frame. 'I wonder what happened to the picture.'

'Miss Caswell probably burned it.'

Jill thought: *Suttee by proxy?*

'But it doesn't matter,' Edith went on. 'All we have to do is put the frame back in the music case. Then everything happened as it really did. June came up here while I was looking through Miss Caswell's things. She saw the edge of the frame in the case and went berserk. She tried to get it away from me by violence, started chasing me. I ran away from her, tripped and sprained my ankle. And as I fell, I threw the case over the edge of the cliff. It stuck on that little ledge a couple of feet down. She leaned over and tried to get it. But she leaned too far.'

'And knocked the case off the ledge as she fell?'

'Yes. That's it. Or it slipped off of its own accord.'

Jill opened her handbag again, angling it away so Edith could not see the book inside. She took out her case and lit another cigarette. Edith, her face calm, was watching her. You never really knew how a crisis would affect someone, Jill thought, because an emergency scraped away the veneer of routine and what was underneath could surprise everyone, including the person concerned.

But perhaps it wasn't entirely a matter of temperament. Perhaps running a family and a home was a better preparation for coping with the unforeseen than being what the Sunday papers referred to as a career woman. Jill picked a shred of tobacco from her lips and glanced at Edith, who was now lying on her side, supporting herself on her elbow. Here they were, two women of much the same age who in other circumstances might have been friends.

If she agreed to Edith's plan, Jill supposed that would be breaking the law. Though apart from misleading the police, it was hard to see what crime had actually been committed. It was nothing more than a slight modification of recent history. After all, they said history was written by the victors. And it should involve no risk for herself. Supporting Edith's story would make Edith's life much easier. And Richard's. Jill felt guilty about Edith, always had, and this might help to lighten that load.

'Miss Caswell's — what did you call it? — trousseau. Does anyone else know about it?'

'That's all right. There was a witness when Miss Caswell told me about it and said that she wanted me to have it. An old friend of mine, as it happens. Jack Graig.'

Jill thought for an instant that there was a trace of self-consciousness in Edith's voice when she mentioned Major Graig's name. She wondered again if there was any truth in Nurse Lindor's unbelievable insinuation: *With her fancy man, I've no doubt, poking around in Miss Caswell's things.* If so, who was she to judge?

'We'd better get things organised,' Jill said briskly.

Edith's face lit up. 'You'll do it, then?'

'I think it's the best thing, on the whole. Should we burn the letters and so on? Just in case.'

'They're safer out of the way. You've got your lighter, and it shouldn't take long. Someone had a bonfire near where Miss Caswell had the oil drum. You could do it there, then no one would notice the ashes. But perhaps you should put the frame in the music case first, and throw it over. Just in case someone comes.'

Jill stubbed out her cigarette and stood up.

Edith stretched out a hand for the case, winced and stopped. 'Sorry – I wish I could help. But I don't think I can move at all with this ankle.'

'Don't worry. What about the hat?'

'Throw it over the edge,' Edith said. 'Perhaps it was somewhere in the Loyseys' car after all.' She stared innocently up at Jill. 'Come to think of it, Mrs Loysey was wearing it. That's it. She probably put it on to keep the sun off.'

Jill smiled. 'You've got an answer for everything.'

'No,' Edith said quietly. 'I wish I had.'

For the third time that afternoon, Jill wondered what Edith was really saying. It was a relief to be busy: to plant the frame and the hat in the quarry – though there was a heart-stopping moment when she feared the hat would fall directly on top of the body.

When she returned, she found that Edith was going through the pocketbook.

'I'd better keep this,' she said. 'The ring binder's metal, and of course the leather won't burn easily. I've torn out all the pages with writing on, and there's an old bus ticket, too. There's nothing to link it to Hugh.'

Jill took the photograph, the letters and the loose leaves from the pocketbook up to the charred circle in the lee of the hillock. The first letter lit easily. Pale flames ran like water over the yellowing paper, turning it briefly to gold and bringing the words that Rufus had written back to life.

*My darling boy, I am counting the hours, no, the moments, until . . .*

The flame licked up and caressed Jill's fingers. She swore and dropped the letter. Soon everything was burned. She broke up the charred pieces with a stick and ground them down into the older ashes. She went back to Edith and sat down beside her. Her skirt was ruined with creases and grass stains. They were a pair of scarecrows.

She sighed and said, 'I suppose I'd better go and fetch someone. It's rather like waiting for the curtain to go up, isn't it?'

Edith nodded. She was attacking another blade of grass with her fingers, whose tips were now stained green.

Jill said, 'It's lovely up here, isn't it? Like being on the top of the world. I shall miss the countryside when I leave Lydmouth.'

'You're leaving?'

'Yes — I've been offered a job in London. Do you know Randolph Haughton?'

Edith nodded. 'Slightly. I saw him at the funeral. He used to come to Trenalt in the old days. He was a friend of Hugh's.'

'Of course. Well, he's bought a magazine, and he wants me to be features editor. It's a wonderful job.'

'I . . . I hope you'll be very happy.'

'Well, I shall miss Lydmouth, of course,' Jill said brightly. 'But I never like staying in one place for any length of time. I like to have a change.'

'I think you're very sensible,' Edith said. 'Of course, it's a shame you're going.'

'Yes.'

The odd thing was, Jill thought, that both of them meant it.

Part of her wished she weren't leaving, and not simply because of Richard. She stood up.

'I'll go and fetch help.'

'Would you leave me with a cigarette?' Edith said.

'But I thought you didn't.'

Edith's hands fluttered over the little pile of ruined grass. 'You know how it is. I need something to do with my hands.' She watched Jill fumbling with her case. 'By the way,' she said, 'I know it's a silly thing to say at a time like this, but I do like your hat.'

# Chapter Forty-six

The funeral of Miss Cicely Caswell took place at St Mary's Church, Trenalt, on Thursday, 4 September. There had been a wedding the previous weekend, and scraps of confetti danced like overexcited children among the graves. It was a dry but blustery day. Gusts of wind eddied round the crowd in the churchyard, lifting up skirts and coat-tails, forcing people to hold on to their hats.

Before the committal, while everyone was still in church, Edith glanced round from her seat halfway down the nave at the rest of the congregation. She established by a series of furtive exploratory glances that Jack was sitting at the back on the other side of the church with Mrs Solly and the landlord of the Bear.

There were even more people than had turned out for Rufus Moorcroft. Sitting at the front were the family. Lord Vauden, a quiet little man who looked like a retired prep-school master, had come with one of his daughters. Two other cousins had put in an appearance, a man and his wife, both thin, grey, elderly and slightly dusty. It was hard to connect them with the princely virtues recorded in marble splendour on the Vauden memorials in the south aisle.

In the block of pews immediately behind the family sat Dr Angmer with selected staff and guests from Fontenoy Place.

Among them was Nurse Lindor, who sobbed quietly and persistently throughout the service. The Chief Constable himself represented the police; he sat with the Lord Lieutenant and Sir Anthony and Lady Ruispidge. George Shipston was not there. He had had a stroke the previous weekend.

When they filed out into the churchyard, following the coffin to the open grave, the sunshine was unbearably bright. The confetti swirled around their feet and speckled the naked earth like coloured rain. Edith limped along, leaning heavily on Bernie's arm and supported by a stick on the other side. Jack was a safe distance away, talking quietly with the rector's sister.

They had given Miss Caswell the plot beside Rufus Moorcroft's. That was natural enough – Miss Caswell was the next person to be buried at Trenalt. The flowers were rotting on Rufus's grave.

'She'd have liked being near him, at any rate,' Bernie said. 'When I saw her here the day after Moorcroft's funeral, I reckon she'd been talking to him.'

An idea stirred in Edith's mind. It was nothing more than a hint of inconsistency. But it stayed with her while the rector was speaking and distracted her from the man's words. She glanced across the open grave and met Jack's eyes. His face was worried. She smiled at him and watched his anxiety fade away when he smiled back.

Afterwards, Nurse Lindor, with the help of Mrs Solly, provided tea and sandwiches in the village hall. Tradition had dictated the seating arrangements in church but, to all intents and purposes, Miss Lindor had been tacitly accepted as the principal mourner. After one cup of tea, Edith hobbled outside. Jack was sitting on the churchyard wall smoking his pipe. He smiled at her and walked quickly across the road.

'How's the ankle?' he asked.

'Mending. But it's still rather painful. Shall we walk? The doctor says exercise is good for it.'

He offered her his arm. 'I hoped you'd come. Where shall we go?'

'Could we go back in the churchyard?'

They went together through the lychgate.

'I've missed you,' he murmured, his face darkening. He cleared his throat. 'Edith, what happened – it . . . it wasn't just a flash in the pan, you know. Not for me.'

She squeezed his arm. 'Not for me, either.'

'I bottled you up, you see,' he said. 'For all those years. Like a genie.'

'I think more than one genie came out.'

'I don't think I'll ever get it back inside.'

'Oh, Jack.'

They walked slowly round the church. Near the far boundary of the churchyard were the whitebeam and the yew sheltering the graves of Miss Caswell and Rufus Moorcroft.

'Miss Caswell wasn't a fool,' Edith said suddenly. 'She wasn't mad, either.'

Jack sucked his pipe. 'She acted very strangely sometimes.'

'She just had a different sort of sanity from most people's. I was thinking about the painting.'

'I thought she'd destroyed it.'

'No one knows what she did with it. But the confetti gave me an idea.'

'What?' Jack stopped, his face bewildered. 'The confetti? They've obviously had a wedding recently but—'

'They'd had a wedding just before Rufus's funeral. Mrs Solly's sister's youngest.'

'I'm sorry. I don't follow.'

'Miss Caswell liked to be clean. Do you remember, Nurse Lindor told us? But when Bernie met her on the day of the funeral, she wasn't wearing gloves and her hands were dirty.'

'I still don't—'

'And then there's the trowel,' Edith went on in a rush. 'The one we found in her trousseau. It had mud on it, and bits of confetti.'

'But why — why would she want to be digging in the churchyard?'

'She gave Rufus a portrait of her. And it hung in his house until he died. It was part of her that could be with him. You see?'

Jack nodded.

'I think she took it back after he died. She wanted to stay with him. And if she couldn't stay with him in person, then the portrait would have to do.' She swallowed. 'As it did before.'

They walked on until they came to the whitebeam and the yew. The undertaker's men had finished filling in Miss Caswell's grave. She and Rufus Moorcroft lay side by side under their flowers, like a couple asleep under patchwork quilts in a twin-bedded room.

'So what exactly are you saying?' Jack stared down at the carpet of decaying vegetation rising in a hump over Rufus's grave. 'You think *Lady with Fan* is somewhere there?'

'Yes.'

'But, Edith — we can't very well dig up the whole thing.'

'She can't have put it far down. And I think I know where. About two feet down from where the marker is, and a little over to the right.'

'How do you know?'

'Because it's roughly where his heart would be.'

'That's ridiculous.'

'Not to Miss Caswell. It's the way she would think.'

Jack took out his pipe and chewed his lower lip. 'Do you want me to—?'

'Yes. Please, Jack, would you? I want to *know*.'

'All right. If you really want. But only for a moment. Anyway, one really needs a spade.'

'You can use my stick.'

He knocked out his pipe and tucked it in his jacket pocket.

He crouched beside the grave. Edith glanced over her shoulder. They were alone. She handed him her walking stick.

'There,' she said, pointing down. 'Try *there*.'

Jack pulled aside the wreaths and poked the stick into the loose earth beneath. He was frowning. Suddenly his face changed.

'Good God. There's something here.'

'What is it?' Edith came forward, resting her hand on his shoulder.

'A roll of something . . . Could be canvas, I suppose.'

Jack pulled it out and shook off the loose earth. The roll was about ten inches long. It was held together by a carefully knotted length of string, and the canvas was already stained with damp. He folded back one of its two visible corners.

'That's it, we've got it — look, you can see oil paint.' He rummaged in his jacket pocket. 'Hang on, I'll cut the string.'

'No,' Edith said. 'Please don't.'

'Why not?'

'I think we should leave it there. It's the best place for it. That is, if you don't mind. I suppose legally it must belong to you.'

'If you want me to put it back, that's what I'll do.'

While Edith kept watch, Jack dug down with the stick to scrape a deeper hole to hold *Lady with Fan*. He dropped the painting into it and smoothed the earth around and over it with his bare hands. Afterwards he replaced the wreaths and stood up.

'Satisfied?' he said gently.

'Thank you.' She put her hand on his shoulder, reached up and kissed his cheek. 'For everything. I wish—'

'No,' he interrupted. 'It's all right. Really it is.'

'It wouldn't work, you see,' Edith said. 'You and me. Or not for long. We have to put the genies back and do the best with what we have.'

Jack turned away, feeling for his pipe. She could not see his face.

'Poor Miss Caswell,' he said in a voice that sounded muffled. 'What a life, eh?'

'Better to have loved and made a fool of yourself,' Edith said, 'than not to have loved at all.'

# Chapter Forty-seven

It seemed to Richard Thornhill that he spent his life waiting, usually for something he didn't want to happen. Slowly the seasons changed, the days shortened, the temperature dropped. When he met Jill in the clearing in the Forest, he noticed the leaves drying out and changing colour. The ground underfoot became muddier. Groups of trees looked like the flames of a bonfire.

Rain forced them to cancel some meetings or to fumble dangerously in parked cars. Once they drove independently to Gloucester and hired a room for the evening in a seedy hotel near the station. The experience was so depressing that they did not repeat the experiment. Twice they went to the cinema together and held hands in the darkness like teenagers. More often, though, they met in the Forest, where at least they could be alone.

Now the waiting was nearly over. Jill was due to depart for London the following morning. Church Cottage was empty. Most of Jill's possessions had been sent in advance up to London, some to the flat in Randolph Haughton's cousin's house in Lancaster Gate and some to be stored. She was spending her last few nights at the Wemyss-Browns'. Her replacement, a youthfully middle-aged man from the *Bristol Evening Post*, was already working at the *Gazette*. The Wemyss-Browns were sad to see Jill go, though in Charlotte's case, Jill said, there was an element of satisfaction mixed in with the regret. Charlotte had never quite forgiven Jill for allowing her husband to find her attractive.

They had arranged to meet at five o'clock. When Thornhill reached the clearing he found that Jill was there, walking up and down to keep warm and smoking a cigarette. She ground it out and ran towards him. They kissed as the starving eat. It occurred to him that his desire for her was so intense that it was no longer sexual.

Jill pulled away from him and touched his face. 'You look tired.'

'I've not been sleeping very well.'

'You haven't been sleeping properly for months.'

He kissed her again.

A moment later, she said, 'It feels like the last day of the holidays. Only worse.'

'Which train will you catch?'

'The—' She broke off and began again: 'Don't come to the station, will you? I couldn't bear it.'

'Then don't tell me which train.'

'Have you heard about the job yet?'

He shook his head. 'But I haven't got it.'

'You can't know that.'

'The Appointments Board was meeting this morning. I'd have heard by now.'

'There may have been a delay. They may not want to announce the appointment immediately.'

'I have to face facts,' Thornhill said. 'I've never really fitted into this town. I've trodden on too many toes.'

'You've got results.'

'You're only as good as your last case. Nobody got much glory out of the Caswell affair.'

'That wasn't your fault.'

'But they're not going to want me running their central office for serious crimes.' He shrugged. 'Let's not talk about it. You're what matters. Will you be all right?'

The question made her cry. He put his arms around her again. They had run out of things to say. All that was left was the need to comfort each other without words.

'I can't stand this,' Jill mumbled into his coat. 'I must go.'

He tightened his grip. 'I can't bear not to see you.'

'I can't bear it either. Could you sometimes come up to town?'

'Yes,' he said recklessly. 'Of course I could.'

'Then this isn't an ending,' Jill said. 'It's a sort of beginning. That's what will make it bearable.'

They kissed again and he watched her walking away. She did not turn to wave. There were tears in his own eyes and he rubbed them with the back of his hand. Was it a beginning, he wondered, or just a form of words chosen to make an ending more palatable?

When he could no longer hear her footsteps crunching through the fallen leaves, he set out for his own car. He walked slowly. It would be six o'clock by the time he arrived home. The children would come running. He was humbled by their capacity to forgive his inattention, his irritability and his absences. And Edith would be there too: though in her case it was hard to know whether she was equally forgiving.

He drove back to Lydmouth. As the car crawled through the evening traffic up the long hill from the station, he came to a decision. Instead of continuing down the High Street, he turned right into the car park of Police Headquarters. There was no hurry. There might even be a letter from the Appointments Board. Better to know the worst than to fear it.

He went upstairs, exchanging automatic greetings. There was nothing in his in-tray. In the CID Office, Kirby was packing up, ready to go. No one else was in earshot.

'Any news, guv?'

'None that I've heard.'

Kirby looked at him. Thornhill wished he had thought to check his face in the mirror to see if any sign of his tears lingered.

'If you ask me, they'd be bloody fools if they gave it to someone else. Do you fancy a pint? It's my ma's birthday, and I'd like to drink her health.'

'Yes,' Thornhill said. 'Why not?'

He was a man who rarely drank very much but at this moment nothing seemed more attractive than a row of glasses, pints of mild-and-bitter interspersed with large whiskies, lined up on a bar counter. A few minutes later they clattered down the stairs. Thornhill caught Brian Kirby looking at him and wondered, not for the first time, exactly how far his sergeant could see.

'I hate autumn,' Kirby said. 'Gloomy time of year, and you know it's only going to get worse.'

The evening air was sharp and smelled of coal fires. Smoke poured into the sky from a hundred chimneys. Thornhill and Kirby crossed the High Street and walked down Lyd Street to the Bathurst Arms, where the new landlord was a retired police sergeant from Hereford. They found a table in the lounge bar. Thornhill sat down and glanced at the *Gazette* while Kirby fetched the drinks.

When Kirby came back, both men drank deeply before saying anything.

'Happy birthday, Ma,' Kirby said.

They drank again. Thornhill was already halfway down his tankard.

Kirby jabbed his forefinger at the byline at the head of one of the newspaper columns. 'Les Fields – that's the new bloke on the *Gazette*. Met him today. Seems all right. In fact I introduced him to Ivor Fuggle. "Actually, it's pronounced Fewgle," Ivor says. And Fields comes back, quick as a flash, "And is it spelt with a Ph?" '

Thornhill laughed. He wondered whether it was a coincidence that Kirby had mentioned the new reporter on the *Gazette*.

'As a matter of fact, I've got a piece of news,' Kirby went on. He swallowed more beer. 'And a bit of a favour to ask.'

'Ask away. But what's the news?'

'Me and Joan have decided to get married. And I was — we were — wondering if you'd be best man?'

'Congratulations.' Thornhill forced a smile. 'Wonderful news. I hope you'll be very happy. And of course I'd be honoured to be your best man.'

'Thanks.'

'When did you pop the question?'

'Yesterday evening.' Kirby looked about sixteen. 'You're the first person I've told. I got this ring for her, a real diamond with a sapphire on either side. Had to sell the bike to pay for it.'

'Good God.'

'Mrs Thornhill said I should get her the best I could manage.'

'I see — so you asked her advice?'

'Yes. Sort of. In a roundabout way.'

'This deserves a drink,' Thornhill said firmly. 'Several drinks. We're going to celebrate.'

# Chapter Forty-eight

It was not the most convenient time in the evening for paying an unannounced call, but wealthy relations are allowed a certain amount of latitude in these matters. Edith limped ahead of Bernie into the kitchen, which fortunately was looking fairly tidy apart from the washing hanging over the boiler. Elizabeth was already in bed, and Edith packed David upstairs for his bath.

'Richard not back yet?'

'No,' Edith said. 'He's having a drink with Brian Kirby.'

'Shame. I wanted a word.'

'He phoned about a quarter of an hour ago. They're celebrating. Brian's getting married.'

'Oh ay? To that little policewoman of his?'

'Yes – Joan Ailsmore. It's about time Brian settled down. I thought he might turn into one of those eternal bachelors.'

Bernie chuckled. 'Like me.'

Edith smiled at him and offered him a chair and a drink. He accepted the first but declined the latter. Max clawed his way up Bernie's cavalry twill trousers, purring hysterically.

'Can't stay. In fact I'm driving up to London this evening.'

'On business?'

'Well, I might see a few fellows here and there. I'm thinking of buying a car, too.' Bernie scratched Max's head. 'Randolph

Haughton knows a chap who's got a showroom in Berkeley Square. He's got an Aston Martin there and a Bristol. Randolph thought I might like to have a look at them.'

'You seem to be seeing quite a lot of him at present,' Edith said.

'Oh, there's a lot to him. Man of many talents. Besides, it's an interesting place, London. Loads of opportunities up there. Trouble with Lydmouth, you see, you can only go so far. But in London, well, the sky's the limit, isn't it?'

'Yes, I suppose it is.'

'In fact I might even take a little service flat up there. Cheaper than hotels in the long run.' He patted his pockets, looking for matches. 'You heard that Jill Francis is moving up to London?'

'Yes, she mentioned it.'

'You must have seen quite a lot of her because of that business with June Loysey.' He began to look for his pipe. 'Glad all that's over. Still, it's a shame we're losing Miss Francis.'

'When is she leaving?'

'Tomorrow. The nine-seventeen to Paddington. I offered to run her down to the station, before this London trip came up. But the Wemyss-Browns are going to do it.'

Bernie struck a match. Edith looked at him. She had known him all her life. The thought of his buying a flat in London was unsettling.

'Personally, I've had enough of London,' she said. 'I'd rather stay in Lydmouth. But of course that depends on Richard's work.'

Bernie grinned. 'I thought it might.'

'Have you — is there any news?'

'That's why I was hoping to have a word with him.'

'Well? Have they decided?'

'The Appointments Board met this morning. They made the selection, but had to refer it to the Standing Joint Committee for confirmation. There's a subcommittee that looks at appointments. Nothing to worry about – just a rubber-stamp affair.' He beamed at her. 'Your Richard's got the job if he wants it. With promotion, of course. So you'll be a chief inspector's wife.'

She felt the blood rushing to her face. 'I'm – I'm so glad. He's been very worried recently. He thought he wouldn't get it.'

'I gather he was far and away the best of the applicants.'

'But this business with Miss Caswell––'

Bernie waved away smoke and waved away the objection. 'They looked at his results as a whole. He's done a lot since he came to Lydmouth. Drake likes him, and that's half the battle. He can handle the administration side of it, which a lot of the applicants wouldn't have been able to do. They even had a word with old Williamson – off the record, of course. He thought Richard was the man for the job.'

'I thought he didn't like Richard.'

Bernie shrugged. 'Appearances can be deceptive. Especially in Lydmouth, eh?'

# Chapter Forty-nine

Richard Thornhill wasn't sure what the time was. He thought he was late. But how late? He propped himself up against the lamppost on the corner of Victoria Road and tried to read the dial of his watch. The light was not good enough. He held the watch up to his ear. He heard nothing but his own breathing and the engine of a solitary car in the High Street. The watch must have stopped.

'I'll ask Edith,' he said aloud. 'She'll know the time.'

He staggered along the pavement, occasionally nudging against a parked car or a hedge. At last he reached his own house. To his surprise, the Austin was not outside. Perhaps it had been stolen. Then he remembered it was still in the car park at Police Headquarters. He had a distinct memory of Brian Kirby sitting on the steps outside the public library and saying earnestly that it was a fine night for a walk.

But Brian had to walk. He had sold his motorbike for the love of a good woman.

Thornhill hiccoughed. Had he imagined it, or had Brian said he had sold the bike on Edith's advice? That was another question to ask her.

He pushed open his gate and reached the porch. He kicked over two empty milk bottles and sat down on the step while he searched his pockets for his latchkey. At last he found it. He stood up and tried to put it in the lock. This went on for some time. He gave up and looked for the bellpush, but couldn't find it. Then, to his relief, a light went on in the hall, and the door opened from within.

'Edith,' he said. 'Hello. I had something to ask you.'

'Where've you been?'

'With Brian, at the Bathurst Arms. Didn't I phone?'

'Yes,' she said. 'Some time ago. But it's all right.'

She laid his arm over her shoulder and pulled him into the kitchen. She swept the kittens off the Windsor chair and pushed him gently into it. He sat back with relief, suddenly tired, and closed his eyes. Something puzzled him but he couldn't think what it was. Something else to ask Edith, when he remembered what it was.

'Don't go to sleep,' she said. 'I'm going to get you some water and some aspirin. And then I'm going to make you some coffee.'

'Thank you,' he said. 'You're very kind. But I don't want any.'

'Yes, you do.'

'I want to ask you something.'

'Later.'

She went away, and he dozed in the chair by the boiler, with Max and Tom on his lap. Edith came back with water and aspirin and woke him up.

'Did you have a lot to drink?' she asked.

'I'm not sure. Probably. We were celebrating, you see. Brian's getting married.'

'I know.'

'You know everything.'

'It's not like you to have too much to drink.'

He tried to focus on her face, and for an instant succeeded. 'Not every day Brian gets engaged. Good bloke, Brian. He's asked me to be best man. What was I going to ask you?'

'I don't know.'

'There were lots of things.'

Edith went away and came back with strong black coffee. She made him drink two cups.

'I wonder if I'll be sick,' he murmured.

'I shouldn't be surprised if you were. I'll put a bucket by the bed. I think it's time I got you upstairs. Try not to wake the children, Chief Inspector.'

'What?'

'Come on.'

So that was something else to ask Edith, when he felt less sleepy. Somehow she got him into their bedroom. He felt like a man in a suit of lead. She sat him on the bed and took off his clothes. He was a child again. He felt the cool of the pillow against his cheek, and the bedclothes coming to rest over his naked body.

'Goodnight, dear,' he said. 'Are the children all right?'

'Yes, they're fine. Fast asleep.'

She kissed him. Then the light went out and the blessed darkness lapped around him. He was swaying gently, sliding down a chute into an even greater darkness. He was happy, and part of his happiness was the knowledge that it wouldn't last.

He tried to remember all the questions he was saving for Edith in the morning.

What was the time?

Did Edith tell Brian to sell his motorbike for the love of a good woman?

Why had she called him Chief Inspector?

Finally, for the first time since that dreadful day up at the quarry, she had been walking normally, without a stick. So was her ankle all right now?

# Chapter Fifty

The whistle blew. A moment later, the train inched its way out of Lydmouth station. Jill waved at the Wemyss-Browns, whose mouths moved silently like those of tropical fish on the other side of the glass. Smoke billowed past and the train picked up speed.

Jill sat down in her corner seat by the window, facing the engine. She watched Lydmouth unrolling like a ribbon. The train rattled north along the line parallel to the Lyd and left the houses behind. She craned her neck for one last glimpse of the church spire.

Soon the train was running through open country, faster and faster, the wheels clattering on the rails with increasing urgency. She was glad she had caught the 9.17, the one train of the morning that ran direct to Paddington. Since Lydmouth was near the end of the line, it was still relatively empty, and she had the compartment to herself. She opened her handbag and took out *The Blue Field*.

*To J. from R., with best love on your birthday.*

She rested the book on her lap and ran her fingertips over the cover. She tried and failed to imagine what it might be like to meet Richard in London.

The door of her compartment slid open. She looked up,

expecting the ticket collector. It was Edith Thornhill, leaning on her stick.

'Oh, hello,' Edith said. 'Well, what a coincidence.'

Jill smiled at her. They had not met since the inquest on June Loysey. 'Are you going up to town too?'

'No – only as far as Gloucester. I need to get some towels and there's a far better choice than in Lydmouth.'

Jill wasn't sure that she believed in this sort of coincidence. But it was a relief to know that she wouldn't have Edith's company all the way to London. She watched Edith putting her coat and shopping bag on the rack. Seen in profile, she thought, her face resembled Bernie Broadbent's, with the same long jaw.

'The towels are a bit of an extravagance, actually,' Edith confided as she sat down heavily opposite Jill. 'But we've got something to celebrate. We've just heard that Richard's going to be promoted.'

'He's got the job?'

'You knew about it?' Edith said sharply.

'I wrote a piece about the police reorganisation in the *Gazette*,' Jill said. 'Mr Drake said they were setting up a central office for serious crimes, and that they were going to appoint a senior detective to run it.'

Edith nodded, apparently satisfied. 'We're delighted. Richard, especially. It's not been easy for him in Lydmouth. Being an outsider, that is. It's taken a while for him to settle in, but I think the promotion sets the seal on it.'

'Yes, indeed. Do pass on my good wishes.'

'Of course.'

'And how's the ankle?'

'Much better, thank you. It was a bad sprain, though. And it was so inconvenient being in that wheelchair. I felt such a fool at the inquest.'

'You didn't sound like one.'

'I can't wait to get rid of this stick. Then things can really get back to normal. But I think it will be a week or two. I still can't go anywhere without it.'

'At least it's all over.'

'Yes,' Edith said. 'All in the past now, thank heaven. To be honest, I'm trying not to think about it.'

Jill's fingertips traced the outline of the book on her lap. Had Edith seen the dedication inside the flyleaf? Was that why she was here? Making sure that Richard had not come for a last fond farewell?

There were too many questions for comfort. How would the *Berkeley's* job work out? Would she see Richard again? If yes, would they meet as lovers or friends or as the sort of social embarrassments you avoid at parties? And if Edith had really been completely immobilised by the wire and her sprained ankle in the field by the quarry, how had she known that there was a ledge a few feet below?

The two women smiled at each other. Of course, Jill thought, Edith had often been to the field. She must have seen the ledge on many occasions.

There was no doubt that June Loysey had been responsible for Miss Caswell's death and probably her brother's as well. Indirectly, too, she had brought about the suicide of Rufus Moorcroft. Her death was a convenience, a gift from fate. Edith had made a wonderful witness, too, explaining the details of the accident with just the right mixture of clarity and womanly reticence. There was no reason why the police should look such a gift horse in the mouth, especially when the horse in question was the wife of a soon-to-be-appointed detective chief inspector and Bernie Broadbent's cousin.

'I hate to say it,' Edith Thornhill said placidly, 'but perhaps it's not a bad thing that Mrs Loysey died. She was a very nosey woman. And once she got her claws into someone, she wouldn't let go. As poor Mr Moorcroft found.'

'So you think — you think she might have tried to blackmail other people?'

'Sooner or later I'm sure she would have done. People are very vulnerable, aren't they, especially somewhere like Lydmouth.'

But which people would have been vulnerable to Mrs Loysey's attentions? Herself and Richard? Jill could hardly ask Edith outright. It might have been closer to home if Nurse Lindor were to be believed. Mrs Thornhill and her *fancy man?*

*No better than she should be, that one. I've seen her with—*

With Jack Graig? But Nurse Lindor was a cantankerous woman who at the time had been having the next best thing to a nervous breakdown.

The train rushed farther and farther away from Lydmouth. The two women talked amicably about the price of towels and about the quality of gloves compared with their pre-war counterparts. They discussed the pros and cons of living in London as opposed to living in the country. Jill described the job she was going to do in London. Edith described the alterations she planned to make to 68 Victoria Road.

'You must let me have your address,' Edith said as the train slowed before Gloucester. 'It would be a shame to lose touch.' She took a pocketbook from her handbag. 'You could write it in here, if you like.'

Jill jotted down the Lancaster Gate address in Hugh Hudnall's pocketbook. She helped Edith get her bag down from the rack. The two women shook hands as the long platform at Gloucester station rolled past the window. Edith hesitated in the corridor and poked her head back into the compartment.

'And if you're ever down in Lydmouth, of course,' she said, 'you must pop in and see us.'

'Thank you,' Jill said. 'I'd like that.'

They smiled at each other. A moment later the train stopped. Jill waited in her corner seat, her hands resting on *The Blue Field.*

She stared out of the window and in a while she saw Edith Thornhill walking slowly along the platform, leaning heavily on her stick.

The whistle blew.

Just as Edith reached the barrier, a burly man rushed through and charged towards the train. He stumbled into the walking stick and sent it skittering several yards across the tarmac. Edith darted in the opposite direction, avoiding a collision. A porter shouted. A door slammed. The train began to move.

Edith walked over to her stick and picked it up. She wasn't limping.

## AN AIR THAT KILLS
When workmen discover the remains of a newborn baby
in an old inn, Jill Francis becomes an unwilling partner in
Detective Inspector Richard Thornhill's investigation.

## THE MORTAL SICKNESS
When a spinster in the parish of Lydmouth is
found bludgeoned to death in St John's church, the
finger of suspicion points at the new vicar.

## THE LOVER OF THE GRAVE
A man's body is found hangingfrom a tree on the
outskirts of town. Suicide, accident . . . or murder?

## THE SUFFOCATING NIGHT
A right-wing politician is found murdered in
the Bathurst Arms and Detective Inspector
Richard Thornhill is called to investigate.

## WHERE ROSES FADE
When Mattie Harris's lifeless body is found in the river, some of
Lydmouth's leading citizens are very anxious to establish that
her death was accidental. Do they have something to hide?

## DEATH'S OWN DOOR
When a widower is found dead in his summerhouse the
verdict is suicide. But the investigation leads to many
surprising suspects, including Thornhill's own wife.

## CALL THE DYING
Unpleasant and bizarre things are happening in Lydmouth.
Can Detective Thornhill and Jill Francis restore peace?

## NAKED TO THE HANGMAN
When a retired police officer is found dead in the
ruins of Lydmouth Castle Detective Inspector
Thornhill comes under suspicion of murder.